Born Lucid

Christopher C. Evans

ISBN-13: 978-1518731068

ISBN-10: 1518731066

DEDICATION

This book is dedicated to my beautiful wife and daughter, who are the inspiration for all of my labours.

May this create a safer and more comfortable world for us all to live in.

Healing, Love and Enlightenment.

CONTENTS

ACKNOWLEDGMENTS

I would like to thank my wife, friends and family for their patience and tolerance as I laboured on extracting this story from the depths of my mind. I hope that now my work is tangible, they will see that it was worth it.

I would also like to offer my sincere gratitude to Richard Davies and Terry Power for proof-reading and providing their feedback on the manuscript, literally chapter by chapter and page by page, as it was being written. Their encouragement helped give me the confidence to persevere.

My thanks also to my wife, Lisa, for lending me her artistic eye and helping me to finalise the beautiful cover design, which catches the eyes and imaginations of readers all around the world.

Finally, I want to thank and pay tribute to all of the truth-tellers and whistle blowers around the world who have endured hardships and put themselves and their families at risk by warning the rest of us and speaking out. Without them, (and the alternative media outlets which carry their voices), we wouldn't even be aware of the problem. I hope that in the days to come, whistle blowers are celebrated for being the heroes they are and that the internet and other platforms they rely upon, remain free and uncensored.

"Some of the biggest men in the United States, in the field of commerce and manufacture, are afraid of something. They know that there is a power somewhere -- so organized, so subtle, so watchful, so interlocked, so complete, so pervasive -- that they better not speak above their breath when they speak in condemnation of it." - President Woodrow Wilson

"For we are opposed around the world by a monolithic and ruthless conspiracy that relies on covert means for expanding its sphere of influence -- on infiltration instead of invasion, on subversion instead of elections, on intimidation instead of free choice, on guerrillas by night instead of armies by day. It is a system which has conscripted vast human and material resources into the building of a tightly knit, highly efficient machine that combines military, diplomatic, intelligence, economic, scientific and political operations. Its preparations are concealed, not published. Its mistakes are buried not headlined. Its dissenters are silenced, not praised. No expenditure is questioned, no rumor is printed, no secret is revealed." - President John F. Kennedy

"There exists in this country a plot to enslave every man, woman and child. Before I leave this high and noble office, I intend to expose this plot." - President John F. Kennedy, 7 days before his assassination.

Chapter 1

The curfew drone hissed by in the predawn gloom. There was little to give it away beyond the lambent glow of its infrared searchlights and the metallic patter of rain on its black carapace. It paused to direct a rapid scan of laser light through the breach in an abandoned guard tower, then it moved on.

The tension eased in the men concealed around me. They were too experienced to release a sigh or any comment, as everyone knew drones tended to patrol in clusters, but through my implant, I could detect their heart rates falling back to resting levels as the mechanical killer passed out of scanner range.

It seemed like only yesterday when citizens were outraged by the tinny notifications broadcast by the drones whilst enforcing curfew, but dissention was soon crushed by the authorities. Now, those screechy little tannoys would be seen as a gift.

Instead, death hovered around midnight streets with no discrimination and no warning. Everyone knew citizens who had fallen to the merciless curfew drones, but whilst resentment simmered in almost every breast, open criticism of the authorities resulted in a one-way trip to the re-education centres, on the way to goodness knew where.

But tonight we would change things.

I felt the attention of one of my men focus on me. Darius. He was wondering whether to ask if we should be moving on to our target, so I saved him the breath.

"We have a 78% probability that the drones will be clear from this quadrant now. It's as good as we can hope for. Tell the men we move in five."

I smiled sardonically at his surprised expression. Born without even basic implants, he couldn't get used to my apparently supernatural abilities and it gave me a glimmer of pleasure to keep him guessing at my limitations.

The recent drones had kept on their patrol, so the chances were also good that we would avoid any incursions with 'the lost' or any of the other forms of sub-culture living in the ruins of the under-city.

In these deserted outer reaches of the city, known as the dead zone, there were far too many ruins to shelter the surviving remnants of the authority purges. So we still weren't safe. In a perverse Darwinian fashion, only the most lethal had survived the collapse and subsequent purges, so even the authority forces had given up trying to reclaim the territory.

Our world was divided between the wild places inhabited by mutated beasts or errant killer A.I.'s and the stifling 'embrace' of the authority. Any citizens with backbone had been recruited to be authority enforcers or else cowed through propaganda and conditioning. Everyone else was either dead or had escaped to almost certain death in the under-city or surrounding gamma wastes. My men and I walked the hazardous barbed-wire line between the sheep and the wolves.

As worn boots scuffed on the rubble under the collapsed overpass we sheltered under, the resulting micro-echoes obliged my implant to form a 360 degree image of our surroundings in my mind. It often made sleep almost impossible, as man wasn't born to be able to see through the back of his head. But this extraordinary technology had kept me alive on too many occasions to list and would be the key to the future of mankind.

I gently 'suggested' to my implant that some endorphins would be helpful to ease the effects of my recent inactivity. I couched the thought in terms of it being an aid to the success of my mission - helping to increase my mobility and reaction speed against unknown threats. I didn't have the capacity to micro-manage all of my implant's functions - nor did I truly know them - but suggestions that encompassed the nebulous concept of mission success were often heeded.

My implant didn't have an ego, it seemed to function with its own in-built logic, so within moments I felt not only the gentle bliss of an endorphin rush and the cold receding, but I also felt my muscles develop the tonus you get for a day or two after a workout.

The creak of leather and shifting of backpacks left echo-images in my mind as my men parted for me in the darkness so I could take the lead. We had the blueprints for an A.I. substation that had been lost in the dead zone years before and we were attempting to recover whatever drone technology and control codes we could find, along with any other abandoned intelligence. With luck, we could use this to access other restricted areas of the inner city. In time, we could perhaps hack the rest of the drone network and turn the tables on the authorities.

The view of the surrounding streets showed nothing beyond the rusted hulks of burnt-out vehicles and the gentle shifting of scrub in the breeze. There were no other signs of life. My implant briefly overlaid heat signatures and scent analysis, but my own assessment was right. It was time to move.

I gestured for Chavez and Harris to take point and we advanced along the ruined streets and through the more exposed and open derelict buildings. Every scent of machine oil, paint, gunpowder or wildlife carried on the breeze twitched my implant into an assessment of the potential hazard, but I had learned over the years to relax through it. My men weren't so blasé, as they knew they didn't have the preternatural speed or reactions that I had, so they spent as much time watching me for clues as they did their surroundings.

As a case in point, as I was scanning a bridge to my left, Decker, a grizzled former drone mechanic, almost stepped on a stiletto-like spike of steel thrusting up amongst the debris of a collapsed machine shop. The first we both knew of it was when my right arm flashed out like a striking snake to stay his forward motion. We were both surprised at this sudden reaction, but as we turned and looked down at what he was about to tread on, moonlight glinted along it's razor length and he was suddenly both embarrassed and grateful.

My implant didn't always look out for others, but Decker was lucky - as a drone mechanic, he was obviously considered to be mission-critical personnel. Sometimes I felt like a fraud, taking credit for actions that were a product of my implant taking over. But it was events like this that built and maintained my close unit of men and their unwavering respect and loyalty for me. This would no doubt turn into yet another campfire tale that grew in scope with every retelling. But if my rag-tag community of 'Freemen' wanted to elevate a figurehead, and this boosted morale for them and their families, then I wasn't going to argue.

We risked cutting through numerous abandoned buildings, scaled rubble piles spined with contorted rebar and skirted deserted streets and avenues, where the empty window frames gaped darkly like the eye sockets of sun-bleached skulls. The dead zone certainly earned its name.

As we covered the ground, the personalities of my team were evident in how they moved from position to position, some boldly, some reluctantly, but every member knew the importance of our mission and pressed on.

We were almost at our target location when I became aware of a high pitched chittering. Some of my freemen heard it too and ducked into doorways, crouched behind low walls and wreckage, or else dropped to one knee where they stood - every one of them sighting down their energy rifles in the darkness.

White knuckles creaked on firearms and flashes of grimacing teeth were visible in the fleeting moonlight, as clouds scudded intermittently across the night sky. Of course, I could see better than most and the echoes of every rustle of wind-blown litter passing down the street augmented my implant-enhanced vision.

My implant flashed the assorted dangers of sub-city rats through my consciousness as it identified the source of the noise. But as the commotion intensified, it was obvious by the number of rats and the urgency of their calls that we had something else to be afraid of.

My men shifted nervously and more than one flinched reflexively as handfuls of terrified rats boiled out from under some battered sheets of corrugated iron, which lay resting up against the side of a building. I was relieved that they didn't fire, as clearly the rats weren't a threat - and our energy rifles, even on their lowest power setting, could draw disastrous satellite or drone attention.

I glided forward silently and gestured for everyone to hold their fire. I hoped that all twelve could see my signal well enough in the dark. It was time for me to earn my reputation once again.

As the rats spilled out from under the sheet metal and fell over each other in all directions, a heavy thud sounded from deep beneath the pile and a deep wail of frustration followed. Something big down there had reached a dead end in its pursuit of dinner and it wasn't pleased.

I could hear bull-like inhalations as something quested for the scent of prey. A brief moment of stillness was starkly contrasted by an enormous pounding under the debris and, all at once, the whole pile of iron sheeting, girders and broken cinder blocks shifted toward me like a house of cards collapsing. With rhythmic pounding, muffled hooting and deranged bellows, the pile shifted forward and our likelihood of detection by the authority increased. We really didn't need to pick a fight with any sub-culture tonight.

The reverberations were too many to get clear echo-images in my mind, but those I received were of a monstrous torso and thickly muscled arms beating a way out of a narrow passageway.

No sooner had the image formed in my mind, then the hulking mutant burst from cover to stand blinking dust from its distorted face, as its massive head swung from side to side. The creature's face was a drooping parody of a man's, with fleshy eye sockets clearly too large for the rheumy, weeping and bloodshot eyes within. It was partly hairy and partly pig-like in its bare skin, but aside from the distorted muzzle of a face, it was man-like. It had only turned recently, as the characteristic wet sores were not yet present. Its 7 foot frame sported the remnants of ragged overalls and one thorny foot protruded from a torn and tattered work boot. I felt pity for him as I caught sight of the plastic name badge, swinging at an angle from the breast pocket of his overalls. This must be what was left of a salvage or engineering crew sent down into the under-city to retrieve lost technology or parts.

I stepped towards him and softly spoke the name on his badge to draw his attention.

"Jed."

The mutant's head shot up, partly in recognition of prey and partly in recognition of his name. For an instant, indecision vied across Jed's mutagen-ravaged face. Drool at the prospect of feeding swung from his slack jaw as he started to turn away in shame, but just as quickly, a towering rage at being forced to endure shame overcame him and he lunged toward me. I suppose he reasoned that if I was dead, then I couldn't pity him. But who knows what he thought?

I relaxed into my peaceful place... which was a form of mental escapism that I practiced when I knew that extremes of violence were sure to follow. My implant would handle the combat in the most efficient way possible and all I had to do was detach my mind so that it did not slow my body down.

I suppose I could liken it to deliberately falling nervelessly to the floor when someone is trying to carry you away as a child. The more you sag onto the floor like a limp sack of wet washing, the harder it is for someone to manhandle you. But in my case, the more I relaxed and distanced my mind, the more inhuman my speed and strength became.

I usually visualise something to take me away from the actual moment of killing, because my heightened senses taunt me with every gruesome detail in 3d and surround sound against my will. Every fibre tearing, every vascular collapse, every bone screeching in protest in the fractional moment before catastrophic failure, and the sigh of release as the last breath wheezes from my structurally incoherent foe.

It gives me no joy, other than some pathetic appreciation for the clinical simplicity by which my implant destroys any threats to me. I suppose this is just a self preservation mechanism to hold the weeping at bay, but I have endured so many deaths at my own hands that often it just makes me feel numb. I had years of self loathing, due to being made to commit despicable crimes which would steer the course of humanity, but things changed when I found I could fight for good.

But today I was feeling melancholy. Jed didn't deserve this. He was yet another victim of the authority regime and their subsequent purges and none of this was his fault.

But he was a threat to me, my men and the success of my mission, so my implant would impassively eliminate him, regardless of my opinions.

To avoid the seemingly inevitable emotional connection, this time I visualised becoming a slick drop of oil, lost in the vastness of a high pressure pocket under the sea - all crushed and merged with my brother and sister droplets of oil. We were one. All we knew was blackness and the immense pressure that drove us together.

As Jed bulled forward, arms outstretched and teeth bared, I pictured release. Now I was a molecule of oil cascading through a pipeline. We were a collective, but entirely outside of our own control and resistance against the inexorable pressure was futile. We flowed, we dispersed and rejoined a million-fold as we rushed like liquid rocket fuel out of the deep, toward an open drill-head. After millions of years, our freedom awaited... so we surged forward.

As I visualised, my implant was simultaneously showing me, in graphic detail, my inhuman grace as a killing machine. I shifted my stance mere inches as my body swayed and turned around Jed's groping arm. As he pushed forward into the empty space where he expected me to be, one of my hands ripped his flailing forearm towards me while my other upward arcing elbow simultaneously smashed up through one of his triceps, stunning the nerve and stress fracturing the underlying bone. A fraction more of a pivot with my feet and hips and the bone and joint would have sheered. But my implant was efficient in its economy of motion and not unduly wasteful of energy. It only needed to incapacitate the arm, not destroy it.

As these abstract thoughts intruded upon my attempts at escapism, one of my hands was already retrapping his mangled limb and the other arm was chopping the heel of my palm up under his slack jaw to bunch his trachea up round the side of his throat with a sickening crunch.

Poor Jed was already falling to one side like a poleaxed steer, as my footwork shifted and one of my boots tore a vicious stamp through the cartilage and tendons of his rear knee. Jed looked to have had enormous strength, but clearly bionically enhanced skill was the winner on the day.

I detachedly wondered why my implant made the extra effort to kick out his knee, when he was already dead - barring the death-throws - but as he flailed on the ground, throttling on the wreckage of his mashed throat, I saw how he had fallen away from my men and therefore decreased the risk to our mission.

My men stood silently, plainly stunned by the three swift, brutal movements that had left Jed sprawled in the dust, making the urban jungle equivalent of a snow angel in the grit and dirt. I had dressed down the magnificent but monstrous Jed like a scolded child, apparently with no mercy, sportsmanship or remorse.

This wasn't combat, it was rank, humiliating slaughter and I was ashamed. He had looked unstoppable, but in mere seconds he was reduced to carrion, heels drumming against the concrete and choking his life out in the dust.

Darius must have seen the look on my face and was the first to break the silence. "You did what you had to do, Chris. Any one of us would thank you for it if the time came and we were 'lost'."

The other men nodded their agreement and a few murmured ascent, but I still felt soiled by the whole affair. I mentally offered up a prayer for Jed's passing, but he was only offered the scant burial that a few sheets of corrugated iron could provide.

As it turned out, Jed had offered a service to us by opening a concealed tunnel to the under-city, as we were now very close to the A.I. substation below the streets and were picking up incoming drones on the scanners. We needed a quick egress, and this was it.

I ducked into the tunnel without a backward glance. My implant was displaying a dozen heartbeats behind me, all falling into single file without hesitation. One remained behind briefly, but as I advanced in a crouch through the dusty, tiled service corridor, I could hear another sheet of iron being hastily dragged across the entrance.

After a few hundred yards of twists and turns down the sloping tunnel, the height of the walkway increased and, every so often, we encountered disconnected junction boxes or rusted grates over running water. The LED lights and infrared goggles of the men behind me highlighted the industrial pipes mounted on the walls or ceiling which followed our course. At intervals, some pipes left the passageway through L bends, exiting the walls or ceiling. Just as frequently, we encountered new arrivals, making the tunnel look like an enlarged circuit board.

The occasional whispered comment or scuffed boot echoed up the tunnel ahead of us, but I couldn't detect any sentient life ahead as I extended my senses. I was still marvelling at how intricately my implant could map out the tunnel from just the sounds we were making and the flashes of light past my shoulders and calves, when I became aware of electro-magnetic fields surrounding some of the cables. This part of the under-city was still operational. We hadn't counted on that, assuming that the abandoned A.I. substation would be out of action. I wasn't sure if this was good or bad news, but I shared my discovery with the nearest man behind me so he could relay it back along the group.

If there was power here, there could also be cameras, alarms, automated defences or even a hostile Mech. I had handled mechanised defence droids more than a few times before, but that was when armed, armoured and with the element of surprise - but certainly not in the confines of a tunnel that would be a lethal shooting gallery.

I extended my awareness as we progressed, hunting for any sign of a trap. We trailed the electro-magnetic fields, which clouded along the length of some of the cables and junction boxes. Eventually, we reached an intersection where an equally non-descript tunnel traversed the one we were in.

There were orange numbers stencilled on the walls of each branch of the tunnel at eye level. These were accompanied by a large, greasy smear along the wall, ending in a hand-print. This marked the tunnel that Jed had evidently come from, as he had crashed through the darkness in pursuit of a rat supper. How he had lived in the barren darkness of these tunnels, I had no idea.

Darius came forward with his nav-band and with a swift stroke of his finger over his wrist, a small hologramatic schematic appeared, hovering inches above his outstretched arm. It was the blueprint for the A.I. substation. He peered at the markings on the wall, and with a series of deft movements he searched the nav-band to see if we were on track.

With a frustrated scowl, he muttered "we're off the blueprints, but we're heading in the right direction. If I had to guess, I'd follow the slime". He nodded toward the trail that Jed had made, and with the curl of his stubbled lip, made it clear what he thought of that.

Darius was a seasoned veteran and I trusted his instincts. Jed's glistening trail also painted a route that mirrored the electro-magnetic fields, and therefore the flow of electric power, so with the loosening of pistols in holsters and a few muttered curses, my men followed me deeper underground.

My implant hummed in the back of my mind as it enhanced my sense of smell, which I could have done without. Now the epitaph written in Jed's filth was so pungent that I could almost taste it. I could have followed his trail blindfolded. Some of my Freemen were none too fresh either, but now wasn't the time to pass comment.

The further we travelled and the more junctions we passed and checked, the higher the tension was ratcheted in my men. There were additional signs of life now, either past or present, in the form of litter, a discarded hard-hat and tracks in several different directions. At one intersection there were the relatively fresh remains of a dead cat. Its tangled ragdoll positioning, combined with the dried blood smatters on the tunnel wall showed it had not died of natural causes. Nearby, we also found the partial remains of either a small adult or a child. There were enough parts missing to prefer not to check. Within reach of the corpse, lay an overturned shopping cart spilling out a scattering of junk - presumably the sad scraps and debris that passed for possessions down here. The way they were strewn hinted at either a lethal robbery or just random violence followed by some curiosity.

Clearly, these tunnels weren't as separate from the rest of the under-city as we had hoped. My men were largely inoculated against the most lethal pathogens that the authorities had used in the purges down here. But there were no public records of all of their sadistic experiments, so you could never be sure.

As the authority had found it harder and harder to clear out the under-city, eventually anything went. The authority's best scientists had had a field day as the constraints of morality were entirely stripped away. Combine a group of lab-coated nut jobs with a god complex, a state of the art laboratory and a standing mission to create the most lethal biological weapons, and you have a recipe for hell on earth. The population down here never stood a chance.

If you didn't end up frothing at the mouth and trying to chew on your loved ones, you could look forward to spontaneously haemorrhaging to death. And that was if the genetically engineered parasites didn't get you, or the assorted shapes and sizes of killer A.I.s. So we certainly didn't want to run into any live infected whilst trapped in such close confines.

After perhaps an hour of tracking the live cables, we came across a natural void in the bedrock that the tunnels bored through. The tunnel was replaced by a railed steel platform which turned at a right-angle and traced the wall of the ink-black void. The cavern wall was to our left, connected to the rusted metal walkway with thick bolts and plates. To our right was what could only be described as an abyss, leaving more than a few of my men hastily crossing their hearts or stroking the hilts of knives for luck in the dark. The air that rose to meet us was damp and musty and it seemed that water was seeping from the rock wall and running down it in rivulets into the darkness below. Perhaps it vaporised before it hit the bottom, as even my enhanced hearing could not detect it.

I felt sweat break out on my forehead and palms as I gripped the rail and leaned over to look below. A few test jumps on the walkway by some of the more headstrong men assured us that at least this section of the platform was secure. But as we began to advance along the gantry, it was almost impossible not to focus upon the blackness visible through the aged metal grates that made up the platform.

It had been many years since I was forced to confront my biggest fear - the mind numbing terror brought about by falling through the darkness, never knowing when you will be dashed upon the rocks. Just darkness and the rushing wind, with the sickening inevitability of a crushing impact.

Darius had noticed the subtle change in my demeanour and without wanting to draw it to the attention of the other men, he urged Jacob and Chavez forward to take the lead. They eased past me with tight smiles, clearly not relishing the task. But no complaints. They clipped a line between themselves and advanced in turns, ahead of the rest of the men, testing the footing as they went.

"What's on your mind Chris?", Darius whispered, concern etched upon his face. He knew I could hear him, even if he spoke under his breath. I stood for long moments in the darkness, listening to the seeping water running down the eroded face of the cavern and the metallic staccato as eleven sets of boots moved off along the gantry.

In that still moment, I weighed up how much I was willing to share with Darius. He had proven himself many times and obviously had been tactful enough to separate me from the rest of the men before speaking. But was I ready to reveal any vulnerability to him?

I wrestled with my emotions and came to a conclusion. No man is an island, however strong he thinks he is, and it had been so long since I had allowed myself a true friend. So in the terrifying darkness, with a few concerned words, Darius had finally earned that position.

"This place reminds me of how I got my implant", I breathed.

My mind flashed back over 94 bitter years of trauma, turmoil and grief to 7 years before the collapse. It was 2010 and I was in the San Ferago mine, near Pretoria in South Africa.

Chapter 2

We were in! I couldn't believe our luck. The fake contractor passes hadn't been questioned, the guards had been diverted as planned and the third mine elevator was now rumbling us down into the bowels of the earth. The security system outage had been mis-timed, but some quick thinking on the part of my accomplices had kept us in the game.

I pushed back my mining helmet as I rubbed the sweat from my brow and grinned at my small team. This would be the YouTube disclosure video to rule them all and we would make history! I dropped my pack and clipboard and started to remove my night vision camera equipment from the concealed compartment in the sidewall of my seismic survey rig.

"Don't get too excited, Chris", David Jennings drawled in his gruff South African accent. "We still have to make it out with the footage."

There were three of us. Along with myself, there was Dave Jennings, our company insider, and Ric Parcell, our hired muscle. He was an ex-marine and martial arts instructor who had built up a healthy resentment of authority, having seen too much corruption in his recent tours of duty.

To maintain our secrecy, nobody on the outside had been told, but I did leave a spare mobile phone with a scheduled text addressed to my lawyer, over a dozen of my colleagues and industry counterparts, along with numerous UFO disclosure sites and alternative media contacts. As long as I was back in my hotel room in the next 24 hours, I could cancel the text - but if anything should happen to us, it wouldn't go unreported or uninvestigated.

The lift continued to vibrate through the soles of our work boots and we all shared the altered sense of gravity as we descended for some long minutes. It was hard to overcome the feeling that mankind was not meant to pierce this deep into the earth. This wasn't our realm and we were trespassing.

The lift jounced on its cable as it reached the end of the shaft and Dave pulled back the inner and outer doors of the car. I let out a breath that I hadn't even been aware I was holding and pulled the trolley of equipment out of the lift car into the gloom of a rough-hewn passageway. Ric bent to lodge a piece of 2 by 4 in between the doors of the lift to prevent it from being recalled from above and Dave eased his way past us both to lead the way.

"It's this way" he murmured as he clicked on his LED mining lamp and headed off into the darkness. As he exited the pale pool of illumination produced by the interior light of the lift car, both Ric and myself hustled the trolley of kit after him.

We had both seen the hand-drawn maps and heard Dave's descriptions, but the strange way that sound travelled this far under the earth was a new experience that left me on edge. To this day, I'm still not sure if it was the millions of tons of rock above us or the anticipation of what we would find that made me feel uneasy, but my excited anticipation overrode my caution and what little prudence that youth allowed me.

David had already described, in detail, the three chambers that he had been ordered to seal over the last few years - including the peculiar remains that had been removed in two cases. The third case had been too difficult to conceal from the rank and file workers, so it had simply been blasted with explosives to cause a cave-in and the mining operation had declared this branch of the mine to be unsafe. But keeping quiet about a mystifying sheer-sided cylindrical borehole in the deep earth had not sat well with David. It showed no tool marks, was a perfect cylinder and was so deep that they had to use laser range-finding equipment to measure the depth. They hadn't believed the results at first - after all, who on earth could bore a perfect hole 18 thousand feet deep?

The shareholders and senior management had too much at stake to allow expensive delays in operations, or even worse, to have this site declared to be of any archaeological significance. The crews knew it and were sufficiently attached to their jobs to help maintain the fiction. But that seemingly wasn't enough for the mining company. A string of accidents and unlikely mishaps subsequently befell the crews that had been present during the excavations, leaving David Jennings the last man alive with any first-hand knowledge of the chambers or the shaft. But he was a good foreman and a very productive one at that, with a charismatic demeanour and the genuine respect of his men. Not to mention the childhood friend of one of the major shareholders.

Perhaps that was enough for them? He had given 25 long years of service to the company, through good times and bad. But David knew he was a loose end and his only safeguard was if the information were to be made public.

A few weeks later, when one of David's crews had discovered a fourth chamber, complete with remains, artefacts and possibly a second shaft, they had unanimously agreed to keep its existence a secret from the mining company under pain of dire retribution driven by numerous company agendas.

But David had many friends, one of which was a retired professor of archaeology who put us in contact. I was already in the area, working on the Adam's Calendar site under the supervision of Michael Tellinger himself and our mutual friend knew I would bend any rules to get at the undiscovered truth - especially if it challenged the arrogant and unyielding academic dogma that stifled the progress of mankind.

It took a long time to reach the location of the fourth chamber and David appeared to get increasingly anxious with every step. We were committed now, but he would be the one living with the greatest consequences of what we would find today. Or so we thought.

Ric and I grunted as we manhandled the boards, signs and surplus supports that David's crew had placed in front of the breach and David intervened to drag out the hastily stacked rock debris, as he had a clearer knowledge of the opening to the chamber.

The ragged breach was only just wide enough for a man to squeeze his torso through, but this had been enough for David's crew to stare wide-eyed into the chamber, following the roving spotlight. As we stood now, recreating that moment, we could see the chamber ceiling arching out of the line of sight of our lantern and the intermittent mounds on the chamber floor. The shadows that these mounds caused lurched crazily as David and I swung our beams to get a better look. Most significant to my mind was the single massive stone pillar looming up and out of sight above. It was far too smooth to be natural and appeared to be made from one continuous piece of rock - and this was not at all like anything I had seen or read about in the area.

Ric peered past our shoulders then backed up a few feet to give us the space we needed to work and presumably to keep watch - although my excitement glossed over the details of the moment. I hastily dug out my face mask and goggles with fumbling fingers, along with my digital camera. We would also take Polaroids to help prove the legitimacy of our pictures, but that would come later and I was desperate to get into the chamber for a closer look.

David and Ric clipped a line to my harness and helped boost me through the chest-high gap in the passageway. My crumpled and dirty high-vis jacket pulled a shower of dust and small rocks with me as I wriggled through the opening. The chamber was much larger than I had first believed, and I could see not one, but potentially two cylindrical shafts. On the left side of the chamber, one dark void indicated a shaft in the ceiling leading upwards, but toward the back wall, there appeared to be a shaft in the floor leading downwards. To my right, the void extended off in an arc and I was unable to see the extent of it from where I stood.

The air was totally still and I took a moment to assess the floor around me before I disturbed anything. My field work and training had taught me to be careful and meticulous, but the nature of this hit and run exposé meant that I couldn't be so precious, or else the entire site may never come to light. I was here in the capacity of a journalist and not purely an archaeologist.

The mounds on the floor caught my attention, because although they were covered with the same rock dust and rubble as the rest of the chamber, they were distinctly human sized.

"What can you see?" hissed David, as he craned his neck through the opening? I stepped aside, my boots crunching on rocks and dust that had remained untouched for unknown aeons. The light from David's camera shone over my shoulder, so I brought up my own camera and started to dictate what I was seeing.

"As I record this footage, we are 850 feet below the mine, in a previously unexplored cavern. Around me, I can see no footprints, nor tools, but can see two potential shafts, several mounds on the floor and a pillar that does not appear to be natural. As I approach the left shaft, it appears to have a diameter of approximately 8 feet, and I am surprised by how smooth and uniform it is. The shaft seems to run vertically upward, out of range of my camera and light source. Looking back at the mounds on the floor from this perspective, I can now see what looks to be remains of a biological nature in the first mound." My heart was now pounding as I edged forward, watching my step to be sure I didn't disturb anything critical.

As I got closer, I steadied my camera, took a deep breath and continued. "The nearest mound appears to conceal a person of above-average height. I can see a gloved hand, an exposed leg and perhaps a boot. It looks as though the person's skull is crushed - either at point of death, or since. The remains are desiccated and only partially visible past the clothing. The clothing is hard to see in this lighting, and it is hard to see past the overlying dust and debris, but any exposed material appears very smooth to the touch. The individual seems to have shoulder length red hair and..."

As I moved closer, my camera dimmed, flickered and died. The last thing on the display being the intermittent flash of the battery warning light just as the screen went off. The air noticeably cooled and over the top of the sound of the camera shutting down, I heard my mobile phone doing the same in my pocket and a shocked gasp and cursing from outside the chamber, as presumably David and Ric suffered catastrophic equipment failures of their own.

The next few minutes are hazy for me, with just flashes of recollection, but I remember a high-pitched metallic whine that squealed up above the range of human hearing so quickly it felt like hot electrified pins being jammed through my ears and skull. My knees buckled involuntarily and a blink took me from being on my knees in the shadowed chamber to being face first in the grit, with my breath blowing small moats of dust away from my slack jaw as my eyes attempted to focus. I was lying just feet away from the first body and, in my dazed state, it was all I could do to turn my head towards it. My forehead and face were numb from the impact with the floor and one of my eyes was watering to clear the dust.

A soft thump and skitter nearby was accompanied by the neon illumination of a thrown glow-stick that came to rest just inches from my face, and I could hear raised voices from the passageway outside the chamber. Some heated words were being exchanged between David and Ric, but my attention was focussed on the strange sinuous motion of something undulating beneath the figure-hugging suit of the desiccated corpse in the nearest mound.

Gripped by a terror as age-old as mankind itself, I desperately tried to focus and back away from the horror unfolding before me, but, despite my panic, I could only summon the breathless strength of a tickled weakling.

As I pushed myself back along the floor, my fingers and the chest of my jacket were exposing a strangely polished surface, not in the least bit similar to the passageway outside. But as this detail and the surprise that went with it flashed through my ailing consciousness, it was brutally swept aside by the sight of what emerged from the neck of the dead man's suit.

Words fail me to explain the movement, as it was the most peculiar thing I have ever seen, then or since, but what emerged appeared to be thousands of fibre-optic filaments - but not as we know it. Some strands were finer than spider silk, and some as thick as deep-sea fishing line, but they appeared to flicker in and out of existence as the flailing mass lurched across the floor toward me with a mind of its own. It's movements were similar to that of an octopus under water, but the peculiar flickering meant that to my eyes, it swept towards me along the floor in jittering bounds, both sensuously smooth and yet freakishly jarring.

A dark organic module of some sort trailed behind it, which glistened like the obsidian eyes of a cave spider - making it impossible to rationalise if this was machine or creature. But regardless of its nature, it swept inexorably toward my head as I squirmed backwards and tried to thrust it away with tattered hands. The cable clipped to my belt pulled taught as either David or Ric tried to drag me backwards, but it was not enough. With my hands warding protectively in front of me, it was like watching a swarm of flies evading a clumsy child's flailing limbs as the mechanical horror flowed around and winked out past my hands, to swing into position behind my neck. I felt both searing heat and the skin-welding freeze-burn of sub-zero steel, followed by a horrendous violation down the length of my spine as the thing swept into position and thrust under my clothing.

My helmet pushed forward and tumbled from my head as the writhing cable-like limbs of the creature wrapped around my face. Every time it flickered out of existence it reappeared deeper under my skin and the metallic tang of copper filled my nose and mouth. I writhed and flailed with every fibre of my being, but I was helpless to prevent this thing from piercing me wherever it had a mind to. As I rolled and heaved on the gritty cavern floor, my own shrieks growing fainter in my ears, I was dimly aware of boots landing hard on the floor behind me and then sprinting toward me. Then everything went silent and dark.

Blackness, blackness, then sudden frantic awareness.

My eyes flicked open to find myself in mortal combat with Ric, his eyes wild and a bloodied shovel in his hands. My hand gripped his lower bicep in some sort of pinch against his nerves, whilst my body hunched under his reach to deliver a devastating upward elbow into his solar plexus. Air whooshed from his lungs as he careened backwards, shovel dropping from nerveless fingers.

My body moved of its own volition and my upper body pitched toward the ground as my rear leg shot out backwards to strike David's chin with sickening force. He had evidently been barrelling up behind me with arms outstretched to embrace me in a bear-hug. I only had a moment to see him crumple before the cavern flared in strange supernatural brightness and the sounds of the struggle began to boom in my ears. All this, in a strangely elongated split second, before the blackness took me again.

Blackness.

I had to follow my orders. No, that wasn't even a fraction of it. My life WAS to follow my orders. Nothing else mattered. In a flash of panic and confusion I realised I no longer had contact with my commander. I had to make contact. These were not my thoughts. It was like I had an alien personality overriding my own. Perhaps more of an uncontrollable compulsion. More like my body had been hijacked and my screaming consciousness was only along for the ride.

My eyes flicked opened again as I hurtled down the cavern at a full sprint into the darkness, hurdling the mounds on the floor and leaving my incapacitated friends behind. My harness was now unclipped and I despaired at the loss of my only connection to my friends. As my footfalls crunched the grit and shale underfoot, I had a peculiar visualisation in my mind from the echoes around me, and I realised that I wasn't relying on my discarded mining lamp to navigate the twists and turns of the cavern. I didn't understand it yet, but the functions of my new implant were gradually kicking in as alien connections were being established with my central nervous system. I was confused, out of control and barrelling along at full tilt with no rationale behind my actions. But what was most horrifying was that I was heading for a wide shaft in the stony floor.

Just as my horror registered with gut-ripping force, my legs bunched beneath me and propelled me up and over the rim into the abyss below.

My screams preceded me down the shaft as I hurtled downward, the wind whipping tears from my eyes. I felt my sanity being stretched thin to breaking point, then the blackness claimed me.

I have no idea how long I fell. My consciousness was winking in and out just like the implant had done. Of course, I now understand and have some mastery over my implant, but at the time it was like something out of my worst nightmares. To be parasitically invaded, plummeting into unknown depths and trapped hundreds of feet underground with my body no longer entirely under my control, filled me with mind-numbing terror.

Each time I blacked out and snapped back into howling, wind-whipped consciousness, I felt I was starting awake from a dream, only to find the terror was real and I was still firmly wrapped in the embrace of this nightmare.

But as I fell, despite my raw panic, I could detect sudden and shocking changes in my senses. I can now rationalise what was happening to me, but at the time I thought my mind had cracked. My implant was settling in and establishing millions of new connections with my central nervous system, adding delirium and confusion to my feelings of horror.

Without augmentation, people can only detect 1% of the visible and audible spectrum, which means we spend our brief lives grubbing about in the proverbial darkness, hunting for clues about the confusing universe we live in. But my new implant seemed to be mercilessly expanding my senses to accommodate greater input from my surroundings. It was also configuring it's links to my twitching and flailing body.

My awareness was being brutally inflated like a water balloon attached to a fire hydrant, which, I assume was why I kept blacking out. Seemingly detecting this, my implant eased back on the process. Nevertheless, it was hugely disorienting suddenly being able to visualise everything from surface heat, to radio waves, to the radioactive decay of elements within the walls of the shaft. It was in the delirium of this adjustment that I realised how amazingly interconnected everything was. I distractedly remembered reading how even the ionisation of rocket fuel creates radio waves, so at the speed of light you can detect and triangulate the launch of missiles around the world, but this abstract concept was entirely different to it actually happening in my head!

But no sooner was the concept formed, it was lost as the range of my hearing began to shift. My awareness moved from the persistent rush of air from my descent, through to processing the micro-echoes from the shaft upon my passing, all the way to being almost deafened by the base hum of the resonance of the earth. Just like the ancient Sumerians claimed 6,000 years ago, the earth rings like a bell - and I hurtled uncontrollably toward its sonorous depths.

During my descent I was cycled through every physical sensory extreme you could imagine from mind-numbing cold through to delirium inducing fever; from skewer-sharp piercing agony through to the embrace of all-encompassing ecstasy, as my implant tested its new environment. I don't know how I knew, but I sensed my implant was struggling to fully integrate with me, as I was clearly different to its previous host.

As I neared the bottom of the shaft, my mouth yawned open of its own accord and I emitted the strangest cry I have ever heard. It was in fact, the first time I had heard both ultra-sonic and infra-sonic vocal tones, which were combined with a pulse of electromagnetic radiation from within my skull. My implant had clearly anticipated a reply from below, but none came. It repeated the signal several times, with increasing urgency. Something was very wrong.

Below me, in the distance, I began to perceive a soft neon glow - a symbol glowing in the darkness. The symbol, a cross within a circle, (which I recognised from ancient Sumerian tablets), was growing brighter. It was then that the bubble of my absolute despair was pricked by the sudden realisation that my implant hadn't leapt suicidally into the abyss - it had counted on some ancient mechanism being below me at the foot of the drop.

But whether it was some incompatibility between my implant and myself, or the effects of aeons of inaction of the mysterious technology below me, it became apparent from my implant's repeated and unanswered calls that I was doomed after all. It had made a desperate gamble and it had lost.

I had mere moments to lament my fate - the cruelty of not bringing my incredible discovery to the world, the anguish that my family would go through at my passing, my never having children, my fear of the unknown when I died... It all seemed too much to bear.

As the symbol rushed up to meet me, I could detect it was emanating from a gigantic metallic plate which spanned the bottom of the shaft. This was the end of the line.

Abandoning calls to the device below, my implant had evidently run out of options to save me from the rushing embrace of cold metal and did the one remaining thing it could, despite the huge risk.

As I screamed toward the final crushing impact, all of my senses dimmed and retreated, then sprang back with vicious clarity as my body was wracked with the most horrendous electric charge. My body flinched violently from the shock and went limp with every shred of my being afire, but I almost completely decelerated mere inches from the plate. But it came at a terrible cost.

I didn't understand it at the time, but my ancient implant knew the true nature of gravity and had improvised an emergency landing for me. The government had rediscovered and suppressed this technology decades ago in their clandestine test facilities, but my implant was clearly advanced well beyond our current understanding of physics.

Gravity isn't a function of mass, which is what mainstream academics would have you believe, it is in actual fact electrostatic in nature. Which is why rubbing a balloon on your hair to create static allows you to stick it to surfaces like magic. My implant knew that massive electrical voltage, combined with angular momentum (often using liquid metals such as mercury) could create an artificial gravity well, and in turn act as a form of antigravity.

Unfortunately for me, despite all the technological know-how, my implant still didn't have the raw materials it needed. So, in the moments before my imminent death, it improvised a solution which gambled a fine line between electrocuting me to death, cooking me alive, or allowing me to be smashed to a pulp. So I experienced a little of all three at once in its blundered efforts to save us.

In the absence of mercury, it had used the iron in my blood, which wasn't enough to actually stop my fall without rupturing every blood vessel and red blood cell in my body. In the absence of the required angular momentum (from the rotation of an outer shell, or an electrical circuit built into a suit), it had discharged the electricity directly through the sweat across the surface of my skin to slow me down via a very brief antigravity pulse. But when I still hit the metal plate, this electrical discharge had earthed, causing massive electrocution along with the damage from the impact.

I lay unconscious, steaming at the foot of the shaft, some of my bones shattered, my skin a seeping, mottled and charred mess, with my labouring lungs burning from the effort to oxygenate my thinned blood. But I was alive.

Chapter 3

As my heart rate quickened uncontrollably and my memories threatened to overwhelm me, my implant pulled me back to the present. It seemingly dialled up the brightness of my vision and boosted my serotonin levels so that my mood elevated to the very edge of euphoria and suddenly Darius stood as clear as day in front of me, still evidently waiting for me to elaborate on what I had said. I visibly shook off the sense of panic that had been welling up inside me and mumbled that I wasn't ready to talk about it... not down here. I unclenched my fists and fastened my jacket and harness by way of a distraction. "But it doesn't affect our mission" I concluded.

Darius looked relieved that I was pulling myself back together and straightened, sensing that nothing more would follow for now.

"I take it that it wasn't a pleasant experience then?" he quipped with a wry smile. But his face soon fell into a look of consternation as his eyes scanned the void. "Does this change anything?" He said, nodding toward the inky darkness.

I considered it for a moment. "No" I sighed. "We still have a job to do". I felt determination growing within me as I reminded myself of the importance of our mission and so with a companionable nod of thanks that Darius probably couldn't see, I turned on my heel and set off along the gantry to catch up with the others. Darius followed a pace behind, watching my back.

As we trekked through the darkness, illuminated only by the lurching beams of light carried by the men, it was impossible to keep my mind in the present.

The narrow openings in the rusted grills beneath my feet seemed to gape at my every tread, filling me with an anxiety I should have addressed years before. My implant-enhanced senses wouldn't allow me to feel vertigo, but I had every right to.

The further we travelled, the more it became apparent that this metal gantry was constructed before the collapse. After nearly two miles of it, I had idly calculated the weight of the steel and knew that even the authority forces couldn't have gathered enough raw materials to build it. As each enclave had been cut off from the rest, an undertaking of this scale would have been impossible without co-operation - and after 2021 that was in extremely short supply.

Every 500 metres, there were narrow buildings for the storage of tools and supplies, but these were long since abandoned and left bare. Only occasional pieces of debris or scattered bones remained. Even so, the approach and investigation of each structure slowed us down.

The walkway was largely in good condition despite the rust, but the persistent erosion from the water running down the rock face sometimes undermined the beams and thick riveted plates which held us aloft over the void. So whilst the structure didn't perceptibly move, the occasional cascade of rocks falling from around the supports put us all on edge.

As we inched along and my thoughts turned introspective, I used the time to work on my growing anxiety. It was time I confronted my fear head on, so I asked my implant to access my memories and the source of my terror. But as my implant replayed the scene, instead of dwelling on the mind-numbing terror of hurtling through the unknown darkness, I focused on what came out of the experience.

Chapter 4

I remembered starting awake violently, in the middle of an anguished yell, with my eyes flashing open and my hands reflexively coming up to shield my face. But instead of the final impact I anticipated, I felt the jarring and sudden restriction around my wrists of hospital bed restraints. Instead of the rushing blackness, I was met with a dazzling well-lit clinical ceiling and a green surgical screen to one side of my hospital bed. The stench of hospital disinfectant and the sudden eye-catching movement of a slender masked nurse by my bedside hit me a moment later.

I was sore, confused and disorientated, and momentarily believing this to have been a bad dream, when the nurse raised a gloved hand holding a gleaming hypodermic needle. My implant suddenly flashed a visual threat assessment overlay over it like something from a head up display in a fighter pilot's cockpit. It detailed the needle's likely trajectory, an assessment of its content, followed by an instant analysis of the nurse's facial expression, pupil dilation, likely intent, heart rate and assumed physical capabilities. This was bewildering, but upon discovering that the needle was attached to an empty vacutainer, ready for collecting a blood sample, we both relaxed.

The nurse saw my reaction to the needle and hastily set it aside on a gleaming steel trolley and wheeled it across the room away from me, where she pushed a wall-mounted intercom button with her finger.

"The patient is conscious" was all she said before turning to remove her gloves and pull the mask down around her neck. She wasn't unattractive, but a hawkish aspect to her features marred her beauty. A hesitant smile crossed her face as she straightened and smoothed her uniform. "Hello, how are you feeling?" she asked, as her bedside manner kicked in.

As she stood before me, framed in a semi-transparent diagnostic overlay, my implant noted her nervousness via her elevated pulse, the light sheen of perspiration across her brow, the increased blinking and occasional glance toward the surgical screen, behind which I could detect a steel framed doorway.

There was no insignia or other sign to indicate which hospital this was, but in response to her question, my eyes were soon straying down to my own body beneath the sheets as I tentatively flexed my toes, ankles, knees, hips and back. My skin felt unusually tight and sensitive to the air and cotton, but I was relieved that I hadn't been paralysed in the fall. In fact, it was an absolute miracle.

I tested my restraints again, taking in the bag of saline dangling from a stand beside my bed and linked to my arm through an IV drip, and the assorted monitors attached to me. As I pondered how I was physically, a schematic appeared to overlay my vision with an assortment of grievous injuries I had sustained, along with a progress meter detailing how well healed each area was. Despite the drip, the diagnostic overlay showed that I was dehydrated and lacked the nutrients and raw materials for a full recovery without cannibalising other tissues. As I looked up to respond to the nurse, she was already glancing at the screen again, clearly uncomfortable.

I had been torn between blurting out everything that had happened to me and the fear of making my position worse, but her demeanour and the restraints said it all! So I opted to keep my responses minimal until I knew more.

"I'm fine. Where am I?" My voice was hoarse and my skin itched where the intravenous cannula entered the back of my hand.

"The doctor will be here in a moment. I only draw the blood." She had evaded my question, but I was happy to take a moment to gather my wits about me. The alien and overwhelming urgency to report to some kind of superior, or to carry out orders, that I had experienced in the mine, had left me. So I was under no compulsion to move, thank goodness! I had no idea what my implant would have done about the restraints otherwise. I could only assume that the failure of the technology at the foot of the shaft was the key factor. Every movement I made now seemed to be my own, and my implant appeared content to simply assist wherever I directed a mental question. This was a huge relief, but I still felt like I had a sleeping rattlesnake down the back of my shirt, which could bite at any moment.

The sound of footsteps outside the door reached my heightened ears before the nurse was aware. Five sets of feet. Two booted, who remained outside, either side of the door, and another three sets belonging to the men who entered the door behind the screen, with a soft click of the latch. The nurse stepped back to give the newcomers room. With her head bowed and eyes lowered in unconscious supplication to the men, she was dismissed by the eldest man wearing a pristine white doctor's coat.

No sooner had the nurse glided behind the screen, the doctor came forward to stand beside my bed. He was in his late 50's with greying temples and had the bearing of a military man - not your typical paunchy "do as I say and not as I do" pill-pushing, TV dinner doctors that I was used to.

"I am Doctor Levine. May I examine you?"

This was more of an announcement than a question, as clearly my consent was already assumed. His air of authority gave me the sinking feeling that I was in deep trouble. Trespassing into the mine was one thing, but getting into the position where a massive rescue effort and huge medical expense would be required was something else altogether. This was not what I had planned at all.

I nodded and remained still as he laid one open hand on my forehead, whilst he probed for a slim-line torch in his breast pocket with the other, his steely blue eyes never leaving mine. He leaned in to study the response of my pupils to the motion of his light, whilst partially obscuring my view of the other men, who had halted behind him.

One man sported an expensively tailored suit with leather loafers, the other wearing a dark green military uniform littered with ribbons and medals on the breast.

The doctor ran through a very brief series of examination techniques, asking a few terse questions about my health, whilst the others looked on impassively. It gave the impression that each man had his own function or area of expertise and would professionally wait his turn.

I attempted to enquire about my restraints, my location and my friends, but Dr Levine did not waste his breath on pleasantries and curtly batted away any questions I had by saying "All in good time. These gentlemen will address your questions. I must address your health."

Dr Levine finished off with a glance at the bank of machines I was hooked up to, apparently assured that I was undamaged. "Remarkable! Over to you gentlemen. There is no turning back with this one. He has fully assimilated the relic." At this news, a look and a nod passed between them.

'The relic!' I wondered, my mind racing. They knew what had happened to me. I hadn't counted on that!

Levine stepped back and made a few hasty notes on a clipboard hanging on the end of my bed, before departing without a backward glance through the door behind the curtain. The other men moved round into position, next to my bed.

The thick-set and heavy-browed military man identified himself as Major Winters and his primped and polished companion as just "Hiram". Rather than explaining away the omission of Hiram's surname or the capacity in which they were here, Winters pushed on. He got straight down to business, but underlining it all he seemed earnest and friendly, so I listened to what he had to say as I studied the two men.

"We extracted you from the San Ferago mine almost 9 days ago. You were injured but have received the most extensive medical attention that money can buy and should not experience any ongoing adverse health issues. We know why you were there, as we have your two companions, Ric and David, in custody and they are safe and well."

My implant, which had remained quiet until now, flashed up an alert at the mention of the word 'safe'. Voice stress analysis - micro-tremors detected. I didn't know for sure what this meant, but I assumed it wasn't a good sign.

Both Hiram and Winters evidently noticed my brow furrowing and after receiving a dark look from Hiram, Winters elaborated. "They are held at a secure facility and no harm will come to them if you are co-operative". This statement appeared to leave a bad taste in Winter's mouth, but had the ring of truth.

"You have been exposed to classified technology and, as a result, you are now required to co-operate with us." I opened my mouth to interject a question, but Winters raised a finger and continued. "I represent a covert agency that has, amongst other things, been gathering ancient technology from around the world for many decades. We also study the paranormal, the occult and other unexplained phenomenon."

As he spoke, he studied my reactions and I am ashamed to this day that I was taken in. They had done their research and profiling of me and knew exactly what buttons to press to have me come to heel like a lapdog. I was born to uncover the truth and the most incredible door was opening for me.

"We would like to involve you in our work as a field agent".

With a sly smile, Hiram added "Yes, a cross between Indiana Jones and Fox Mulder from the X Files". I couldn't tell if he was mocking me or just pulling my strings a little too hard, but I started to get the uneasy feeling that Hiram didn't like me. Maybe he didn't like anyone. Nothing so overt that you could put a finger on, but the slightest narrowing of his eyes and the crocodile smile which dripped off his face when I looked at Winters.

The Major continued. "You will receive training, meet others with your unique... gifts, and undergo tests to determine your capabilities before being offered any assignments. Our Agency has considerable resources, which can and will be put at your disposal during your assignments, so I suggest you embrace this opportunity. We are unable to remove the implant, but you will meet other personnel who have completely embraced the change that this technology brings."

In the blink of an eye, I had gone from being in a world of trouble to having access to the world's most closely guarded secrets. I felt giddy with the possibilities. But where was the catch?

I looked at Hiram, and said "But I stand against secrecy." I was being naively idealistic, but I meant it.

He shrugged nonchalantly and with an oily smirk said "It's just a matter of timing. We are gearing up for disclosure anyway. The sooner your missions are successful, the sooner that will be. You will be instrumental in the process. But that is Major Winters' department, not mine."

"So, are you in?" Winters asked.

I was so bowled over that I didn't even think to ask about the alternative. I had been swept up in the moment. Having insider access to the world's most tightly kept secrets and being part of the disclosure process had me hooked. It was all I had ever wanted.

But it suddenly occurred to me that I had left a mobile with scheduled text messages in my hotel room. "I scheduled some text messages before we left," I said. "They will have notified people where I have been." My look of consternation must have been evident.

"All taken care of." Winters replied.

"What do you think the NSA does all day? Eat donuts?" Hiram added with a self-satisfied smile.

Winters leaned forward and started to unbuckle my restraints. "An alternative message was sent to your family, informing them that you were heading out on a new, privately funded expedition. You will be out of contact for the next 3 weeks, but that you were having your $17,000 retainer paid into their account for safe keeping and that although you won't have the facility to use the emergency satellite phone, your base camp will send periodic messages home and will notify them if there are any issues".

They had made all the right noises. So while Major Winters was symbolically unbuckling my restraints and offering me freedom, I was actually putting my own head into the agency's noose as I replied. "I'm in."

Chapter 5

For the next two days, I was moved to a larger ward, where I was fed, watered, provided books and magazines and encouraged to rest. But aside from two or three different nurses, who worked in shifts to monitor me on the hour, I didn't have any more visitors. The ward still had armed guards wearing dark uniforms stationed at the door and I could plainly see the infra red flare of two ceiling-mounted night vision cameras, so I was under no illusion that I was free to go. But despite my captivity, I was relieved that I wasn't being intensively studied like a lab rat.

There were no windows in this section of the medical facility, except for internal wire mesh reinforced ones which allowed me to see through to another adjoining room where the nurses were stationed, so I assumed that we must be underground.

On the first day, I was still not fit to move about my ward unaided, so tried to get what little rest I could despite my mind racing. I had no idea how my implant could have helped me heal so well in such a short period of time, but I didn't want to overtax myself. I was vulnerable and I knew it. So when I wasn't dozing fitfully, I was turning my perspective inwards, trying to learn what I could about my new implant.

I attempted to address it directly with a series of questions aloud in my mind, such as 'Who are you?', 'How old are you?', 'Who made you?', 'Are you from Earth?', but I didn't even get a flicker of a response. So I tried to issue specific commands to myself, hoping that the implant would facilitate my demands. This worked much better.

The thought 'Please display a schematic of my implant' brought up a 3d revolving diagram of such complexity it made me giddy. No wonder Dr Levine said the implant couldn't be removed. It had threaded filaments throughout my entire body - so although it was more concentrated around the glistening black module I had seen in the cavern, which was now nestling close to my heart, it was absolutely everywhere! Larger filaments of it ran and up and down the length of my spine, but tendrils ran along every bone, blood vessel and nerve. It looked as though my entire body was laced with cobweb.

I looked down at my body in consternation. I didn't know how to feel. In some respects, I felt I should view this as a gift, but that was easier said than done, as I was afraid. So after some deliberation, I resolved to view this experience as a roller coaster ride I couldn't get off. Either way, I was committed, so I hoped it would be a thrill ride rather than a sentence.

Both 'Please display a schematic of my health status' and 'How is my health' triggered the diagram that I had seen when I first awoke, but I was making definite progress. I was back up to 64% of my original health.

The thoughts 'Please display user manual', 'Please list your functions', 'Please display your battery level', all brought up a notice which said "Unable to comply - Classified". This was alarming to me, so I asked myself who had classified these areas of enquiry. The answer to this was the same.

My mind reeled. Whatever this implant was, it hadn't withheld anything from me when I was in the mine. It certainly hadn't given the impression that certain things were off limits - in fact, I had been largely just a vehicle to enable the implant to do what it had to do.

I had a growing suspicion that the classified notices had the agency's grubby fingerprints all over them. So I attempted some detective work by posing what I thought would be insightful questions in a process of elimination. I resolved to ask my implant to replay memories from before, during and after my exposure to the implant.

'Please display my earliest conscious memory' yielded not at all what I had been expecting. Suddenly, I was in the darkness, floating in warmth and softness, feeling my mother's blood rhythmically coursing through my umbilical cord. My newly developed ear drums were near deafened by her heart beat and the muffled conversation she was having - or was she singing? I didn't wait to find out. With a startled jerk of my head, I was back in the ward. My heart racing. It had seemed so real. Thank goodness I hadn't tried to recall my birthday!

After taking a moment to compose my thoughts, I concentrated again. 'Please display 1pm on my tenth birthday'. This immediately thrust me into the dappled sunshine under the oak trees in my local park. My young arms and legs were pumping and my sides were heaving with laughter as I chased along behind a football. I was laughing to the point of wheezing as my older sister caught up with me and grabbed me by the ribs with tickling fingers. I tumbled to the grass and moss with a squawk and a giggle. As I rolled over, squirming, my elbows reflexively defending my sides, her grinning face was half silhouetted against the sunshine above me and she pushed off me to run for the ball...

I pulled back from the memory with the ghostly sensation of my face aching from laughter and my ribs contracting away from teasing fingers. This was so intense.

Tears came unbidden to my eyes, as I realised the enormity of what I had just experienced. What a gift and what a curse. I could relive any memory I chose - good or bad. I could revisit times with my grandparents before they passed away... I could relive every golden moment, every mistake.

I angrily cuffed the tears away, reminding myself that I had to stay focussed and decided to replay my conversation with Major Winters and Hiram. It didn't yield any new insight except for the fact that my memories were accessible at will. With this critical piece of the puzzle. I asked the question I had been leading up to.

'Display any available memories or information within the first 9 days since my fall'. The result was what I had feared. "Unable to comply - Classified". No wonder the agency wasn't treating me like a lab rat. They probably already had! I realised that when Winters said that I had received "the most extensive medical attention that money can buy", he wasn't kidding.

I was disgusted, but didn't know what to do about it, so I resolved to stow the information away. I certainly wasn't going to let them know what I had discovered for myself. Maybe I would make a good agent after all, I thought with a self-satisfied smile.

Chapter 6

At 6am on my third day on the ward, Major Winters arrived unannounced, accompanied by a new subordinate. Winters looked like he had slept worse than me, but his uniform was still crisp and he was as professional and to the point as before.

He gestured to his white lab-coated colleague as he introduced him. "This is your new agency handler, Professor Thomas Sanders".

Thomas Sanders was everything Winters wasn't. He appeared scatterbrained, dishevelled, a touch nervous and clearly wore his heart on his sleeve. He appeared very young for a professor too. He held out his hand, which I accepted with a firm shake. Disappointingly, his limp hand folded damply in my grip, but judging by his demeanour, it was a confidence issue rather than anything more sinister. It made me feel a little sorry for him.

"I have had to pull strings and call in favours to pair you two up" Winters continued, "so make the most of it whilst it lasts".

Thomas nodded emphatically and I felt my initial assessment of him was correct.

"In due course, the agency will become your family. But as in life, you will discover that some siblings get on and some do not. Some are favoured and others aren't. I put you two together so you may be better prepared before being exposed to the other students in our unique 'academy'. If it had been left to Hiram, you would be bunking with your peers today with no preparation. But as I say, I pulled some strings." He fixed me with a beady eye.

"Do not take advantage of Thomas' generous nature and he will prepare you better than any other man I know." Winters tapped his temple with a meaty index finger for emphasis. "What the professor can put in here with the aid of your relic, is worth ten years of active duty - and I'm not exaggerating". He glared at me, one eyebrow raised for extra emphasis .

There it was again! My mind seized on the mention of the word 'relic'. Whilst Winters was brusque, he came across as fair - perhaps a man who did what he had to do, but he did it for the right reasons. I felt that if I could earn the trust of this man, then maybe I could unlock the keys to my implant and the mystery behind it. Either way, if I was picking sides, I was with Winters and not the snake in the grass, Hiram.

Apparently satisfied with my nod of response, Winters, turned to Thomas. "Thank you Professor. Over to you."

He turned on his heel and purposefully swept from the room. I watched him through the meshed glass as he passed the nurse's station, where he clearly made some small joke, as the nurse on duty smothered a grin and blushed. Her eyes followed him from under her long eyelashes as he left, with one delicate finger tapping thoughtfully on her lips.

My attention returned to Thomas as he cleared his throat. "R-Right" he stammered. "We'd better get started".

Chapter 7

A few minutes later, I had been provided with fresh clothes and shoes and we were being escorted through a series of well-lit corridors to Thomas' laboratory and quarters. There were numerous other doors along the route, each with back-lit Perspex signs. The whole complex came across as industrial, with well-laid concrete floors and riveted, prefabricated panelled walls. Occasional ventilation ducts blew filtered and temperature controlled air into the corridors.

We passed numerous different types of personnel, all going about their duties, each with different coloured uniforms, which made me think of the underground lair of some mysterious James Bond villain. It would have been comical if it wasn't real.

I was expecting to go directly to the Professor's lab, but as we passed the sliding steel door to 'Lab 14', he pointed it out, but suggested we first go to his quarters next door. When we pulled up at his accommodation a few moments later, one of our armed escort raised an eyebrow questioningly, prompting Thomas to say to everyone and nobody in particular, "I just have to collect some necessary items. We'll be just 5 minutes".

He swiped a key card through a reader on the side of the door frame and the latch clicked open. He held the door wide open with one hand and ushered me through with the other as the guards took up position outside.

Inside Thomas' quarters there was an eclectic mismatch of furniture and items from different eras - a sort of magpie's collection, where the only link was Thomas' own personal interest in them. He appeared to have a suite, rather than just a room, with a central living area, off which three doorways led into adjoining rooms.

After hastily pushing some clutter to one side, he offered me a seat on a carved stone bench on one wall of his living room. "Do you recognise this?" he asked with an excited look on his face. As I cast my mind back over my archaeological studies, grasping for inspiration, my implant stepped in.

"Babylonian, circa 1700 BCE" I blurted out, feeling as surprised as I must have looked. Thomas's eyes lit up. "Excellent! It is always a pleasure to work with a student who is well-read. This is your first lesson."

My puzzlement must have been evident, so he elaborated. "Anything you have ever seen, heard, touched, tasted, smelled or felt is stored in your mind. Therefore, your relic has access to it. We will make use of that."

I nodded thoughtfully as he handed me a shiny black tablet computer. As I took it from him, he was already patting the pockets of his lab coat as though searching for something and looking around his quarters distractedly. "The limitation seems to be the number of saccades your eyes and brain can manage per second and the size of your foveal focus - oh and the flicker rate of the screen you are looking at, but I have already taken care of that".

I wasn't entirely sure what he had just explained to me, but he gestured for me to hold the tablet at arm's length. As I did so, he said "As I say, I like a well-read student. Don't blink or you'll miss it!"

To the room, he called out "Computer, my student here is curious about saccades. Please display all topics under 'S' in the encyclopaedia".

I resisted the urge to blink as the screen in front of me lit up and flickered at blistering pace through every topic under the letter 'S'. I believe my implant was as hungry for information as I was, because after a few moments I felt myself settle into the process and the urge to blink went away. My eyes went almost numb. Even my breathing slowed to keep my head still.

Thomas continued to rummage around his quarters, apparently looking for some other items. Almost two minutes passed. I was conscious of snapshots of information passing before my eyes, but I couldn't hold on to it. So I just relaxed. I was almost in a trance when the tablet bleeped and went blank.

"Eureka! Thomas said as he came back into the room proudly brandishing a large box, labelled Sumerian artefacts. "Now ASSIMILATE!" he commanded.

In the fraction of a second it took me to sub-vocalise the word in my mind, my implant dumped the general knowledge of the human race under the letter 'S' into my brain. But not just there to be retrieved at a later date, it was now in my consciousness and part of my understanding - just like anything else I had ever learned the conventional way.

I was totally blown away. I looked up at Professor Thomas Sanders from my seated position in a state of shock and awe.

He had a broad grin on his face. So I humoured him by regurgitating facts like a model student. "Saccades are quick, simultaneous movements of both eyes in the same direction. They are the fastest movements produced by the human body and our vision is made up of millions of them. A saccade can last as little as 20 milliseconds, meaning that without blinking and with an appropriate device, I can read as many as 50 pages per second. The only limit is the size of my foveal focus, which is the portion of high resolution right in the centre of my vision."

"Correct!" the Professor exclaimed. "Now we have proof of concept, we just need to input the right material. We'll have you up to agency standards in no time!"

Winters was right. This man would change my life. As I looked back down at the tablet, I knew that this genius of a man had already selected the maximum screen size for foveal focus at the length of an average human arm. His bumbling exterior belied the keen intelligence I now saw within.

A look of mutual understanding passed between us, as he held up the box of Sumerian artefacts. "Well done Chris. So, now that you have a newfound encyclopaedic knowledge of all things 'S', perhaps you can tell me what this artefact is?"

He positioned the box on the ground before me, so that I could see inside, where he also placed his hands as though rootling for an object. As I watched, his face turned more serious and he covertly started to sign out a message using sign language. "We are watched and listened to."

I immediately schooled my reaction. To anyone else eavesdropping on us or observing, this would have seemed like an innocent enough conversation between two enthusiasts of archaeology, but Thomas had artfully commenced my education with my studying all topics beginning with the letter 'S' so that I would cover saccades, sign language, Sumerians and subterfuge - not to mention surveillance, security, spying and secret societies.

Out loud, I responded carefully, "How fascinating... might I get a better look at it closer to the light?"

I randomly selected and lifted out some inconsequential nik nak, albeit no doubt irreplaceable, and looked around the room as though looking for the best light source with which to study it. I opened up my mind to search for the source of his concern. My implant promptly responded by cycling my vision throughout the full visible spectrum and beyond, and overlaid the detected electromagnetic frequencies and magnetic fields associated with wiring. My ears strained for high pitched audio signals. With all of my heightened senses, combined with my newfound knowledge of security and surveillance systems, I detected microphones in the light fixtures, which also housed systems to modulate the flicker rate of the bulbs (in order to wirelessly interface with computers, or alter mood) and no less than 3 tiny hidden cameras just in the room we were in.

Now that I had gone "full spectrum", I also noticed that every 25 seconds, a pulse of EMF lit the room like a beacon for mere fractions of a second. It was the same microwave frequency as Smart Meters used in people's homes, but from the after-image it left on my senses, I knew it could be used to map out these rooms like sonar and could disturb the sleep cycle and healing.

Whether it was subconscious choice, coincidence or pure good fortune, I didn't know, but I couldn't have picked a better piece from the Professor's collection. I chose my words carefully as the Professor looked on expectantly. "It appears to be a statuette of Nergal, the great watcher. He was the Sumerian god of war and pestilence, but also presided over the underworld. He stood at the head of the special pantheon assigned to the government of the dead, which gathered in a large subterranean cave known as Aralu."

Outwardly, and no doubt for the cameras, the Professor congratulated me for my astuteness, but from the subtle fall of his features, it was clear that the blatant parallels between Nergal and the Agency itself were not lost on him. If this facility represented Aralu, were we the dead?

I made one last show of holding the statuette up to the light with both hands, holding it between fingers and thumbs as you would a camera, which was sign language for 'camera', and said aloud "I have seen three of these before, but heard of others. You must be very pleased to have such exquisite pieces in your own quarters."

"Indeed! Thomas replied brightly, "and I have so many other fascinating things to show you. It will be a joy to have a like-minded soul around who appreciates them".

I nodded with a smile. "Well, I have a passion for such things, so please consider me your faithful student".

Thomas took a moment to gather the last of the items he needed. "Excellent. Well, we must build the foundation first. Let us go next door and get started".

Chapter 8

The Professor's laboratory was a brightly lit clean-room environment, split into four long parallel workspaces with large lozenge shaped windows dividing them. A corridor linked them all, a little like the palm of a hand linking four fingers.

Once the outer door closed behind us, leaving our guards at their usual positions either side of the doorway, we both relaxed somewhat. In the short time I had spent around them, I had revised my assessment of them being my guards, to them being our guards. They were men of little imagination and they certainly had no affection for the Professor. I suppose in their eyes he was the reason for their tedious babysitting duties. But what they failed to grasp was that it was the Professor's brilliance and enormous value as a top-secret research scientist that made him worth guarding and worthy of their respect.

Thomas led me past the reinforced glass doors of each room so I could get an overview of our workspace. "The agency doesn't spare its resources! This is one major consolation for being so isolated - having the best facilities tailor-made to my requirements."

He seemed genuinely pleased with his lab, so I felt a little better about his lot in life. Having the ability to experiment and research without the fetters of expense, politics or poor facilities would be liberating to many scientists.

The first section housed books, documents, parchments, numerous ancient artefacts and magnifying lenses on stands, along with several computer work stations and a large television screen at the far end. The second workspace contained an electrical workshop, with tools, machinery, spools of wiring, a series of test rigs and trays of components stacked in metal racking.

The third and fourth spaces boasted their own airlocks and complex ventilation systems. One was set up as a microbiology lab, with vacuum cabinets, incubators, microscopes and other related apparatus set along white counter-tops. Occasional wheeled stools, were left abandoned in the centre of each room. I imagined that Thomas wouldn't stay still in one place long enough to use them.

The fourth and final sealed clean-room was evidently geared toward chemistry. A periodic table was displayed on the wall and glass fronted cabinets were filled with bottles and jars containing chemicals and reagents of every colour. At the far end of the room was a great steel cabinet, complete with the controls for two armoured robotic arms within. Thick glass portholes were held in place by riveted steel plates.

Thomas saw my gaze linger, and nodding toward the cabinet he said "that is for testing novel explosives. It can withstand over 22,000 atmospheres of pressure. It is of my own design. The glass is modelled after the samples that were brought back from the ancient domes found on the moon."

My eyebrows shot up at this, but he ploughed on before I could interrupt. "You see, glass formed in a complete vacuum is over ten times stronger than steel, yet totally transparent. Amazing stuff. Hemp plastic is almost as strong, but it is ten times lighter."

He paused, clearly arriving at a conclusion. "This is all very inefficient. Let me get you set up in front of the big screen. You have a lot to learn. THEN we can talk."

A few minutes later, I was reclining in an ergonomically designed leather chair in front of the large television screen I had seen earlier. The professor was displaying text in ever decreasing sizes, attempting to discern how small the text could be presented with my implant still able to read it. As it turned out, very small indeed, even from a distance.

Thomas was amazed and said it was more than twice as small as the limit for other 'relics' he had worked with. In fact, it was almost at the limit of the resolution of the display. I didn't know how significant this was, but I hoped I would have the edge over my future peers in other ways too.

When the professor was satisfied, we got to work. We began with general knowledge, comprising the full encyclopaedia to complete my basic education. As I sat there, entirely absorbed in my learning experience, the professor had been preparing me a nutrition shake, with antioxidants, omega-3 essential fatty acids, egg yolks for cholesterol content and numerous other compounds to support brain function. He told me that during this process, my brain would require major nutritional support. This wasn't magic, it was just shortcutting a normal biological process and that my neurons would still be forming billions of connections. All of this would require raw materials that I would still have to consume the old-fashioned way.

I sat for hours, glued to the screen like a video game addict, sipping the formula from a large cup with a straw. I took time to blink and refresh my eyes in between sections and whilst I periodically assimilated the new information. But despite this, my eyes were becoming raw. When I mentioned this, Thomas provided me with eye drops which would slow down the evaporation of fluid from my eyes, but which he said would not be suitable for longer term use.

We were running on borrowed time and neither of us knew how long we would have before I would be placed with the other relics.

I had wondered what the fuss was all about, but the professor explained that there was a lot of competition between relics because it was possible to rob each other of certain modules, which enabled specific features and abilities. Relics had not been created equal, so I needed to be able to defend myself.

Thomas confided in me that this competition was encouraged, in order to force us to be the best we could be. However, he admitted it was no secret that certain distinct factions had formed within the academy.

Loose associations had formed due to quarrels, truces, rivalries and even relationships, but there seemed to be overriding loyalties related to whomever your sponsor was.

Sponsors were usually the person responsible for bringing you into the agency, but some sponsors traded relics with each other - particularly if they didn't like what they had found or if it could result in advancement or a serious favour. There weren't many of us relics and only the top tier of the agency personnel could be designated as a sponsor, so I imagined the favour would have to be pretty huge.

Thomas let slip that Major Winters was in fact my sponsor, which left me a little irritated that he hadn't told me something that important himself.

"That's Major Winters' way." Thomas mused. "He would rather have your loyalty because you stand for the same principles, rather than because he saved you from certain death!" He emphasised this last point with a warm smile. It was clear where the professor's loyalty lay and his gentle rebuke blew my annoyance away like only so much smoke on the breeze.

The professor explained aloud that Hiram's relics were powerful and were to be respected, whilst simultaneously flashing me the sign for "bullies". I read him loud and clear, even if the hidden microphones didn't.

Reading between the lines, I guessed that Hiram's plan to throw me in with general population was just a thinly veiled way of enabling his relics to upgrade at my expense. In order to maintain some balance within the academy (and no doubt the agency), Winters didn't want that to happen.

As I concluded my general education, the Professor breathed a sigh of relief. "Well. At least now I have someone to converse with without having to explain myself".

I knew how he felt and said as much. My passion was for forbidden archaeology, which completely challenged the mainstream paradigms. I had only found a few select individuals prepared to pursue the truth professionally, as it rejected the politically entrenched academic narrative, which seemed to ignore all the evidence that human history was very different to what our text books said.

Yet I had soon discovered that if any scholars openly investigated such matters, they would be pilloried by their peers or institutions and would risk their academic careers. Heaven forbid that they undermine theories their colleagues had built their careers upon.

My frustration was particularly piqued by the mainstream establishment ignoring, dismissing or even actively suppressing, such things as mechanical objects discovered in the middle of undisturbed coal deposits millions of years old, or sophisticated tools found partially fossilized in rock that takes millions of years to form. No, whatever was revealed to me as part of my Agency duties, I KNEW, knew to my very core, that human history was not what the general public believed it was.

I could see some suppression of evidence was likely due to the lack of imagination of the academics involved, such as in the case of solid gold pre-Columbian brooches which perfectly resembled aircraft. These had been catalogued as jewellery resembling insects and stored away. Yet, decades later, when they were rediscovered in an archive, German engineers manufactured large scale replicas which could not only fly, but they had the aerodynamic perfection and manoeuvrability of fighter planes.

Mistakes were one thing, even wilful ignorance was another, but far more blatant was the systematic recovery and suppression of hundreds of skeletons and desiccated remains of 7 to 9 foot tall red haired inhabitants of the US, discovered throughout the 1800's. All that remained of these buried giants were the hundreds of newspaper articles, complete with eyewitness accounts and photographs before the Smithsonian institute swooped in and cleared the scene.

Well now I was within the Agency, I hoped I could be privy to what they had found. Better yet, I could be a champion for the disclosure of this and other equally sordid cover-ups.

It was simply infuriating. But whilst I felt apprehension at the thought of the dog eat dog ethos of the academy, I had high hopes for the places I could visit and the things I could discover.

As the Professor advanced my education on to agency manuals and protocols, I daydreamed of visiting ancient monuments such as Baalbek in Lebanon - a structure made from granite blocks weighing upwards of 1200 tons! With today's modern equipment and engineering expertise, we couldn't even move half that weight, let alone lift these blocks 17 feet in the air and place them atop other stones so precisely that the blocks cannot fit a human hair between. All done by savages with stone age tools, ropes and wooden rollers? How absurd! Yes, I fantasised, I would shine a light on these delusional theories and self interests.

As I began to assimilate more of the agency manuals, my eyes widened in disbelief. Thomas had included material from the FBI, CIA, KGB, MI5, STASI, SS, MOSSAD, and other security agencies worldwide, past and present. I was surprised not only by the content, but also the fact that the Agency was so far reaching in its access to information. The professor explained that if I were to be effective in the field, I would have to be able to understand and second-guess personnel from other agencies who may be competing for the same prizes. If I understood their strategies, I would have the edge.

As my education continued, I soon realised how serious this all was. I wasn't just getting myself into a comic book tale of Indiana Jones style adventures. I was being made privy to EVERYTHING these agencies were involved in. The smile soon falls off your face when you are learning advanced interrogation techniques and how to resist them, and then how to overcome that resistance, like some horribly macabre version of rock, paper, scissors. Or how to 'suicide' people so their deaths looked like accidents. Or how to form, operate or dismantle drug cartels, or terrorist groups. Arms dealing, staging false flag events, rigging financial markets, siphoning off public funds to create black budgets, blackmailing everyone from high court judges to politicians to heads of industry. You name it, if it was sinister, it was in the manuals. These weren't history books, but you don't make standard operating procedures for such things unless they are standard practice.

I was in a distinctly sombre mood when a balding, middle-aged man dressed in the uniform of a porter arrived with some food and drink for us on a steel trolley.

The day had flown by and whilst my middle was bloated with nutrient drink, I was embarrassed that I hadn't even considered that the Professor hadn't eaten all day. He had been slaving away, feeding grist to the mill of my mind.

When the porter had gone, I apologised for my selfish oversight, but the Professor waved away my concerns and apology with a dismissive flick of his hand and a shake of his head.

"Think nothing of it!" Thomas replied around a mouthful of food, which evidenced his pressing hunger. We ate together companionably, with Thomas telling me more of his background and upbringing. It turned out that there was little to say about myself which wasn't already in my file, so Thomas did most of the talking.

He had been born to a couple of government scientists and raised on government bases and secure facilities all over the world. His parents had been gifted humanitarians, one working in the field of free energy research and the other in medical imaging, who had been brought together due to the stifling patent laws of the US. He explained to me that in the States, there were in excess of 5000 patents suppressed and stifled with gag orders in the interests of "National Security".

In such cases, the inventors were not allowed, on pain of imprisonment and huge fines, to even tell people that their invention even existed.

Generally, inventors in this position had four options. Blood money to keep silent, an offer to work exclusively for the establishment, prison, or death - the latter being fairly common when particularly hard-headed scientists didn't read between the lines. Having read the assorted agency manuals, I now had an intimate familiarity of how this was handled.

Both of Thomas's parents had independently chosen to continue their work on behalf of the government. Until their deaths in 2004, they had harboured unrealised hopes that circumstances would change and their work could benefit mankind.

It put my petty resentments into perspective. Where my fury had been directed towards archaeologists and academics over disclosure and censorship of archaeological finds, Thomas and his parents had built up well-founded resentment towards the government due to their career-long treatment and the innovation stifling consequences of US patent legislation.

"...but inevitably it was easier for them to become insiders than to fight the system" Thomas went on. "But I still have faith that what I do, and what my parents did, will matter. After all, imagine five times more patents than Thomas Edison and Nicola Tesla combined. Without them we wouldn't have electricity, x-rays, radio, light bulbs, lasers, and a thousand other such marvels."

He was right. The mind boggled at how different the world could have been if there hadn't been decades of mankind's innovation shovelled under the carpet.

"But the good news," Thomas said brightly, "is that much of this suppressed innovation forms my playground here!" He made a gesture which fondly encompassed his lab.

We shared a smile. "...and once you have graduated from the academy," he continued, "if I do not presume too much, I think we could be an unstoppable team. With you in the field and me in the lab, we can set the world to rights."

This was dangerous talk in hindsight, but despite our careful skirting of sensitive topics, we were still full of the exuberance of youth and were thrilled to have each found a counterpart in the other.

Unfortunately for us, we hadn't yet experienced the pessimism and paranoia of people in real power, so we weren't careful enough.

As the saying went, 'men in power would rather make two mistakes than admit to one', and allowing Winters to take Thomas off Hiram's special projects team and assign him as my handler was a strategic mistake Hiram would regret... and men like Hiram didn't tolerate regret well. His second mistake would be attempting to sever our connection after it was made. But I get ahead of myself in the telling of my tale.

As the remainder of the 'day' drifted away, (for there was no evidence of time passing in this facility), my education moved on from intellectual to practical.

Through my grainy-eyed 'learnathon', I had covered languages (both modern and ancient), all forms of engineering (including mechanical, electrical, chemical and biological), combat, weapons training, computer programming and more.

Thomas had even thrown in art appreciation, musical theory, sacred geometry and the golden ratio.

With an earnest smile on his face, he told me that in experiencing all of the ugliness that the agency would require of me, with this addition to my training I would still have an innate appreciation for things of beauty.

I was naive at the time and didn't appreciate the gravity of his comment, but I often now reflect on how much I owe that man. In truth, far more than I could ever repay.

So, as evening transitioned into night and as we burnt the midnight oil, Thomas began to demonstrate some of his gadgets and, between us, we fashioned ways for me to achieve the same result using my implant.

The first was a laser microphone. I was now familiar with parabolic microphones used to eavesdrop from a distance, but a laser mic was able to measure the reverberations from sound on glass - even from a considerable distance. As long as the laser microphone was mounted to a stable tripod or held still on a solid surface, it was able to translate the detected vibrations back into sound.

Thomas explained how agents had been able to eavesdrop from hundreds of meters away, even on the most secure locations where bugs had been searched for. The downside was that it required laser light, which was detectable with infrared cameras.

Thomas set a computer playing audio in one of the neighbouring workspaces and had me concentrate on all visible glass in the location. I asked my implant to translate whatever vibrations I could see into sound and, remarkably, it duly complied.

I smiled broadly as Mozart sprang into vibrant life within my mind, despite completely bypassing my ears. It was surreal and magical to me, but it wasn't perfect. However, it didn't require laser and amazingly, my implant was able to compensate for my own body's movement.

"Mozart", I murmured with reverence. But Thomas, always the gifted teacher, leaned toward me with a twinkle in his eye and said "don't tell me, show me! EXTRAPOLATE!"

I didn't know whether it was my own thought, or a product of my implant making use of all of the day's input, but I felt compelled to reach out with my index finger, and rest it on the Professor's brow.

My finger tingled as I pressed it firmly against the Professor's skull, which almost caused me to withdraw it. But it was the Professor's turn to smile.

"Ah yes, Mozart" he agreed. "You are quite the student! Major Winters will be pleased with your progress. As should you be."

I realised what I was doing just moments later. Back in the sixties, a thirteen year old prodigy by the name of Patrick Flanagan had invented a device called a Neurophone. It took sound and converted it into high frequency vibrations that could be played back through special pads that would be placed against the skull of the user. The user could then hear without the use of their ears. This was due to the saccule, a hearing organ that evolution had left behind in the human inner ear. Only humans, dolphins, whales and bats had them, because they were necessary for echo location.

Just like Patrick Flanagan's invention, which allowed the deaf to hear without functioning ears, my implant had vibrated my finger against Thomas' skull in order to vibrate a signal to his saccules.

No wonder Thomas was being congratulatory, for an agent after just one day in the making, I was proving to be very effective, even if I couldn't personally take the credit for it.

After a few more experiments, some more successful than others, Thomas decided it was wise to call it a night. We shut down the equipment in the lab and wearily trudged back to his quarters, escorted by a different set of guards.

I silently noted that Pinky and Perky had been replaced by Tweedle Dumb and Tweedle Dee, who were just as bad, but perhaps less overt in their disrespect for the Professor. The Professor seemed not to notice. After all, he no doubt had experienced years of this.

As Thomas was fumbling for his key card, probably due to his exhaustion, three well-built young men happened to pass down the corridor.

They strutted like peacocks, expecting even the guards to make room for them, despite the ample width for all of us to pass by with space to spare. My implant could detect alcohol on their breath as they passed and their sniggered remarks boomed in my ears. "Looks like Thomas has a new boyfriend" one joked, referring to me.

I had a sinking feeling that these puff-chested bantams were my future class-mates, so I would have preferred to keep a low profile, but the leader's disrespectful sneer as he looked me up and down and his deliberate attempt to intimidate Thomas on his way past stung my ego and fired up protective instincts in me for my newfound friend.

I really should have stayed quiet, but my anger was piqued and demanded justice.

I turned to our guards and, with the same tone of voice that the brash young men had used, I declared "I see that the facility kindergarten has just kicked out the slow learners."

The eyes on my guards veritably bulged as what I said registered. Everyone went suddenly still and silent. All except for the apparent leader of the young men.

Clearly, he was used to the palpable nervousness coming from those around me but I held my nerve and my ground. I had dealt with bullies before.

"What did you say, Bitch?" he snapped at me, starting forward with his friends in his wake.

I stepped away from Thomas' doorway, unconsciously putting the leader between me and his entourage, but caught Thomas' look of horror as matters unfurled before him. "No Chris, you will not fight…" was all Thomas could get out before the biggest of the bullies was rounding on me.

"It's time YOU were schooled, son", was all the leader snarled out before his fist was flashing toward my face and his accomplices were fanning out with their fists also raised.

As before with the hypodermic-wielding nurse, my implant overlaid likely trajectories as the action unfolded. It also slowed my perception of time, but despite this, the leader was inhumanly fast. Without thought, my implant bobbed my head to one side, allowing the incoming knuckles to slip by, mere inches from my ear. My right arm came up to fend the punch away, in a move I now recognised as part of Wing Chun kung fu.

No sooner had I done so, then more blisteringly quick strikes were incoming and it was all my implant could do to keep me in one piece. Worse yet, I was now mindful of Thomas' reaction, and in my uncertainty, neither I nor my implant made effort to strike back and escalate the situation.

My diagnostic overlays were detailing the enormous forces within each strike thrown at me and the likelihood of internal injury or broken bones if they came into contact, as my forearms, elbows, shoulders and shins diverted every strike and kick.

By now, the leader's cheerleaders were crowding in behind him, disrupting his flow. The shorter, more pug-faced of the two, began to call encouragement. "That's it Flint, break his face."

The frustration began to show on Flint's face as he couldn't land a solid blow.

Although I might have bitten off more than I could chew, I marvelled at how my implant flawlessly switched from Kung Fu to Pencac Silat, to Dirty Boxing, to Aikido, but my lack of physical fitness and conditioning was showing as my body slowed.

One of Flint's devastating uppercuts brushed my ribs enough to push the air from my lungs and I almost failed to bob beneath a crushing right cross. My back slid along the wall of the walkway as Flint's fist smashed masonry in my wake.

The guards were now shouting frantically down their radios for backup and Thomas was waving his arms. "Stop this at once I say! Kester, Jarrod, Flint. Report to your handlers."

Thomas' uncharacteristically strident orders had cut through the red fog of battle, and the young men began to grow less sure of themselves.

But it was Flint himself, apparently as fickle and unpredictable as a flick-knife in a baby's crib, who suddenly straightened, all outward sign of anger sloughing off him.

The only evidence of our combat being the sheen of sweat on his muscled arms and boxer's brow, along with the broken blood vessels beneath the skin covering the knuckles of his right hand. He ignored his hand and the damage to the wall and I couldn't tell if this was a result of his relic or his pride.

That hadn't gone well at all. I had made enemies, stirred up a hornet's nest of security and undermined the Professor's authority. The only positive thing I could take from this episode was that I had burst my own bubble about being superhuman. Whilst I had put on a great show for a first effort, I was literally a couple of bob and weaves away from having my head taken off.

Flint and his cheerleaders stalked off before further security details arrived and a dismayed and rattled-looking Thomas advised we do the same.

Thomas showed me a small spare room within his quarters, along with his bathroom, and after leaving me with a clean towel and a toothbrush still in its cardboard-backed bubble, he retired and strongly suggested I do likewise. We would speak of this in the morning.

As I lay awake in my bunk, I contemplated that all of my initial assumptions about the agency had been well short of the mark. Knowing what I now knew, there would be no turning back. I would never be allowed this deep into the agency and back out again alive. But not only that, I had also let down my friend and mentor, which would likely reflect badly on him.

The icing on the cake was that I had also undoubtedly created some powerful enemies, even before my first day at the academy.

My last conscious thoughts were a request to my implant to awaken me refreshed in 8 hours, having consolidated my learning experience and healed my body.

With a heavy heart and yet more bruises to add to my collection, darkness took me.

Chapter 9

In the morning, the Professor seemed surprisingly upbeat about the whole affair. I had started with an apology, but Thomas dismissed it with an apology of his own.

"It is I who should apologise. I shouldn't have hamstrung you the way I did" he said, "it was dangerous and thoughtless of me."

My brow furrowed as I considered the Professor's unanticipated direction of thought. "Flint is lethal and once battle was joined, asking you not to strike back was naive of me." Thomas was genuinely sorry, as though he had wronged me. "Naive and dangerous of me. I could have got you killed. I really will try to do better. I just need to adjust from my own way of dealing with conflict to behaving like the handler of a relic should."

When the breakfast that Thomas had ordered arrived, we seated ourselves around his kitchen table to eat. The professor placed another nutrition shake in front of me as an accompaniment to my meal.

When I asked him what was in it, he responded with a simple "You tell me!"

No sooner had the request been uttered, my implant sprang into action. The wavelengths of light being reflected from the fluid were analysed, stimulating a long list of elements and molecules, much in the same way that astronomers used light refraction to study distant stars. Then my sense of smell took over to validate my findings. I took a sip and my vision lit up with additional information.

"It is a modified version of yesterday's brain support formula, but spiked with additional protein, nutrients for bone and joint support". I smiled and added "plus a liberal helping of the precursors of testosterone and anabolic steroids." The Professor really was trying to make amends if he was preparing my body for future combat.

"Well, it looks as though you have sufficient mastery of your implant to hold your own with the other students." Thomas' gentle smile faded a little.

"Your fine display with Flint attracted attention from our superiors. I was messaged this morning to confirm that you will be joining the academy later today. You are being fast-tracked".

I started to protest, but the Professor continued. "I have not been entirely forthcoming. We have never had a student make such swift progress as yourself." His lips pursed together as he formulated his words.

"Your relic appears to be somewhat unique. It has similarities to the others, but they look like clumsy toys in comparison. I was selected as your handler partially due to our compatibility from a personality profiling perspective, but also because I was one of the scientists who studied you after your recovery."

I knew he was referring to my missing nine days, where I had no memory and even my implant could only return 'classified' notices.

I felt a flicker of anger, but my loyalty to Thomas held my tongue in check whilst he unburdened himself.

"My colleagues believe your implant is much newer than the rest, due to its blatant superiority, but I believe it is much older and the other relics are inferior copies."

This really piqued my interest. To learn that there was some concealed portion of our history was to be expected, but the prospect of yet another earlier epoch was even more tantalising.

Noting my body language, the Professor looked somewhat relieved. He perhaps hadn't known how I would react. "I am not authorised to cover certain academy topics, so you will have to bear with me until you join your peers. But in due course I will have answers for you."

I nodded thoughtfully and after a moment of contemplation I assured the Professor that I trusted him enough to wait.

Emboldened by my response, Thomas added "Hold that thought. I have more to confess. You haven't grasped the full extent of what having a handler means. The agency have discovered how to secure the obedience of relics."

The added emphasis on the word 'obedience', and the subtle elevation in the Professor's heart rate did not bode well and I felt the walls closing in around me.

"Relics are comprised of a central system which enhances almost all aspects of physiology, but there are various additional interchangeable specialisation modules. Many relics are incomplete, including yours, but we have discovered specific modules for strength, speed, healing, combat and weapons, rapid learning, surveillance, communication, engineering and more. But all of them possess a control module, which corresponds to a command module."

My eyes narrowed as I followed this chain of thought to its logical conclusion. "Handlers have a command module for their relics?" I surmised with perhaps less venom than I felt.

I didn't even wait for Thomas' response. I knew the answer. My mind cast back to every command he had given me. "Assimilate...", "Extrapolate...", "Do not fight...", "You tell me...". I had jumped like a lapdog, due to the Professor's easy teaching skills, without realising that my implant would have compelled me regardless.

"How strong is the compulsion?" I asked, fearing the answer.

"Absolute. Even down to the cellular level. You are not a drone, you have your own thoughts, but your implant can override every single nerve impulse. The Agency could not afford to have such living weapons around without safeguards. You are a very valuable, but dangerous, asset. With that said, you have my word that I will not abuse my position as your handler while I have a say in the matter. But I had to explain it to you before you found out the hard way. I'm sorry my friend. We are both tools of the agency now."

Thomas meant every word. He believed it, but I wasn't willing to give up so easily.

I asked how long I had to prepare and what other skills I would need, to which the Professor replied "We have another three hours. In terms of skills, in all honesty, I do not know." Thomas looked crestfallen. "I have only ever worked with relics from the perspective of a researcher. I've never been a handler before." But after a contemplative pause he added, "There are powerful relics within the agency, so if you are able to excel in your studies and subsequent duties, then you may have a greater say in both our futures."

With that carrot left dangling before me, we concluded our meal and spent the rest of the morning in the Professor's laboratory, focused on suppressed and covert patents and figuring out how my implant could improvise novel uses for the technology. It wasn't necessarily going to help me as a student of the academy, but it was a pleasant distraction while I waited.

Chapter 10

After lunch, an instructor from the academy arrived to escort me to my new quarters. Tall, thickly muscled and dangerous looking, he was serious and straight to the point. There was no slouch to the man and his dark, chiselled features framed hard eyes as blue as chips of sapphire.

"You may call me Canis. It is a name bestowed upon me by my brothers of the academy. It was earned through blood, sweat, fire and service. Today, you will begin your journey and, in due course, forge your own name".

It was all very dramatic, but he was deadly serious and from his sinuous efficiency of motion, my implant silently rated him as a lethal threat.

"When you come with me," he continued, "you leave your old life behind. You will be remade. We will trim the fat and be left with the iron core. With that metal, we will shape a tool fit to save humanity."

Save humanity?! I had been straining through my implant to scavenge every possible clue from this taciturn man. But every word he uttered, he fervently believed to be true. I felt like my very foundations had been knocked sideways. What didn't I know?

Beyond his initial speech, Canis seemed a man of few words and not given to explaining himself, so I temporarily stowed my curiosity. I had no possessions to gather, so we left for the section of the facility specifically reserved for the academy.

As we left, like a doting mother hen, Thomas promised to attend me later to check on my progress. He also asked that I make what progress I could in his absence. I noted with relief that he had not obliged me to obey my new instructors at the academy. At least I had some discretion.

Canis glided ahead of me to an elevator which, after scanning his retinas, took us down deeper still into the earth.

The academy was a marvel of engineering which housed a great vaulted floodlit arena, along with several tiers of rooms overlooking it. The area was currently divided into different training zones, but it gave the impression of a versatile space, adaptable to the needs of the academy.

As we stood upon a broad mezzanine in between the living quarters and the training ground, my eyes were instantly drawn to a dozen or so individuals, each wearing snug black uniforms, in the midst of various simulations and exercises.

Canis turned to me and saw me watching. "Your new family will hold you to a higher standard from now on. Let's assign you some quarters, then you can be introduced to your peers and the other instructors."

The rooms that Canis ushered me towards were the self-contained quarters for the relics, but to my mind, they seemed little more than glamorous detention cells with kitchenettes and ensuite bathrooms.

As Canis pointed out trivial features of my new accommodation, I replayed in my mind the scene from the arena, as the other relics persevered in their training.

I recognised Flint and his cheerleaders, Kester and Jarrod, who were in the middle of manhandling human sized mannequins across an assault course whilst a Nubian giant of a man was laying down suppressing fire with plastic rounds. The relics were ducking and weaving in turn, drawing his fire as they each advanced through the course. I noted them occasionally twitching aside to avoid being struck by unanticipated rounds when the instructor wasn't fooled by their feints. Kester grunted as he was struck in the shin, but they continued undeterred.

Across from the assault course, a wiry, lean woman with iron-grey hair pulled back into a tight bun was instructing a group of four relics in the subtleties of knife combat. She held the arm of a balding relic with one hand as she demonstrated to the others the correct angles for a blade to more easily bypass a ribcage. A metal rack, positioned close by, housed numerous conventional weapons, along with an assortment of improvised ones. Battered chair legs were lined up with snooker queues, hammers, rolled magazines, chains, improvised flails, home-made garrottes, knuckle dusters, bats and more.

In the central portion of the arena was a mock-up of a high-tech secured facility where three more relics were working together to breach and navigate through without triggering the security lasers, pressure sensors and cameras. As I looked on in my mind's eye, a beautiful nymph of a girl was propelled upward in a graceful arc by the other two relics. Her somersault perfectly evaded the mechanical swing of the security camera and she sprang off the wall to brace herself into a corner, supported only by the toe of one outstretched boot, pressed against a marble worktop. No sooner was she airborne, then her two comrades were melting aside, out of view of the roving camera.

The gymnasium, pool, climbing wall and firing range lay empty, but a further three relics were seated in front of a bank of computer monitors, furiously interfacing via keyboard and mouse. Thanks to my rapid education by the Professor, I could recognise the login screens and system menus of various industrial software applications, such as would be found in power plants, robotically automated factories and banking institutions.

I was wondering what on earth the agency would be expecting of us with such training when Canis snapped me back to the present. "We are already familiar with the configuration of your implant, so much of your training will be more geared toward building muscle memory, teamwork with other relics and conditioning your body. Your fellow relics aren't all as fortunate as you in terms of modules, but they have made up for that in upwards of six months' hard training."

I nodded as he went on. "We do not have the luxury of starting you with another class, so you will have to catch up as best you can." Canis showed neither sympathy nor pleasure in what he was relating to me. It seemed that to him, facts were facts, black and white. No wonder he saw us as tools to be honed, as he himself was perhaps little more than a mechanical killer for the agency.

"We have an hour before your classmates get a break, so let us begin with some background information. I would personally rather put you to work with something more practical, but your sponsor believes you would be more... responsive... to our efforts to mould you if you were in full possession of the facts."

He gestured for me to take a seat as he turned to the black flat panel monitor on the wall of my quarters. A few deft finger strokes later and my first official academy briefing began.

Chapter 11

As my briefing completed, I became aware of Canis standing at ease, his thick arms folded across his brawny chest and his face an impassive mask. He was waiting patiently for me to assimilate the information.

As my assimilation completed, the magnitude of what I had learned hit me like a ton of bricks. In fact, I physically rocked back in my seat, my mind ablaze with more questions than answers.

Canis grinned at me wolfishly, knowing the perverse mix of horror, anger, urgency and determination which must be coursing through me.

"One more of us, one less of them!" he intoned with mock gravitas. It was the first sign of any humour from him, as he waited patiently for my response.

"There could be another six billion of us if we played it differently" I shot back at him with genuine anger.

Chapter 12

Of course, it is common knowledge now, but back in 2010, the general public didn't know about the Anunnaki or their planet, Nibiru. Only NASA insiders, or those who had read Zecharia Sitchin's translations of the 6000 year old Sumerian tablets even considered that humans could have been a genetically engineered slave race, abandoned on earth by their creators. TV shows of the era, such as 'Ancient Aliens' presented watered down evidence for the masses, to condition people for future disclosure, but nobody took it very seriously.

In fact, more accurately, anyone even discussing the topic in those days was mocked as a conspiracy theorist, such was the success of government sponsored disinformation programmes. Subtle propaganda had been in full swing since the late 1940s, and by the 21st century, with over 1500 TV stations, 9000 radio stations, 1500 newspapers, 1100 magazines and 2400 publishers owned and controlled by just six corporations, it wasn't hard for the Agency and its masters to restrict the flow of information.

You have to remember that back then, such theories undermined religion, academic institutions, governments, the financial system and more. People weren't ready to ditch their firmly held beliefs. So even when mainstream archaeologists failed to locate our evolutionary 'missing link' (because there wasn't one) and scientists had clearly shown upwards of ten thousand transcription errors in the human genome consistent with genetic engineering (not present in other primate species), it didn't matter. Because as they say, who lets facts get in the way of a good story?

I was already familiar with the alternative archaeological research prior to my briefing, but having it confirmed by the Agency was still completely mind blowing. I remember thinking that Lloyd Pye, and his groundbreaking book "Everything you know is wrong", was pretty well on the money.

But what gave this Agency briefing some real sting in its tail, was the fact that planet Nibiru, with its vast 3600 year elliptical orbit, was almost ready to pass earth again. The Agency knew that with media control or not, they weren't going to be able to conceal a planet, 8 times larger than Earth, tearing through our solar system - let alone the inevitable return of Anunnaki forces.

With Nibiru's passing, we could face tidal calamities, a potential shifting of our poles, along with conflict with the Anunnaki themselves, if they intended to reclaim their planet. After all, as far as they were concerned, they were here first, and as our creators, we were their property.

There was no escaping it, we faced a monumental crisis. Not every passing was a disaster, but 13,000 years ago, when Nibiru passed through our solar system on the same side of the sun as Earth, the extreme gravitational forces caused a huge section of polar ice to break away and slough into the ocean, triggering a tsunami of biblical proportions, literally. Every culture in the world now knew this deluge as the great flood, and it changed the face of our world.

All of the wonders of the ancient world were largely scrubbed from the face of the earth, or else buried under great depths of silt, with no record of them and almost nobody to remember. Only the global network of pyramids, gold mines and temples remained as mute testimony to the Anunnaki occupation.

More disconcerting was that the Anunnaki themselves had known of the coming calamity and yet had callously allowed the disaster to thin out our population. Where they couldn't reach democratic consensus over our deliberate extermination, they still agreed to a policy of non-intervention, which led to the deaths of untold millions.

I agreed with the Agency's conclusion that the Anunnaki were no friends of ours!

The briefing had continued with details of how the remaining Anunnaki had fled Earth with Nibiru's last passing, in the midst of civil war and nuclear calamity, leaving behind one last remaining royal Anunnaki named Marduk, along with his retainers. Marduk's victory was hollow, however, as his prize was a radiated wasteland inhabited by hostile humans.

The final broadcast from the departing ships, which is carved to this day into the 19 foot granite slabs of the Georgia guide stones, was a list of commandments, which began "Maintain humanity under 500,000,000 in perpetual balance with nature". This was something we clearly hadn't adhered to as a species.

Although the Agency believed Marduk to have been subsequently overthrown and killed during Roman times, Earth's ruling elite still tremble at the echoes of that last broadcast. The Anunnaki were tremendously long-lived and they would not forgive and forget.

The briefing concluded with a stark warning. “That was 3562 years ago. Nibiru is almost here. We have a choice. Establish a one-world government and thin out the population in the hopes of meeting the Anunnaki's final directive and becoming a vassal planet, or else establish a one-world government in readiness for war with a technologically superior foe.”

My mind churned furiously. It appeared that opinion within the agency (and the power behind it), was divided. But whichever side I took, the outlook for mankind appeared pretty dire.

The thought of wiping out over 6 billion of our own species and throwing ourselves on the mercy of our former oppressors sickened me. It was a dark betrayal by sly men, used to skulking in the shadows. Yet to ready ourselves for global conflict, we would need to gain the support of the masses, which in turn would require disclosure and the monumental chaos that would entail.

I now understood that disclosure of the existence of extra terrestrial life wasn't the problem - especially if the so called aliens looked like us. It was the very real threat of extermination or slavery that would panic the populous and hamper any resistance at all.

Chapter 13

Canis was unphased by my outburst. He clearly expected a strong reaction from every new relic he dropped this bombshell on. In fact, I think he used the response to profile which side of the fence you would be on.

"We have more ground to cover before you meet the others," he said sternly. "The Agency likes to believe that all the decisions are down to us, but in reality, there are still three separate blocks of power in this world". He had my attention.

"The agency is part of the Anglo-American-Israeli block. We have infiltrated both the Russian and the Chinese blocks, but we do not yet control them." His eyes watched my every reaction and he no doubt listened to my heart rate as well. Satisfied by what he detected, he went on. "Each block has their own relics and believe me, all the manuals in the Agency won't prepare you for contact with them. You see, we don't just hunt buried relics, we also hunt live ones - and so do they!"

To illustrate his meaning, he set his feet and drew himself up to his full height in front of me. With a deep inhalation, he extended a hand in mid-air towards me, palm upwards. As his fingers began to close in a beckoning gesture, a dull hum and an ache tickled the edge of my senses. I could discern the crackle of some form of energy forming in the air between us, but my education hadn't covered whatever it was.

As I sat and looked on, perplexed, the world seemed to slow and the background noise receded from me. It was a strangely relaxing sensation at first, but the dull hum gradually intensified into a throb and a slight dimming of my peripheral vision. It was like being a candle flame trapped under a glass as the oxygen gradually burns away.

I felt a stab of panic as my skin began to bead with perspiration and as my mind grew increasingly confused. My internal organs felt as though they were tugging at the connective tissue which held them in place and this feeling was intensifying at an alarming pace.

Canis now stood over me, filling my vision, his arm still extended, an intense scowl furrowing his brow. As I looked on in mute horror, his hand was closing into a grasping miser's claw. It was like he was calling to parts of my implant and they were reluctantly obeying. With every passing moment, the force grew and the disturbing ripping feeling inside me ratcheted to new heights. The throb became a sharp pain, the sharp pain became a shooting agony and the agony soon began to blur what was left of my vision. Just as I felt I would burst open like a rotten melon, I panicked out of my inaction and my implant lashed out violently.

Evidently, my implant knew what Canis was doing, even if I didn't. My vision snapped back into focus with a sudden tensing of my abdominal muscles and ribcage and using this same mystery force, my implant pulled back. But not just with a gradual pressure. Instead it snatched violently at my own internal modules and all of the implants and modules in Canis' general direction, seemingly with extra focus on the modules at the base of his spine.

With a grunt, Canis staggered forward, one meaty hand slapping down on the furniture next to him to keep from falling. Behind him, across the mezzanine, my suddenly enhanced hearing picked up startled cries, followed by a buzz of conversation.

"Careful!", Canis cried, his voice a whip crack, anger bubbling through his stony exterior. "That is how training accidents happen".

I think I was as shocked as he was about what had just happened, but I couldn't tell whether his ire was directed at my clumsiness or at his own failure to maintain control of his demonstration.

Before I had rationalised what had happened, I was hurriedly getting to my feet and stammering an apology as I went to help him. My gut reaction was to feel mortified. It was as though I had slapped my instructor full in the face during a martial arts class.

But Canis was a professional. As he straightened and regained his composure, he waived me away. "I will accept responsibility for that one. I didn't set boundaries, nor explain the demonstration. But you will NEVER, EVER strike at an instructor without invitation. Do you understand me?"

"Yes Sir", I nodded, my face flushed with embarrassment.

"And in any event," Canis continued, "it is bad form to pull the plug on a fellow relic. We might fight dirty out in the real world, but here, that was a low blow".

I now understood what my implant had done to Canis at the base of his spine. It had tugged sharply on one of the modules responsible for powering his relic, temporarily disrupting his efforts and distracting him. I couldn't take any credit for the move, but I guiltily tried to hold on to what I had done, in case I ever needed to use the move again.

As I tried to settle and relax, my implant refused to do the same. Instead, it drew a series of vibrant red lines, each as thin as a thread, to every relic within range. The lines overlaid my vision and rather distractingly, they passed through walls and objects. I tried to blink them away, but I could now detect each of the relics around me, including Canis, even through my eyelids.

"OK. Well. We are done here for now." Canis concluded, his scowl fading. "I was going to walk you through some other basic defensive techniques before you met your peers, but I think that little demonstration will be enough to make them wary of you for now."

'Was that just a demonstration?' I wondered, or was it a test? Or was Canis trying to take advantage of a rookie recruit to upgrade his own implant? Either way, my implant's response had just exposed this whole confusing encounter to the entire population of the arena.

I was bewildered and disappointed, but before turning on his heel to leave, Canis added "Only Paredo has a 'siphon' as strong as yours, so don't throw your weight around here unnecessarily. Save that for out in the field. I have built a well balanced team here and don't need you to change the dynamics. Your uniform is already in the drawers beneath your bunk. Join us in 20 minutes".

Without a second glance, he puffed up his chest and sauntered out onto the mezzanine as though nothing had happened. As he moved further away, my implant dimmed the red overlays until they were gone. Well, that was one thing to be thankful for.

But with my instructor's departure, my mood grew darker. However much I thought I knew before, I had discovered that this new world of intrigue was made of riddles inside of mysteries, all wrapped up in lies. Who could I trust, as everyone seemed to have their own agenda. Thomas had eased my passage into the academy and I felt inclined to trust him to a degree, but ultimately, I felt I was on my own.

Chapter 14

As I crossed the mezzanine, freshly dressed and bathed in the harsh white glare of the overhead floodlights, I expanded my senses in every way I knew how. I wanted my wits about me and any clues about my peers, however subtle, would be welcome.

I reached a wide set of stairs, leading down to the arena itself, where the other relics now rested in groups. Some were seated on benches, holding muted conversation, others were leaning on whatever was near whilst they stretched out tired limbs. Jarrod and Kester were lying on the ground, bathed in sweat and lungs still heaving. But Flint stood, almost fully composed, directing a hard, challenging stare toward me as I approached. It reeked of territorialism, but he didn't appear to be as volatile as he was the last time we met.

It struck me in that moment, that whilst the other students were yet to be named by their brother and sister relics based upon their character traits and deeds, Flint had walked in with a name that was already appropriate.

Eyes followed me as I approached, and Canis beckoned me over to where he and the other two instructors waited.

With a perfunctory nod toward his sister instructor, who managed to look elegant despite the uniform, he said "This is Sericum, our hand-to-hand combat specialist. And this..." he turned to the black tower of a man to his left, "is Acertas. He is our ranged weapon and explosives expert."

With a generous and gleaming white smile, Acertas nodded his blocky head in my direction. Acertas meant 'force' in Latin, and I could tell exactly why his peers had named him so. At almost 7 feet tall, he must have been at least 350 lbs of dense muscle. My implant helpfully supplied 348 lbs as it took in and assessed every figure near enough to pose a threat. But for now he seemed jovial and friendly.

But it was the graceful Sericum who was first to break the silence. "Welcome to our humble training ground, Chris. Please, join us and make yourself at home." Sericum was everything her name implied - 'Silk' in Latin. She was attractive, yet refined, with just a hint of a conspiratorial sparkle that never left her eyes. She made you feel as though you both shared a private joke and that built an intangible aura of trust in very short order. She had the unlined face and physique of a much younger woman, but the steel-grey hue of her hair confused the eye and put her at some indeterminate age around the mid 50's.

"Let's allow your fellows to regain their composure whilst I show you the facilities" she said as she led me away from the group, toward the training zones. She kept her explanation of the facility brief, as my peers were no doubt as curious about me as I was of them. Despite giving no reason to doubt her sincerity, I couldn't quite bring myself to relax in her presence. Silk from a soft, alluring negligee could as easily be used as a garrotte, and from what I had seen on the training ground, I knew Sericum would be just as versatile. Nevertheless, she was charming and I warmed to her.

As we approached the group again, she casually dropped that usually, this would be where she would attack new relics without warning, in order to test their current level of skill and integration with their implants. Fortunately for us both, she had already watched the security footage of my encounter with Flint and felt my 'siphoning' with Canis from a distance. She couldn't contain a rich throaty laugh at Canis' expense about that.

"No. I see it's wise to operate more openly with you, to prevent... unnecessary complications. Your new family have already formed that opinion." Her eyes slid to my peers as we approached. "Verity here was almost lost for words". Sericum teased as she laid a hand on Verity's arm with a warm smile. "Almost!"

Verity was one of the relics I had seen operating the computers. She had the plain look of a librarian about her, perhaps in her late twenties, but she cut a fine figure in her dark suit. In fact, as my eyes panned around, I noted that they all did. There couldn't have been more than 5 lbs of spare flesh amongst them all.

I looked down at my own suit self consciously. Whilst I wasn't sporting a spare tyre around my middle, I didn't have the hard and compactly muscled body common to my peers.

Verity offered me a hand to shake, which I accepted with a smile and some small pleasantry. I moved along the group, greeting people and exchanging nods or smiles as I went. Some relics came in closer to greet me, but others did not.

Of course, I was already familiar with Jarrod, Kester and Flint, who just offered non-committal nods or mock salutes. In Flint's case, he simply said flatly, "We've met", which triggered some stifled laughter from the other relics, who must have heard about our encounter. Flint's complexion darkened, but beyond that, he pretended not to hear.

The warmest of the other students was Oliver, the balding relic I had seen helping Sericum with her demonstration. He was a former structural engineer from London, who had been implanted when he had been inspecting a collapse in the London Underground subway system which led to the discovery of buried remains. He was by far the most talkative of the group and did his best to bring me up to speed with my new peers.

He explained that amongst the group, we had people from all walks of life, including a museum curator, a deep sea diver, a farmer, two soldiers, a paramedic, a seismologist, a police officer, a digger operator... even a drug smuggler. But the common theme was that as soon as they had come into contact with their relics, they had been swiftly intercepted by the agency and brought to this facility.

The exception to this was Hector, a fierce and swarthy Hispanic in his late twenties who had been involved in digging tunnels under the US / Mexican border for one of the Mexican drug cartels.

He had been an urchin raised by the streets, earning him the respect and loyalty of the underbelly of society. As a result, he had evaded the various Agencies for almost three months before capture. But to my eye, he still looked aloof from the group.

As Oliver's loose tongue wagged, he received some smiles and some dark looks from the other relics, but he was tolerated. I suppose he served as an unofficial notice board for life in the academy. He clearly loved to talk and went on to say that several of our class were already on field assignments, so you could never predict what each day would bring. Interestingly, he also explained that the instructors were all currently serving operatives who were cycled in and out of the academy, so it was best to learn what you could, when you could. Any lessons missed, may be missed for good.

Equally, they only taught the skills they used, so I wouldn't be burdened with any useless outdated theory.

As the break time came to an end and the other relics hastily gulped final mouthfuls of water from their canteens, Sericum returned. As Oliver's enthusiastic welcome had begun, she had given me a knowing smile and discreetly withdrawn to the company of the other instructors. But now, with her arrival and a crisp clap of her hands, she restored interested silence within the group.

"Right, ladies and gentlemen", she began. "On behalf of my fellow instructors and myself, I would like to congratulate you all on excelling in your studies and developing your remarkable abilities." She paused, allowing her words to sink in. "I have no doubt that you will make fine agents in the coming days. But today, we have a new initiate into our brotherhood. He doesn't have the luxury of your hard training, nor your experience, yet he will be working alongside you in the field sooner than you might think. You have all strived and competed to prove yourself the best in your own unique ways." Meaningful looks passed between her and some of the students.

"But as I have often said, such competition in private, must yield to teamwork and trust in the course of our duties in the field. Out there, we have to rely upon each other. It is no exaggeration to say that although many missions are mundane, I have saved the lives of other agents in the field, and they have saved me." The importance of her words stretched on in the silence.

"It is in such times that all of our training and dedication to teamwork makes the difference between life and death. Winning and losing. Success or failure. I ask every one of you to consider this. We each strive to be the best we can be and to prove ourselves unique and indispensible to the agency and a boon to mankind. But in the field, your new brother may be your only lifeline, just as you may be his. So today, I would ask you to put aside your personal feelings, set aside the politics of your sponsors and bring your new brother into the bosom of our family."

At this my heart surged. The lovely Sericum was smoothing my way into the group. But no sooner had I lapped up the honeyed words, then I began to realise that they were tainted and turning more sour by the moment.

A few brows had begun to crease at this unanticipated direction of Sericum's speech, but we all looked on as she triggered the trap she had just laid. "Today, YOU will be the instructors. You will work your new brother hard and drill him to the standard you would expect from yourself. If you ever require his proficiency in the field and he is found wanting, then you will only have yourself to blame. This young man may one day hold the lives of your brothers and sisters in his hands. Help him earn that trust."

Her manipulation of the group was masterful. Those relics with a genuine affinity for the group would train me to their utmost ability, whilst those with vested interests and a mean streak would work me like a dog - each side thanking her for setting up the opportunity.

"Return to the stations where you bear the highest proficiency. You may practice your own preferred disciplines until Chris works his way around the arena to you. Ben, Zoe, Omar, as your stations are last on the circuit, you may take two hours' free time. Return here fresh to deliver your instruction".

Some of the relics refused to meet my gaze, whilst others shot me apologetic glances as they jogged off to their posts. Of course, I anticipated the triumphant crowing from Kester and Jarrod, but I didn't know how to read the pursed lips on Flint as he locked unblinking eyes with Sericum. Perhaps he didn't know how to play the ball she had just thrown him.

Chapter 15

I was snapped out of my reminiscence and back to the present by an urgent whisper from Harris, as word came back along the steel gantry that we had encountered something new. I heightened my senses and strode forward through the darkness.

Going over my memories had helped with my anxiety, but my implant still cautiously assessed the steel grating beneath every footstep. I passed some of my men, who had unslung their weapons and taken a knee in anticipation.

It wasn't long before my enhanced vision picked out the source of their concern. Ahead, the gantry was twisted and splayed and the long-dead remains of authority soldiers, (or perhaps more accurately, parts of them), littered the way. My implant overlaid likely trajectories of the shrapnel and shells embedded in the structure and neighbouring cavern wall and confirmed that both conventional and energy weapons had been responsible.

The way looked passable if we went single file, but that didn't address why the authorities hadn't cleared their dead. Such a scene undermined their apparent superiority and would allow their weaponry to fall into enemy hands. At worst, after a victory they would toss the remains into the void, but would never leave such a scene behind.

I hoped the combatants were long gone, but with the rise of artificial intelligence and the resulting drone wars, whatever or whomever had done this could still be ahead, patiently standing sentinel for all eternity.

I carefully considered our options. As brave and loyal as many of my men were, blundering into a killing field wouldn't help, so I asked them to stay put whilst I ventured on alone.

I am sure some wanted to protest, but harsh whispers exchanged with their brothers-at-arms kept them silent. I took an additional coil of rope from Chavez and a much more high-tech retractable nanofilament line offered by Darius, before edging out onto the damaged walkway.

Every sense screamed at me, as I left the safety of the rails, but my footing was sure and within moments I was across the damaged section. That's not to say that the remainder of the gantry wasn't pitted and pocked with small arms fire, artillery shells and plasma grenades.

As I made progress, I could now detect the hazy beginnings of the cavern wall in the distance to my right, across the abyss. Clearly, whatever chasm yawned beneath the earth was narrowing to a close ahead.

The walkway was arcing out of sight to my left in a vast crescent, broken intermittently by desiccated corpses in their sunken-chested uniforms. Just as frequently, there were missing grates that had been dislodged during the fighting to drop to the unfathomable depths below.

The further I progressed, the nearer the opposite cavern wall became, until I could make out a narrow walkway running along its edge, back the way we had come.

I reached out with my senses and was just about to hurl a rock across the gap to trigger some echo mapping by my implant, when I was startled by a sweep of infrared flare coming from round the bend up ahead.

As the bright glow licked up the gangway to within just inches of my feet, I flinched back as close to the cavern wall as the gaps in the railing would allow and waited with baited breath. Another few feet and I would be lit up for all to see. But as swiftly as it arrived, the spotlight swung away.

The glow swept back moments later in the exact same place, so I didn't need my implant to tell me that the source of the light was stationary, nor that it had the predictable mechanical rhythm of a machine.

I knelt and, putting fingers to the steel walkway, felt for vibrations. I felt no footsteps, no motors or generators. Just the subtle action of the water running down the rock at my back. Added to this, there were none of the usual scents of people. The area ahead seemed to be as lifeless as the unfortunate authority soldiers scattered along the gantry.

But whether the roving glow was the product of a camera or some form of mechanised defence system, I wasn't going to step into the line of fire to find out.

The old fashioned tricks, such as using a mirror to look around corners would only give away my position if any automated systems were using pixel tracking technology. I had to be out of sight altogether.

I cast my eyes around for inspiration. But finding none, I backed up until I could reach the outer rail of the gantry without exposing myself to the mysterious mechanical observer. I was going to have to advance underneath the gantry.

The thought made my stomach churn, but the prospect of walking into a hail of bullets from an automated gun turret was worse. I think my implant was wearying of my persistent fear, because it shot me with a gut-full of adrenaline.

I reached for the nanofilament line that Darius had given me. My implant helpfully highlighted the most structurally sound anchor point, so in moments my harness and the steel gantry were connected by an 80 metre line that could withstand five metric tonnes of tension. The line would deploy from its case automatically, but a fall would trigger magnetic braking. The only downside was that the line was far too narrow to climb after a fall and the enclosed motor only had enough charge to hoist a man's weight once. It would have to do.

With my Kevlar impregnated gloves creaking quietly as I tested my grip in the darkness, I climbed over the rail.

As I hung beneath the walkway, I found the corrosion from the running water was much more extensive than above, but even so, there were enough reliable hand and foot holds to advance supported by fingertips and toes.

But each time I shifted my grip, a small shower of rust flakes fell away, making me wince at the clatter against my clothing. I had to keep reminding myself that only I could hear it.

After thirty metres or so, my forearms were beginning to burn, so I decided to edge in towards the cavern wall where there were more beams and potential places to rest and reconnoitre what lay above.

To my right, the opposite side of the cavern was now just a mere 20 metres away and, up ahead, I could see that the walkway turned a sharp right to span the gap, where it was reinforced by stone and concrete. At this point, the gantry appeared to join a road wide enough for vehicles, so I assumed that there must be another main entry point to the cavern above me.

As the roving spotlight passed overhead and swept well behind me, I pulled myself up so my face was close to the corroded underside of the walkway and chanced a quick glance through the grating above me. My heart sank.

A few feet away, towering a good 9 feet tall stood a battered titan series mechanised defence drone. Its grinning steel skull was turning in time with the infrared illuminator mounted on its shoulder. It was tarnished, dented, burnt and its grenade and missile hard points looked to be empty, but the midigun mounted on one thick forearm looked fully functional. These units were the utilitarian workhorse of the drone wars.

They were relatively simple to maintain, operated reliably in the worst conditions and were as lethal as anything that came later. Early models were designed with the same bipedal skeleton and proportions of a human to gain acceptance, but as the drone wars raged on, they had been made increasingly large and menacing. Later models dwarfed their operators and, in all fairness, this one was no toy.

I knew from experience that they couldn't be trusted with any sophisticated missions, but if you wanted something dead or defended, the titan series were good units.

It stood sentry in the darkness, it's metallic frame stylised to appear grotesquely muscular and threatening.

I should have known that an abandoned A.I. substation would be too good to be true, but we were desperate and grasping at straws.

I was no match for this mechanical killer head-on and only lightly armed, but I could have attempted a hack if I still had a communication module. Unfortunately, I had severed my comms module decades before as part of my escape from the agency.

Looking up through the steel walkway I knew that this infiltration was going to be harder than I thought.

The only good thing I could salvage from this situation was that the substation was definitely not in authority hands.

I was about to turn back and retrace my route to my men, when I caught sight of something over the armoured shoulder of the titan. Something I hadn't seen in years.

Emblazoned across the wall behind the titan was a multicoloured patchwork of materials that formed a symbol. Well two symbols in fact. The first was the symbol for the Academy, but the second, as if graffiti tagged over the top of it, was the symbol for the Zeta Mexican drug cartel. Both had been gone for almost 50 years, so how was this possible?

The answer hit me like an icy slap to the face from beyond the grave.

I was looking at the scene in 'full spectrum', hence the multicoloured appearance of the symbol. As I cycled my vision through the various wavelengths of heat, light, radiation and more, parts of the symbols disappeared into a patchwork of seemingly random parts.

To anyone else, even someone with advanced technology, the symbol would appear as just a few random patches on a wall. But to a relic who had gone 'full spectrum', it would form a complete image as plain as day.

This could only have been put together by a surviving relic. But I only knew of one relic who would have used the Zeta gang sign. 'Solus', or as I once knew him, Hector.

Hector was like a brother to me, but what I was seeing was impossible. Hector was dead. I should know - I killed him.

Chapter 16

As I hung, suspended by my fingertips in the darkness, I searched my mind for clues to explain what I saw.

None of it made any sense. I shifted my weight to one side to get a better look at the symbols, but the shift in my grip crunched against the corroded steel and sent a tiny cascade of rust fragments tumbling down my clothing.

It should have been barely perceptible over the noise of the water, but to my alarm, I was suddenly bathed in the titan's spotlight as its head whipped around with a hiss of servos to glare straight at me.

Time slowed as we both reacted simultaneously. The titan's arm-mounted midigun began to rotate up to speed as it's arm extended menacingly towards me. I am sure my implant's intent was to just let go and free-fall until my nanofilament swung me clear, but my grip had tightened in horror at the prospect.

In that fractional hesitation, the percussive thump, thump, thump of 50 calibre rounds began exploding from the titan's cluster of barrels and high velocity lances of lead began stitching through the grating towards me.

We were both bathed by the strobing muzzle flash and the buzz of glowing steel splinters as the searing cascade of shells carved through the steel gantry between us.

My implant changed tactics and jerked me to one side behind a thicker supporting beam, leaving a trail of molten destruction in my wake, but this forced the titan to break off its assault momentarily to track my movement.

Before the smoke was even clear, the titan sprang forward towards me with the harsh screech of steel on steel.

My precarious grip under the gantry was tested to its limits when the titan landed heavily and thrust oversized mechanical fingers into the grate I clung to. The fingers bunched into a fist, crushing ripples into the rusty steel above me and suddenly both the panel and myself were lifted straight upwards.

I hung, suspended face to face with the titan, who stood with one arm outstretched and legs braced, its steel toes biting into the protesting walkway below it. Smoke still belched from the barrels as its arm-mounted gun raised toward me. Whether it intended to crush me in its grip or mow me through with white-hot lead, I didn't wait to find out.

My implant and I acted with unified purpose and did the only thing we could. We had to tangle the mechanical killer in the nanofilament line still clipped to my harness.

My legs scissored out in front of me to wrap about the extending arm as I used the droid's own strength and momentum to corkscrew myself forward, feet first. I managed to bypass the questing fingers and the end of the canon, but felt the immense contrast in temperature between the cold steel arm and the gunpowder-heated barrel against my legs as I slid forward, over and around the titan's arm.

No sooner had I released my grip then I was slipping over the groping limb and down the titan's slick armoured flanks. As my feet hit the deck, one hand went to my belt to unclip the small case containing the nanofilament line whilst the other fended the droid away from me. I couldn't match its strength, but whilst I could keep from its crushing grip I stood a chance.

I had already heard shouts of alarm from my men back along the gantry and hoped that some small measure of suppressing fire would be enough for the artificial intelligence to prioritise them over me. I only needed a small window of distraction.

As the clip of my nanofilament case came free, my other hand yanked the loop of filament taught about the arm as I depressed the emergency retraction mechanism. The fraction of a second it took for the safety line to take up the slack almost cost me my life as the titan reached for me. But before it could unleash a lethal strike or grab a fist full of flesh and clothing, the line thrummed like a string on a base and the titan was twisted about.

With a whine of servos and a hiss of hydraulics, one chromed foot stepped sideways to brace against the unanticipated force of the nanofilament motor, but the other foot was tangled into the shredded metal grate at its feet.

The towering machine looked down at its feet, then back towards its trailing arm, then back at me, it's baleful glowing eyes boring into me accusatively.

Unable to bring its gun to bear, and with me hastily backing away as I drew my sidearm, the titan made another lurching grab for me. It stupidly used the hand still clutching the metal grate. I was close enough to be buffeted by the air it displaced, but the increasingly encumbered titan didn't have the sense to release its fingers.

Fortunately, with every shift of its bulk, the titan was being ratcheted toward the hole in the walkway whilst the tiny motor on the nanofilament line squealed and smoked.

I brought up my sidearm and drew a bead on its eyes and illuminator and squeezed off a dozen tightly clustered shots.

As fragmentation rounds blasted pits into the droid's face and shoulder, it was wise enough to duck its head and turn its one remaining good eye away from me. It even brought up the grate in its hand to protect itself.

I could now hear booted feet beating up the gangway, but knew my men were still precious seconds away.

The titan was obviously piecing its predicament together and changing its strategy. It looked back at its trailing arm as the forearm-mounted barrel began to rotate again, but instead of attempting to bring the gun to bear on me, it began to spray a wide strafing arc across the gantry in an attempt to shear the nanofilament.

I was now standing clear, but if the titan broke free, there would be no cover. So, brandishing my tactical knife and my pistol with just four remaining fragmentation rounds, I sprinted back towards the titan.

I fired as I ran, my implant targeting the remaining known weak points, if you could call them that. Blowing out a hydraulic hose behind one armoured knee, I caused the hampered drone to stagger slightly, but fortune favoured me when it tried to take a backward step.

With a frustrated heave of its immobilised leg, both the grate and foot came free together. To my eyes it was as though the titan was sporting a ludicrous oversized snowshoe. With several clumsy attempts, it tried to place its foot, but the steel panel caught in the gap in the gantry and toppled the huge automaton backwards.

How the nanofilament line hadn't been destroyed in the Catherine wheel of lead spewing from the titan's midigun, I will never know.

But as I sprinted the gap between us, tactical knife in hand and pistol now discarded to the deck, the floundering titan was being dragged like a turtle on its back toward the gaping hole I had been lifted through.

Metal screeched, sparks flew, servos whined and the percussive thump, thump, thump of the titan's canon filled my senses. But just as the titan kicked its foot free of the metal grating, it was pulled backwards into the hole left by the missing grate.

It would have been swinging at the bottom of Darius' nanofilament line if the grate in its hand hadn't spanned the corner of the hole, leaving the impotent droid hanging by its fingertips, whilst being spread-eagled by the filament attached to the other arm. It dangled like a fly caught in a spider's web, gnashing its chromed teeth and out of combative options.

When my men burst onto the scene, guns drawn and breathing heavily, I was standing over the immobilised titan series, feeling amused at the strange quirks of fate that had allowed us to trade places in a few frenzied moments.

I had my knife poised to pry the mechanical fingers loose, when the tension in the men around me exploded into course laughter and sheer disbelief.

To my men, all hell had broken loose in the darkness. Yet in a fireworks display of midigunfire, I had seemingly marched in, trussed up a mechanised defence drone with my bare hands and hung it out to dry.

A few warm claps on the back later, with some raucous jokes thrown in for good measure, my men settled enough to secure the area.

More than one man asked for the privilege of prying the droid loose and dropping it to the depths of the void, but Decker quietly informed me that he could rig a good enough connection to hack the titan series.

As dangerous as it was, it was worth the attempt. This kind of hardware would be invaluable in the war, even if it was just to guard our ragtag community while we took the fight to the authority.

Chapter 17

While Decker worked in the darkness, the rest of us took a well-needed break.

For now, morale was at an all-time high, despite the recent lows and resistance toward this mission.

After all, not everyone in our community believed it was worth the risk. So I intended to enjoy the goodwill whilst it lasted. With any luck, bringing home such a prize would grease the wheels of my leadership and quiet some of the more vocal naysayers.

They weren't a bad bunch, but you couldn't please everyone.

I took the time to thank Darius for lending me his safety line, but apologised for the state it was in now. The only way I could make up for it was to roundly give credit to him for our victory over the titan in front of the other men. He seemed pleased with that and assured me there was more hardware where that came from, but I knew how hard it was to come by good tech.

Some of the men took the opportunity to pass out ration packs and water, which I was grateful for, as I sat in the darkness contemplating the relic graffiti on the wall. No doubt more than one of my men assumed I was simply staring into space, because I didn't share my findings. I would lose the confidence we had just built up if they thought they might be up against another relic like me.

But what could it mean? I wondered.

As I stared, the mystery nagged at me and drove my implant to review my memories of the Academy for clues. My vision swirled and decades fell away as I mentally returned to the Academy arena.

Chapter 18

There is an old Chinese saying - "you never truly know someone until you have fought with them". It took my first day within the Academy to really show me how true this was. Perhaps 'fought' isn't always the right word, but to compete on a visceral level opens up aspects of personality you wouldn't otherwise see in another. In mundane day-to-day living, where people are rarely at odds with each other, let alone fighting for survival, it is very hard to see what they're truly made of. But during conflict or fierce competition, the thin veneer of civility is stripped away and you get to see the true core of a person.

Sericum guided me to every section of the arena, where I faced a new challenge with each of my fellow relics. At every station, I was shown a new skill.

Some relics took extra care and attention to ensure I learned the lesson well, whilst others were vague and dismissed my questions with off-handed responses. "You'll pick it up, or learn the hard way" was a common response amongst Hiram's relics, and I expected no less, but Sericum's subtle scowl was an interesting thread I resolved to pick at later.

But in every case, no sooner was the lesson delivered, then I was expected to immediately put what I had learned into practice. To my relief, not every challenge was physical, but every one carried an element of pain, danger or both.

In some instances I would be paired up with my tutor to act as a team, whilst in others, I would be set against them head to head.

It became apparent that Sericum was choosing the order of the trials to make it possible to complete them, by interspersing physical lessons with mental ones, and any trial requiring specific knowledge had typically been addressed by the earlier trials. In this way, I was able to make a decent showing of myself and not come away with too many injuries.

My first trial was with Jesse, the delicate wisp of a girl I had seen evading the security systems in the arena. She seemed shy, but her warmth soon shone through as she explained the lesson she was to give me. There was no guile in her and her openness made you want to reciprocate. She led me to an aluminium box on a table, labelled 'Biofeedback'. She unclipped the catches and casually flipped the lid open. Reaching inside, she surprised me by pulling out an electric stun gun for subduing cattle during slaughter.

This wasn't looking good.

She took a step towards me, idly tapping the chromed side of the device with a finger nail, before saying "Studies conducted over the last 35 years by scientists in the public domain have shown that precognition of future events is rare and sporadic. However, 'presentiment', or the subconscious 'feeling' of future events, is real and VERY predictable." She paused to note my interest in what she was saying and then continued.

"Test subjects shown traumatic images, or who are exposed to unexpected loud noises, have blatant, measurable physiological changes anywhere from 1 to 10 seconds prior to the actual event. They don't consciously perceive the changes beforehand, but with the right monitoring, the body responds every time. This information is pretty useless, unless you are a relic. Fortunately for us, we can monitor our physiological responses all the time and get a very small warning prior to any event of major emotional or psychological impact."

Jesse began to pace around me in a circle as she spoke. I turned my head to follow her as she moved, but rather than twist around with her, I turned back to face the front. If I was going to be tasered, I would at least try to do it with dignity. My implant wasn't so impressed with my stoic attitude and began to overlay echo-images triggered by her footsteps. They weren't very detailed, as she was almost silent in her motion, but they were better than nothing. The occasional tap of the stun gun in her palm added to the tension, along with ambient sounds coming from the other stations where relics practiced.

As she completed a full circle, she smiled at me and said "I suggest you relax as much as possible and clear your mind. Start monitoring your heart rate, breathing and galvanic skin responses."

I tried to do as she said, as she continued her circuit about me with a resigned smile forming on her lips. "Let me know when something changes".

After almost a minute of her pacing about me and my apprehension building, I was suddenly alerted to some subconscious physiological changes by my implant. "Biofeedback alert" was all it said.

"Now", I rasped reluctantly, feeling as though the admission would trigger my own doom.

But Jesse continued pacing about me. "Really?" She asked brightly, excitement in her voice. "Are you sure?"

At my nod of confirmation, a broad smile lit up her face and she broke into a childish skip around me. It was bewildering, as I was bracing myself for a brutal stunning. She managed a full 8 circles about me, giggling gleefully before skidding to a stop in front of me. Her laughter was infectious and my own bafflement about her behaviour was overcome by my amusement.

As we stood, facing each other, grins on our faces, the long stun gun in her hand almost forgotten, she had just enough time to breath "18 seconds!", before her hand thrust the stun gun up under her own chin and a brilliant white arc of static electricity jolted through her face.

Time slowed for me as her sweet smile contorted grotesquely and her eyes bulged and rolled up in their sockets. Her rigid body convulsed as she slumped to one side and the stun gun clattered to the floor from nerveless fingers. If I hadn't been so near, she might have dashed her brains out on the polished concrete floor, but I managed to step in close to limit her fall.

The disturbing contrast of youthful joy and exuberance, followed by the horror of the self-destructive attack she inflicted upon herself, left me shocked and rattled. As I stooped, cradling her in my arms, my eyes snapped up to see Sericum standing by with hands on hips and a sly smile forming. I was about to call out for a medic when movement in the delicate bundle in my arms drew my attention.

My adrenaline was up and I didn't know what was going on when Jesse's eyes opened and she pulled free an arm to wipe drool from her chin with the back of a slender hand. "Yuck! You can let me up now." She grinned, all sign of the electrically induced seizure falling away. I was confused, but she ploughed over my reaction.

"Come on silly, help me up", she chided with a twinkle in her eye. She took my hand and I pulled her to her feet, still feeling bewildered. She felt as light as a feather and in a slightly awkward moment, she didn't relinquish her grip, but instead gripped harder and used her other hand to reach behind my neck to pull me closer. I was so relieved she was OK, that I lost concentration on my surroundings. We stood, frozen in that moment, my hand in hers, as she looked intently into my eyes. She was fascinating to me. But as I looked at her, my implant picked up sudden changes in her skin, pupils and heart rate. Before I had time to register what this meant, I was alerted by changes in my own.

"Biofeedback alert" flashed through my mind, but Jesse's reassuring smile seemed so genuine, I hesitated. Time dragged on for a few seconds and so I began to straighten. But before I could release myself from Jesse's increasingly firm grip, two steel darts ripped through the back of my suit into my flesh and 5,000 volts of pulsed current flashed through me. Every muscle in my body tried to fibrillate with the flow of the electricity. I might have fallen, if Jesse hadn't held me so, but my implant stabilised my body and soaked up the majority of the current.

I turned my head to see Sericum standing behind me, taser in hand, with a pair of coiled steel wires sagging across the gap between us. She was looking down at the device and dialling up the power setting with her free hand. I was about to reach behind me to try to pluck the steel electrodes loose, when a high pitched squeal jagged through me as my implant took matters into its own hands.

My back flashed with scorching pain between the two darts and the smell of burning flesh was suddenly in the air, but Sericum yelped as the unit exploded in her hands and the wires between us vaporised in places.

My shock was turning into fury at this attack, as I spun to confront Sericum when Jesse's excited voice rang out. "6 seconds!".

I felt like a caged animal between the two of them and hastily stepped to one side to keep them both in view. Sericum was now nursing scorched fingers, but looking up to see the thunder in my eyes, she blanched and said "this lesson is over now. You can relax".

"You did wonderfully" Jesse delighted. "Hold still. Let me tend to your wounds".

Moments later, as Sericum and I sat side by side at the table where the Biofeedback box still lay open, my anger had subsided somewhat. Jesse was fussing over our wounds with a spray she told me was made from various natural disinfectants, modified stem cells (which would massively accelerate healing) and a form of skin glue which would also act as a barrier. It stung, but as it dried it did offer relief.

"You really are a conundrum" Sericum admitted. "The biofeedback test doesn't always generate the results you expect, but this was something new altogether." Jesse nodded at this, but let Sericum do the talking.

"You see, presentiment requires you to have an emotional response. If you were a sociopath, you would have barely had a reaction when Jesse shocked herself. Unless something directly affects them, sociopaths don't care. So a reading of 1 to 4 seconds would have been an indicator that either your implant was poor at monitoring biofeedback, or that you had no empathy. A reading of 18 seconds means that either you have the most sensitive biofeedback monitor ever developed, or that you empathise a lot. Or both. That isn't always ideal in our line of work", she said as she gave me a pointed look, "but the results could be skewed if you had a greater interest in Jesse than in other relics".

I cleared my throat, feeling a little embarrassed. Jesse was lovely - and friendly towards me too, but we had only just met and she came across as too slight and youthful for my tastes. I was just relieved that her implant had been able to eat up the stun gun current nearly as well as mine had.

"No", Sericum went on, not expecting a response, "the first test doesn't concern me. But the second one does. Six seconds is a respectable time for self preservation purposes, particularly when the event is not life threatening, but you took no evasive action when you were alerted. You allowed yourself to be distracted. I accept that you don't always know the source of the threat, nor whether the target is yourself or someone you empathise with, but standing there canoodling will get you killed in the real world!"

I nodded and took the rebuke in good grace. It was sound advice and coming from the right place.

But Sericum wasn't done. "The one saving grace is that I have never seen a relic handle a taser like that before. They wouldn't normally have the power to vaporise the wires, let alone overload a battery like that. I will be asking the Professor what he has to say on the matter. But for now, you can move on to your second lesson. Just use what we have taught you."

...And so the day went on. Sericum led me to each station in turn, where she stood by with a critical eye. She didn't ever interrupt, but she did offer her evaluation afterwards. She was firm, but fair in her appraisal and I retained a grudging respect for her throughout the day, despite the hell she put me through. It was exhausting and the more tired I got, the more prone to making mistakes I was.

We covered marksmanship, trajectory analysis and evasion, siphoning, body morphing, wireless electronic interaction, using retrieved relic technology, underwater survival, hacking and more. Every lesson was a genuine life-saver in the field, but without my time with the Professor I would have been completely exposed as a green, ill-equipped rookie.

As much as I learned about the various unique and incredible relic skills, I felt I learned just as much about my peer group - and they learned just as much about me. In some cases that was a bad thing, as some of them initially misinterpreted my friendliness as weakness. Certainly, I found that competing with my fellow relics was no game. They all wanted to win, except for Jesse, who had preferred to demonstrate upon herself.

Of all the relics though, Flint surprised me the most by being very diligent in his tuition and not overly cruel despite every opportunity to be so. His was the last lesson of the day - compromised combat.

By this point, I was already wet, bruised, nauseous and weak and had attracted a small crowd of relics who now followed me from station to station. I was becoming oblivious to their calls, taunts and cheers. Flint could have capitalised on my weakened state, yet he treated me with a grudging respect. He didn't give me an easy ride by any stretch of the imagination, but he was civil and fair.

Compromised combat involved surviving various attacks despite being handicapped in assorted ways. Being bound, or blind-folded, or hung upside-down, or crushed beneath a pile of fellow relics, whilst drugged, disorientated or sick due to sonic weapons, or any number of other unpleasant options.

No wonder this lesson was the last of the day, as I couldn't imagine anyone being fit for anything afterwards. Thank goodness that Hector had already trained me in body morphing, so I could mobilise my ability to heal and relieve pain to a degree.

Body morphing largely involved gradual implant-assisted changes to my body over time, in order to change appearance, physical attributes, strength, endurance and more. But as a desperate measure to survive this ordeal, I was riding my implant hard to facilitate healing, pain relief, enhanced strength and more.

I had given my all, and my implant had happily thrown my body under the bus in an attempt to win each round of the ordeal. Many people don't realise that human muscles are 6 times stronger than our brain allows them to be, because our tendons and ligaments are only 4 times stronger. So in times of crisis, your body can take the brakes off and do the seemingly impossible, but we cannot keep that up without tearing ourselves apart.

As the last exercise of the compromised combat was drawing to an end, I stood, with one leg unable to fully support my weight, one eye swollen shut, a nasty flap of skin hanging from my cheek and my mouth filling with blood where my front teeth had been half driven through my lower lip.

I held a Desert Eagle handgun out in front of me, drawing a shaky bead on Flint, as he stood with a remote detonator in his hand. I was at the end of my strength, with my chest heaving and I didn't know how many more exercises I would be pushed to do.

In this scenario, I had begun the simulation zip-tied to a chair, about to be tortured for information. The three supposed torturers, now stood to one side, having been 'eliminated', watching me complete the escape. They had yet to remove their riot gear and Oliver was still rubbing at his elbow. Of course, I had been instructed to avoid using breaks during combat, but when I had spun Oliver into his team-mates and kicked a desk over the top of them, he had landed badly. In the back of my mind I regretted it, but I didn't have the time or the energy to worry about people's feelings. Fortunately, he was still in good spirits, understanding the nature of the game and was taking in all the details.

Flint was edging backwards away from me, putting furniture in between us, so I advanced. The briefing was that I was supposed to capture him alive. I only had three rounds left in the Eagle, but the weight of it made my arm tremble and I struggled to keep it aimed at Flint as I shuffled forward.

I was slightly disorientated by the dull, rolling thump of the large metal resonator tubes they had wheeled over to this section of the arena to confuse my echo location abilities. None of the students liked those, because it is surprising how quickly you begin to rely on echo location as an additional sense and it felt bizarre to be without it.

The other relics were a low buzz of conversation to one side of me, barely audible over the base background rumble and I did my best to ignore them as I advanced. But Flint's widening smile was disconcerting as he backed up. In this scenario he was not allowed to use his relic abilities, but I still had to disarm him without blowing us up. It was laughable really, as I shuffled forwards, feeling the urge to wince with every step.

But as I angled toward Flint, I noticed Hector off to one side of the small crowd. He was leaning back in his chair, tattooed arms folded across his chest and scowling at Flint. There seemed to be no love lost there. Hector noticed me watching and with a slow smile of satisfaction, he uncrossed his arms and raised a single index finger to his eye before looking back at Flint. Nobody else saw as his hand fell away.

I wasn't certain of his meaning until my gaze returned to Flint. We locked eyes and his intense gaze never left mine as his grin widened further still. But then I saw it. Reflected in his eyes, like tiny circular TV screens, I could make out the shapes of 3 other relics advancing behind me.

Without hesitation, my implant overlaid my vision with a zoomed in version, similar to having rear-view mirrors on my vision as I studied Flint's eyes. This was yet another debt of gratitude I owed the Professor for his training. Literally any photo of a person taken on a 40 megapixel camera or greater can be zoomed in to see a whole new image in the light reflected in the people's eyes - in effect making high resolution photos become 360 degree images.

My implant added trajectory lines ready for execution and the thin red threads which linked to nearby relics when I siphoned, but I was too exhausted to marvel at the effectiveness of this accelerated learning process.

Flint and I stood on opposite sides of a desk, as Kester, Jarrod and Omar moved into position behind me, believing themselves to be unseen. I didn't know what to do. Four able-bodied opponents, one with a detonator held low in front of him and I only had three rounds. This was impossible.

I was pondering what to do, without giving away my awareness of those behind me, when the time ran out. Flint's pupils twitched. The movement was subtle, but the lighting hadn't changed. My own heart thumped in my chest. He was receiving biofeedback. I cursed inwardly, knowing I had seconds before a brutal conclusion, one way or another.

I didn't have long to wait. It was like Flint had fired a starting pistol, as everything happened at once. All three relics behind me rushed forward simultaneously, weapons in hand, so I did the only thing I could think of. I thrust the Desert Eagle under my arm pit and cracked off three deafening shots in quick succession. My implant had already taken care of the targeting, so the rubber bullets slapped home onto the ceramic chest plates of the vests that each relic wore. But no sooner was the last round clear of the barrel, then my arm whipped round in a violent arc as I hurled the pistol with my last vestige of strength toward the detonator in Flint's hand.

It spun lazily in the air between us and I watched Flint's eyes widen as he calculated it's trajectory. Without meaning to, I had check-mated him. Where he held the detonator, he could either wrench it aside and take the 4 lbs of carbon steel in the crotch, or he could let me win.

I knew before it struck what he would choose. His presentiment had only been 3 seconds. He would take the injury and embarrassment over failing a mission. I had lost.

All that was left to do was to watch the show play out and hear the gasps and laughter from the other relics and instructors as Flint doubled over whilst hitting the detonator. A series of LEDs lit up along its length, indicating the activation.

"That's enough for today!", Canis boomed over the noise of the crowd. "Get those damn resonator tubes turned off, pack up the gear and someone help Flint and Chris to the Medic Station."

The chatter was slow to subside, as this was probably a break in the tedium of day-to-day training, but as the small crowd dispersed, I noted Hector's look of feral glee at Flint's misfortune and the daggers Flint was sending me as he did his best to straighten and shrug off Kester's unwanted assistance.

I would have apologised to him, but Oliver and Jesse each took one of my arms and half lifted, half dragged me toward the small infirmary. Flint ignored Canis' orders and left in the opposite direction.

Chapter 19

I lay in my quarters, bandaged, sprayed, splinted and sore, reviewing what I had experienced. My mind was a whirlwind, unable to settle, as I sifted through my thoughts and emotions. The trouble was, I felt completely torn. On one hand, I was trying to learn as much as I possibly could about my fellow relics and the lessons they had taught me, but on the other hand, I was stressed and homesick. So I divided my time between reviewing my time thus far at the Academy and exploring my memories of home and wondering how everyone was doing.

The cover story that had been concocted to explain my absence was plausible, but it wouldn't stop my parents from worrying about me. But there was little I could do about that at the time and the weight of the world was on my shoulders. I resolved that I needed to be at the top of my game to be able to make any difference, so I set about instructing my implant to improve my bone density, muscle mass and aerobic efficiency. These things would take time, but it was clear from my numerous injuries that my body needed work.

I was still lost in my thoughts when my door intercom sounded.

"Just a minute" I called, unable to reach the panel on the wall without standing.

"It's me, Thomas", came the Professor's muffled response

I didn't have time to get out of my bed before he opened the door with his swipe card and bustled in bearing a tray loaded with my evening meal and a nutrition shake he had prepared.

"Hope you don't mind visitors?" He said cheerily. " I missed all the action and wanted to make sure you were being looked after". His smile told me he was pleased with what he had heard.

"You don't do things by halves, do you?" He asked, noting the state of my face. "But well done all the same. By all accounts you will fit in fine".

Thomas sat with me whilst I ate, idling away the time talking about some of his latest experiments and quizzing me on what I had learned during my encounters with the other relics. It was a pleasant distraction and in several instances he was able to provide a better explanation or a different interpretation of what was said. It was useful to have him as a sounding board, and I think he gained pleasure from feeling useful. I don't mean him to seem needy, but the Professor was largely isolated in those days and it made a nice change for him to interact with people, rather than computer simulations and test rigs.

After an hour or so, the Professor and I had chewed over everything to be gleaned from my recollection and moved on to what he knew about the coming days. He told me a little bit about some of the lessons I would be learning and how some of his latest prototypes would feature heavily in our training, but he kept his explanation light on detail to avoid spoiling the 'surprise'. I was growing weary as my body healed, so I didn't press him.

Thomas bid me good night and let himself out, but before the door clicked shut behind him I heard Hector's voice. It sounded as though Thomas was trying to buy me some privacy, but after a moment he relented and Hector slipped through the door and closed it behind him. He had changed back into his civilian clothing, a white vest, bandanna and baggy jeans. He looked every inch the gang banger, complete with his tattoos, shaved head and goatee, but he was smiling as he leaned back against the door.

I pushed back the covers and swung my legs round to get up, but Hector started to object.

"Hey Homes, relax. I come in peace. You rest up." His brown eyes flashed and the beginnings of a sly smile tugged at his lips. "You did good today. Put that puta in his place."

Having Hector visit was unexpected, so I just nodded as I gathered my thoughts.

"Yeah, you shoulda seen his face. Ha!" he crowed. "It's a wonder he took what was coming. Because he's fast, I'll give him that." Hector was gleeful at Flint's expense, so I began to relax.

"Yeah Hector, thanks for earlier" I said.

He waved it away. "Don't thank me, man. I wasn't helping you, I was settling a score. And I'm gonna keep on settling. But I thought I would come to an understanding with you."

"Okay? What did you have in mind?" I prompted.

"Nothing as formal as an alliance, but to let you know you're not on my radar. It's a start, Homes." He regarded me, looking more like a bird of prey as his humour fell away.

"People round here mistake me for an outsider. That's fine. I ain't gonna correct them. But I have influence. You saw my influence today. But for now let's just leave it this way..." He paused. "If your luck hinges on the toss of a coin, if I'm in a position to nudge it one way or the other, I'll push it in your favour."

"Thank you. And in return?" I asked, still adjusting to the clandestine way of doing things in the Agency.

"Likewise Homes, you do likewise. This place ain't so different from the streets. Human nature is human nature. Implants don't change that, they exaggerate it. So all I am offering is an understanding."

"What's your problem with Flint, Hector?" I asked, trying to buy myself a moment of thinking space.

Hector looked surprised. "Same as yours, Chris. He has it in for me. Just like he has it in for you. Not because you mean anything to him, but because you mean nothing to him. And because he doesn't like people getting in his way or taking his glory. Just like his old man."

"His old man?" I echoed.

"You didn't know? Well here's some useful intel for free." Hector grinned. "Hiram isn't just Flint's sponsor, if you get my meaning. The rest of us were 'infected' by this god-damned technology without a say in the matter. But Flint was bred for it. Hiram was gonna put this electronic bullshit in his kid from the start. Part of the new generation of humans. Human 2.0." he sneered.

I knew Flint was different from the other relics, but I had assumed it was to do with his behaviour and attitudes, combined with his physical prowess, not his connection to Hiram.

"Thanks for the heads up Hector, but it has to be more than that?"

He studied me for a moment. His eyes narrowed as he calculated whether it served his purposes to divulge more. "Okay," he conceded. "Oliver told you that we get to go out on training missions right?"

I nodded.

"Well, Flint and his old man were involved in my capture. So Hiram's my sponsor. But he doesn't take kindly to having a dog that tries to bite him whenever he throws scraps. I can't strike back directly because of my control module, and his threats against my Homies back home. But he won't let me go. It gives him a sick thrill to keep me on a leash."

"So you piss up his leg whenever he isn't looking?" I finished for him.

"Right!" he grinned. "So we have an understanding?"

"We have an understanding", I agreed.

Hector left me with a million and one more things to consider. I would make more enemies throwing my lot in with Hector. I couldn't trust him, but I decided to humour him until I knew more.

Chapter 20

The next two weeks at the Academy rolled by as a never ending cycle of training, studying, team building and intrigue. I had healed by the following morning, barring some stiffness in my joints and, as time went on, my frame had packed out with another 17lbs of dense, functional muscle. I was certainly starting to look the part and I had even cut my hair short to keep maintenance to a minimum.

As much as I had tried to resist it, the place was starting to feel more like home and the familiarity of my surroundings and fellow relics took the edge off my home sickness. What's more, every new skill and secret technology I experienced fuelled my thirst for knowledge and although I felt like a naughty child eating stolen cookies, they were delicious nonetheless.

I sat at a dining table in the mess hall enjoying some breakfast with Oliver, Jesse and Verity. Oliver was laughing at Ben's expense, who wasn't there to defend himself, and was mercilessly teasing Verity about her new suitor. Both were still smiling, so he hadn't gone too far yet.

"In all fairness, Ben is a nice guy..." Oliver continued around a mouthful of fruit, "if you like simple country boys". His other empty plates were stacked in front of him and he pushed them to one side in order to lean casually on one elbow. "But yesterday he just creeped me out."

He was referring to an incident in Verity's quarters the night before. Poor Ben had been working his way up to telling Verity of his feelings for her, but his romantic gesture had fallen horribly flat when it was inadvertently triggered by Canis during an impromptu visit to Verity's quarters.

"Well I think it was sweet", Jesse chimed in, smiling at Verity. "In a bizarre stalker kind of way," she added, her laughter joining Oliver's.

We had been crossing the mezzanine back to our quarters after dinner when Canis had arrived, asking Verity for some encrypted flash drives she had been working on for him. What none of us realised was that during dinner, Ben had broken in to Verity's quarters and filled them with scented candles, rose petals and soft music. He had set himself up as the centrepiece, half naked with a rose between his teeth. Who knows what strings he had to have pulled to set this up.

More to the point, I can only imagine what went through his head when the first person through the door was a red-faced and furious Canis and not Verity. As mortified as Ben was, even I couldn't help laughing when Canis emerged, trailing rose petals from his combat boots, with a half naked Ben scuttling before him.

In all fairness, Ben had been flirting with Verity for over a week and she seemed just as keen as he was. In fact, the more Oliver goaded her, the more she came to Ben's defence.

"Well, Mr. Lover-Man, what would you have done to get my attention? It seems to me that all you can do is criticise like a backseat driver. You haven't done any better with Zoe". She took the barb out of the riposte with the flash of a smile as she flicked some of her drinking water at him.

Oliver blushed, but took the rebuke in good grace. He was about to respond when the mess hall intercom sounded. It cut through the chatter in the room like a knife.

"All personnel report to the Arena Proper", came Sericum's melodious voice, made tinny by the speakers. "I repeat, all personnel please report to the Arena Proper *immediately*".

This raised some eyebrows and sparked a few groans from about the mess hall, but all of the relics present left their seats. Some moved with trays in hand to drop off their leftovers on the way past the chef's station, whilst others abandoned their meals where they lay. This was unusual.

Chapter 21

We stood together in a row at the front of the arena, facing the three instructors - Sericum, Canis and Acertas. They had replaced their usual dark academy uniforms with military fatigues and this had created some apprehension amongst the students. I could hear the elevated heart rates about me and detect the tang of adrenaline in the air. Something was happening and some of my fellow relics must have known what, but they weren't talking.

Canis stepped forward and, soberly clasping his hands behind his back, began our briefing. "Early this morning, four of the Agency's relics on field duty were apprehended by enemy Agencies. These operations were clearly planned in advance and coordinated simultaneously in different countries to hamper our response. Three relics are still unaccounted for, but intelligence from the location indicates that they may have evaded capture. All available evidence currently points towards the Chinese, but this is, as yet, unconfirmed."

A vein throbbed in Canis' temple as he spoke and, behind him, I could see that Acertas had entirely lost his usual jovial good humour. He looked to be made of stone, which almost vibrated with pent up rage.

"Today, you are all being placed on active duty. Ready or not, this is what we have trained you for. We have given consideration to your skills and assigned your missions accordingly. In most cases, your handler will travel with you, but local Agency support will be provided for everyone."

Several relics broke protocol by nudging each other or exchanging looks, but Canis didn't remark upon it. He had bigger fish to fry.

"My fellow instructors and I", he continued, "are very pleased with your progress within the Academy. We believe that the determination and aptitude you have demonstrated during your training will carry you through any missions you are set. However, your education is incomplete."

Canis inclined his head towards Sericum and stepped back, as she simultaneously stepped forward.

"I would like to echo Canis' sentiments. But given the pressing matters at hand, we must greatly condense the final stages of your education. You will be leaving today, but before this is possible we must discuss your acclimatising to the outside world. A couple of you are well aware of the importance of what I'm about to share," she said as she glanced at Hector and Flint, "but for the rest of you, visiting the surface without any prior preparation can be a jarring experience. We need you at the top of your game, so please focus your full attention on this briefing."

Acertas cleared his throat and stepped forward, his voice a bass rumble as he addressed us.

"Many of you have not seen the outside world since receiving your implants. When you do, you will understand exactly why we train you underground. In recent years, the world has become completely filled with electromagnetic smog. Wi-Fi, cell phone signals, television, radio, power lines, smart meters, CB radios and more, completely fill our atmosphere with electromagnetic wavelengths that your implants will be able to detect. This can cause a certain level of overload if you have not already guarded against it. Imagine 1000 voices in your head, all talking at once. For most types of equipment, they specifically filter relevant wavelengths and ignore the rest. However, your implant technology is so sophisticated that it can decrypt almost anything it is exposed to. Without actively suppressing these signals, you can experience a form of shell shock. When you return to your quarters to assimilate your mission-specific briefings, you will note agency protocols on how to deal with various electromagnetic wavelengths."

As he spoke, he pierced us all one by one with his gaze, commanding our absolute attention. His sheer size and intensity put him in a new light, as we had only ever seen him in good humour, or with a strange form of battle lust during training. He was the kind of man who would embrace an enemy whilst holding a hand grenade, his laughter booming in the face of the other man's terror.

"There is also a section of your briefing which strictly relates to paranormal phenomena. For reasons which should be abundantly clear, we do not progress onto your paranormal training until we have evaluated all other aspects of your personality and skill set. But in the interests of brevity, I will say that whilst the rest of society clearly separate science from religion, this is purely a product of man's traditionally narrow perception. As relics, we are able to experience far more sensory input." He paused allowing a murmur amongst the students to pass.

"Paranormal activity for us, falls largely into the category of super science. It is all simply a matter of perspective and ability to experience it. However, not everybody is psychologically suitable to open those channels, so in the interests of successfully performing your duties during this time of increased pressure within the agency, your briefing shall specify certain wavelengths that you are prohibited from accessing whilst away from the Academy. Your briefing will explain how to disable those wavelengths. I can assure you, that your training shall be completed and that these additional areas of study will be open to you in due course, but for now, this could be detrimental to your missions."

Acertas acknowledged the nods from many of the relics and stepped back, as Canis once again stepped forward.

"Thank you Acertas. One final point. Once you're topside, particularly at night, I don't want you gawking at the skies like country bumpkins visiting the big city for the first time." He ploughed on, overriding the sniggers coming from Kester and Jarrod. "Your enhanced vision completely changes the nature of the night sky. You get used to it, believe me, but at first it will be a distraction. Secondly, you will notice the substantial traffic in our upper atmosphere. This is normal and the agency is entirely aware of it, and, in many instances, responsible for it. Now, return to your quarters, access and assimilate your briefings, then make preparations necessary for travel. In two hours, we shall be receiving Paredo as our honoured guest and to preside over your naming ceremony. You are dismissed."

As Canis turned on his heel, Sericum and Acertas followed him towards the briefing suite, set aside for active agency staff and instructors.

The subdued buzz they left in their wake was a mixture of concern and fear of the unknown, with a dash of exhilaration and excitement. Kester and Jarrod, never ones for decorum or tact, high-fived each other, completely ignoring the fact that up to 7 of our brothers and sisters could be dead or being tortured for information. Several of the other relics apparently had the same thought as me, as they shook their heads in disgust.

We dispersed in small groups, with Oliver caught up in conversation, spreading what information he had as we walked. "I can't believe Paredo would be involved in our naming ceremony!" He stammered excitedly.

"I heard he's too valuable for babysitting the likes of us. They didn't name him the devourer for nothing. My sponsor told me that he is one of the first generation of relics and only answers to the highest echelons of the Agency. But, by all accounts, he eats enemy relics for breakfast..."

Oliver's chatter faded with distance as Hector caught my attention. As usual, he was hanging back from the rest of the group, leaning up against one of the walls separating the training zones. A flick of his fingers, held behind his back, was enough to draw my eye without anyone else taking notice. His facial expression didn't change, but the length of eye contact was enough to know he wanted to speak with me. I continued to drift out of the arena, and he fell in line with me as I passed.

"Oliver is right you know," he said, looking over his shoulder to see who noticed us talking. "Paredo is a killer. They don't just have him liberating enemy relics. He gets stuff done. The kind of stuff you don't trust to the likes of us."

As we walked, Hector began to loosen his shoulders and throw some jabs and uppercuts, his smile belying the seriousness of our conversation. "I hear he is an agency enforcer, like a sergeant who cracks skulls when the rank and file don't listen to the officers."

I didn't look at him as I walked, knowing he preferred it that way. "We've all heard the rumours about him Hector. They are probably just short staffed whilst they try to recover our agents."

Paredo was almost an urban legend at the Academy. A cross between the bogeyman and a figure of national pride. He held the agency record for the number of enemy relics captured and the highest scores for most of the training exercises we laboured at, which made many of us feel as though we were always walking in his shadow. But there was a much darker side to his legend. He was supposed to be old. Very old. Nobody knew for sure what that meant, but to be the last of the first generation of relics, meant that he was a tough man to kill.

There were also rumours that some elements of the agency didn't approve of his methods. During training, Canis had once intimated to me that Paredo had taken body morphing and siphoning to a new level, but the tone of his voice and slight curl to his lip indicated he didn't mean that as a compliment.

Hector was not mollified and continued to work out his frustration as we walked. "Nah Homes, you're wrong. I don't like it. It's just like the cartels. They don't send in a cold-blooded killer for something like this. This isn't a favour to us, it's a favour to them. They want something."

I considered what he was saying. It had the depressing ring of truth about it, and I respected Hector's insights. He had been true to his word since my first day in the Academy, and you don't survive a life on the Mexican streets without staying sharp and learning how to read people.

"Okay Hector," I said. "I'll go and get debriefed, then I'll tell you what I know. Maybe we can spot a pattern. It's not going to be hard to find out what Oliver's mission is, and maybe I can get Jesse and Verity to share too."

Chapter 22

When I returned to my quarters, I found my wardrobe had been kitted out with casual travel clothes and cold weather survival gear. It was off-the-peg civilian clothing, albeit expensive and good quality, but much of it was undoubtedly designed for harsh conditions. I wasn't a big fan of the cold but assumed that for a first mission, they would want me away from urban environments until they could be sure that I could be trusted.

I left the wardrobe door open and sat on my bunk for my debriefing.

"Computer," I called out, "begin debriefing".

The flat panel monitor on the wall of my quarters lit up with the Academy welcome screen and, within moments, several hundred pages of text were being assimilated by my implant. I was an old hand at this now and sat for a moment contemplating everything I had just learned.

The instructions for adjusting my implant to cope with the outside world were there, as I had anticipated, but despite the content of my wardrobe, I didn't foresee the nature of my upcoming mission.

I was going to the Antarctic.

Chapter 23

As I left my room, I expected the whole mezzanine to be abuzz with relic chatter about our first missions, but things were strangely quiet and many of the doors to the relic quarters were still closed. It occurred to me that not all of the relics had the ability to learn as quickly as I did. I secretly hoped that the lack of activity simply meant that many of the relics were checking out their new gear or that their briefings were more extensive than mine.

I made my way to Oliver's quarters, knowing that he would be happy to share his new insights. As I was approaching, his door opened and an uncharacteristically sombre Oliver emerged, evidently still deep in thought. His brow was furrowed, but he looked relieved to see me.

"Hey Chris," he began. "What a mess! They think we're ready for this, but I'm not so sure. Did you see the pictures? This wasn't just some hit or miss raid, this was planned."

I started to raise a hand. "Whoa, Oliver. I didn't get the same briefing as you," I said as he trailed off.

"You're not going to Rome?" He said, looking crestfallen.

"No, Antarctica! Although I suspect we shouldn't be discussing it."

"Well there was nothing in the briefing about keeping this from other relics within the agency." He replied, brightening at the prospect of more gossip. "I have multiple missions in the area. One at Tivoli, where several miles of underground tunnels have been discovered under Emperor Hadrian's mansion, but then I head back to Rome for further debriefing. We lost Reperrio there, but he didn't go down without a fight. It was carnage."

This whole situation appeared to have burst Oliver's bubble. It wasn't a game for him anymore.

"We should talk to the others and see what else we can find out." I suggested. "But first, can I take a look at your briefing? After all, two heads are better than one." I was chancing my arm, but Oliver had always come across as an open book and he liked me. Oliver looked up and down the mezzanine, and seeing nobody around, quickly retreated back to his room and beckoned me to follow.

Chapter 24

Oliver wasn't wrong about the carnage. The crime scene photos showed signs of an intense struggle. Blood and broken furniture was everywhere. Without visiting the scene it would be very difficult to determine if Reperrio was alive or dead and the forensics reports weren't included in the briefing.

From the file photographs, Reperrio looked to be a scholarly academic, with round steel-rimmed spectacles, a beard and corduroy jacket and trousers, atop a chequered shirt. But despite the window-dressing, he was still a 200 lb relic who knew how to handle himself. Reperrio meant 'to discover', 'to find out', so I assumed he must have been investigating the possibility of ancient technology in the area - particularly if several miles of undiscovered Roman tunnels under the Emperor's mansion had been unearthed.

He had been staying at one of the agency safe houses in the area, but his abduction occurred when he was visiting the home of an informant, who was also still missing. Reperrio could have been accidentally caught up in the abduction of the informant, but in the agency's line of work, nothing was coincidence, especially when such a large and highly trained team would be required to pull it off.

As initial lines of enquiry, the briefing suggested that Oliver look into the recent communications between the informant and Reperrio, but to scan the underground tunnels in Tivoli before the opposition got there first. The site was on temporary lockdown, with the general public being denied access under the guise of preservation work. Given the fact that these tunnels were nearly 2000 years old and belonged to the Emperor of Rome, it was a good chance that hoarded ancient technology could be there. Scanning from the surface would have been conducted by the agency many years ago, but range was a limitation. Having several miles of tunnels would greatly increase the possibility of discovering something new and previously undetected.

"Well Oliver", I said, "Reperrio's Academy scores and combat record were good and he's been in the field for several years. So if he can be apprehended like that, you'd better be sure to take good care of yourself. But I don't think the agency would put you straight into harm's way. We're too valuable for that."

He nodded, and the slight reduction in his heart rate told me that he was feeling more at ease now.

"I hope you're right" he said, rubbing at his chin in thought.

I turned to leave his quarters. "We still have an hour or so before the naming ceremony, so I'll keep thinking on it. Maybe Verity or Jesse will have a missing piece to the puzzle?"

I didn't hold much hope of that though, as I assumed that Canis, Sericum and Acertas would have been privy to all of the briefings - and they would be taking orders from someone else higher up the chain. The Agency supposedly had hundreds of analysts and operatives who would be working in the background, but the relics were the tip of the spear. If there was some common thread, someone else would surely be following it up already.

Oliver followed me out onto the mezzanine to find that more relics were moving from room to room and were caught up in hushed conversations. I heightened my hearing and was able to pick out discussions related to Bosnia, Alaska and Japan, but not enough to discern anything meaningful.

Jesse and Verity were already in Verity's quarters. Clearly they had decided to share information in the same way that we had and Jesse was staring at the monitor as it flickered. Verity was thumbing through the new attire in her wardrobe.

"I like to see you getting your priorities straight, Verity." Oliver joked.

She shot him an annoyed glance, but didn't stop. I dismissed their conversation in favour of watching Verity's briefing over Jesse's shoulder. The flicker rate was quite a bit slower than I was used to, but it would have been unreadable to anyone without an implant. It appeared that Verity was going to Indonesia, except in her case it was not to investigate an abduction, it was to cover for one of the missing relics named Adamus.

Adamus meant 'hard' or 'adamant' and could refer to something like Diamond or steel, which gave me a broad clue about Adamus' character. I was beginning to appreciate the way in which relics were named, but I did carry some concern about my own name. After all, who wanted to carry a codename that was derisive or patronising? The naming ceremony had been shrouded in mystery and nobody seemed to know much about it.

As the panel on the wall went dark, it became apparent that Jesse had been thinking along the same lines as myself. She turned from the screen and said "your mission looks straight forward enough to me, Verity. I would be more worried about the naming ceremony. Is anybody else worried about it? I have enough trouble choosing my accessories, let alone a name to carry around for the rest of my life. I don't want to end up being called Kitten or pixie!"

"Yeah, tell me about it!" Oliver shot back. "Try 'cue ball' on for size," he joked as he rubbed his bald head with one hand. This lightened the mood somewhat, and I was relieved that Verity's briefing was almost as thin as mine.

She was being sent to Gunung Padang, an ancient megalithic ruin in the Cambodian jungle. It had been discovered in 1914, but recent Agency-funded seismic surveys and core samples had shown that the structure went well below the top terrace, complete with a network of underground tunnels. What was more impressive, was that just like the recently discovered pyramids in Bosnia, soil and wood samples from within the structure carbon dated back as far as 26,000 years old.

"How about you Jesse?" I asked. "Where are you being sent?"

Her shoulders were slightly slumped and she was now chewing her lower lip. Her teeth gleamed white in the glow of the monitor. "They're sending me to Berlin. Nobody was kidnapped there, but communications from three of the missing relics mention it. I don't like it at all."

"They're sending you there alone?" Oliver asked, sounding incredulous.

"No, with Carmine and Jarrod of all people," she replied miserably.

I could understand them choosing Carmine, a dour, middle-aged Austrian relic with a military background and experience in seismology. That made sense. But handcuffing anybody to Jarrod was a dirty trick in my book. He was incapable of taking anything seriously, and his persistent gallows humour and sarcastic comments were enough to wear you out. He had been a grunt in the U.S. Army, but there was no trace of any discipline that this should have instilled. I could only assume they were tolerating him long enough to make him cannon fodder!

"Yikes!" Oliver commiserated. "Take some earplugs and maybe Jarrod's constant mocking and Carmine's complete lack of humour will cancel each other out. With a bit of luck they'll both totally disappear," he finished with a grin.

"Yeah," I joined in. "When humour and anti-humour collide, you get an explosion of pure energy and not much else. So maybe everything happens for a reason?"

Jesse finally smiled. "Well I hope you're right, Chris. Otherwise, I'll be tearing my hair out before the plane has even landed."

As Oliver and I trailed after Jesse on the way to her room, she explained that her briefing had detailed some newly discovered records of lost Nazi tunnels leading to a hastily abandoned research facility below Berlin. It had been sealed off prior to the storming of the Reichstag at the end of World War II and anyone with any knowledge of it had been killed to hide the truth.

"After faking his death", Jesse continued, "Hitler escaped to Argentina via submarine with some of his core advisors and a fanatically loyal crew. He may not have been able to take the objects of his research with him, but he would have kept important records from the secret research that was carried out in Berlin."

As we walked, the bustle and murmur of the other relics was now evident across the whole mezzanine. This gave the illusion of privacy, but I knew there was no such thing in this place and I grew nervous that Jesse might get herself in trouble by talking about her mission so openly.

"Perhaps it would be better if you show us?" I whispered to her as we neared the door to her quarters. We had both noticed Flint and Kester, standing outside Flint's quarters, like spectres at the feast. Kester scowled at us and turned away to say something. We couldn't see his lips and there wasn't enough glass nearby for me to eavesdrop on what he said.

Moments later, safely behind closed doors, Oliver and I were absorbing Jesse's briefing. I was amazed that we had been allowed to share, but our curiosity was greater than our caution, especially in light of being observed. The wartime phrase 'loose lips sink ships' sprang to mind, but I felt protective over Jesse and wanted to offer what help I could to keep her safe.

Jesse stood by, with her hands on her hips, waiting as we assimilated the briefing.

"Well?" She queried, as we both snapped back to the present and refocused on her.

The briefing had covered how, in 1945, General Zhukov, commander of the Soviet armies occupying Berlin, had reported that Hitler and several Nazi leaders had escaped, presumably to Spain or the Americas. Stalin had advised the U.S. government of this fact but they ignored it, much to his frustration.

The Allies had decided that it served their interests to have a neat conclusion to the war, rather than a worldwide manhunt and continued German resistance, and were happy to publicise Hitler's death, whether real or staged. They cited the remains found in his bunker as evidence of his death, but those bones were later DNA tested and found to be female - they couldn't possibly have belonged to him.

But where the public narrative left off, the Academy briefing continued. Sightings of the two U-boats carrying Hitler and his accomplices to Argentina were corroborated by eyewitness testimony from German sailors who helped unload them.

But when the notorious war criminal Adolf Eichmann, was captured in 1960 outside Buenos Aires by Israeli commandos, his interrogation by the Agency was able to reveal the sites that had sheltered Eichmann himself, Hitler, Martin Bormann, Joseph Mengele and all of the senior personnel who had escaped via submarine.

Certain elements within the agency had demanded to expose Hitler, or at least to eliminate him and gather any secret intelligence that was available. But unfortunately, under Operation Paperclip, the US and British governments had helped many thousands of Nazis to escape from Germany in return for sharing their assets, knowledge and research. Exposing Hitler's whereabouts and their complicity in his escape from justice would have been disastrous for numerous high-ranking officials within the intelligence community and the Argentinean government. So despite knowing Hitler's exact whereabouts in San Carlos de Bariloche in Patagonia, Argentina, the Agency sat on the information.

Naïvely, they believed they had already taken all of the assets and intelligence from Nazi Germany. They were wrong. They hadn't known about the tunnels and facility under Berlin, nor the remarkable research it potentially contained.

What had seemingly brought this matter to a head was the discovery of a journal belonging to Nazi captain Erich Priebke, who had been extradited to Italy from Patagonia in 1995 to face his crimes. It had taken nearly 15 years, but when this secret journal finally surfaced, it was found to contain references to relic technology studied under Berlin and, more importantly, it contained coordinates.

Information regarding this journal had been forwarded by informants to at least three of the seven missing Agency relics and they, in turn, had reported it to the Agency.

"I think you're right. The facility in Berlin is definitely linked to the abductions. It is too big a coincidence otherwise. But why send details of the journal to those relics in particular?" I asked. "And who else received information about the journal?"

"The Agency must have looked into this already, Chris." Oliver said, his faith in the organisation lending him confidence.

"Yes, I would have thought so too," I replied, "but making assumptions can be dangerous. After all, who would have thought that the Chinese could field as many relics as would be required to pull off all these abductions simultaneously. Just think how much surveillance that would have required, let alone having enough implanted assets to get the job done."

"Unless they were just highly trained spooks and not relics?" Jesse interjected.

She had a point. But with all of this, we were out of our depth and just working with the bare minimum intelligence that had been forwarded to us at short notice.

"If our relics have been intercepted, then so has the information concerning the journal. Every enemy Agency could be making a beeline for Berlin. It seems risky for you to be there, Jesse." I concluded.

Oliver nodded in agreement.

Jesse's eyes narrowed. "I'm not made of porcelain. I can take care of myself." Her pursed lips spoke volumes. "I will do my duty. The agency needs boots on the ground and who knows what would happen if this technology gets into the wrong hands. The enemy clearly places a lot of value on it - whatever it is."

I paused to think for a moment. She had a point.

"Okay," I conceded. "But I suggest you raise this with Sericum before you ship out."

Chapter 25

Oliver, Jesse and I separated to discover what further intelligence could be gained from amongst our peers, but I soon found that many of the other students had now left their quarters to visit their sponsors or handlers.

Being unable to locate Jesse, Ben, Hector or Omar, I headed back towards my quarters to see if I could raise the Professor on my intercom. Given the news, I was surprised that he hadn't made contact already.

I had only been able to gain rudimentary gossip from those I passed, when the arena tannoy system sounded. Sericum's melodious voice once again summoned us to assemble in the arena proper immediately, which left me with a distressing sinking feeling. I was totally unprepared and had no idea what was to come.

Chapter 26

Sericum and Canis kept order amongst the group as we assembled. This in itself was not something new, but their repeated glances toward the closed door of the briefing suite lent them an air of nervousness which was entirely uncharacteristic. I am not sure what the others made of it, but it put me in mind of seeing a nervous great white shark. Firstly it is not something you normally come across, but secondly the question arises 'what on earth could put a dead-eyed killer like Canis into a state of apprehension?'

Hector was the last to arrive, with a face like thunder. I would have made some form of contact with him, but Canis wasted no time in calling us to order.

"Relics! Your attention please." He began and a hush descended over the group.

"My fellow instructors and I have done what we can, in the time we have, to forge you into weapons. You may not have appreciated our approach, but strength comes from adversity and the strongest steel is forged by the hottest fire. The iron we began with was full of impurities, but every hammer stroke within the forge of the Academy had a purpose. Every new element we folded into you improved your mettle. The fire we stoked gave you power and flexibility and every hammer blow gave you strength. A good blade embodies all these aspects and is able to withstand every test a battle may hold."

Canis paused briefly and looked towards Sericum, but she just nodded for him to continue.

"We have transformed you into something new. We have given you the edge you need to be of service to the agency and to mankind. But your final quenching will be outside these walls. As instructors, we must hope and trust that we have done enough - that you will become an agent worthy of our sacred obligation."

Sericum now stepped forward, alongside Canis, who's sturdy build emphasized her lithe proportions. "Leonardo da Vinci once said 'Where the spirit does not work with the hand, there is no art.' You have experienced the hand of the Academy, but what my brother is building up to, is that it is time you experienced the spirit".

Everyone's attention was on Sericum as she turned towards the polished mahogany door of the briefing suite and with high ceremony she intoned "It is time you were named".

At this, the door to the suite swung inwards and in the dim interior, I could make out Acertas, clad in a dark hooded robe. It would have been slightly comical if it wasn't for the ominous reverberations I could now detect within my implant. Something dark and sickly seemed to be in the atmosphere and a sense of foreboding oozed out of that room. The nervous glances from my fellow relics told me they could feel it too.

Sericum and Canis both took a couple of steps backward, placing themselves one on either side of the doorway and gestured for us to file in. The dark sense of foreboding was building and nobody seemed willing to take the lead until Flint scoffed at their cowardice and strode toward the darkened room. This seemed to break the spell enough for everyone else to follow suit, but the nearer we got to the doorway the more intense the sensation became.

Of course, darkness posed no obstacle to relics with heightened senses, but the briefing suite, usually containing a large conference table surrounded by plush leather chairs, had somehow taken on some reverential quality which discouraged the use of our gifts.

There were 14 chairs in the room, spaced equidistantly around the polished conference table. One stood a good 18 inches taller than the others and marked the head of the table. My fellow relics filed around and took their places, with a clear preference being as far away from the head of the table as possible. The mood in the room was almost palpable as waves of fear, reverence and a shared purpose coursed through us.

Even Jarrod had ceased his joking and all traces of his usual smirk had been replaced with a wide-eyed seriousness.

Looking back on it, the occasion had a dreamlike quality to it as though we were mesmerised. Flint took one of the last remaining spaces right next to the head of the table, so I took the other, opposite him. More than one other relic breathed a sigh of relief at that, although none of us yet knew the source of our discomfort, which rolled through us in waves.

I had been expecting Acertas, in his ceremonial robes, to take his position at the head of the table, but instead he closed the door and put his back to it. With his arms thrust deep into his sleeves across his broad chest and the cowl of his robe low across his eyes, his voice rumbled in his chest.

"Be upstanding, for you are in the presence of a master of our order. A keeper of the mysteries. The Lethal Hand of the Committee of 300. Bow your heads before 'the devourer'."

We all stood behind our chairs, our heads bowed, as the sense of dread built within us. Jarrod now wasn't the only student with wide eyes.

I was wondering if anyone would break for the door, when a ripple to my left startled me. Right in front of my eyes, a powerfully muscled figure began to materialise out of thin air. Like Acertas, it stood a good 7 feet tall, with broad shoulders and muscular arms folded across its chest. But instead of robes, it wore a slick black trench coat and a stylised helmet, which seemed to take on the hues of our surroundings.

Opposite me, Flint was growing pale and, next to him, Zoe visibly started as the figure emerged seemingly from thin air. Soon, the attention of the room was focused on the figure at the head of the table.

"Children," it rasped. "Allow me to introduce myself. I am Paredo."

The figure stood just over a head taller than me, but was substantially wider. It paused as it reached up to remove the helmet. The face revealed underneath had strong Roman features and dark hair. Beyond that, however, there was nothing normal about this man. He wore thick soled steel-reinforced boots and Kevlar impregnated trousers. I could make out ridges within the fabric which contained polyalloy reinforcements. His trench coat clearly incorporated the agency's latest optical technologies to help its wearer blend in with surroundings, but more alarmingly, the skin of Paredo's arms and neck was thick and scaly like the hide of a rhinoceros.

"My reputation may have preceded me." He continued. "But do not be concerned, for today I am here to raise you to our noble brotherhood."

It appeared that he had taken body morphing to a new level, enhancing his height, musculature and even skin texture to ensure his survival. He alone knew what other modifications he had made internally. Only his face and hair appeared normal, if you could call Hollywood good looks normal.

Paredo's words rolled over us like crashing waves. I'm sure the other relics felt it too. I couldn't understand how, just moments before, we had been standing calmly, but now we were almost quaking in our boots.

As Paredo continued, my implant helpfully supplied that it had detected abnormal levels of pheromones and infra-sonic pulses, along with a very subtle siphoning action coming from him.

Before I even voiced a command in my mind, my implant was counteracting his influence. It was as though someone had thrown a stone into the pond of my perception, shattering the illusion that he was creating. I felt the palpable fear and reverence fall away and now, before me, stood a vain man in a silly costume. His subtle manipulation of the group had been masterful, but with the fear fading, the deception irked me.

My momentary relief was short-lived, however, as Paredo's dark eyes flicked toward me ominously in acknowledgement of my realisation and the actions of my implant, but he continued to speak to the rest of the group, who stood there staunchly whilst every nerve told them to cower.

"I have set aside vital agency business to help you find your names. At the same time, your eyes will be unveiled and you will behold the true mysteries of our order. But enough talk." He concluded. "Please be seated".

All but Flint and myself scurried to obey. Flint woodenly took a seat at his own pace, although he did not meet Paredo's gaze. I, on the other hand, with the arrogance of youth and overconfidence in my training, locked eyes on Paredo as I took a seat. Catching him out in his showmanship during the ceremony, took away some of my caution, as I reasoned that much of his reputation could be based on smoke and mirrors such as this.

But if I had reasoned things out more thoroughly at the time, I would have dwelled more closely upon his unbeatable test scores and exalted position within the agency. It certainly wasn't worth risking his ire for my pride. But as we locked eyes, there was something within me that refused to submit to his dominance.

I was expecting his anger, but as his penetrating gaze eventually slid away from mine and roved across the rest of the group, a slow smile played across his lips. He was enjoying his showmanship, and what did it matter if one of the audience was in on the act as long as they didn't spoil the show for everybody else?

"You came to this place as individuals". He went on. "As so many grains of sand scattered to the winds. But destiny chose you to be different from the rest. Your relics chose you."

A ripple of acknowledgement passed around the table.

"You are the product of the perfect melding of man and machine, making you something more than either. In your time here at the Academy, you have experienced a mere fraction of what this truly means. As relics, we have the unique privilege of experiencing the world in a different way. We are the pinnacle of human development where man's interaction with the universe traverses from the seemingly magical into the quantifiable realms of super science. We are pioneers at a time where our unique gifts can help us to unlock the secrets of the universe."

The group was riveted, hanging on Paredo's every word. I could detect that the field he was projecting was changing subtly and my fellow students were now looking more comfortable and sitting taller in their chairs.

I felt a renewed effort in his siphoning to work around my relic's defences, but Paredo made no outward sign that would give away his intentions.

"But we are at a crossroads where the future of mankind hangs in the balance. This opportunity for extraordinary progression and the liberation of mankind from our limitations is threatened by a perfect storm. A storm of greed, stupidity, unwillingness to work as a collective unit and of course an outside threat." Paredo's eyes intently searched us all, as his rich baritone voice commanded our attention.

"We represent the dawning of a new age. But without unity of purpose, this new age is threatened. So today, I invite you to join our brotherhood. Please join hands." He said, as he took his seat and extended his bare hands toward Flint and myself.

I noticed that the first two fingers of each hand were subtly different in their proportions from a normal human hand. They reminded me of the talons of an eagle, which have the biomechanics of a ratchet. I wondered if this would also give him a similar grip strength and this made me reluctant to take the proffered outstretched hand. An eagle's grip strength was measured in the thousands of pounds per square inch, so taking Paredo's hand could be the equivalent of putting my hand in a guillotine.

A look at Flint told me he had noticed the same thing, but he defiantly stared at me as he took Paredo's hand. I turned to Paredo and his sly smile gave me no comfort. I felt Carmine's hand slip into mine on my right hand side, which meant that I was the last link in the chain around the table. So with a deep breath and a silent prayer, I reached for Paredo's hand and took hold of my future.

As I made the connection, palm on palm, a wave of motion around the table, caught my attention. Opposite me, Flint's body arched up rigidly, his head tilting backwards and his jaw falling open. All around the table my brothers and sisters went rigid and yawned towards the heavens in some form of macabre Mexican wave. In truth, it must have happened within a second or so, but my shock at this sudden development slowed my perception of time. Paredo's grip was vice-like and although it did me no harm, my unconscious flinch response was stopped dead in its tracks.

From the corner of my eye, I watched helplessly as the reaction of my peers flowed rapidly around the table toward me.

Carmine's grip intensified and went rigid as he jerked upright and the breath he must have been holding wheezed out of his chest past a slack tongue.

My implant had just a fraction of a second to superimpose the red threads of siphoning across my vision before I too was hit by a tidal wave of psychological force. It felt as though every muscle in my body simultaneously tried to wrench itself free from its neighbour, but as I was brutally expelled from my own consciousness, the last thing I saw was the shadowed light fixtures adorning the ceiling of the briefing suite as my eyes rolled back in their sockets.

Chapter 27

I snapped back into awareness with a sudden jolt, to find myself floating in a formless void. Around me, were tight clusters of energy of all different colours, all linked together by the red threads of force emanating from Paredo. Or at least, I assumed it was Paredo. Each cluster of energy glowed in different colours and configurations, which seemingly mirrored the power and type of our implants and modules. I was surprised by how few modules some of my peers had, but also by the sheer volume that Paredo had hoarded within himself. He must have had upwards of 30 different modules, compared with the least of us, Omar, who had only three.

This fleeting glimpse was not meant for me, as form and substance suddenly materialised around us and we were now clad as Knights Templar and standing in the fire-lit stone hall of a draughty Castle. I tried not to register my surprise, but I could feel the weight of my chainmail and armour, the icy touch of it against my skin where my padded gambeson didn't entirely protect me from the steel.

The gauntleted hands of Carmine to my right, and Paredo to my left, felt every bit as real as the waking world. I could even feel the faint blush of warmth against my skin emanating from the fireplace, contrasting with the cool stirrings of air breezing through the open arched windows of the hall, and smell the smoke, leather and oil.

Paredo's rich voice began again, but this time it was accompanied by a chorus of 12 other voices, all speaking in unison.

"Join us. Why do you remain apart?"

I hadn't been aware that I was holding anything back, but this comment highlighted a tugging, nagging feeling that the back of my mind. I focused on my surroundings, and looked at the faces of my fellow relics. All heads were turned towards me as they stood hand-in-hand, a look of peace or even rapture on their faces. My heart ached to join them, but something held me back. I started to feel woozy, as though the dream was beginning to claim my consciousness again, and the scene shifted.

We still stood, clasping hands, but now we were dressed as Druids on a wooded hillside, surrounding a large silver bowl filled with fresh, clear water. As I watched, the surface flickered strangely, as though it reflected something beyond the clear blue sky overhead.

"We are one". My brothers and sisters intoned in a chorus. "Join us."

I was confused. Confused to the point where I was losing sight of the fact that this was a ceremony. For some reason, my experience in the Academy, my knowledge of my brothers and sisters, had fallen away and I was left with just raw uncertainty.

As I dithered, I felt the wind begin to stir and our coarse woollen robes began to flap and brush against our legs. The sky began to darken, and the intensity of their plea began to grow.

"Join us. Relax and become one with us." Their voices seem to come from all directions, both outside me and within me.

As I looked on, the sweet green meadows surrounding the wooded copse we were within began to wither. The vegetation wilted, dried and crumbled to dust, exposing cracked and baked earth. Dust moats eddied above the surface of the ground, as the wind picked up and as the decay gradually encroached upon our grove.

I shook my head violently to ward off the confusion, but I was clearly being absorbed into the dream.

As the wind whipped the skeins of dust across me, I blinked to clear my watering eyes, to discover that the scene had shifted again.

We were now all floating in the void once more. But this time, the thoughts and fears, the hopes and joys of every relic around me were laid bare and open. Just by looking from face-to-face, I could read my brothers and sisters like an open book.

They still had physical form, but they were naked and translucent. As was I, as we hovered in formless space, the vastness of the universe all about us. But instead of embarrassment at our superficial nakedness, all I felt was bliss at the passing of my physical form. I was now free to explore all possibilities of what was, what is, and what will be.

I tried to withdraw my 'hands', but I was gripped tight by my neighbours.

"No." The chorus sounded within my mind. "We are one. Join us."

My confusion was increasing as I lost touch with my own personality, my own being. As I watched the group of spirit forms around me, they seem to shift and change like a carousel circling about me. Each face moved on to the next position, as I was lulled into deep relaxation. But seeing my own face and body in front of me jarred me into some level of alertness as I realised the spirits around me weren't moving, it was my own consciousness jumping from body to body.

I tried to relax, unable to do any more than go with the flow. But as the pace increased, not only was I jumping from body to body physically, but I was also feeling the overlay of their individual minds upon me.

"That's right. Join us. We are one." Was the last I heard of the chorus as the dam of my mind broke and the flood of my consciousness rushed into the group.

It is impossible, as a unique and individual being, for you to understand what I experienced. But the only way I can describe it would be to say that we were all part of one collective consciousness who had merely experienced itself in various different individual, separated facets to see what would happen. An experiment, if you will.

In this form, we were whole - I was whole. We still could recollect our individual experiences, but they were shared. I knew my brothers and sisters as intimately as I knew myself, if not more, because we were one. And in that moment of pure and unreserved acknowledgement, I had a name for each experience. Almost like a filename for each experience saved on a computer.

I was formerly Lucidus - which meant clear, transparent, easy to understand and unable to conceal the truth. But my name had a dual meaning. If the world in which I had lived was but a dream, then I had been a lucid dreamer, able to recognise and distinguish illusion from reality. I had been born lucid - with eyes wide open whilst all around me clenched their eyes shut.

But that was another time and another place. My consciousness, *our* consciousness, turned inwards as I reflected, in turn, upon all the lives I had led. I fondly recalled my life as Jesse - or Cordis, as I now knew her - a sweet girl, who lived life as a free spirit, always led by the heart. My awareness moved from lifetime to lifetime, absorbing and reliving my experiences and dwelling on the rightness of each name.

My life as Renovo, or Flint as I had been, was particularly harrowing. The years of abuse at the hands of my father's masters had almost left me a desiccated, soulless shell. At the point where almost nothing but hurt remained, well beyond humiliation and self-loathing, a final spark of fury had fanned to life within me. I had resolved to fight back. To crush any remaining softness left to me and to renew, to restore, to revive. On the day I stabbed one of my abusers to death with a pair of scissors, the child I was, Carmi, died and I assumed a new name of my own devising, Flint. Hard as stone and a sharp, cold-blooded killer when I needed to be. There was no give in me. There could be none, for to show compassion would be to acknowledge my own suffering.

My father had cried that day, not because he risked falling out of favour with his masters and their syndicate, (because he had already brokered more than enough power, influence and leverage from my abuse), but more that he wept because now he could truly see me as his son. I was finally worthy to follow in his footsteps.

My awareness cycled through my collective memories and I relived the highs and lows of my lives as Solus, Colligatio, Balatro, Verum, Alumnor and more, my consciousness caressing every tantalising memory until I reached my life as Paredo.

As my awareness tried to touch upon those memories, my first impression was that the memory file was huge. In fact, it was many times greater in size than any I had experienced so far. But as I delved, pain unexpectedly lanced through me - through us, pushing my focus away. I couldn't understand why this would happen, why I would be denied. Uncertainty flickered across my consciousness, but experiencing all those lifetimes was like a drug - indulgent, maybe even self-destructive, but so addictive. So as quickly as the tendrils of my awareness retreated from the pain, they strayed back. Tentatively at first.

It is hard to explain the sensation of pain when you are able to exist without physical form, but what I was experiencing was designed to repel my attention. Just like a Jonesing addict though, I was hungry for knowledge. Even just scraps, so I persevered.

Two successive attempts were more successful than the last, as I was able to fleetingly experience a snippet of Paredo's life as an adult. But each time I tried to delve into what I considered to be my "own" memories, I was rebuffed.

Despite the pain, I bore down on Paredo's memory file one last time with all the force of my collective willpower and snatched at the information it exposed.

I reeled back in agony, retreating into the void from the violent response I had received for my intrusion, but I didn't come away empty handed, and snaffled hungrily at the intellectual titbits I had stolen.

Unbeknownst to me, my consciousness and those of my brother and sister relics were slowly beginning to unravel, because Paredo had lost control of the ceremony. His siphoning was much stronger than the other relics, so previously, this had never been an issue for him. But with 13 minds pulling in different directions, he couldn't hold everybody together.

In his arrogance, he also hadn't counted on the strength of my ability to siphon rivalling his own. Stripped back to my raw consciousness, I was impulsive and tainted with the alien personality traits of all my fellow relics, so I wasn't being rational.

Paredo had recognised the danger of having his consciousness forcefully ripped from him by an untrained relic, to be left drifting in the void. So in order to preserve himself, he had firewalled off his own awareness. The pain I was experiencing as I grasped at his memories was the equivalent of him callously trying to pry our cold, dying fingers off his lifeboat as we all drifted at sea.

As I sucked appreciatively at the tattered memories I had snatched from Paredo, my awareness was rewarded with fragments of experience. I had visions of the dig site of an underground pyramid which lay buried under nearly 700 feet of soil, snow and ice, deep in the Alaskan wilderness somewhere between Nome and Mt. McKinley. I somehow knew that the site had inadvertently come to light during nuclear tests, when strange seismic readings had been detected by a crew of geologists looking for rare mineral deposits. The dark pyramid was exactly twice the size of the Great Pyramid at Giza, but was now surrounded by a vast underground facility where agency experts were hard at work trying to harness the beam of energy which was constantly being emitted from its peak.

I also received several flashes of Paredo's mortal combat with Russian relics upon the discovery of the site and was nearly swamped by his monumental hatred of them. What had they done to him to make him hate them so? The feeling burned like a firebrand.

As I continued to sift through the scraps, this feeling soon gave way to Paredo's frustrations of being at the beck and call of a schizophrenic master. Things used to be different, but now the agency was so divided and split by corruption and politics that his orders were becoming confusing at best and contradictory at worst. He was certainly not being given the leeway he felt he needed to drive the agency toward its main over-riding objectives.

As the flashes of Paredo's stolen memories disintegrated between my 'fingers' I was left with one last brief snapshot in time. The image of Relikviya: Smert' Pyat' - a powerful and stern-looking Russian relic, codenamed 'Death-5' - which seemed to burn feverishly in Paredo's memory. But eventually, even this faded.

Chapter 28

We drifted in the darkness for a time, savouring what we had learned from this last set of memories. We were at peace now. Content.

But a faint vibration in the darkness was disturbing our slumber. It wasn't enough to rouse my awareness fully, but as we drifted, we tried to remember.

The vibration went away for a time, and we were pleased. But when it returned, it came back stronger - and with that renewed strength, the vibration in the depths took form.

Everything in this universe is made of energy, but what distinguishes an electron from a photon, or anything else in the universe, is simply a matter of how the vibration within that energy is organised.

This vibration took the form of a red light - pure, polarised and true. It sparked in the far distance, but as our attention acknowledged it and reached out to it, we were also obliged to take form.

The distance between us was impossibly vast, but with stoic determination, it sped across the void between us, growing in intensity with every moment. As it took greater shape and form, going from a point of light to a ball of light with a corona, then so did we, our curiosity roused. The ball of light gradually expanded into a dazzling array of activity, as though solar flares were firing off in all directions, until we were bathed in light and became aware of a consciousness calling to us.

As the light filled my vision, I became aware of separation. I knew I had lost something, but I didn't know what. I just felt a sense of loss as I looked around to see my brothers and sisters in their spirit bodies, held together by a lattice of red threads of light. Their energy twinkled and pulsated in the receding darkness, and this was the last thing I remember as I was crushed back into the physical constraints of my body.

Chapter 29

I slumped forward, my face slick with sweat, to feel the reassuring cold gloss wooden finish of the conference table. My whole body was a grateful wash of sensation. My toes gripped the innersoles of my combat boots, the edge of my leather chair was pressuring the back of my thighs and I could feel the hands still gripping mine. To my right, Carmine, or Severus as I now knew him, breathed heavily and licked his lips. He looked ready to vomit, but a weak smile from him was a surprise.

It wasn't until that moment that I realised how close we had come to having our conscious minds severed from our bodies. I had no idea what that would have meant, but I turned my fury to the figure grasping the hand on my left.

I drew a furious breath and was about to lash out with a tirade, when it registered that I no longer held Paredo's hand, but instead held a much more slender hand belonging to Sericum.

Flint was also looking down at her hand dazedly, but colour rose in his cheeks as he noticed eyes upon him.

"Welcome back." Sericum said, a smile on her lips. She looked tired and dark circles were beginning to form around her eyes.

All about us, my brothers and sisters were stirring and bursting into a buzz of conversation, but we could hear raised voices outside the briefing sweet as Canis, Acertas and Paredo exchanged heated words.

"...Why you deviated from the ceremony, I don't know". Canis growled. "We could have lost a whole crop".

"Any loss," Paredo countered "would be down to your failure to prepare them. They didn't even know how to maintain their own integrity. It was like herding kittens in the void".

"Hold on Paredo", Acertas intervened, "you knew that we were cut short by a couple of months. What did you think we could achieve with just us three?"

"I assumed that surely Textor would have been recalled to handle their siphoning? After all, Lucidus was show-boating by casting off my manipulations before I pulled everyone into the void. He shouldn't have even been able to sense them. I had to co-opt the group to overwhelm him"...

The voices had been fading as they moved further from the suite, and the groans and muttered conversation within the room began to drown out any hope I had of following the Instructor's conversation.

Sericum had observed my eavesdropping, and with a gentle squeeze of my hand before releasing it she said, "That really was most unexpected. Paredo has never lost control of a group like that before." I could tell there was more that she wasn't saying, but I wasn't going to push her after she had just dived in to save us.

"He isn't the most skilled at siphoning", she went on, "but he has always been able to make up for that with sheer brute force. It is just as well that I knew you all well enough to find you".

"Were we really in danger?" I asked. "And how did this happen?"

"We have taught you the physical skills you need. But siphoning is a new skill that nobody has mastered. Textor - the weaver - is more proficient than any other relic and keeps pushing back the boundaries. We taught you the combat applications of siphoning between relics - what we consider to be the basics. But when Paredo broke the circle and told us that you had merged the group and pulled them from his grip, it showed once again how little we know about it."

"But aren't we supposed to merge? I asked in surprise. "How else are we supposed to gain our names?"

Sericum paused a moment, then looked me squarely in the eyes. "We use a bit of showmanship, use the siphoning to create some shared experience, then douse you in a sense of empathy. It is usually enough to then lift the names from your superficial consciousness."

I nodded, as she continued. "But when you wrested control of the group from him, he was drawn with you as you siphoned the life story of every relic in the group. It scared him. Nobody has ever done that before."

The chatter from the other relics in the room had died out as she spoke and Sericum had suddenly become aware that all of our focus was upon her.

"Let me just say that when it was his turn to be stripped and dissected by you, he bailed out. He has secrets that he cannot share with a class of fresh recruits. Whatever the cost." She concluded lamely.

The room stayed quiet as we each processed her meaning.

"He didn't just bail out though. Agency relics also use siphoning as a form of wireless communication to convey large volumes of information quickly, and he showed me what had happened - so I could bring you all back."

Some of my peers still looked disgusted, at both myself for triggering this whole debacle and at Paredo's behaviour - despite Sericum's effort to put a brave face on it - and they made their excuses and left.

We had missions to finish preparing for, but now none of us were under any illusions. If it served the agency's interests, any one of us would be thrown under the bus to serve the 'greater good'. So much for a brotherhood. I secretly hoped that our shared experience would at least bind our class together, even if we couldn't count on loyalty from elsewhere in the agency.

Chapter 30

"Don't you see?" Thomas exclaimed excitedly. "If you can experience the lives of other relics, you have just become invaluable to the agency! You can extract information in a way unlike anything we have ever seen before. You could train new relics in a day! Think of the possibilities!"

He sat on the end of my bunk as I stood at my wardrobe, filling an expedition bag with my new clothes.

"No Thomas". I responded acidly. "I have just shown that now I am a danger within the agency. At any point, I could learn something I am not supposed to."

Never one to adequately conceal his emotions, the Professor's face fell as the realisation dawned on him.

"And what's more," I went on, "I have potentially humiliated one of the masters of the order. It is just as well I am being shipped off to the arse-end of the world. At least there, I can watch my back."

I was being unfair on the Professor and perhaps more acerbic than I meant to be. I suppose my frustration at the outcome of the naming ceremony had been compounded by the fact that Thomas wasn't coming with me. Hiram had made it clear that the Professor was still required to fulfil his duties in the development of special weapons.

"Don't worry." Thomas said, trying to mollify me. "It will all be forgotten about by the time you get back".

He remembered who he was lying to at the exact same moment my implant alerted me to the micro-tremors in his voice. My half-smile exposed the white lie between us, but it was enough to chip into my dark mood.

"Look," I said, letting out a sigh that relieved some of my frustration, "I now have the memories and confidences of every relic in my class stuck in my head." I paused in my packing and turned to face Thomas.

"There's some seriously dirty laundry in here," I said, tapping my temple for emphasis. "Things that people will want buried. My only protection is that EVERY relic at the naming ceremony now has the exact same memories and secrets that I do. But I am reliant upon our sponsors and handlers reasoning that out before I am targeted. It's thin ice, but it's all I have to work with."

Thomas' face was a study as he rationalised what I was saying.

"You mean, they know everything that WE have discussed too?" He blurted. "They also have your memories?" I could see his mind racing back through every one of our conversations, concern etched upon his face over what he may or may not have said aloud.

"I'm afraid so." I went on. "I have lived up to my new name, Lucidus. I've made our entire class transparent. As things stand, we have no secrets from each other." I paused to think about it. "In any other setting," I wondered aloud, "it would be therapeutic to have gotten everything off your chest."

But in the agency? That was another story. I think Thomas was only half listening at this point, as he stressed over the ramifications of what I had just told him.

"But beyond this debacle," I continued, "my abilities could be very polarising within the agency. Think about it. I could facilitate incorruptible politics amongst the relics. If we all shared the same memories, there would be no mind games, no hidden motives, just a general consensus of how to move forward."

The Professor's eyes widened. "Oh dear. I see what you mean. Some will leap at that opportunity, but many will not. If you could meld the relics into one consensus, all of the power-games within the agency over the years could have been for naught. Alliances would be uncovered. Blackmail, corruption and deception could suddenly be out in the open! Goodness knows what plans would be undone or how power might shift."

I was now in severe danger and we both knew it. I zipped the bag I was holding and dropped it at the Professor's feet as I took a seat on the bed alongside him. "All I've done is put my head in a noose." I said. "I might have been better off staying in the void."

The Professor's head snapped up at this. "Come now!" He said fervently. "You must never think like that. Where there is life, there is hope. You should consider what good can come of this. Think of the research possibilities!" The Professor was clearly slipping back into his own comfort zone.

"What if linking so many relics together could create some form of hive mind?" He went on. "With your implants combined, the relics would have more processing power than any supercomputer ever dreamed of. And what about life extension technologies? If you can suck up the life experience of a relic, and deposit it into another..."

With a frustrated shake of my head, I cut the Professor off. "Look Thomas, on one hand I may be the key to every transhumanist's dreams, but at the same time I have just made every relic expendable! If I don't end up dead, I'm going to be caught in a monster tug of war between the masters of the agency. Your research isn't going to stop that. I need to get this target off my back, not sit here discussing more theory."

I knew it was just a matter of time before others within the agency came to the same conclusions. Would I be a figure to rally around for the betterment of mankind? Would I be a tool to be studied or abused to further the agenda of the darker half of the agency? Or would I simply be too dangerous to keep around?

I felt like a cat on a hot tin roof.

Thomas stood up, and bent to brush off the front of his trousers with the palms of his hands. He was already spotless, but he often fiddled with his clothing whilst deep in thought.

"Okay." He concluded. "I'll talk to Major Winters right away. He will know what to do."

Thomas smiled at me, in an attempt to reassure me. But a nervous tic in his cheek completely marred the effect and made me feel worse.

We exchanged our goodbyes, but as the Professor swung the door to my quarters open wide to leave in a hurry, he almost crashed into the broad chest of Paredo, who had evidently just arrived to call upon me.

"I do apologise!" Thomas stammered in surprise, before backing up and out of the way.

Paredo smiled at this show of deference on Thomas' part, but graciously stepped aside himself and ushered Thomas through with a curious gesture akin to a bow and a flourish of his hand.

On his way out, Thomas shot me a nervous glance, then hurried off. He must have known that there would be nothing he could do, besides contact the Major.

I was already on my feet before Paredo 'invited' himself into my quarters.

"There's been a change of plans." He said flatly, his smile slipping from his face. "You're coming with me".

Chapter 31

I sat in a plush cream leather chair, on board one of the agency's private jets. My eyes scanned the horizon as I looked out of a porthole over the wing, watching a full spectrum sunset for the very first time. It was majestic. That's the only way I can describe it. In fact, I could have been brought to tears, letting loose the stress I had pent up throughout the day, if it wasn't for Paredo's occasional glances as he carelessly lounged in the chair across the aisle.

I had been too up-tight to enjoy my brief tour of the private Boeing 757 when we had boarded, but 5 hours later, still alive and after a fairly frank conversation with Paredo, I had resolved to make the most of it. If I were to be executed, he wouldn't have taken me half-way across the North-American continent in luxury to do it.

The Boeing had luxury seating for 43 passengers, a dining room, master bedroom and bathroom, guest bedroom and VIP lounge. Paredo hadn't mentioned who mainly used it, but I could tell from his cavalier disregard for the leather and mahogany that he rested his boots on, that it wasn't him.

The Rolls Royce engines hummed in the background. They were far less intrusive than the roar made by the usual commercial aircraft I was used to, so I ignored them as I cast my mind over the last few hours.

We were beginning our descent and our steady loss of altitude, combined with the incessant pings coming from GPS satellites overhead, told me that we were heading for Anchorage airport. In all honesty, I wasn't surprised, given that Alaska had clearly been on Paredo's mind when I tried to siphon his thoughts during our naming ceremony.

What was a surprise, however, was that the Academy, and the vast agency facility which contained it, had been housed under Denver International Airport. I had simply assumed that because I had lost consciousness after my fall in Africa, that I would still be on the same continent when I woke up. After all, the area was home to numerous US bio weapon research labs, so why not deep underground military bases? It was an ideal location to avoid unwanted oversight.

When Thomas had left me, Paredo had been very curt in his responses and had led me straight to the lift with my bags. I had felt like a man going to the gallows, not even being able to say goodbye to my friends. But as the elevator scanned

Paredo's retinas and the steel doors quietly eased closed, I knew that I was committed to whatever happened next. But I certainly wasn't going to give Paredo the satisfaction of seeing me afraid.

We had stood side by side, staring straight ahead at our dull reflections in the steel doors. The time seemed to drag by as we ascended, but fortunately for me, after 30 nerve-wracking seconds of silence, Paredo began to speak.

"You are coming with me, because it is no longer appropriate to leave you to your own devices in the field. Especially whilst you remain unschooled."

My spine stiffened with indignation at that. Paredo harrumphed softly at my reaction, but went on. "Listen boy. When you rack up as many years implanted as I have, everyone seems unschooled. Don't get tetchy".

I must have given off some sign that I had acknowledged his point, because he turned his head slightly to put me in the corner of his vision.

"Besides. I am honouring a favour."

"A favour?" I asked. "A favour to whom?"

I was still angry at Paredo's behaviour in the void. So, despite carrying a cold shard of fear down the length of my spine, I was being impudent. For all I knew, he was just lulling me into a false sense of security before he eliminated me.

He considered my question a moment, but his brow furrowed at my tone. "Let's just say, a certain little bird didn't risk her sanity to pull you out of the void to then leave you vulnerable. There are forces at work that you are unfamiliar with, and besides, I said I would complete your education."

Sericum. His words had the ring of truth about them, however reluctant he might have been to nursemaid me.

I hoped that I could detect if Paredo were lying, but I didn't know for sure. If he was as old as the rumour-mill made out, then who knows what tricks he had picked up over the years.

"And what's in it for you?" I asked, emboldened by his candid responses.

"Easy pup. Remember who you are speaking to." Paredo snapped back, irritation finally showing through. "My reasons are my own. If you earn my trust, I may tell you more. For now though, your adrenaline stinks to high heaven. Shut it off."

I was embarrassed into complying and, after a moment, he mastered his irritation and continued.

"I'm not going to eat you. You can be on your guard all you like, but you are coming with me to be useful. If I wanted you dead, you would be."

I still couldn't detect any lies from him, so Paredo must have had absolute confidence in what he said. I suppressed a hard swallow and just scowled at my reflection instead.

"Besides. You have just made the game a little more interesting." He added obliquely.

Any further conversation was made impossible by the elevator drawing to a stop. The lift pinged and the metal doors slid open on to a pale marble-clad atrium, which was divided down the middle by bullet-proof glass and reinforced security booths. There were armed guards on both sides, bathed by bright overhead lighting. More steel elevator doors were set into each wall.

Several corridors later, and having repeated Paredo's retina verification more than once, we exited the facility through some thick steel blast doors. We emerged into a rough-hewn rock tunnel. Tunnel is perhaps the wrong word, because this passage through the bedrock was the width and height of an aircraft hangar and stretched on as far as I could see. It was lit with high-powered floodlights suspended overhead and was lined with bay after bay of unmarked agency vehicles. These were mainly dark SUV's, but also some more heavily armoured vehicles, along with numerous prestige cars. My implant highlighted that a high proportion had Colorado plates, with several marked Denver County, but as surprised as I was, I made no comment.

Paredo was still clearly vexed about having me with him, but his irritation seemed to subside as he emitted a broad spectrum signal from his implant, which caused at least three of the vehicles in sight to flash their indicator lights as they unlocked their doors and disabled their alarms.

He selected a black SUV with keyless operation and used his implant to mimic the key fob . I was still climbing into the vehicle as his thick finger pressed against the starter button, causing the throaty V8 engine to roar into life. We had set off with an impatient squeal of tyres. Paredo had navigated us through several miles of 'tunnel' where, in places, heavy goods vehicles queued to deliver supplies to heavily guarded goods-inwards points.

Eventually, we had pulled into another agency parking area where we had accessed an elevator up to the private hangar where we had boarded the jet I now sat in.

"Have you thought about my offer?" Paredo asked, drawing my attention back to the present.

He was referring to our brief conversation a couple of hours earlier. He had grown weary of my silence and having gulped his way through half a decanter of 25 year old scotch, he had stalked over and sat in the seat opposite me. You couldn't tell from his physiology that he had been drinking, but he stank of it as he propped himself on an elbow.

"I told Sericum I would look after you for a time. But I am not holding you hostage. Nor am I going to babysit you." He fixed me with two dark, intense eyes, which would have wiped the smirk off even Jarrod's face. "We have two ways of doing this. I can cast my shadow over you for a while, whilst you *play* at being an agent. If all is well, that will be sufficient to keep you out of harm's way whilst the dust settles." The subtle twist of his words didn't do much to hide his disdain for this option.

"Or," he continued, "you can embrace this opportunity and learn agency business from a master."

He watched me, but not receiving a clear indication from me, he elaborated. "Hiram sold you a pipedream. The world doesn't work the way you want it to. It doesn't work the way *I* want it to. So if you apprentice with me for a time, I will expect you to take the rough with the smooth. I will not shield you from anything, however ugly. Then, maybe in due course, you will be in a position to make a change from within the agency."

This was exactly what Thomas had laid in front of me. Were these people all reading from the same script? I had nodded thoughtfully. Did I want a sugar-coated, insulated experience until some dark faction within the agency felt secure enough to eliminate me? Or did I want to stare straight into the heart of the agency, however black it was?

My ideological view of the world had been eroded into something more realistic during my time at the Academy and, thanks to my education by Thomas, philosophy from various sources resonated in the back of my mind as my conscience tried to make sense of the situation. On one hand, Nietzsche cautioned me with 'Beware that, when fighting monsters, you yourself do not become a monster... for when you gaze long into the abyss, the abyss gazes also into you', whilst Machiavelli was counselling me to 'Keep your friends close, and your enemies closer'.

I stood at a crossroads. But whichever option I chose, I risked being nothing more than a puppet on a string for somebody. The question was who? In the end, Sun Tzu won out with 'know thy self, know thy enemy'. If I was to make any difference in this world, I needed to know exactly what I was dealing with - and I couldn't hope to get any closer to the thick of the action than by hanging on to Paredo's blood-drenched coat-tails.

I was about to answer, but Paredo must have taken my brief contemplation for hesitation. He stood, and looking down at me in my chair, seemed even more intimidating.

"Think on it." He said seriously. "*Act in haste and repent at leisure.* That is a saying I should have heeded more myself. So I will give you some time to think. But I *will* have your answer before we leave the aircraft."

Two hours later, to the second, Paredo was demanding my response.

I had been thinking on my answer - long and hard.

"I always thought that Canis was being over-dramatic", I replied solemnly. "But today, I forged my name - and bonded with my brother and sister relics in a way that I could never have imagined. I have always felt I had a duty to serve mankind, but now I also have a duty to the brotherhood. So, for better or worse, I'll play my part within the Agency."

"As for your offer", I continued, "I am both honoured, and daunted, that you would agree to have me as your apprentice. I recognise it as a lifeline, and I am grateful for it." Paredo nodded his acknowledgement. "But I also owe Sericum a debt of gratitude and will repay it, with interest, by being the hardest working and most sincere apprentice you could ask for. So yes, please, I would like to accept."

Paredo smiled, showing straight, white teeth and a trace of satisfaction across his features.

"Very well!" He said, with a clap and a rub of his hands. "A new player enters the game. Better to be a player than a pawn, I always say. Come and sit over here." He beckoned me to him. "We do not have much time before we land. I need to show you how I firewalled myself when we siphoned. I can't have you giving away all my secrets."

Chapter 32

From Anchorage airport, we had shuttled straight across to the neighbouring Elmendorf Air Force Base, where we took a military transport to a much smaller and more isolated base in the Alaskan wilderness. From there, we completed the remaining 30 miles of our journey to the actual facility and dig site via an underground rail system. This enabled the movement of large amounts of supplies and labour with no evidence above ground for prying eyes.

The more I saw, the more I realised that the agency wasn't just the pinnacle of the intelligence services. It represented a breakaway civilisation which had been parasitically leeching labour and resources from the old one for many decades (if not centuries), despite almost nobody knowing of its existence. It was disconcerting to see how incredibly extensive this had become, when 99% of the population was unaware that it was going on right under their noses.

My mind boggled at the expense of such an operation, but as Paredo observed dismissively, "When most countries' central banks have been privately owned by undisclosed shareholders for over a hundred years, fiat currency is just a plaything for the elites. All the markets are rigged and they can print as much money as they like."

It turned out that Paredo was only taking me to the dark pyramid to experience the energy fields and the ancient technology they had found there. He explained that I should then be able to recognise these unique signatures at other locations and suggested that I create a standing request for my implant to alert me whenever I experienced them again.

We weren't granted access to all of the work being done there, but the energy being released from the pyramid was believed to be enough to power the entire continent. The underground facility had been here for decades and even had its own Academy training area and quarters, albeit on a smaller scale than in Denver.

There weren't currently any relic students being trained in this location, but the site did maintain a resident relic named Sagax, who spent his time training with the exotic weapons technology they were working on here - and sparring with the special forces who were rotated in and out on guard duty.

He was very pleased to see us both, and said as much, as it had been a while since he had enjoyed the company of other relics. He appeared to be in his 30's and was lean and whip-like, which was even more apparent when he was demonstrating his novel weapons. His enthusiasm was contagious, but it was a strange contrast with his lethal demonstrations.

Of particular interest to me was a light-weight hand-held baton which used high voltage to generate its own gravity well. This meant that when you swung it, it was light, but when it fired up mid-swing, it would become heavy toward the tip and carry a substantial amount of inertia. The gel-coated ballistics dummy he demonstrated on didn't stand a chance.

Sagax described his ideas to further develop the concept, such as using the electrical discharge to deliver a stun at the same time, but I didn't see the point in stunning someone who was already dead.

It was a clever gadget all right, but I pointed out that maybe this technology could be better utilised in power generation, where you could spin a light-weight turbine using low energy, then energise it to make it heavy like a flywheel, to generate energy via a dynamo as it took much longer to stop.

"Or maybe this technology could be built into reinforced gloves?" I wondered aloud as Paredo hefted the baton experimentally. Despite the flat end, Paredo had no problem driving it through the dummy with a short thrust. He left the baton quivering in the jellied mess as he moved on to another station which housed a hermetically sealed box which contained an unimplanted relic.

Sagax explained to me that this relic was damaged and could not be implanted in anyone. So it was just useful for students to detect what energy signatures they could from it. I was about to siphon when he also added "But be careful, it is hostile."

"Hostile?" I asked, my curiosity piqued.

"Yes," Paredo added. "If a relic dies a violent death, more often than not, his implant will enter some form of defensive mode so it cannot fall into enemy hands. This is why we cannot remove relic implants from their hosts. It makes them worthless scrap."

I considered this a moment. "But my implant came from a corpse with a crushed skull."

"Time is a great healer", Sagax responded with a grin. "We assume that if the relic can no longer detect a threat, it stands down."

"But we haven't been able to trigger this ourselves, so it is just a theory," Paredo added, as I peered into the box.

I felt a tiny thread of Paredo's siphon just as the relic twitched and one of its thin filaments lashed at the confines of its box in response, making me jump. Paredo's deep chuckle at my expense was cut short as the immobilised relic emitted a high pitched squeal, causing us to all cover our ringing ears. I don't know how I knew, but I felt there was something mournful in the cry, however alien it was.

Sagax scowled at Paredo, but said nothing and Paredo ignored him.

Turning to me, he said "We use this one to train our students how to snatch modules from other relics. Spend some time with it. Paredo and I have some other business to discuss."

I was left alone with the relic and the assorted gadgets that Sagax had demonstrated, as Paredo and Sagax headed off through the door to the briefing suite that must have been common to all Academy facilities.

I toyed with the reverse-engineered tech, practicing some martial arts forms with the baton to see how its variable heft affected my balance and flow, but my attention soon returned to the encased relic. The analytical part of me wanted to dismiss it as just a machine, but its behaviour mimicked a caged animal, making me wonder at what point programmed responses blur into intelligent self preservation. And what did this mean where my own implant was concerned?

It occurred to me that everyone who had interacted with the forlorn relic had been pulling and snatching at it. Every contact a hostile grab, always wanting to take something. I knew from my own training that having my modules pulled at was painful and disorienting. Why would this be any different for a relic without a host?

You don't befriend a caged animal by ripping pieces off it, so I did something that perhaps nobody else had tried. I used what Paredo had shown me on the flight and fed a trickle of energy and memories into my siphon and then withdrew.

The relic still lashed its filaments, but didn't cry out this time. The motion seemed more of a warning. I had spent time around horses in my teenage years and having watched their behaviour, it reminded me of when an impatient swish of a tail and the cocking of an ear was enough to warn the other horses to back off. Not as aggressive, or overt, as lifting a leg or threatening a bite, but a warning nonetheless, for those with the eyes to see it.

Maybe this wasn't a battle of wills won by force, but rather a delicate courtship to initiate the most intimate symbiosis?

I waited a minute, then offered up a similar morsel. Energy and good memories, and taking nothing in return.

The relic still reacted with hostility. It was hard to tell if this was any different than before, but it didn't feel right to rip and tear at it like a punch bag. So I decided to test my theory whilst Paredo and Sagax went about their business. I had time to kill and repeated as many subtle variations as I could think of, watching and assessing the reactions I received.

As preoccupied as I was with this process, I couldn't help but wonder who had previously hosted this relic. Was it from an archaeological dig site, or was it fresh from an agent of a rival power block. Worse yet, I thought darkly, it could even be from one of our own dead relics. After all, every government intelligence service had dark secrets and the Agency would be no different.

As I pondered, I considered what the 'makers' of this amazing technology would have been trying to achieve in building in this behaviour. I stood in front of the transparent case, hands on hips, studying the relic, whilst my puzzled features were reflected back at me.

'If it were me', I thought, *'I would want the implant to retain its secrets and definitely not to reward any attempt to steal the technology.'*

But the very fact that these units didn't self destruct seemed to be a clue. Maybe they were simply too valuable to be lost each time the living host died? Or maybe the relics themselves didn't want to die?

I changed my tactic and instead siphoned a simple message.

'I acknowledge you. I do not wish you to reveal confidential information. I do not require any of your components. I am sorry for the loss of your host, although I wasn't involved and I don't have any information about it. Do you wish to communicate?'

I was expecting the usual lashing, but this time, the relic didn't so much as twitch. I didn't get any response at all. It simply lay there, apparently inanimate. But as I studied it, cycling my vision up to full spectrum, I noticed that the temperature had subtly dropped in the immediate area.

The relic itself was gathering in energy from its environment.

'Do you have a message?' I siphoned again. *'Can I deliver a message?'*

I had still received no response, when the silence was broken by the swish of the briefing suite door and the release of Sagax and Paredo's heated conversation into the arena. They were still exchanging harsh words as they approached and weren't at all interested in my activities.

I turned away from the cabinet as Paredo's wrath was boiling out over the hapless Sagax.

"If they truly hold those opinions," Paredo stormed, "they can share them with me *directly*." His words contained cold menace and this wasn't lost on Sagax.

"I am only passing on what I know, Paredo," he replied, stoically taking the brunt of Paredo's anger. "You have my loyalty - which is why I am sharing this with you. We both know they won't move against you openly, but that doesn't mean they won't act at all."

Paredo was turning to respond, when to my surprise, the disembodied relic initiated a short, sharp siphon, whilst simultaneously letting out a piercing shriek twice as loud as before. It was enough to make us all wince and reach for our ears, but I was the most surprised of all, as a packet of information was dumped straight into my implant.

"Damn it, Lucidus!" Paredo snapped. "Stop playing around will you?" Then towards Sagax, in a more civil tone, he said "Thank you for the information and hospitality, but we're leaving."

It seemed that neither of them had noticed what had just happened. They had assumed that I was still just poking and snatching at the broken relic in the same way any other student would have.

"But what do I report to the Committee?" Sagax demanded, his own anger rising.

"Nothing." Paredo shot back. "Buy me some time. You owe me that much. Wait for them to ask - and in the meantime, make yourself hard to reach."

Sagax's eyebrows rose, but Paredo rolled straight over him. "What you say to them is your own affair, *Brother*, but in 48 hours I can give them something more important to talk about."

In the face of Paredo's heated words, I didn't want to raise what had just happened, so I simply instructed my implant to firewall off the mysterious packet of data, scan it, disable any malicious code and await my further instruction. Besides, it felt wrong to break the confidence of the helpless relic until I knew what it had just given me.

"I'll be back," I promised it aloud, and Sagax barked a short laugh.

"Ha! That's the spirit". He said, clearly misinterpreting my meaning.

Chapter 33

Paredo and I retraced our inbound journey. He was evidently vexed by the outcome of his conversation with Sagax.

"Do you want to talk about it?" I asked, as we sped back toward the military base on the underground train.

The carriage we occupied was well-lit and comfortable, despite not having windows to see out of. It made the journey that little bit more claustrophobic, but with the latest developments, I had more pressing things on my mind. An armed operative sat at the other end of the carriage, doing his best to appear discrete.

"No," Paredo responded tersely as he turned away from me, seemingly losing himself in his own thoughts.

But my awareness of his siphoning a moment later confirmed the complete opposite. I adopted a bored look and fiddled with the trim of my jacket as I allowed his communication into my mind.

'This isn't the right place to discuss things', he siphoned. *'But we do need to talk'.*

'I am ready when you are,' I siphoned back, feeling my curiosity vie with my concern.

'I got you out of Denver just in time.' He continued. *'News of your anomalous naming ceremony has travelled faster than I expected. I knew the heads of the agency would take serious interest when they learned of it, but it seems there is a difference of opinion over what should be done with you.'*

'Done with me?' I replied, my welling anxiety only being surpassed by my disappointment at how fast the news had travelled.

'Don't act the fool, Lucidus,' Paredo returned. *'We both know the ceremony opened a can of worms this morning. This even goes beyond the Agency now. Sagax informed me that they have called for the Committee of 300 to be convened. That is the last thing we need, because now I am caught up in the mess too.'*

'You are?' I asked, not understanding the politics involved.

'Yes.' Paredo replied. *'Not only was I involved in the ceremony, but those resentful of my position have called into question my motives for spiriting you away. They have been waiting for an excuse to pull me down - and this turn of events has lined up nicely for them.'* I could sense his bitterness at this.

'The only saving grace is that they won't yet know whose interests I am serving, so they will have to tread lightly. They don't know if I have taken you somewhere for a discrete accident, or whether I am protecting you. But one thing is for sure, it will be obvious that it isn't just standard agency business, or I would have left you to your designated mission.'

I considered what he had just shared with me. Convening the Committee was presumably a big deal and seemed a bit of a knee-jerk reaction to me, when the Agency could handle its own business. It didn't stack up with the rumours I had picked up about the Agency and its masters during my time at the Academy. So I said as much.

'Don't count on getting the facts from Academy briefings!' Paredo scoffed. *'If they told you everything, you wouldn't be so willing to serve. They certainly wouldn't tell you where the power lies!*

Governments are just the playthings of the bankers and elites. The Agency is the manpower that holds together the web of intelligence services, secret societies and institutions, but both the Agency and myself answer directly to the Committee of 300 - a group of 300 people from the wealthiest and most ancient bloodlines who truly run the western world.

Despite their political and financial power though, they aren't at all comfortable having relics around, yet they cannot dispose of us, because we are all that stands in the way of the other power blocks. Not to mention our usefulness for keeping the public-facing world leaders in check and silencing anyone else who rocks the boat. The only reason they don't move against us is because they feel they can control us.'

My mind reeled at his frank admission.

'But believe me,' he continued, *'I know how many of those bastards think - I've worked for them long enough. We aren't from the right bloodlines. They just see us as nothing more*

than upgraded hired help, always looking to steal the silverware when their backs are turned. So anything that could threaten their control is a BIG deal.'

'So now what?' I asked, feeling out of my depth.

'Now, I dig us out of the cess pit we have fallen into. But you are going to help. We don't need any more scrutiny. They are getting jumpy enough as it is.'

His comment left me puzzled, as though we were talking cross-purposes, but over the next few minutes, Paredo outlined his plans. He believed that the only way to avoid being indefinitely confined to an underground test facility, or some fate altogether worse, would be to demonstrate that I was far more useful in the field. At the same time, I could show my loyalty and vindicate Paredo's decision to take me with him, killing two birds with one stone.

Paredo had several different European leads we could explore, including a trip to Berlin to assist in the search for the lost underground facility. But we didn't have much time and needed a spectacular result to make any difference - something that would demonstrate the usefulness of my unique talents.

Paredo had outlived the rest of his generation, and several generations since, because he was audacious, unpredictable and acted decisively. More importantly, he knew how to dance his way through the politics of the Agency and cultivate a fearsome reputation. A smooth combination of blunt force, dark favours and fear. For his own reasons, he had taken me under his wing and if anyone could get us out of this situation, it was him.

As the train began to decelerate, indicating our arrival at the base, we gathered our few belongings and stood in anticipation of the doors opening.

I nodded and smiled a neighbourly farewell across the carriage to the operative, but, as if in rebuke, Paredo not only outwardly ignored the guard, but as we approached him, Paredo's implant began to pulse a base frequency below the range of human hearing. Sound frequencies of 18 to 19 Hz can cause eyeballs to resonate and trigger strange visual phenomena, along with a feeling of unease, which can lead to intense fear and even panic attacks. So as we moved towards the guard's position in order to exit the train, I detected his heart rate rising. He hastily stepped aside, despite there being plenty of room and averted his gaze.

I heard his deep swallow and the outflow of his pent-up breath as we left the carriage.

'You have a lot to learn,' Paredo chided me through his siphon, before getting back to business.

'So how is your Russian?'

Chapter 34

Thick snow squeaked as it compacted under the heels of my new leather boots. My breath didn't have time to mist in the frigid Russian air, as it was whipped clear by the decelerating rotor blades of the Kamov KA-60 Helicopter on the landing pad, some 60 feet behind me.

My Officer's woollen greatcoat and Ushanka fur hat did a reasonable job of shielding me from the cold, as I waited for the flustered lieutenant to hurry across the gravel walkway between us.

The eddies of sound bouncing off our surroundings painted me a clear picture as the Kamov's engines wound down. Paredo stood behind my left shoulder, as tall as a barn door, and almost as wide, in his matching greatcoat and Russian aviation Officer's uniform. Unlike me, however, he was wearing a black special forces beret with the black, red and gold chimera insignia worn by Russian relics.

"Major." The young officer greeted me in his native Russian, after snapping me a crisp salute. "What a pleasure to see you." The micro-tremors in his voice gave away the lie.

"What brings you to our humble facility? We were not informed of your intended arrival, otherwise we would have prepared a warmer welcome for you and your esteemed colleague." He looked slightly sick as he sized up Paredo, who stood as impassive as a statue, with his eyes unreadable behind mirrored glasses.

I too, stood there with my face a static mask, not a trace of softness about my features or in my manner.

"Take me to your commanding officer". I ordered, looking impatiently past his shoulder to the reinforced metal door of the concrete bunker. "I am not in the habit of discussing state secrets with subordinates."

The lieutenant was not a great deal above a green recruit, presumably with insufficient connections to prevent him from being stationed in the furthest reaches of Far East Russia. So although his mouth fell open at my harsh dismissal, and began silently working to formulate a response, another uncertain glance at Paredo made him think better of it. Instead, he promptly turned and gestured for us to accompany him.

I could feel Paredo's satisfaction through his siphon as we headed toward the beckoning facility entrance.

"Bold plans are always the best ones," he had said as he had explained our mission back in Alaska.

We had returned to the Agency jet in Anchorage in order to collect our luggage, along with several different passports, each claiming a different nationality. From there, Paredo had chartered a twin turboprop aircraft through Bering Air, to take us to Ugolny airport in Russia.

Bering Air were one of the only airlines to have breached the "ice curtain" between Alaska and Russia since the Cold War. With over 95% of inbound Russian flights being Moscow-centric, and much of Far East Russia being a "closed" region within the Russian Federation, it was no wonder Paredo had chosen this route into the country. The small number of chartered flights coming in to the remote Siberian town of Anadyr were largely overlooked by the Russian intelligence services, because they simply didn't have the manpower to scrutinise every tourist coming in through the back door.

Paredo had evidently used Bering Air's services before, because the manager came out from his office to personally thank him for his custom and wish him a safe flight back home. A warning look from Paredo had ensured I kept quiet, as he responded in a perfect Russian accent, complete with new mannerisms which seemed totally alien to me - but they were very convincing nonetheless.

For this trip, he had styled himself as a Russian oligarch named, Alexey Tumanov, a moderately successful defence contractor with numerous ties to the oil and gas industry. It was no doubt just one of his many covers and manufactured identities, but he admitted to it being one of his favourites.

Although it was only a relatively small aircraft, we still made good progress as we cruised towards Anadyr. The three hours it took seemed to fly by, as Paredo carefully briefed me by siphon.

Until this point, my Russian language education had comprised entirely of phrase books, grammar guides, Russian dictionaries and a smattering of movie clips from my past. So when I engaged my implant to speak Russian for the first time, Paredo winced, saying that I sounded like the Russian talking clock.

To add authenticity, he dumped several hours of his memories of a particular Russian major he used to know, into my implant and had me assimilate his style of language, mannerisms and air of authority. He had picked a great man for me to study and emulate, but the memories somehow seemed tinged with an indefinable sense of loss. Paredo made no comment about that and soon brightened when I spoke in Russian again, this time with the correct intonations and accent.

Ugolny airport at Anadyr was a mixed-use military and commercial facility, so it was an ideal location to meet with one of Paredo's native contacts who had a reputation within the Agency for solving problems on red soil. Despite his excellent track record though, today he seemed most uncomfortable to be doing business right under the nose of the military. But the three quarters of a million dollars Paredo had wired to his account in Zürich several hours before, had overcome his reservations and bought us the use of a Russian helicopter, a discrete pilot to fly it, and a suitable change of clothes for our mission.

"So good to see you again Alexey," the ageing Russian had begun.

"You too, Vadim!" Paredo responded. "You have the pilot and the chopper I asked for?"

Vadim nodded. "All fuelled and ready to go. But I had some difficulties with the uniforms at such short notice. Your associate here, was not a problem," he said, nodding towards me, "but we don't see many of your prodigious size. So although I have Officers' clothes for you, they don't all match. But you should be fine if you keep your greatcoat on."

So, several hours later, we had successfully retraced Paredo's previous steps to visit one of the last occupied Sharashka's in the region. Siberian gulags, or forced labour camps, had officially been phased out, because you couldn't easily hide crews of political prisoners working to cut lumber, lay railways, mine gold and more. However, secret research and development laboratories, utilising highly skilled prisoners to work on scientific and technological problems for the state, were much easier to conceal.

Paredo had visited this Sharashka eight years before, whilst inserting a deep cover Agency operative to eavesdrop on both the research, and whatever dirty secrets Mother Russia had wanted buried here.

My mind was drawn back to the mission at hand as the young officer slammed the metal bunker door behind us, sealing out the sub-arctic chill. Paredo had been forced to duck under the low lintel, but at least the corridor had sufficient ceiling height to accommodate him.

The officer eyed us warily, perhaps anticipating some criticism, but upon receiving none, he said "the Captain Lieutenant's office is this way".

It was time for us to action the weakest and most vulnerable part of our plan.

We followed the officer through several corridors, lined with dark steel doors. Each doorway was designated by a white spray-painted stencil and some also had machined name-plates screwed into the concrete lintels.

Within Paredo's siphon, I felt him initiate a bridge. We had practiced this several times on the flight here, but it was one of the harder things I had done with this incredible new skill. The easiest way to describe it would be to say it allowed several relics to join together their abilities, whilst just one of them could control the flow of the siphon. It is what Paredo had done at our naming ceremony.

But despite my cool exterior, I was filled with both nervousness and exhilaration and this heady combination was interfering with the process.

'Concentrate, damn it!' Paredo chided me in my mind.

We passed several guards, going about their business, who, upon seeing us, hastily tucked in shirts or straightened their uniforms before stepping aside and snapping salutes. Their unkempt appearance highlighted the sense of abandonment that this place had. The facility was a ghost of a former age, where the inhabitants were now just going through the same old motions, but with no real conviction. What was the point in going the extra mile if nobody would ever check - because nobody cared.

As we reached the top of a wide flight of stairs, Paredo and I managed to complete the 'bridge' and Paredo hastily began searching for sign of his contact. To the eyes of the guards we passed though, we were taciturn officers on the warpath, our eyes boring holes into the unlucky lieutenant's back.

The boosted strength of Paredo's siphon flared all around us and, to my eyes, it seemed peculiar that the officer could be totally oblivious to it, as he led us through the facility.

As we passed doorways to offices, store rooms, barracks, armouries and more, the softly whistling overhead air vents, (which maintained life within the lower levels), also carried snatches of conversation and other signs of life too quiet for a normal ear to hear. My implant was keeping tally and displayed a confirmed count of at least 26 potential hostiles so far.

With a sinking feeling, I could detect that Paredo's siphon was drawing a blank. This could be a disaster, because I was reliant upon the information our spy held to inject insider knowledge into my discussion with the commanding officer. If we reached his location empty handed and clueless, then everything could unravel.

'Well, Araneus is either not here, dead, or dimming himself.' Paredo concluded, his words carrying more frustration than concern.

Dimming referred to our ability to suppress and stifle our relic signatures. We had trained extensively in the Academy to both dim and flare our implants. Flaring helped us locate each other and co-ordinate on the battlefield and dimming helped us to infiltrate locations undetected by enemy relics. It was almost impossible to hide from a powerful relic determined to smoke you out, but most students could evade passive detection by dimming.

Araneus had no reason to conceal himself from us and, judging by this dingy dungeon, he should be counting down the hours to his extraction. Where was he? We hadn't even reach the workshops and cells of the inmates, yet I already wanted to leave.

With an outward grunt of frustration, which drew a concerned glance from our guide, Paredo took it upon himself to flare with the combined force of our implants.

'This is Relic: Death-13. Report', he boomed into the ether.

We both strained to detect a response from Araneus, but a long moment later, the distant, scratchy message that came back from the bowels of the bunker below our feet was certainly not what we were expecting.

'This is Relic: Enforcer-32, with Handler: Control-376. Go ahead.'

If my implant hadn't been keeping tight control over my facial expressions, my eyes would have bulged. What was a Russian relic doing in this far flung facility? There weren't that many of them to go around. Surely they had more important business to attend to?

No sooner had my unguarded thoughts blurted across my consciousness, then Paredo had slapped me behind a firewall. He still maintained a siphon bridge and was drawing on my hardware and power, but he was ensuring that I didn't do anything to compromise our disguise.

All Russian relics were kept under the heel of dominant handlers and were much more tightly controlled than in the West. They were stripped of their humanity with merciless 'conditioning' and behaved more like organic machines. Paredo had explained to me, with disgust, that the Russian handlers were almost like jockeys, riding in the minds of their relics at all times. This was my role in the whole deception. I was to take the lead and act as his handler - not to fire off random thoughts which could blow our cover.

The burning question was whether the relic and his handler were there because of Araneus, or was it purely coincidental and Araneus was simply lying low. I hoped for the latter.

Having an enemy relic on-site made our mission that much harder, and I wasn't confident that I could maintain my cover both under the scrutiny of a relic and minus the intelligence that Araneus would have provided.

If anything could be salvaged from this situation, it was that at least we knew we were only dealing with an 'Enforcer' class relic - and there were two of us. 'Enforcers' were the lower grade relics simply used to back up the secret police and coerce compliance domestically. Relics designated as 'Death' were the elite, semi-autonomous assassin units which were considerably more lethal. 'Talons', Paredo had told me, were the equivalent of super-soldiers, complete with rudimentary exoskeletons and heavy armour, purely for battlefield missions.

Paredo couldn't leave the communication hanging any longer, so with a boldness that surprised even me, he siphoned *'Relic: Enforcer-32. Handler: Control-376. You are both relieved of duty. We have your new orders. You have fifteen minutes to conclude your business and report to us in the Captain Lieutenant's office.'*

Whether Paredo meant to buy us some precious time, or to bring matters to a head, I didn't get to find out, because the lieutenant, blissfully unaware of the psychological turmoil behind him, offered over his shoulder, "Captain Lieutenant Stavka's office is just down here".

It was crunch time and I was running out of options, so I took a gamble. I knew that Araneus had been set in place as a Supply Sergeant, so he could scrutinise all of the materials coming in and out of the facility. So I did the nearest thing I could to getting him a message.

"Thank you." I replied. "I trust your Supply Sergeant can prepare the necessary requisition documents to have our transport refuelled? We shall be leaving in a couple of hours."

I felt Paredo's sense of approval leak through our bridge, but the Lieutenant's response swiftly doused that like a bucket of iced water. "I'll see what I can do." He said. "But he may not be in a position to oblige you. He is with your colleague from

Moscow, downstairs. They've been down there almost an hour. It seems someone is being questioned about fiddling the books!"

My initial horror at hearing this made the lieutenant's air of smugness even more distasteful, but no sooner had the thought crossed my mind, then it dawned on me that Paredo had just inadvertently instructed the Enforcer to 'conclude' his business. Poor Araneus. After almost an hour with an Enforcer, goodness knows what we would find. And even if he was still alive, could we extract him from the very depths of the facility, with so many soldiers above us to keep us penned in? The siphon bridge had gone cold and analytical as Paredo was perhaps also calculating our odds. My mind raced.

But the moment of indecision was taken away from us, as Captain Lieutenant Stavka emerged from one of the doors ahead. He was still as drawn and pale as Paredo's memories showed him, but he was now perhaps a little more stooped and was carrying yesterday's stubble about his jaw. His shirt looked slept-in and this whole section of the corridor was tainted with the smell of his fear.

His shoulders slumped almost imperceptibly in resignation at the sight of us, but our guide either didn't notice or pretended not to.

"There you are Lieutenant Vysadili." The Captain Lieutenant said. "I was just heading up to the surface. But no matter. Please bring our esteemed guests through. I suppose we should get down to the matters at hand."

He turned around, without looking to see if we followed, and went back into his office.

I was still frantically trying to figure out how to get to Araneus, but blowing our cover in front of the base commander wasn't going to help any of us. So as we entered the dim interior of Stavka's office, my mind raced furiously to pull the pieces of the puzzle together.

Several grey filing cabinets lined the walls, above which hung a series of maps dotted with labelled pins. A worn rosewood desk took centre stage, with a lamp casting a pool of light over some old ledgers and the three crystal tumblers that Stavka had just set down. He stood behind his desk, rummaging in one of the deep filing cabinet drawers for a bottle of spirits.

"We are not here for your liquor, comrade Stavka." I began.

Vysadili still hovered at the doorway, perhaps unsure whether to excuse himself, or whether further orders would be forthcoming. But his expression, pupil dilation and elevating heart rate, soon made me suspect that he was anticipating something new or exciting taking place. Combined with Stavka's evident dejection at our arrival, Vysadili looked like he was waiting for the fireworks to begin. Maybe he hoped today would result in his advancement at Stavka's expense. The little cockroach left a bad taste in my mouth, so I dismissed him.

"See to our request, Lieutenant," I ordered, without taking my eyes off Stavka.

He moved somewhat reluctantly, but didn't need telling twice, as I was the ranking officer here and Paredo's stern presence added a sense of menace.

There were two leather upholstered chairs set at the corner of Stavka's desk, but when the Captain Lieutenant gestured for us to take seats, I peremptorily dismissed his request and remained standing, with Paredo at my shoulder.

Stavka blanched at this and swallowed thickly. "You don't mind if I take a seat?" He asked. "I would rather do this seated, if I may?".

I nodded, buying myself a moment to think.

"Our colleagues from Moscow are downstairs with one of your subordinates. Enforcer-32 already has him singing like a canary." I hedged.

Stavka's hand trembled slightly as he poured himself a deep glass-full of vodka. I could tell that it wasn't his first and his increased nervousness meant I was on the right track.

"Would you like to talk to me? Or should we await Enforcer-32?"

Something had unravelled horribly for Stavka, and my best guess was that he was involved in skimming the supply budget. Presumably, Moscow had found out and sent an Enforcer to take care of business. Paredo and I had simply walked in at the critical moment.

It was standard protocol for Araneus to spread corruption within his field of operation, in order to garner favour, (or blackmail opportunities), and to provide a realistic cover in case he was ever discovered. Better to admit to corruption than to being a spy. But it would have been risky for Araneus to attempt to involve the commander of the whole facility - unless Stavka was already dirty?

Stavka took a deep swig from his glass, ignoring the burn of the alcohol down his throat, just as much as he was ignoring regulations and protocol. This must be more serious than I thought. What was he involved in?

"What will happen to my family?" He asked, looking like a broken man.

"That will depend on if you make this easy for us, or difficult". I countered.

I was hoping he would offer up a confession of some sort and give me something to work with, but instead he swivelled in his chair and pulled a large cigar box out of one of his draws. He hefted it in his hands briefly, then laid it on his desk, almost reverently.

"Anya will be heartbroken," he said, "but I will cooperate fully." He lifted the hinged lid on the wooden box, releasing the smell of tobacco, but my implant flashed a sudden alert as it detected the scent of gunpowder combined with the magnetic field disruption associated with an all-steel construction firearm.

But Stavka's movements were not threatening as he carefully removed a Makarov PM pistol, a loaded clip and a large Cuban cigar and laid them out in front of him.

"She has family she can stay with, and my boys will look after her," he continued solemnly, as he loaded the pistol. He didn't draw back the slide, nor click off the safety, but instead laid it in front of him on the table as a mute testimony to his pending compliance. I was secretly appalled that the reputation of the Russian relics could be enough to drive a man to suicide, but I had no intention of making him go through with it. I just needed cooperation.

"What do you require of me". He asked.

Paredo softly siphoned some suggestions to me, relating to the release of certain research records, inmates and prototypes, but I was concerned that it would look suspicious if I opened with that.

"You can start by telling me who else was involved and fleshing out some of the details," I responded.

Stavka knew he was finished. Assuming I had the full weight of the state behind me and fearing for his family, he didn't hold anything back. He listed the names of his co-conspirators, his contacts, the scale of his operation - even the location of his ill-gotten assets. He detailed how excess inventory was being sold on the black market, how wages were being drawn for personnel who had been dead for years and a number of other ways his small team had milked the system. He wasn't in any effort to hurry, perhaps savouring what he believed were the last minutes of his life, but he was true to his word.

If the emotions I could detect through Paredo's siphon bridge were anything to go by, he would have been tapping his foot in impatience as Stavka doggedly droned out the details of his corruption. Paredo wanted to retrieve Araneus' body before the Enforcer and his handler realised what they were dealing with, or else to siphon the information from him before he died. The cold fury ebbing through the bridge made me nervous, however, because I could sense his overwhelming urge for retribution.

My attention was drawn away from Stavka's confession as Paredo and I detected movement in the Russian relic. The vivid red thread that my implant overlaid across my vision to locate him in three dimensions, began to shift it's angle. As I watched, the thread repeatedly traced a rectangular pattern across the floor at my feet, as though Enforcer-32 was ascending a stair well.

'Cut to the chase, damn it!' Paredo siphoned to me.

I too was aware that our window of opportunity was closing, so I cut Stavka off mid-flow.

"Enough Stavka!" I interrupted, my voice a whip crack.

He flinched slightly, but then his face reddened, both with annoyance at my rudeness and in embarrassment at his own reaction. He was still a proud man, preferring to go to his death with dignity than to beg for a deal to be struck.

It was a dark business, which left a greasy film on my soul, but I continued. "It will go easier for your family if you sign for the release of certain research records prior to your... resignation. We will also require the release of some of this facility's scientists into our custody."

Stavka's chin lifted at this, as it was no doubt an unusual request which wasn't following the correct channels. But the swiftly changing angle of the red thread of siphon made it clear that we didn't have long before we were joined by the Russian relic and his handler, so I pushed my luck.

"We will also require the release of the body of Sergeant Petrov." I added, referring to the unfortunate Araneus.

Stavka's eyes widened in surprise, then his eyebrows drew together as his surprise turned into anger. "Petrov? But why? Leave him out of this." He leaned forward in his chair and his thrusting finger emphasised his words as he jabbed it towards us. "I gave you the names of everyone involved," he spat. "Petrov's too squeaky clean to be involved in this. And now you will kill him too?"

I had realised my mistake as soon as he reacted. We had misinterpreted Vysadili's words in the corridor, yet my implant still replayed them to me anyway, as Stavka vented his fury at this injustice.

The ghostly echo of the lieutenant's comment now stood in a completely different light. *'He is with your colleague from Moscow, downstairs.'* He had said. *'They've been down there almost an hour. It seems someone is being questioned about fiddling the books!'*

But what a glorious mistake to make - for it meant that Araneus was alive! The relief was visceral, but Stavka could only have taken my twitch of a smile for the smirk of a cold-blooded killer.

'So who was being questioned?' I shot through my siphon to Paredo, as I pondered how to salvage something from my blunder.

I was only saved from having to respond to Stavka by the sudden sound of boots pounding along the corridor toward the office. Evidently, it was also loud enough for the Captain Lieutenant to hear, because his eyes flicked towards the door in anticipation.

A moment before there was a hurried rap at the door, I felt the thinnest tendril of a siphon caress my awareness, along with Paredo's muted relief as Araneus joined our siphon bridge.

He greeted Paredo like a long-lost brother and acknowledged me with gratitude.

"Come", I called aloud, just a fraction of a second before Stavka.

In the time it took Araneus to open the door, step inside and snap a respectful salute, he had uploaded a wealth of information in the form of documents, plans, observations of prototype technologies, prisoner rosters, personnel records and other details of the inner workings of the facility. Most important to him was that he was also warning us of the approach of the enemy relic and his handler. But of course, with our siphon-tracking that was redundant.

I felt Araneus' relief at our arrival give way to his concern about the impending showdown with Enforcer-32, but the look on his face was priceless as my implant reached out across the bridge and greedily snatched a copy of the last 8 years of his memories and assimilated them into my consciousness. It only shared the last 2 months of data with Paredo through the bridge, because despite his abundance of modules, such large amounts of data would take more time for him to assimilate.

I almost physically winced at my new memories of Araneus' last hour with the Russian relic, as he desperately dimmed his signature for all he was worth. Araneus had been forced to look on helplessly, whilst the relic and his handler had brutally interrogated one of his colleagues, knowing that at any moment, he could be next.

But whilst Araneus was perspiring and looking somewhat haggard after his experience, he was still a consummate professional.

"I just received your request Sir," Araneus began, addressing myself, "and have authorised the refuelling of your transport." To Stavka, he turned and said "Enforcer-32 and his colleague will be with you shortly Sir."

The thin red thread pointing to the Russian relic was almost horizontal now, indicating that he was nearly on the same floor as us.

"It seems I may have been premature in my assessment of Sergeant Petrov," I back-tracked. Araneus affected a nervous flinch at the mention of his name, but Stavka looked relieved.

I now knew from Araneus' memories that Stavka had tried to catch him out as a crook in the first week of his arrival. But Araneus was a cautious man by nature, so he hadn't fallen for the ruse and instead had seen opportunity to build his reputation as someone Stavka could trust. Over time, Araneus, or Petrov, as Stavka thought of him, had become indispensible as an advisor. He had fabricated a background as an accountant and financial advisor, prior to his service, and offered to help the Captain Lieutenant to invest portions of his 'income' in offshore trusts and other clean assets for the benefit of his family. It was this turn of events which had helped keep 'Petrov's' name from everybody's lips when the Enforcer and his handler applied pressure.

But despite the heady relief that our brother was alive, we still had to get out of here in one piece.

'Suggestions anyone?' I siphoned through the bridge, as the red thread of Paredo's siphon-tracking indicated that the Enforcer was now less than sixty metres away and closing.

'Dim yourself' was all Paredo offered up as he no doubt readied himself for combat.

Unaware of how close the Enforcer actually was, Stavka got back to business and asked Araneus to provide him with the appropriate documents to authorise the transfer of inmates and research materials.

He knew the deal could change if he didn't conclude our business before the other relic arrived, so he offered to sign blank documents for us to use at our discretion in his 'absence'. Araneus retrieved the appropriate documents from various cabinets and shot us a questioning look as Stavka pushed his pistol to one side to sign each of them with a bold flourish of his pen.

The whole situation was fast becoming just too appalling to think about, because as crooked as Stavka obviously was, he was still demonstrating extraordinary bravery and sacrifice for his family. I was left feeling that maybe there were no black and whites in this world, only varying shades of grey. And one thing was for sure, playing at being spies was much more stressful than I had expected.

The whole situation was becoming even more poignant as Stavka trimmed the end of his cigar and lit it. His cares seemed to fall away as he sat back in his chair puffing smoke. For him, it was time. He silently toasted to his family with what remained in his glass, then reached for his pistol.

Paredo's grudging respect leaked through the bridge, but it was overridden by both Araneus' and my feelings of horror at what Stavka was about to do.

Araneus was nearer than myself and, with a lunge, his hand clamped over the grip of the pistol a second before Stavka could reach it. Stavka clutched at it, but Araneus' relic-enhanced strength and skill wrenched the pistol clear like he was pulling it from a child.

"Damn you, traitor!" Stavka hissed bitterly, just as the door burst open and the Enforcer filled the doorway.

The scene that greeted him couldn't have been more perfect. To the eyes of the Enforcer, a Death-class relic and his handler stood looking on, whilst the Sergeant he had sent ahead now held his suspect at gunpoint. Yet clearly the self-important little popinjay who controlled him wanted to throw his weight around some more. His blood must have been up after his session of interrogation and torture downstairs.

The office was a good size, yet as the giant Enforcer stalked inside, immediately squaring off against Paredo, suddenly there didn't appear to be much room at all. The two colossal men stood facing each other, awaiting the smallest instruction from their handlers to unleash savage violence. I suddenly knew why Paredo had such hate for the enemy relics.

My own fury suddenly boiled up and ripped past my better judgement as I bellowed "What is the meaning of this Control-376! You will stand down."

The handler arrogantly sauntered in behind his relic.

He was slightly smaller than myself, but under a shock of dark hair, his tanned face was marred by a scar that ran from cheek to chin. It had the unfortunate effect of pulling his mouth into a permanent sneer on one side, but judging by his attitude, it suited him. Next to his gigantic Enforcer, he was made to look more like a child, but with him being permanently resident in the giant's mind, it had obviously given him delusions of grandeur where his own diminutive presence was concerned.

"You have no authority here, *Brother*," he said, the oily words dripping from his sneer as he looked me up and down. He ignored Paredo as nothing more than a tool and gave the others even less consideration.

I didn't have the experience to know how to act realistically around another 'handler', and Paredo, in his pent up fury, wasn't being much help.

My implant was now overlaying threat assessments over my vision, which was more of a distraction. I didn't need to know the precise dimensions, weight and physical attributes of the Enforcer, nor the nature of his bulletproof and stab-resistant clothing. He was a monstrous pig of a man, with a shaved head and the overgrown brow ridges and jawbone born of gigantism. His oversized hands were spasmodically clenching and unclenching as he stared at Paredo with undisguised hatred. Clearly, whoever had controlled his body-morphing was clumsy and impatient - and had ridden his pituitary gland too hard, in order to grow the biggest and baddest relic.

"This is my jurisdiction," the handler went on, as he strutted into the centre of the room and proceeded to circle the two massive relics. It was though he was assessing two prize fighters before placing a wager.

I wondered if this odious little man would still be so cocky if he realised his relic, massive though he was, was out-numbered three-to-one, or if he didn't have his command module.

"Your relic is a mess. He isn't even wearing correct uniform," he concluded smugly as he pulled up alongside his own specimen. "I don't know you, and therefore I outrank you. You will stand aside."

He looked up at his relic, then jerked his head at the seated Stavka.

The Russian brute obediently turned from Paredo and set his beady eyes on the horrified Captain Lieutenant, who was now cringing into his chair, with nowhere to go. This wasn't how it was supposed to be. Not on my first mission. I just wasn't going to let it happen.

No sooner had I cried out in anguish within my mind at what was about to happen, then a new orange overlay sprung up within my vision, spanning between the popinjay and his brute. It was similar to the usual red siphon-tracking thread, but it must have indicated the flow of information from a control module. Incredibly, as fast as I could comprehend what I was seeing, my implant was already taking it upon itself to hijack the siphon-bridge, pulling an almighty flow of power from the other relics in the room. The action caused all three of us to flare brighter than I had ever seen, filling the room with a vivid red glow, as my implant lashed out, overloading the handler's control module and severing his bond with his relic.

The handler's eyes only had time to widen in disbelief as he comprehended the last instruction my implant had blasted down the connection with an urgency and fury he had never been able to deliver.

'FEED ON ME,' it had boomed into the Enforcer's consciousness as the link severed.

The brute had wailed in pain as he immediately lurched into action, his lethal speed belying his great bulk. The hapless handler was within easy reach of those monstrously powerful hands and they were already tearing at him as the Enforcer's open jaws descended over his face. They both went down in a collapsing heap, the crushing mass of the relic on top, as he relentlessly chomped and savaged his erstwhile handler from nose to sternum. Control-376 was only able to leak one muffled shriek directly into the gnashing mouth of his beast before the breath was crushed from his body and the blood pumping from his ruined throat reduced his cries to gurgles.

Under the frenzied mass above him, the handler shuddered. A few agonising moments later, his desperately clutching fingers relaxed and fell away from the last embrace he would give in this life, landing wetly in the spreading pool of crimson.

We all looked on, frozen in that gruesome moment, trying to make sense of what had just happened. Through the bridge, Paredo was more puzzled than disgusted, trying to make sense of what I had done. Araneus was baffled but experiencing a sense of divine retribution. But poor old Stavka had scooted his chair backwards with his heels until he had butted into the cabinets behind him.

The animal noises coming from the heaving mass in front of us, as Enforcer-32 chewed and gulped, were sickening. So I tried to salvage what I could of the situation.

"Enforcer-32! Stand down!" I barked. Nothing happened for a moment, but then an orange thread from our siphon-bridge sprang into view as my implant emulated the action of a control module.

'Do you know what you have done?' Paredo blurted incredulously through the bridge before he could contain himself. I turned toward him questioningly, but he shook his head dismissively. So I took that to mean '*not now*'. Araneus was also looking at me speculatively.

The Russian relic had gone still, so I imagined him getting to his feet and standing to attention. No sooner had I done so, then he turned my thoughts into reality. I had him go and stand in the corner, facing the wall, so the gore down his face and chest didn't terrorise Stavka any more than it already had.

What now? I wondered, feeling shaken at what had just happened. I was awash with adrenaline and felt light and jittery. It made it hard to think clearly.

Fortunately, Paredo broke protocol and spoke to Stavka for the first time to fill the gap.

"I apologise for this unfortunate... situation," he said, as Stavka's head shot up, wide-eyed to stare at Paredo with renewed horror. "This malfunction puts us all in a difficult position. If word were to get back to Moscow of this, we would all find ourselves at the sharp end of some difficult questions."

"I see," the rattled base commander responded mechanically, although in his current state, I am not sure that he did.

"Yes," I joined in, following the lead Paredo had given me. "In light of these developments, I propose we collect the personnel and materials we came for and leave you to your business."

Stavka's eyes strayed back to the confiscated pistol hanging forgotten in Araneus' hands, clearly wondering how he was supposed to take his own life without it.

"No," I clarified. "That will no longer be necessary. Neither my colleagues, nor ourselves, were ever here. You were never investigated. But Petrov here, will accompany us with the prisoners and cargo. He will be returned at a later date if he is no longer useful in Moscow."

Stavka's eyes searched his Sergeant's face for clues about his opinion on all of this, but Araneus simply nodded in acknowledgement, with a pursing of his lips that fell short of a smile.

Stavka let out a shaky breath and steadied his hands by placing them firmly on his thighs in front of him.

"Agreed," he said, regaining some of his former aplomb. "Petrov, please make the necessary arrangements for your departure." Then to me, he added, "We have body bags and a gurney in the infirmary, unless you would recommend we use our incinerators?"

Chapter 35

Paredo had called in every favour he could to get us out of the country. It would have been much easier with official agency support, but he hadn't wanted to telegraph what we had been up to, prior to the official meeting of the Committee of 300.

He told me that some decisions were already as good as made in advance by the careful lobbying of certain Committee members ahead of time, but dropping hot new information just before a vote could often disrupt any decisions that would otherwise have gone against us.

Ten of us had left the godforsaken facility in the Kamov helicopter - three allied relics, the Russian relic (under a close eye), the pilot and five scientists that Araneus had selected for their current knowledge and future potential.

The rest of the space in the chopper had been taken up with chunky military storage cases, loaded with carefully selected research materials and some of the smaller prototypes that the scientists had been working on.

I had been horrified at the prospect of trying to smuggle our precious cargo back into North America, but Paredo had scoffed at my concerns, reminding me that the Agency held the other branches of government in the palm of its hand.

True to his word, Paredo and I now sat in relative luxury, back on the Agency jet, cruising towards Denver at maximum speed.

Paredo was tucking into a lavish meal delivered by an attractive attendant and the liberated Russian scientists were abuzz about their change of fortune. But their excited chatter didn't do anything to lift me from my pensive mood. I knew that they were simply fleeing from one cage directly into another, but I didn't have the heart to kill their good mood.

On a personal level, I was still trying to process how I felt about my part in the death of the Russian handler. During my naming ceremony, I had 'experienced' a total of 22 different murders and deaths through the memories of my fellow relics, but this was somehow different. I was directly involved and I had experienced it in the moment and not through the lens of hindsight.

I was well aware that the Russian handler, Control-376, wouldn't be losing any sleep if our roles had been reversed, yet I wasn't certain where the autonomous actions of my implant left off and my own subconscious urges began. It was a horrible way to die, but how much culpability did I have?

The grizzly scene of the Enforcer munching on his handler was all too easy to replay over and over in my mind, even without the assistance of my implant. But I tried to ignore it, especially as I watched Paredo contentedly shovelling great forkfuls of steak and asparagus into his mouth.

I tried to rationalise that this one death would prevent many more, but I still had blood on my hands. The question was how much. Was sin found in the thought or the deed?

Although the handler was a nasty piece of work, I hadn't consciously thought of killing him, yet the result had been the same as if I had. My crime had been wanting to prevent him from hurting or killing Stavka.

Finding more questions than answers in my own thoughts, I even turned to the extensive mental library of philosophy and religion that the Professor had given me. But I still didn't find the answers I was looking for.

In the end, it had been a soft snoring coming from my right, which had helped to distract me from my self-indulgent wallowing.

I looked over to see the great big Russian relic snoozing in his chair. He spilled over it in every way, but was still sleeping soundly.

As docile as he seemed now, I couldn't help feeling nervous about what would happen in such tight confines if my control slipped, so I had instructed him to sleep for several hours whilst I practiced maintaining control.

His face was relaxed in sleep and with his bald head and wet lips, he was more reminiscent of a colossal toddler than a mind-controlled killing machine. But I suppose each handler saw in him what they wanted to see.

My implant maintained a thin thread of siphon between us, which meant that I knew his whereabouts and status almost as well as my own, but checking on him visually helped me to relax a little.

Paredo had urged me to attempt to pass the bond to him, but it hadn't worked how we had hoped. I had been able to create a standing order for the Enforcer to follow Paredo's instructions as though they were my own, but it was far from perfect.

It would have to do. The fact was, we were in new territory and would simply have to improvise. We had no idea how much of the relic's own personality could be recovered. He may be permanently dependent upon a handler.

Araneus wasn't troubling himself with any of this. Instead, he was in deep conversation with the scientists he had befriended during his stay at the Russian facility. It was strange for me though, because having accessed Araneus' memories, I felt casual familiarity with the scientists and would smile at their jokes, only to have them look at me blankly with no recognition beyond that afforded by the brief introduction

Araneus had given me. I had to remind myself that they were Araneus' friends, not mine, but it still felt a little like my own friends had completely forgotten me.

But I cast all of my musings aside as Paredo came over to sit with me, still wiping his fingers on a white linen napkin.

"Mind if I take a seat?" He asked, as he cast the cloth onto the table between us and took one anyway.

I smiled and nodded my acceptance. He shifted his bulk, trying to find comfort in the narrow confines of the aircraft.

"You did well." He said, after a moment. "But it does get easier."

I wondered about trying to justify the murder as not of my doing - of it being the action of one relic being controlled by another and that I had only been present as a bystander. But I would be lying to myself and wasting my breath besides. Paredo saw life in black and white. He believed in taking action and then just wearing the consequences. My feeble excuses would only diminish me in his eyes, so I held my tongue. Besides, to him the mission was a resounding success.

"I won't let it get in the way of my duties," I replied, "but I don't want it to get easier."

I didn't want my humanity to trickle away, one mission at a time.

"Well said." Paredo went on. "Better to be an honest killer with a conscience, than to end up like some of the dead-eyed psychopaths I've worked with… and for!" He added with a grin.

Interestingly, this must have meant that Paredo didn't see himself in the same light. He had many hundreds of confirmed kills on his Agency record, yet he still separated himself from the other agency hit men. It made me wonder about him.

"Anyway," he went on, "we need to be clear on a few things before we get back to Denver and I have to report to the Committee."

I felt him initiate a siphon-bridge and allowed him to communicate covertly within my mind, as the hum of the engines accompanied us toward Denver and my uncertain future.

Chapter 36

The Academy facilities I had grown to be so familiar with, seemed bare without my peers around to fill the arena with the sounds of competition and friendly banter.

I missed the company of Jesse, Verity, Oliver and even Hector, now that I understood him. But they were flung to the four corners of the globe on their various missions.

Instead, after a short rest and time to refresh myself in my quarters, I was graced with the company of Canis and a couple of new guards I hadn't seen before.

Canis had greeted me as a brother, returning victorious from the field, but it was hard not to see him as my instructor, after several weeks of hard training and being barked at.

He informed me that Sericum was now also away on Agency business, but that Acertas would be coordinating relic missions in the briefing suite, whilst we were required to be on hand to address the 300, should they require it.

I was appalled to have drawn the attention of such lofty individuals so soon, as I had no political connections of my own to draw upon. No greased palms, no favours, no leverage and no clue. It wasn't a good position to be in to defend myself.

I could only hope that my fledgling bond with Paredo was sufficient for him to speak up for me.

"I'm to escort you to Major Winters first though," Canis informed me over his broad shoulder, as he led us through the warren of bland facility corridors. The steady drumming of four sets of boots triggered a continuous stream of echo mapping within my implant as we walked along, being trailed by our security detail.

I noticed how my guards no longer concerned me as they once had. Having undergone Academy training and seeing firsthand what combat-ready relics could do, I realised that the guards were just an affectation to provide a flimsy sense of reassurance for our non-relic colleagues and masters. The truth was, either Canis or myself could have broken these clumsy soldiers across our knees blindfolded and unarmed.

The usual porters and maintenance staff occasionally crossed our path, but eventually we were covering new territory. My implant created a small map to overlay my vision, showing my location in relation to the other known areas of the facility, but I dismissed it as we arrived at a sturdy set of steel doors.

The guard detail detached themselves and took up position either side of the doorway as Canis thumbed the wall-mounted intercom impatiently.

"Yes?" Came a voice, made metallic by the microphone and speakers.

"I have your prodigy here to see you, Major Winters", Canis responded as he shot me a quick wink.

"Thank you Canis," came the response a moment later. "Send him in."

Canis stepped aside as the steel doors parted with a hiss.

The room Major Winters occupied was more of a small conference room than an office, but numerous reports and files were strewn across the tabletop of the central conference table. He had shunted several of the chairs to the outer edge of the room to give him better access to the information as he sorted through it and tried to make sense of it all.

My implant passively vacuumed up the visible information as I entered the room to await his attention.

Winters seemed to remember my abilities and belatedly turned a couple of files over with a frown.

"Paredo has briefed me," he began. "It seems you have potentially turned quite a clusterfuck into a coup."

He pulled a chair out for himself and took a seat, but didn't offer me one, so I remained standing.

"It shouldn't come as any surprise to you that Hiram has been campaigning for your liquidation, but that oily little weasel only has so much sway. Not everyone has the 'appetites' that he relies on for leverage."

Major Winters looked disgusted. It was unusual to see him being outwardly critical of another sponsor. I could only assume that this series of events had brought matters to a head.

"But that aside," he continued, "you do represent something we have never seen before. A new generation of relic with even more alarming abilities! I'm not going to lie to you son, you are a hot potato to have in my stable. But, as your sponsor, and as someone with a certain amount of sway, I will put my weight behind you."

He paused to fix me with a steely gaze. "But mark my words, Paredo doesn't answer to me. So I cannot vouch for what he is going to say to the Committee. But he doesn't answer to Hiram either, so we shall see."

He glanced at his watch. "They will be convening soon. I suggest we head to the Committee chambers."

I mutely nodded my agreement, but Major Winters wasn't finished. "Equally," he continued, "I must insist you not say or do anything to further inflame any precious sensibilities today. I am getting tarred with your brush as it is."

In all fairness, nothing I had done so far had been intentional, but I resolved to abide by his request, where I could.

The Major corralled his paperwork into a single stack, then donned his uniform jacket with a heavy sigh.

He asked if there was anything I needed to let him know before we officially assembled, but I hedged that Paredo had been privy to everything we had encountered since leaving the Denver facility, and that he was sure to have relayed anything he considered to be of importance.

"Well," Winters concluded, as he gestured for me to exit through the door ahead of him, "for both our sakes, let's hope your first outing was successful enough to keep you in the game!"

Chapter 37

The Committee chambers weren't entirely what I expected. I had anticipated the vaulted ceiling and the three steeply tiered rows of crimson leather chairs which arched round in a tight circle. But for some reason, I hadn't anticipated that the Committee members would be represented virtually.

The chairs were there so that members could physically attend, but each chair also sported a set of holographic emitters positioned over the shoulders so that attendees could either conceal their identities, or else attend from remote locations, represented by holographic avatars. Project Blue Beam had evidently advanced well beyond anything that had been leaked to the public in declassified government documents.

This whole setup was yet another indication of the largess of the ruling elite, presumably having hundreds of these chambers secretly dotted around the world to suit the needs of the Committee.

Winters led me along an aisle which ran through the centre of the rows of tiered seats, almost dividing them like two hemispheres of a brain. Hiram and some of his cronies that I didn't recognise, occupied some of the padded benches in the central section at the foot of the chairs, but Winters made a beeline for Paredo, who was sitting alone on the left hand side.

Winters offered a curt greeting before taking a seat, but as usual, when Paredo was in public, he only offered a hard, stony face to the world. He was an executioner and looked the part.

Looking about me before I took a seat on the bench next to Winters, I imagined what it would look like as a full house, with all those sets of ruthless eyes gazing down at me from all sides. It put me in mind of an aviary full of owls, watching a dormouse who had been dropped in the middle.

I had some of Flint's knowledge about the event itself, but he had never attended in person. So I sat with an outward air of patience, which belied my churning belly. I had done nothing wrong. Now all I needed was for the Committee to come to the same conclusion.

When I looked up at the chairs surrounding me again, I almost jumped to see that some of them were now occupied by hovering emblems, or shadowy figures. It wasn't the occupants that surprised me, but the fact that they hadn't registered on my echo mapping. It made it seem like I was in the presence of spectres, who were both there and not there.

As I watched, a new gentleman dressed head to toe in Savile Row's finest tailoring gradually materialised above a glowing plate embedded in the floor at the front of the chambers. He wasn't in ceremonial dress, but he was wearing a scarlet sash as a mark of his office and next to him, a mahogany podium held a thick metal gavel. What was disturbing however, was that his features were hazy and indistinct, and his eyes glowed yellow like those of a wolf in a spotlight. It was no doubt an effect he had chosen to include in his avatar, but it was still creepy nonetheless.

"It's almost time," Winters said quietly. A slight pursing of his lips and a tilt of his head was perhaps designed to offer me some small reassurance, but looking around me as more sinister figures materialised, it was small consolation indeed.

Over the next two or three minutes, the Committee chairs filled with a veritable menagerie of avatars. Some were simply dark suited characters with blurred features, whilst others were much more theatrical and reminiscent of the extravagant costumes found at elite costumed balls.

I spotted someone masquerading as Baphomet, the goat-headed demon thought to be worshipped by Freemasons, but my eye was soon drawn away by an equally jarring representation of Moloch, an ancient deity worshipped through child sacrifice and represented by a stylised owl.

My implant idly recalled for me that I had seen a giant Moloch statue on a TV documentary, when the reporter, Alex Jones had infiltrated Bohemian Grove in California, to expose a who's-who list of politicians, presidents and glitterati engaged in bizarre occult rituals, covert networking and policy-making.

As my eyes scanned the growing crowd, and the din of conversation began to build, there were simply too many different characters to list, from Sumerian gods and goddesses, to fictional characters. Some opted to be represented by symbols and most of the secret societies were represented, from the skull and bones club frequented by numerous American presidents, through to the all seeing eye of the illuminati.

I did my best not to gape and stare, but I had never seen such theatrics, especially when such serious matters were to be discussed.

The creatures and characters were perfectly animated and voice-synced in real time through advanced computers, and I marvelled at the processing power and bandwidth this would have taken to enable this to happen simultaneously at hundreds of locations globally.

When the speaker at the front of the house brought his metal gavel down, it was accompanied by an almighty computer-assisted clang, which brought the Committee meeting to order.

A hush filled the room, as everyone settled and waited for the speaker to begin. I was left just listening to the heartbeats of those few around me that were physically present.

The peculiar spell of silence didn't last and was eventually broken as the speaker began.

"As always, a warm welcome to the esteemed and honourable Committee of 300 for this special session."

The speaker's voice was loud, but pleasing to the ear. It was clear that he must have practiced his oratory skills on many occasions, as he paused just long enough for effect, but not long enough to permit interruption.

"I assume that you all have today's agenda," he continued, "but as formality dictates, I shall enumerate each talking point for your esteemed consideration."

It was a bizarre sight to say the least, to see the strange assortment of furred, feathered, suited or silk-clad avatars, look down to study the tablets in their hands as the speaker reeled off today's talking points.

My situation was talking point number 2, to be considered after voting on the continued rollout of genetically modified crops and the associated pesticides that went with them.

He introduced my case as 'the discovery of new relic abilities and their implications in relation to Agency stability'.

Points 3, 4 and 5 involved the timetable for spiking vaccines in third-world countries, the continued manipulation of the global financial markets and finally, the deliberate escalation of war in the middle east.

I am embarrassed to admit it, but at the time, I was being selfish and short-sighted, paying much more attention to my own affairs, but my relic still diligently recorded everything I saw and heard whilst I thought about what I would say.

As I daydreamed, the speaker briefed the Committee on how the FDA had allowed upwards of 170 million acres of genetically modified crops to be grown on the back of study data as flimsy as 90-day studies carried out on as few as 36 rats. More incredible was the fact that these same studies had been conducted by those who stood to gain most by their success. He applauded the efforts by the agricultural giants to suppress the independent studies which showed GMOs to be harmful to human health, longevity and fertility and assured the house that with the senior officials of the FDA now having substantial financial ties to the likes of Monsanto and DuPont, that control of the US market was certain.

"86 percent of the US food supply is now contaminated with GMOs and we have so far resisted calls for labelling. So we are well on target there," he explained, "but unfortunately, Europe and especially Russia have been a tougher nut to crack. You have your briefing notes and the recommendations of our panel of experts in front of you. Are there any questions from the Committee before we put it to a vote?"

I looked around at the myriad of moneyed misfits as they murmured amongst themselves as the speaker waited patiently.

But just when it seemed that nobody would ask a question, a white spotlight lit up over one of the chairs on the third row, and a long-necked lady in an elegant gold brocaded gown got to her 'feet'. Her face was obscured behind an ornate mask of rare bird feathers.

"Are we correct in assuming", she began, "that the vaults of organic seeds are already fully stocked?" Her voice was low and throaty and sounded as though it had also been disguised via complex software. "After all, if cross contamination is as common as our notes suggest, it may be premature to push harder in Europe?"

The speaker seemed to have been anticipating such a question and promptly reassured her that both underground aquaponic systems and seed vaults were already in place to ensure uninterrupted continuity of the food supply for the elites and their staff. Not to mention the vast stockpiles of food and water sufficient for at least 25 years. There would be more than enough to start again after any future collapse.

As the lady sat, the spotlight above her chair went out. Nobody else asked any further questions. Evidently the notes they had been given were thorough enough to satisfy them.

"Very well", the misty-faced speaker concluded. "Using your keypads, please could you now take a moment to select which route forward we should pursue."

It was quite surreal to watch gods, goddesses, lords, ladies and beasts alike, all studying their keypads.

But after perhaps 30 seconds, the Committee chambers were bathed in a kaleidoscope of spotlights. I assumed that the colour indicated the direction of their vote. In this instance, as my eyes scanned the seats, my implant assessed there to be around 65 percent green votes, 25 percent red votes, 5 percent blue votes, a smattering of orange and some seats unlit. But of course, without the notes accompanying the keypads, it meant nothing to me.

"Motion carried" the speaker concluded with another resounding clang of his gavel. "Now onto the second issue of the day."

This was it. My attention pulled into laser focus as the suited wraith presided over the chamber full of freaks and dandies to decide my future. It was sickening, but wishing it weren't so had done no good so far.

Looking up at the many strange faces leering down at me, I didn't hold much hope of a fair trial. These kind of people didn't do fair. They thought in terms of privilege, not ethics or morality.

"It has been brought to the Committee's attention that a newly raised relic has succeeded in drawing vast amounts of privileged information from other relics in his class. Today we shall vote on what shall be done about this substantial breach in security."

I could tell from the framing of my case that it was positioned to fail from the outset. It felt as though the tiers of leather seats and their ghoulish occupants were pressing closer with every breath.

When the speaker began again, he even managed to inject a tone of boredom into his voice, as though this matter was pretty well decided and, in any event, was nothing for the Committee to concern themselves with.

"As before," he said, "you have your briefing notes and the recommendations of our panel of experts in front of you. Are there any questions from the Committee before we put it to a vote?"

His strangely glowing eyes fixed upon mine as the seconds drew out excruciatingly. I was appalled that I hadn't even been privy to the package of notes that they had provided to the Committee members. The unfairness of it all stoked a fire of righteous outrage within my soul.

But as my face no doubt darkened, a murmur amongst the crowd turned into a buzz of conversation as the taciturn Paredo shifted in his seat as though making ready to stand. This seemed to draw some of the unwanted attention on to him.

My lifeline came in the form of a tall bull of a man who appeared to be fashioned entirely from bronze. As his spotlight flashed on, he stood to address the chambers.

"Mr Speaker," he began, his voice carrying a low metallic echo, which was clearly designed to match his verdigreed appearance. "I have no doubt that my esteemed fellow Committee members would also like to hear directly from our lethal hand. I call to ask Paredo for a statement on the matter."

The ruckus that ensued contained enough affirmative noises to give the speaker pause. It appeared that now the request had been made, it would be difficult for the red-sashed speaker to refuse. His eyes panned around the chambers, as the din from the Committee members increased. To any but a relic, it wouldn't have been obvious, but as the speaker's eyes passed over his audience, they lingered a fraction longer on the Baphomet avatar than the others. The horned demon's head tipped in a subtle nod of instruction. My temporary sense of relief was confirmed when the Committee speaker finally acquiesced to the bronze man's request.

"Very well." He intoned with formality. "The esteemed Committee members call upon their lethal hand to address the chamber. Paredo, please stand."

Paredo stood to attention as a white spotlight bathed him from above and the excited chatter subsided. He was every bit as imposing, in his dark relic battle gear, as any of the holographic avatars.

His voice rang out loud and clear as he addressed the Committee with a matter-of-fact confidence that I certainly didn't feel.

"Esteemed members of the Committee. As your lethal hand, and as a first-hand witness to this development, I appreciate the opportunity to serve you with the truth."

The chamber was listening, unsure which way he would go. So he continued.

"As you know from your briefing notes, due to the attacks on some of our relics in the field, this particular class of the Academy had not completed their education before they were raised to full relic status. In my opinion, this data leak was nothing more than a training accident. As the master of ceremonies and as a fully trained relic, I was able to firewall my own data and therefore put it to you that this was a product of an inexperienced student interacting with other inexperienced students and has no bearing on future security."

At this, there were some angry murmurs from the tiered seating, but Paredo ploughed on.

"This isolated breach involved a whole class, not one student, so I would council the esteemed Committee members to consider the cost of losing a whole class."

At this, Paredo pointedly looked across at Hiram, whose face was darkening in anger at his son being dragged into this affair.

"But I must also report that although Lucidus here was involved in the accident, he has a uniquely strong siphon which, when added to mine, allowed us to seize control of a Russian Enforcer directly from his handler, whilst keeping the relic hardware viable."

The buzz of conversation at this bombshell almost drowned Paredo out. Clearly, this titbit hadn't been included in their notes. Paredo had been right to keep quiet about our activities.

"I believe we can use this new strategy to divest our enemies of their relic assets and thereby tip the balance of power in the esteemed Committee's favour."

The ruckus at this grew too boisterous for even the seasoned speaker's taste and so he called for order until the menagerie of avatars calmed themselves.

"Have you anything to add?" The speaker asked, but his tone indicated that he didn't actually want more information released.

"Only that in my professional opinion, the security of the esteemed Committee is better served by utilising this new weapon against our enemies than by containing the source of it."

Paredo left that hanging a moment, then added "I would like to request that I retain the services of Lucidus whilst I complete his education myself and harvest more enemy assets. He has proven himself capable in the field and has already assisted me in infiltrating a Russian Sharashka and recovering numerous captive scientists, plus their prototype technologies and up to 30 years' worth of secret research documents."

This time, the din continued despite the speaker's calls for order. The audacity of our actions was highlighted to me anew by their startled reaction to hearing of it. I was still afraid, but Paredo hadn't let me down. My heart swelled with gratitude for my new master's efforts to keep me from the mercies of this macabre circus.

Finally, the light over the bronze man lit up again as he stood. The other Committee members began to subdue in deference.

"I haven't called for further questions yet." The speaker responded with a touch of irritation creeping into his voice as he perceived his loss of control over the proceedings.

But a stern frown from the bronze man gave him pause. "In light of this new intelligence that was 'omitted' from our notes, I invoke my right to amend the ballot options."

At a startled movement of Baphomet's head, the speaker tried to object, but the bronze man stoically steamrolled over him.

"I propose to add two options. Firstly, to confine the entire class until further notice, and secondly to grant our lethal hand the leeway he seeks to increase our stockpile of relic assets."

It was done. The blessed bronze man had injected some fairness into the vote. As I looked around, trying to gauge the mood of the room, I noticed the sullen look on Hiram's face and the satisfaction evident in the bronze man's posture.

There was clearly no love lost between the mysterious bronze man and the speaker, and I could only piece together that Hiram, the speaker and the member masquerading as Baphomet were aligned where this matter was concerned.

Attempting to conceal his frustration, the speaker turned to his wooden podium and began to type upon it as though it bore a keyboard. Of course, in the speaker's location it probably did. Seeing his wishes being acted upon, the bronze man retook his chair, and with the dimming of his light, the stirrings of whispered conversation began again.

When he had completed his amendments, the speaker once again asked for any further questions. But the murmur from the crowd didn't result in any additional spotlights being triggered.

I suspected that the clash between the bronze man and the speaker hinted at much deeper political manoeuvrings around lines that were already drawn in the sand. Perhaps my case was more of an opportunity for them to flex and test their influence and they didn't actually care about me at all?

I wanted the opportunity to put my own case forward, but with nobody giving me leave to speak, I had to rely on Paredo's performance.

When it was clear that everything now hinged upon the Committee vote, the speaker once again secured everyone's attention.

"The ballot has been modified accordingly. Please could the esteemed members of the Committee vote for their preferred course, or courses, of action."

The matter was out of his hands. I held my breath, but looking about me, a stony, impassive look from Paredo took my attention. There was no expression on his face at all, something you could only achieve with a relic to subdue the subconscious tells that your body gives off, but even so, the twinkle in his eye seemed to be saying 'hold firm, lad! Brace yourself!'

Siphoning wasn't permitted in the presence of the Committee of 300, so I just had my imagination and wishful thinking to go on. Either way, this mountain of a man had proved he was on my side in this matter at least. It was the only reassurance I had. Major Winters just sat stock still, presumably hoping all he had invested in me would not be lost.

But my painful wait was brought to an end as hundreds of coloured spotlights flicked on all about me. The eyes that looked down at me ranged from magnanimous to menacing, but it was hard to determine how much of the original members' features would be translated onto their digital avatars.

This time, there was a much greater variety of responses, with many avatars bathed in more than one light at a time. My implant ran the numbers as I twisted and craned my neck about to assess the outcome of the vote.

"Motion carried" the speaker concluded as his eyes lifted from the hidden screen on his rostrum and the clang of his gavel reverberated through me with grim finality.

He didn't meet my gaze, but instead he addressed Paredo.

"Paredo, as the lethal hand of the Committee, we commend Lucidus to your charge. Your petition is granted. You are dismissed."

The explosive breath I let out was covered by the loud clap on the back that Major Winters gave me, and even that was lost in the clammer of conversation that erupted from the Committee members.

Paredo was clearly not impressed by being peremptorily dismissed. But he drew himself up to his formidable height and stalked off down the aisle, with Major Winters and myself in tow. Hiram and his cronies watched us go, but didn't follow, their faces a mixture of emotions, but none of them pleasant.

From this, I took it that Winters could have stayed, but clearly he had also had enough of the politics and posturing for one day.

Chapter 38

The Agency briefing suite was every bit as hectic as Major Winters' desk had been, as Acertas and Canis did their best to coordinate relic activity across the globe. Reports had been coming in thick and fast.

But despite the sense of urgency, it felt good for Paredo and I to be back amongst our 'own kind' after today's affair. It was hard to put a finger on it, but there was some indefinable sense of security being amongst my brothers. We might have our differences, but we would always look out for one another - which was more than I could say for the back-biting rabble running the show.

In all fairness, I didn't count Major Winters amongst their number. He had been generous in his thanks before he departed and, as a result, my respect for him had grown further still.

He had congratulated me on my narrow escape and thanked Paredo for sticking his neck out for me. Nothing over the top, but he must have felt it needed saying.

Paredo wasn't a big talker, but I think he had appreciated some gratitude rather than being taken for granted like a servant.

Now that I was out of the Academy and on a much more equal footing with my former instructors, I was picking up much more of an 'us and them' attitude behind closed doors.

It put me in mind of the likely attitudes that would have been held by Victorian servants when the masters weren't there to overhear what was said.

Anyone outside of the brotherhood couldn't ever fully understand what it meant to be a relic, but seeing firsthand how our lives literally hung on the whims of our exalted masters, it wasn't surprising that resentment simmered and secrets were kept.

"What do you have for us, Acertas?" Paredo asked as the black tower of a man stood in front of the bank of monitors scanning through screen after screen of maps and reports.

By contrast, Paredo was reclining at his ease, his boots yet again up on the table and his leather chair creaking beneath his bulk.

I had been assimilating everything that passed my vision, but clearly Paredo wanted to siphon the whole lot after it had been processed, very much like copying a friend's homework.

"We are getting much clearer intelligence now we have relics in the field," Acertas said with a wide smile. "Those initial reports were almost useless."

He was right. Relic reports covered so much more detail, as we were able to detect a great deal more using our implant-heightened senses, then report at much higher speeds.

"But something just doesn't add up," he continued, idly scratching at his chin. "I know the Chinese - and aggressively abducting groups of our relics just isn't their style. Their ruling elite are proud alright, and believe their nation and people to be superior, but they aren't into expansion. The west takes over other cultures and assimilates them, but the Chinese don't bother, because as far as they are concerned, you can't turn a donkey into a racehorse, so why even try? Don't get me wrong, if you push the Chinese, they bite back, and hard, but it isn't like them to risk starting a war like this."

Paredo nodded thoughtfully at this. "You have a point," he said. "Who do we have on their doorstep? I think maybe I should head over there and shake the tree and see what falls out".

Acertas paused a moment as he accessed the information. "Sierene, and now Solus." He was referring to Hector. "The others stationed there were recently called away on assorted missions by the 300, or their sponsors."

"Alright," Paredo replied with a slight frown, just brief us on our Agency assets and field contacts in the area."

"Stand by," Acertas said as he collated the information. "But you should know," he went on, "that the reason Solus and his handler were sent was because Sierene was overdue on her report. She is usually most thorough, so we thought it wise to provide her some support. Besides, of all people, we thought she might give Solus more reason to stay on the team."

He was referring to Hector's aloofness from the group. Having all of Hector's memories gave me a unique insight into his attitudes, and in all honesty, I could see why he always kept his distance.

Orphaned at a young age, with very little extended family, he had fallen through the cracks in society and had raised himself on the streets. But without much education and in the sway of the older boys, he had been absorbed into Mexican gang culture, and later, the drug cartels.

Many of his friends had been lost to gang violence, some to black-market organ harvesting, some to drugs, some to corrupt Police, so as a self preservation mechanism it was no wonder he preferred and relied upon his own company. Of course, he had his own clique back home, but he didn't trust easily - especially in a world where you could wake up in a bathtub full of icy water with your kidneys missing because you trusted the wrong person.

Hector was a survivor for sure, but Acertas was right. He probably needed more than the brotherhood to keep him from trying to opt out of a system which had been against him his entire life.

It turned out that Sierene, named after the mythological Greek sirens, was a rare beauty. She was a perfect flower from a wealthy Chinese family living in Hong Kong, who had made their fortune exporting rare antiquities. But now she worked the elite social circles of Hong Kong, loosening all but the most secure tongues.

Hector would be a perfect accomplice, able to go where she couldn't. Besides, great big hulks like Paredo or Acertas would hardly blend in where the average Chinese male was only just over 5 foot 6 inches tall.

When Acertas had gathered the necessary information, he siphon-bridged with us and dropped all of the intelligence we needed straight into our implants, complete with the current reports coming in from around the world.

I was relieved that my close friends were all secure, but still concerned about the level of sophistication, manpower and planning needed to execute such abductions.

Paredo also took the opportunity to properly brief Acertas on our Russian expedition, including my relic's unique intervention between the Enforcer and his handler. Acertas was aware of his presence within the facility, (with several operatives authorised to act as his new handlers), but as the details of his capture and control reached Acertas' conscious mind, his thick eyebrows rose. An unreadable look passed between Acertas and Paredo, but before I could puzzle out its significance, Canis interrupted us.

"Hey, you need to see this. Sierene is missing. We need you in Hong Kong."

Chapter 39

The air conditioning unit rattled and whirred above me as Paredo and I waited for Hector to arrive. We were sitting in one of the Agency safe houses in the Kowloon district of Hong Kong and were impatient to be debriefed after our long flight.

We had put the time to good use, with Paredo siphoning to me a whole host of useful maps, memories, language refinements and techniques. The more time I spent with this man, the more I realised why he was considered such an asset to the Agency.

Don't get me wrong, he could be uncouth and immensely stubborn, but he knew the streets and had a wisdom born of understanding what truly drove people. Furthermore, he had instincts which were uncanny even by relic standards, so it would be a rare agent capable of catching him napping.

The interior of the room we occupied was as run down as the outside, but direct access to the busy marketplace in the streets below made it an ideal location to conceal the comings and goings of all manner of people.

I looked past the flaky yellow plaster and hanging calligraphy, through the doorway into the kitchen where our agency host was still busy preparing tea on a gas stove.

"Cut the crap, Wei", Paredo cut in. "You can't tell me you have no leads at all. Sierene must have maintained some communication with the agency."

Zhang Wei, a diminutive and elderly Chinese man visibly flinched at Paredo's tone, but continued to lay out delicate cups on a tray as he spoke.

"I am sorry sir, but lady Sierene was very private and discrete. Which is why she was able to keep such lofty company. She only reported on matters she had confirmed herself. Never any supposition. Only fact." Wei's English was very good, but his disapproval of Paredo's potential for disrespecting his precious 'lady Sierene' shone through in the tone of his voice.

Paredo was clearly frustrated, but he moderated his tone as Wei poured out the hot tea and carried it through to where we sat in handmade wicker and bamboo chairs.

"So what CAN you tell us then? We know she traded information both sides of the border." Paredo clearly meant that both literally and as a euphemism for sharing information with the other power blocks. Perhaps unbeknownst to Wei, that was actually part of her function. It paid to let the opposition have a few titbits, if you could occasionally salt them with disinformation when it suited.

After passing each of us a fine porcelain cup, which looked like it cost more than the furnishings in the whole property combined, Zhang Wei elaborated.

"I can say that even lady Sierene's enemies needed her. She served a very helpful diplomatic function. Power in Hong Kong is split between many factions including the west, the Chinese, and organised crime on both sides. Much is lost in translation and the usual posturing, but lady Sierene helped act as a very diplomatic go-between." He cleared his chest, then sipped at his tea appreciatively.

I leant forward in my chair to retrieve my cup and to do the same, but Paredo wasn't interested in etiquette. My implant assessed the contents, deeming it to be safe, before my lips had even touched the rim of the cup.

"Wherever the lady Sierene is", Wei continued, "it is more than their life is worth to harm her". He spoke with the confidence born of long-standing tradition and disbelief that anyone would even dream of changing the status quo.

"Unless they want to create tension and rivalry in the region?" I interjected, watching for Wei's reaction.

Wei was very good at concealing his natural tells, but he still reacted with slight surprise. Even so, my implant still extended a wisp of siphon in his direction to ensure he wasn't dimming some relic technology within himself. He was clear, but Paredo still exchanged a glance with me when he felt what I was doing.

"I don't believe it. Maybe one side or another is flexing their muscles, but the lady Sierene is resourceful and will not allow herself to be compromised. Besides, your colleague, Solus, will be here shortly with more information.

Paredo continued to quiz the old man over the next few minutes, until the turn of a key and the click of a latch announced the presence of a new arrival.

At the sound, Paredo had left his seat and moved out of the direct line of sight through the doorway, but Hector's footsteps gave him away before we saw him.

I was surprised when a stooped Chinese man entered, but he straightened and pulled off his hair-piece with one hand and vigorously scratched at his scalp with the other. Hector's brown eyes smiled back at me from within a remarkably authentic-looking oriental complexion. He was now clean-shaven, and with dark glasses he could easily pass for a local.

We exchanged grins, but before we could exchange proper greetings, Paredo was already talking business. Clearly, he was more concerned about Sierene than he was letting on.

"I see why they picked you, Solus. Your body morphing is impressive, especially with the limited time you've had. So, what have you discovered?"

"Good to see you too, Brothers," Hector responded sarcastically, his apparent good humour souring. I wasn't at all surprised that he was still angry with Paredo for the way he had abandoned us during the naming ceremony. But it didn't stop Hector from nodding guardedly at Wei and noisily pulling up one of the wicker chairs.

"It hasn't been easy," Hector began, "but I have been running down all available leads. I've cracked a few skulls and know exactly where I'd like to go next, but the local agency support has been useless. They are more worried about rocking the boat than finding Sierene. I think we are weaker here than we would like to believe."

Paredo nodded at this, hearing the truth in it.

"But a rumour has been growing of an important meeting. I've been told that she is involved. But I think this is something we should discuss in private," he concluded, looking pointedly at Wei, who had been trying to remain as unobtrusive as possible.

Wei had been watching our brief reunion with guarded features, but at our sudden renewed interest in him, he diplomatically offered to give us some privacy and made himself scarce.

Even so, we still feared eavesdropping in some other fashion, so we siphoned and coaxed Hector into a delicate and tentative bridge. He hadn't had as much practice as I had, but the tenuous connection still functioned nonetheless.

I tried to draw upon Hector's memories of the last few days, but they were broken and disjointed. It was like a scattered puzzle, that had been haphazardly slung together. As I tried to make sense of what I was seeing through the bridge, my implant visually overlaid an orange thread extending from Hector, down through the floor at a 45 degree angle. Paredo noted it too, with relative alarm.

'Were you aware you are still being controlled by your handler?' Paredo asked, as he probed through the bridge for more information.

'You mean Brett?' Hector responded, telegraphing his surprise through the siphon-bridge. *'He helped me with my disguise earlier... and he went searching for Sierene with me. He's not all bad for one of Hiram's boys, but he wanted to piggyback off of my relic's senses in case the shit went down.'*

Hector made it sound very reasonable, but having seen how the Russian handlers rode in the minds of their relics, both Paredo and I were angered by this stealthy and undisclosed intrusion. Nobody likes being spied upon, let alone in their own mind. But what was worse was that 'Brett' had made a confusing mess whilst he was at it!

'May I do the honours?' Paredo asked me through the bridge, offering up the impression of a dangerous smile?

Hector's brow furrowed questioningly as he tried to follow Paredo's meaning, but his eyes widened in surprise as Paredo reached through the bridge to draw on my relic's power. The only way I can describe it is that Paredo took hold of the orange thread leading to Hector's spying handler and shook it with ever increasing intensity, until it was oscillating in a disjointed, chaotic rhythm.

Hector let out a gasp as the orange thread promptly withdrew from him and we heard muffled voices calling out from below us in surprise.

"Spy on that, you little cockroach," Paredo growled in satisfaction. I don't think Paredo had even known exactly what he was doing, but it had felt right.

At the withdrawal of Brett's influence, I could feel Hector's evident confusion through the bridge. In fact, it went beyond that. It felt as though he was almost dazed.

"What? Wait... what's going on man?" Hector rambled aloud, as his implant feverishly tried to restore order in his mind.

"That stinkin' little puta!" Hector cried out as he jumped to his feet and lurched toward the open doorway, one arm outstretched to steady himself. "We gotta go! He's running."

He didn't look back to see if we were following.

Understanding reached Paredo and myself through the bridge as some of Hector's implanted memories faded away and the real ones slammed back into place full force. Brett wasn't hitching a ride, he had been manipulating Hector's memories!

I caught flashes of an immobilised Sierene being bundled into a black limousine in an underground parking garage, as Hector and Brett had stood by, watching passively. There were several white men wearing dark suits and earpieces, and an equal number of Chinese, with dark glasses and triad tattoos. I couldn't get a timeframe on the memory, but it felt recent.

Paredo was already following in hot pursuit of the furious Hector as I got to my feet. As we barrelled through the narrow apartment complex toward the stairs, I lost sight of Hector round the bends and behind Paredo's broad back, but through the bridge, he was a roiling ball of Latin fire. Paredo shot me the impression that he had recognised a face within the flash of Hector's recovered memory, but we were all thirsty for a conversation with Brett. What kind of treachery was this?

As we reached the top of the stairwell, I heard the rush of footsteps from the corridor below, from some five or six men, along with some hastily barked orders in Chinese. As my adrenaline began to flow, my implant created a three dimensional visual overlay map, using what it had recorded on my way in.

This was supposed to be an Agency safe house, but it felt anything but safe as the sound of more booted feet came through from the ceiling above us too.

I had caught up with Paredo as the map finished populating itself with red targets where my implant assumed any hostiles might be, having drawn data from a variety of improvised sources. Echo mapping, input from the siphon-bridge and even the vibrations coming up through the soles of my shoes were all used to provide my implant with the data it needed.

I was about to urge caution when gunfire split the sound barrier and wood splinters, plaster dust and lead slugs careened past us.

Hector had been forced to twist aside, but Paredo and myself were further behind.

"Stand down," Paredo boomed in his battlefield voice, made alien to my ears by his use of Mandarin Chinese. He didn't wait for a response, instead drawing a ceramic machine pistol from a shoulder holster as he bulled past Hector to take the lead.

Hector's fiery anger had quenched to red embers, which could still be stoked to life at any moment, but at least he was being more rational now.

"I need information on this venue," I hissed to him as I took a proffered blade and a small Beretta that Hector retrieved from an ankle holster. He himself had reached within the folds of his jacket, and withdrawn an Uzi 9mm, as was common amongst the Triads.

"Numbers of personnel, schematics... anything that would help," I prompted him again.

At last, I sensed Hector initiate the flow of information and I instructed my implant to share my visual overlay through the bridge.

Paredo grunted as additional intel flooded his awareness, but he was already taking the stairs three at a time.

Alarmed cries were already filtering up from the street below, but we were 4 floors up, so it wasn't loud. I could only imagine how the market patrons and vendors alike would be taking cover or fleeing, having heard the first barrage of gunfire. The Police sirens wouldn't be far behind.

Below me, I could hear Paredo calling for a ceasefire and yelling the current Agency safe word, but when another volley of rounds tore up the stair well, I knew the gloves were off.

Paredo swore like a trooper, then, with all other options exhausted, his own pistol began a staccato rhythm of death as he advanced.

On my map, targets were winking out rapidly as Paredo executed our adversaries whenever they presented themselves, and even when they didn't. The stairs were open to each floor, where corridors lined with wooden doors and communal areas stretched away in both directions, so it wasn't as simple as clearing the stairwell.

But as Paredo pushed ahead relentlessly, any combatants who ducked behind furniture, sheltered behind doors, or who tried to observe us from cover which was penetrable by Paredo's firearm, paid the ultimate price.

By the time Hector and I had caught up to provide support, six operatives were already sprawled in their own blood, brains and filth, their bladders and bowels relaxing in death. Four were in their standard casual undercover dress, but two were already suited up in full riot gear, complete with full-faced helmets, elbow, forearm, knee and shin pads.

'These guys were waiting for us,' Paredo siphoned. *'They weren't just kicking it back in full riot gear.'* It didn't look good.

As he pressed on, I wondered if this was what had happened to our brothers and sisters all over the world. I heard Paredo swap out a magazine and wondered how many he had left.

Although I had yet to fire a single round, I stooped to unclip an extendable baton from one of the dead guards and pulled a SPAS-12 shotgun from nerveless fingers. The poor sod who gripped it hadn't managed to get a shot off either, before Paredo had blasted him through the back of his neck and out through his shouting mouth. He had been hunkering down behind a wooden partition, but the cover was an illusion when you were up against relics. His dead eyes had rolled upwards, so he appeared to be staring over my head at an angry God, whilst a darkly spreading bib of blood, bone, teeth and wood splinters adorned his still chest.

Hector gave me a feral look as he hefted a second, freshly looted pistol, and piggybacking off his senses through the bridge, my implant added some additional targets behind us. He had seen the shadows cast by more men following us down the stairs.

This time, they were preceded by the smell of their fear, distinguishable amongst the burnt gunpowder.

Paredo began calling the Agency safe word again, but fresh gunfire from below and calls to advance coming from behind us, were enough to convince us all that the safe house was well and truly compromised. We just needed to get out of here.

My implant showed the stairwell above and below to be a steadily thickening mass of red targets, but that we could make our way across the second floor to a different set of stairs. The second floor contained offices, kitchens and a communal dining area, so it wasn't good for providing us with any cover, but it was even greater folly to remain sandwiched in the stairwell.

This time, Paredo fought a steady retreating action as Hector and I pushed ahead, clearing the way through a cluttered dining area. Hector put three rounds high in the chest of a dark-suited operative with an earpiece, who now lay there bubbling out the last of his life-blood with a look of surprise on his face.

Intermittent bursts of gunfire strobed us with light and debris from behind, but it was still a shock to me when two armoured men burst through a beaded curtain which led into a bar area.

In an automatic reaction, the gaping mouth of my shotgun came up and belched fire and buckshot into the Kevlar and ceramic chest of the lead man. In a strangely comedic moment amongst the carnage, he disappeared backwards through the beaded curtain as fast as he had arrived, as though he was attached to a bungee. The second man's head turned in apparent disbelief, following the trajectory of his partner back the way he had come.

Before I could even rationalise what I was seeing, my implant had kicked the militarized operative square in the sternum with the force of a kicking mule, and now he too was following his friend. But he wasn't so lucky. Before he had even hit the ground, my shotgun had been pumped, aimed and fired, filling the inside of his helmet with shot, skull fragments and scalp.

There was a lull in the gunfire just long enough to push through the swinging door to the restaurant kitchen. Several kitchen staff still cowered beneath stainless steel work benches, but because they were unarmed and made no effort to attack, my implant applied them to the map as orange unknowns.

Hector still menaced them with a glare and a flash of his guns, which made them cower and wail even more.

I advanced toward the rear of the kitchen, past cupboards, racks, pots and pans, where a second set of swinging doors presumably serviced another dining area. But as I drew level with a large steel-clad ice cream machine, sudden movement to my right and a yell in Chinese gave my implant all it needed to have me parry the vicious swing of a large cleaver with the short wooden stock of my shotgun. A bandana-wearing, tattooed kitchen assistant had leapt at me from behind cover, evidently intending to split me from crown to crotch.

As the force of the blow sheared into the wooden stock, my implant capitalised on the momentum and brought the barrel of the gun round in a swift strike that took the yelling assailant in the temple with a jarring crunch. But that was still tame, compared with the counter strike with the butt of the gun as it pivoted around to meet his head coming the other way. He collapsed back behind the machine in a heap, with just his grubby sneakers sticking out.

I didn't spare him a second glance as I booted the doors open into a smaller and better furnished private dining area, but this was empty.

My eyes were drawn immediately to illuminated fire exit signs mounted above a sturdy metal door with a horizontal release bar, but my implant also noted the other doors and windows which could pose a threat.

As my eyes slid across the room, the windows revealed that we had reached the outer face of the building and I could see the colourful canvas-covered tops of market stalls below us and across the street.

"Clear," I yelled, forgetting to siphon in the heat of battle.

Hector and Paredo were close behind me and whilst I covered the doors with my freshly pumped SPAS-12, Hector ran to take cover next to one of the windows. He took a few tentative glances out onto the street, and at the buildings opposite, before announcing that the fire escape was also clear. His implant would have highlighted danger from all but the most mundane of sources.

Paredo backed through the kitchen doors, still firing at our dogged pursuers. Even the gaps between the gunfire were filled with the incoherent wailing of the kitchen staff and the cascade of debris which was set free by the storm of flashing lead.

Paredo's pistol clicked empty, so he holstered it and turned to pluck the spare handgun out of the air that Hector had just tossed him. We were clearly outgunned and running low on ammunition.

The decision to vacate the premises was made for us, as the sound of over a dozen booted feet came thumping up the corridor.

"Time to go," Paredo grinned savagely.

We moved toward the fire exit just in time to hear the telltale tink-tink-tink of a tossed flash-bang grenade landing in the tiled kitchen. As the projectile rolled to a stop and the hapless occupants recognised it, their wails rose in pitch and intensity, but we had already burst out onto the steel fire escape when the blast occurred.

Even so, the ringing it left in my ears was only exceeded by the terrified screams of the last remaining foolish market goers and stall owners who had sheltered in place, and the drumming of our feet on the steel stairs.

We all jumped the last set of stairs, trusting in our relic augmented bone density and sprinted between the colourful stalls of forgettable knickknacks, outdated DVDs and local produce. There was no indication which way Brett had run.

The remaining forces within the safe house must have still been hesitant to step over their dead to follow us, because no shots followed our headlong flight as we weaved through the next three Hong Kong streets. But I still had visions of white-hot lead stitching through me as I ran.

We weren't alone as the herd mentality asserted itself and soon we were amongst a crowd of hurrying tourists, stall owners, shop assistants and street cleaners. Savvy shop owners were pulling down shutters and others had already been dropped at the start of the gunfire.

Car horns sounded, and some cars even tried to use oncoming lanes as the panic spread.

I felt a series of broad spectrum pulses coming from Paredo as we passed parked cars, as he tried to secure us easy transportation.

Back in 2010, Hong Kong had a vast economic divide, where the filthy rich rubbed shoulders with the poor people who serviced them, so it seemed that half the vehicles were taxis and delivery trucks, whilst the other half were prestige cars - with nothing much in between.

So as fortune had it, a shiny new white Jaguar XF flashed its indicators and lit its interior invitingly. Its mirrors were still unfolding as all three of us pulled open doors and slid onto tan leather seats.

The drone and wail of police sirens in the distance was muted as we slammed the doors and Paredo calmly adjusted his mirror and eased his seat back to accommodate his long legs. From the frequencies he was putting out, I think he was still trying to interface with the onboard computer common to modern cars. After all, in a car chase, it was much better, as a relic, to be able to intuitively control breaking to every wheel, stability and many more features.

When he was satisfied, Paredo pressed the pulsing ignition button and the turbo charged engine awoke from its slumber and the air conditioning stirred into life. I was expecting Paredo to hoof the accelerator, but instead, he ambled out of the parking spot with the care of a Sunday driver. But as several Police cars screamed by, blue lights and two-tone sirens in overdrive, I saw why.

"Have you been listening to the Police scanners?" Paredo asked us, referring to the Police radio traffic.

I felt like an amateur for not having done so, but before responding to him, I had my implant assimilate all of the radio chatter it had picked up over the last three hours.

"There weren't any on-air references to this ambush until after it happened," I reported, "but we've stirred up a hornets' nest now!"

Hector whooped at this information and his eyes and teeth flashed as he smiled. This was just another day in the life for him, but admittedly his gang-related confrontations weren't quite on the same scale.

"Solus," Paredo asked, "can you remember where that parking garage was, or any details about who took Sierene?"

Hector covered his eyes with his hands as he tried to pull the images into coherence, but it was no use. "Nah man, it's like Swiss cheese in here," he said, pausing in his efforts. "But Brett left me with the impression of the business district as he bailed out." His nose wrinkled as he closed his eyes in concentration again. "Head for Wanchai and I'll see if I can pick him up when we get closer." He grunted in frustration and slapped his hand down hard on the upholstery.

"Well," Paredo added as he indicated and changed lanes, "one of those men in your memory was a henchman of Jià Zhú Táo, who is the boss of the Jade Needles, a Triad gang operating out of Lockhart Road, Wanchai. Let's see what she has to say about your friend Brett and our lady Sierene."

Chapter 40

It took us another ten minutes to navigate around the bay towards Wanchai, where we eventually parked illegally and abandoned the car.

As we stepped away from the vehicle, Paredo and Hector didn't look back, but out of conscience, I had my implant lock the car.

Hector looked at me like I was mad, and I felt defensive enough about it to justify myself. "It's only common courtesy!" I said as we walked away.

Paredo ignored the whole exchange as we walked along Lockhart Road toward the centre of the red light district. He was too busy looking out for signs of a trap.

Lockhart Road was an eclectic mix of hotels, restaurants and banks, littered with bars, nightclubs and lap dancing clubs. It wasn't quite dusk, yet businessmen and tourists alike were sitting outside bars and restaurants with cool beers and warm 'girlfriends'.

As we walked the street, I noticed that the bigger businesses occupied the most frontage, whilst the sex trade occupied narrow, neon-signed entrances with dark stairways that either led down into basement space or up onto first floor premises.

The angle of the sun was casting long shadows and the height of the high-rise buildings was prematurely darkening the streets.

Groups of pretty, and not so pretty, girls from Thailand, the Philippines and Vietnam stood around doorways or lounged on stools, as middle-aged or older Madams offered their company to passers-by.

Paredo adopted a face like thunder to go with his purposeful stride, but after a couple of the more brazen girls or their Madams had still tried to solicit our custom, he began to generate a sonorous low frequency which induced fear and kept them at bay.

I noticed bouncers, broad-chested and gold-chained, folding their arms defensively and squaring up their postures as we passed, but Paredo ignored them. He knew exactly where we were heading. My implant assessed and tagged them, but didn't bother to display anything, as they didn't pose a direct threat.

Hector's brow was furrowed in concentration as he searched for any hint of the control module which was buried within the body of his handler, Brett. It was a concern, because at any point, Brett could attempt to compel Hector to attack us.

But whilst we maintained the siphon-bridge we would have some small notice and the opportunity to defend ourselves. I assume that after Paredo's little trick, Brett had thought better of making a connection with Hector and giving us a pinpoint location. After all, calling down the wrath of three relics, including the lethal hand of the Committee of 300, would be suicidal.

Rather than speak, Paredo pulled up a map for us through our bridge and pinpointed the location of 'The Inferno', a nightclub and lap dancing bar owned and run by the Jade Needles. He uploaded images, memories and floor plans from his last couple of visits, although I sensed there had been more.

As we drew near, a group of seven men emerged from the club and arrayed themselves about the doorway defensively. The cloud of girls hovering around the entrance were ushered inside, but the two bouncers remained outside with the newcomers and puffed their chests and clicked their knuckles and necks. The tallest was still a hand shorter than Paredo and an arm narrower.

My implant could detect the steel amongst the men, in the form of guns and blades, and tagged the men in order of their level of threat.

Some of the younger men shifted nervously as we came to stand on the cracked pavement in front of them. The older men had more of an air of confidence about them, but even they began to falter as Hector and I both stood as stock-still and stony-faced as Paredo, bathing the group in the frequency of fear.

The apparent leader, a middle-aged man with a badly-set broken nose contrasting with his expensively tailored black suit, stepped forward.

He swallowed discretely before speaking in Cantonese, but our implants adapted immediately.

"Jià Zhú Táo sends her regrets, but she cannot entertain you without an appointment." He let the rebuttal hang there pregnantly, as the men behind him shifted uncomfortably.

Paredo didn't so much as move, allowing his dead-eyed stare and sheer physical presence to go to work alongside the frequency coming from our implants.

But where his men were more cautious, the lead man seemed happier confronting his fear. He stepped forward and laid a hand on Paredo's muscular chest. Paredo's plain tourist style clothes didn't do much to conceal his brawn, especially when flattened against him.

Paredo looked down at the sweating palm, then back at the dark eyes of its owner, before breaking the silence.

"You remember what happened last time you put your hands on me Lee?"

Clearly Paredo and Lee had some history, so I was surprised that Lee was only sporting a badly healed nose.

Paredo began to smile as Lee put his other hand to the hilt of the pistol he had tucked into the back of his belt, under his jacket.

As Paredo's smile broadened menacingly, he lent forward slightly, increasing the pressure of the hand against his chest - just enough to encourage Lee to take a step back. But instead,

Lee made the rookie mistake of pushing forward and locking his arm out to compensate. It was all Paredo needed.

Paredo's motion was completely fluid and faster than a striking snake. With Lee's arm braced straight at the elbow, it had nowhere to go as Paredo's left forearm snapped up to break it. Time slowed for me as Lee's arm folded horribly with a sickening crunch and Paredo completed the embrace by stepping in close and reaching over Lee's shoulder to wrench on his other arm, like he was ripping off a chicken wing through the cloth of the jacket.

In less than a second, Lee was collapsed on his knees in front of his men, with his jacket pulled over his head, squealing like a stuck pig. One arm protruded at a grotesque angle and his other arm, complete with dislocated shoulder, still tangled across his back. In his sudden agony, the pistol Lee had been reaching for dangled forgotten by its finger guard from his useless fingers.

It was so fast, that Lee's men had stood there blankly trying to process what had happened, before Paredo announced. "Here's my calling card. Please take it to Jià Zhú Táo. I'll await her invitation."

For emphasis, he casually tipped Lee onto his side with the toe of one oversized boot, eliciting a mournful cry.

Two of the bigger men stepped forward as if to tackle Paredo, but one of the smaller men in front of them promptly stayed them with an outstretched arm and tried to placate us.

"Discussions on the street are bad for business," he began, his plaited ponytail bobbing as he spoke. "Let us go inside and you can make yourselves comfortable with some of our girls whilst I request an audience."

As he gestured for his men to stand aside, his jacket sleeves rode up slightly to reveal the Triad tattoos spiralling up his arm.

The men didn't hurry to comply, but instead moved stiff-leggedly, with many still fingering the hilts of their weapons.

But cooler heads had prevailed and a groaning Lee was carried up the stairs ahead of us.

I considered the questionable wisdom of marching into a stronghold of armed Triads, but Paredo had set the tone and his feelings coming through the siphon-bridge would likely brook no argument.

The music within the club was pumping and getting louder with every stair we climbed.

Mr Ponytail, as I now thought of him, directed the two men who half carried and half dragged a groaning and swearing Lee to go through to the back of the club, before gesturing for us to follow him.

The first floor of the club was geared up as a nightclub, complete with bar areas and a couple of dance floors. Stools lined the walls, wherever there weren't booths with comfortable sofas and fake pot plants. Black leather dominated the furnishings, combined with pale wooden flooring, but many of the wall-mounted lights featured fans and coloured silk to masquerade as flickering live flames.

The DJ booth was empty, as it was still early and the sound system was just running a pre-recorded mix.

The second, smaller dance floor also housed a stage and three chromed poles for the club's dancers to ply their trade from, or to entice the clientele further into the club. Three long-legged dancers practiced their craft, much to the appreciation of some inebriated patrons brandishing crumpled bank notes. But of the girls who had been ushered inside, there was no sign.

A further flight of stairs led upwards and a black set of double doors led inwards. One would lead to booths for private dances and who knows what else, and according to Paredo's map and memories, the other led to a larger invitation-only section of the club geared specifically toward the gratification of VIPs. The third floor was private and reserved for gang business. This, presumably would be where Jià Zhú Táo would be found.

We followed Mr Ponytail across to a booth near the empty dance floor, were he called a scantily clad waitress over and offered us complementary drinks and a seat whilst he 'informed' Jià Zhú Táo of our request for an audience.

It struck me that he was just buying time to spring an even bigger trap, but Paredo agreed to accept the seat and the drink, so for better or worse, Hector and I followed his lead.

I noticed, as Mr Ponytail departed, that he moved very well for an older man. He had the balance of a martial artist and the grace of a dancer. He didn't project the arrogant swagger that Lee had, but I wondered if Mr Ponytail was a substantial part of the power behind the throne that Jià Zhú Táo occupied. He was certainly more than he had first appeared.

We ordered our drinks and whilst Hector and I admired the departing waitress, Paredo was silently adding the building's wireless security camera feeds to our siphon-bridge. It hadn't taken him long to hack the feed, but personnel were already moving, presumably at Jià Zhú Táo's order.

'Stand firm boys,' Paredo siphoned. 'Jià Zhú Táo just wants to put on a show of force before she meets with us. She knows I represent the Committee, and that we know where she lives. But she is proud and this helps her save face.'

Paredo's reasoning made sense, so having hacked and added all the neighbouring wireless camera feeds within range, we sat there quaffing Champaign and vintage scotch, watching dozens of Triads and bouncers converging on the club.

My implant registered 16 already in the building, but Jià Zhú Táo's quarters were not on a wireless feed and so far there was no sign of her.

After what seemed like an age, Mr Ponytail returned and asked if we would kindly follow him upstairs.

Chapter 41

A couple of minutes later, all three of us reclined comfortably in front of a dozen beautiful dancers at various stages of undress. They were clearly well practiced and their lithe bodies helped dull my alarm at the army of 53 potential combatants that my implant had tallied on the assorted video feeds.

Interestingly, we had observed the gang members being asked to turn in their firearms on the way into the property, although they were allowed to retain all else. So when Mr Ponytail asked us to hand over our guns, it wasn't much of a surprise.

Paredo siphoned that this was asked of him the last time he was here and that he had expected as much again when we arrived. So with the thorough ministrations of six of the more sultry dancers to take the sting out of the process, we were disarmed.

Mr Ponytail was acting the consummate host, as he announced that Jià Zhú Táo would be with us presently, but firstly, for her security, she would feel better with some protection in place.

I detected no lies from him as he concluded with "please do not be alarmed. In fact, I speak on behalf of Jià Zhú Táo and myself when I ask that you take the extent of her precautions as a compliment".

At this, and with a florid bow, he retreated and gestured to one of his men to send up their 'protection'.

Over 50 hardened gang members and experienced club security filed up the stairs and formed a loose circle about us. They were mismatched in every way, except for their uniform look of hatred.

"So, without further ado, may I present the boss of the Jade Needles, Jià Zhú Táo," he concluded.

I had expected her to enter from one of the side doors, or even from behind the stage that the girls had been working, but instead, a colourful bunting hanging against the wall above the stage began to lower, exposing a large plate glass observation window.

The room behind was darkened, but as the lights were raised, a slim middle-aged oriental woman was standing there with a look of imperious satisfaction on her hard face.

"This is new," Paredo said aloud.

Jià Zhú Táo was the Vietnamese name for the Oleander, a beautiful flower with bright pink petals. It was pretty, but every part of the bush, from the roots to the petals was poisonous. You had to even be careful of the smoke if it was burned, or water with the petals floating in it.

When she was younger, I could see how she earned her name, but the emotionally bankrupt ice queen before me was now nothing but poison.

"I see you are still as arrogant as ever, Paredo," she gloated without any preamble, her voice being amplified via the stage sound system.

"I am no more arrogant than your idiot boyfriend." Paredo jibed back loudly enough for her (and everyone else) to hear. "Did he show you the new tricks he can do with his arms? You might just have found your club a new act, now that your own looks fail to draw even dollar bills from your clients."

I couldn't believe my ears. If this was Agency diplomacy, I clearly missed that class at the academy! Paredo was going to get us killed!

I expected Jià Zhú Táo to rant and rave, but instead, she threw back her head and laughed. She seemed genuinely amused.

"Oh my dear Paredo, I shall truly savour this. We both know it was never my looks that put me where I am today. It was my ability to kill without compassion... And my ability to capitalise on the human desire for forbidden fruit." I sensed she wasn't just talking about her girls and other contraband.

"You think this meeting to be a repeat of your last visit?"

Receiving no answer to her question, she continued. "I think not. You see, you are out on a limb… overextended, if you will. I believe that was the word you used last time we met?" Her words dripped with venom.

It was becoming increasingly obvious that this poisonous, pinch-faced harpy was angling beyond a simple show of force. For her, this was revenge.

'What did you do to her?' I shot through the bridge to Paredo, but he casually ignored me. In fact, Paredo felt quite satisfied with the current turn of events.

It was Paredo's turn to speak. "No, hag. I'll tell you what is going to happen. I am going to pull this seedy dive down around your wrinkled ears, and then I am going to physically wring you until you tell me where Sierene is."

His cruel insults and brash threats angered the men around us, who now flexed and readied themselves. They saw three against over 50 and rightly expected us to be broken, bleeding and no doubt dead at the end of it.

But their anger was but a candle flame alongside Jià Zhú Táo's raging furnace. She was almost trembling with it before he was done.

"In this, you are wrong, dead man. A new order emerges and you are a redundant part of the old one. You are a relic in many senses of the word. But I already have a buyer for your corpse, and your soft friends here will increase my profits. You have no backup, and even if you did, Mr Mason will cover up your demise for me. Everything is arranged."

She was referring to Brett, Hector's double crossing handler. Hector's rage bubbled perilously close to boiling point but the most he showed on the surface was one of his fists unconsciously clenching.

"Very well boys," Paredo said, "any last requests?"

"How about some music?" Hector replied as he flexed his shoulders.

"Ha!" Paredo's laughter burst from him with genuine mirth. "Not you, Solus, I was talking to these stringy little bitches!" His predatory eyes cast over the gang surrounding us, but the grin didn't leave his face.

'Great plan, Paredo,' I siphoned sarcastically, as I too readied myself for mortal combat.

'What more do you want?' He responded. *'We have a solid lead upstairs and my plan just disarmed all their men!'* It had a perverse logic to it, but it was beyond reckless.

The sound system interrupted us as Jià Zhú Táo's voice once again overrode the angry muttering and threats coming from the gang of men surrounding us.

"Remember men, I want them dead, but not dismembered. I need their hardware intact. The bounty is five million dollars US, split between the men left alive in the room."

Then to us, she cackled, "but I like your style, Mexican. Your request is granted. Let's have some music for you to die to."

A moment passed, but when the sound system kicked back into action, we were bathed in the thumping beat and rolling vocals of Hispanic rap music, just as the ring of human bone, muscle and steel surrounding us began to contract.

Hector whooped, Paredo grinned, and my own battle lust burst through me into the siphon-bridge, as we kicked our chairs into the oncoming mass of attackers. If they wanted violence, then violence they would have.

Bats, knives, cleavers, knuckle dusters and batons bristled along the hedge of flesh around us, but to my implant, it was just lines of force, angles and vectors - just one big mathematical puzzle to solve as it detachedly calculated and executed the most efficient ways to neutralise any threat.

Paredo, Hector and myself each pushed outwards toward the disruption our flying chairs had created, but our implants kept contact through the bridge, giving each of us triple the input from our senses.

The first man to reach me was still crowded by those around him, so it was a simple thing to block the overhand swing of his billy club and twist it from his grip with a fluid circling of my arm, leaving it trapped under my armpit. The thrusting fingers of my other hand jabbed into the hollow of his throat as I pulled and pivoted. It was hard to distinguish where my own knowledge left off and my implant's skill began, but as the bones of his wrist sheared in a nasty break that spiralled up the bones of his forearm, I directed his dead-weight momentum diagonally into the path of his comrades.

I stamped a knee out from under the second man, as I parried the short thrust of his blade with the flat of my forearm and hastily retrieved the baton I still had trapped under my armpit. But no effort was wasted. In retrieving the weapon, my implant whipped the baton around in a merciless backhand swing that cracked across his nose and eye socket and crumpled him into a tangled heap amongst the press of booted feet.

The hack and slash, riposte and parry, combined with the sheer press of men caused me to back up, but I left behind grimacing or senseless wrecks of men as I destructed limbs, compromised joints, and redirected forces in a merciless flurry of implant-enhanced martial arts.

I could hear Paredo counting his fallen opponents aloud as he fought with berserk abandon. "Nine, ten... Are you next little man? Eleven!"

Hector was slick with the blood of the fallen, but from the siphon-bridge, I could tell he wasn't injured. He had liberated a switchblade and now a cleaver, and was merciless in their application. I tried to ignore the screams and wailing, with corresponding thumps as fingers, hands and sometimes limbs tumbled to the dance floor.

I simply didn't have the stomach for the cruel devastation left behind by edged weapons, so although my implant resheathed several blades in their respective owners, I retained my baton.

Paredo was outpacing Hector and I two to one as he crushed, ripped, rended and even hurled his opponents. He gloried in his raw power, executed in the most innovative ways. It wouldn't surprise me if he would still have come here alone.

Hector had lost himself in his whirling slaughter and was moving to the thumping bassline of the music. It reminded me of Capoeira, the Brazilian martial art that had camouflaged itself in dance when martial arts were forbidden by the slave owners and authorities of 16th century South America. He caught me looking and the flash of his white teeth amongst the crimson splattering on his face, although jarring, still elicited a whoop of abandon from me. We were the masters here - let the wave of fools break themselves against us!

Heaven help me, I suspect these were bad men, but my reckless abandon in that moment was still shameful. I certainly considered nothing beyond the moment.

If men came within my reach, I broke their bones. If a skull cracked under a vicious elbow, or a face flattened itself across the thick bones of my skull, then so be it - as Paredo, Hector and I danced a lethal rhythm to Latin beats in that charnel house.

As the bodies of the dead, dying and groaning maimed began to pile around us and Jià Zhú Táo's forces were down to just over half their original number, her piercing shrieks began to interrupt over the sound system as she tried to direct affairs.

She had gambled everything on this one reckless roll of the dice, and despite all odds, her fortunes were unravelling in front of her. Her men were faltering and the glitter of her offer was losing its appeal. They certainly hadn't counted on this!

"Chou! Jade Needles!" Jià Zhú Táo shrieked, her veneer of calm all but disintegrated. "Finish them!"

At first, I assumed this was more encouragement for her beleaguered men, but from behind the stage, I caught a flash of movement.

The distraction almost cost me an eye, as a burly martial artist thrust rigid fingers into my face. He was good, and with Hector flailing wildly close behind me, my implant had opted to duck my forehead and take the impact, rather than step backwards into the path of a relic wielded blade.

As I ducked under the trajectory of a thrown dagger and swept the legs out from under the yellow-toothed kung fu master in front of me, Mr Ponytail emerged on stage, stripped to the waist and carrying an exquisitely etched Chinese broadsword. So, his real name is Chou, I thought, as I stomped on the hand of yellow-teeth before he could regain his feet. He rolled away from me, clutching his damaged hand, but I thought him lucky as the two that replaced him were swiftly boxed, bludgeoned senseless and booted backwards over their fallen allies.

In the time that had taken, Chou had been joined on stage by the dozen beautiful dancing girls who had performed for us earlier. Each one was still dressed to distract, but this time, they also bore a variety of Wushu weapons. No wonder they had moved so well, I thought, these were Chou's students and probably the real reason for the naming of the Jade Needles.

Their arrival caused a natural lull in the combat, as sweating men backed away from us cautiously, to make way for Chou and his Needles. Jià Zhú Táo had realised that the music wasn't helping her cause, and so she shut it off, leaving the echoes of the music still playing downstairs to filter up to us.

In the relative quiet, the panting and groaning of the wounded became much more apparent.

'Be careful,' Paredo siphoned to us in warning. *'These girls have trained all their lives to fight together. They aren't like the rabble of amateurs that were just sacrificed to soften us up.'*

My implant took a moment to reassess the battlefield. The floor was slick with blood in places and spattered elsewhere, and though many bodies lay still, others rocked or thrashed in pain, or tried to drag themselves out from underfoot. Some of their friends warily dragged them out of our reach and to make way for the combat to begin again.

Hector removed his shirt and, having wiped the worst of the gore from his face and hands, he cast it amongst the dead and wounded.

My own clothes were torn and wet, but I opted to spend the time looting the nearest bodies for a better weapon. My wooden baton was splintered and wouldn't stand up to the fine steel wielded by Chou and the Jade Needles.

"Here!" Hector called, as he understood my need and tossed me a 21 inch steel retractable baton. I collapsed it against the floor and flicked it out again experimentally, as I retrieved a length of steel chain. The limp grip of its previous owner didn't offer much resistance as I pulled on it and retreated.

As Chou and his harem arrayed themselves in front of us with a level of showmanship and flare, Paredo simply stepped forward to stare defiantly at them. He held a hammer in one hand and a dripping machete in the other. His jacket had been discarded, or else pulled from him, and his shirt was stuck to his torso in places.

"Well Chou?," Paredo asked, "are you ready to die for your slattern?"

He was trying to cloud Mr Ponytail's mind with anger, but the frustrated squawk that came back was instead from the harridan behind the glass, whilst Chou seemed unperturbed. But his Needles weren't so calm and three of them broke off from the group and ran at Paredo.

One had a broadsword, one had a spear and the other bore a nasty set of bladed hooks.

Hector was nearest and turned to assist, but Paredo's siphon was forceful and certain. *'Don't crowd me. They are mine.'*

I was feeling squeamish about fighting girls, especially after watching them dance for us, but when I saw their opening gambit, my views changed somewhat. They moved in perfect concert with each other, with a lethal grace that left no room for error nor reprieve. As one stabbed from long range, another harried and the third struck like a bag of striking snakes. I hadn't ever seen speed or coordination like it from non-relics.

Paredo's parries and counter-strikes were every bit as fast, but having already defeated so many and having to respond to the astounding number of simultaneous strikes, the odds of him avoiding injury were diminishing. Having weapons with a much shorter reach wasn't helping Paredo either, but it was still a magnificent display of skill. The whole room watched the furious exchange of whistling and chiming steel in awe, but I was counting the seconds before something went wrong.

Chou was watching his girls proudly, when Paredo decided to goad him further.

"Which of these children is your favourite, Chou?" He called.

"Is it this one?" He asked, as he sidestepped a spear thrust and was suddenly amongst the trio, bringing his hammer down hard onto the wrist of the swordswoman. She hadn't realised he could move so fast and wailed as the bones broke. But her wail was cut short as his vicious shove emptied her lungs and thrust her straight onto one of the hooks borne by her sister-at-arms.

They stood for a moment, locked together in a lethal embrace, and it was all the time Paredo needed.

"Or is it this one?" He asked again. This time, he pivoted and with a clean sweep of his machete, struck the head from sister hook's shoulders, with the look of horror at what she had done still upon her face.

Paredo danced clear of the pulsing fountain that ensued, leaving the third Needle yelling incoherently in remorse.

Paredo once again locked eyes with Chou, as his calm oriental demeanour swiftly began to unravel.

The final straw was when the spear-wielding Jade Needle attacked. I am not sure whether her flurry of strikes was sloppy due to her eyes being clouded with tears, or whether Paredo had been toying with them all along, but she only got one chance at a solid thrust before Paredo casually divested her of her spear and backhanded her smartly across the face. She was lucky that he had already made examples of her sisters, but even so, she landed in a senseless heap with the dying swordswoman reaching weakly for her.

"Only nine more to go, Mother Chou," he mocked.

But that was all it took to take the last of Mr Ponytail's self control.

With a yell of rage, Chou leapt from the stage. He closed on Paredo, his exquisite sword flicking and darting like the wicked tongue of a serpent. He truly was a master.

Many do not appreciate the decades of practice and training it takes to build the perfect balance and muscle memory that turns 4 lbs of razor-sharp steel into an extension of your will. Yet Chou had done this.

His blade kissed and clashed, feinted and needled, keeping Paredo out of reach, whilst constantly testing his defences.

Through the siphon-bridge, Paredo was a curious mix of frustration and appreciation for Chou's skill, but Hector and I couldn't spectate any further as the other sisters grouped to attack us.

Hector and I had three groups of three girls to contend with. I was appalled at the prospect of fighting them, yet I knew that every girl I incapacitated was one that Hector wouldn't have to cut.

But when their blades and polearms were flying with lethal intent, I had no choice but to play to win. It was unnerving for these beautiful girls, who had recently been objects of desire, to be snarling behind every spear thrust, whip-crack and slice of a scimitar.

How my implant kept me intact in those first few frenzied moments, I don't know. But as I ducked and shifted, my baton strikes rapped at knuckles and my chain tangled blades. More than one maiden instantly resorted to fists, elbows and feet the moment I disarmed them, but inevitably, the pressure of combat forced either myself or my implant to escalate the aggression.

Yet with every Jade Needle taken out of the game, the others fought harder, with renewed fury. Some of the men rejoined the fight, but as we steadily added to the butcher's tally, several started to slip away down the stairs. They wanted no part of a fight that wouldn't leave them alive to spend the bounty that Jià Zhú Táo had promised.

As Hector and I whirled amidst a flurry of wicked steel, I saw that Paredo had swept up the weapon of the dead swordswoman, in order to counteract Chou's reach advantage.

It really was a testament to Chou's skill. But despite a couple of the Jade Needles breaking off to harry his back, Paredo had now drawn blood in several places about Chou's person - nothing which would be life-threatening, but the intense look of concentration on Chou's face said it all.

"You don't need to follow her into an early grave, Chou." Paredo breathed heavily as he cleaved a brawny bouncer who had tested his luck by leaping in with a vicious cut. Paredo didn't even break eye contact with Chou as he shoved the windmilling corpse towards Chou's feet. The poor fool, now open from collarbone to hip, didn't realise he was dead and clutched desperately at Chou's foot as he frothed and wheezed for help. But Chou side-stepped out of range with a look of annoyance and took up the offensive again, the ring of their singing steel echoing from the walls.

The girls were more wary now and I used the brief reprieve to glance up at the observation window, where the wild eyed Jià Zhú Táo was urging the last of her men to come down to us. She had severed the intercom connection to the sound system, but I could still discern her acerbic demands through the vibrations of the glass.

'Lucidus! Get up to that booth before the bitch runs,' Paredo siphoned through the bridge. Even with his prodigious appetite for battle, Paredo was becoming anxious to conclude matters and report back to the Agency.

Hector had taken a cut or two, but as I turned to see if he was okay, the dazing head butt he delivered to a gorgeous brunette helped assure me that I was free to go. They were more than capable of taking care of the rest on their own.

Chou saw me break off and did his best to angle round, but Paredo's unyielding pressure left him weighing up his options as he ducked and thrust, sidestepped and parried. His only option was to throw everything into an all-out assault on Paredo.

As I leapt onto the stage, I headed towards where I believed the stairway to be, putting the ringing clash of steel and the grunts of those still fighting behind me. But as I drew level with the curtain at the back of the room, Paredo's biofeedback alert pulled me up short. I looked back, hoping to see the source of the alert, but the animated mass of combatants didn't offer any clues.

"Go!" Paredo yelled, his words simultaneously echoing through the siphon-bridge. The force of his intent snapped me out of my hesitation and drove me through the abandoned backstage area, past dressing rooms and a kitchen, not knowing what was about to happen.

The seconds drew out excruciatingly as I ran, but as I reached the foot of a staircase, Paredo's sense of remorse caught up with me through the bridge. It took me a moment to understand, but as the sound of Jià Zhú Táo's cry echoed down from the stairs above me, I realised the significance. Chou was dead.

To a relic like Paredo, who, over decades, had experienced the pinnacles (and depths) of what life had to offer, losing someone of Chou's remarkable skill was a tragedy - enemy or not. Paredo's remorse reminded me of the creed of the Samurai, where Warriors still respected one another despite being adversaries. Wealth and possessions come and go, but you take honour, knowledge and experience with you, and hopefully hand it down to future generations. But Chou's light was now extinguished - only to satisfy the greed and lust for power of a petty tyrant, jealously ruling over her own tiny kingdom.

'That bitch will pay for this!' Paredo snarled through the siphon-bridge, as I caught the impression of him launching one of the few remaining combatants into his peers. But it wasn't going to be that easy.

As I crested the stairs onto an empty corridor, I heard footfalls coming from around the bend ahead. Although they were muffled by the pile of the carpet and overlaid by Jià Zhú Táo's fury, they were enough to help my implant to piece together a map of the layout ahead. But it was the sound of magazines being driven home into machine pistols, followed by rounds being chambered, that pushed my implant into high alert.

Before conscious thought could engage, my implant had me sprinting for the corner before Jià Zhú Táo's men could reach it. Fortune favoured me, as I encountered two suited gangsters as we converged on the bend simultaneously. The first, who was incongruously wearing mirrored sunglasses in the dim corridor, thrust his Glock 18C towards my chest. My hands flashed out to meet his and I deflected his aim, just as the pistol began to spit out its full clip of 20 rounds. Time slowed for me, as I forced him back into his sweating partner and the Glock stencilled my distorted outline in bullet holes up the corridor wall. His wild arc of fire travelled up one side of me, then down the next, as I twisted the firearm out of his hands, leaving my assailant grimacing with the pain of broken fingers until my vicious crushing elbow knocked him aside, senseless.

His partner, hampered by the press of our bodies and his dark eyes narrowed against the spray of gunfire, tried to bring up the dull grey muzzle of his silenced Uzi, but my implant felled him with a flying knee to the sternum that bounced him off the corridor wall. The sickening crunch of several ribs popping within his chest and the rattle of a freshly punctured lung joined the cacophony as I stooped to retrieve his firearm.

Ahead, two men who had been exiting Jià Zhú Táo's booth, took one look at the scene before them and hastily backpedalled, slamming the reinforced steel door behind them.

Even without my implant-enhanced senses, the sound of deadbolts slamming home and a bar being dropped into place were obvious.

My siphon-bridge connection with Paredo and Hector was growing a little tenuous due to distance, but their sense of satisfaction made it apparent that the situation was under control. My implant shot them both an image of the door ahead of me, as it simultaneously piggybacked the Wi-Fi security feed to send a status report to the Agency. In moments, Acertas and numerous other agency analysts would be alerted to Brett's betrayal and the escalating body count left in our wake. Whatever information we were about to squeeze out of Jià Zhú Táo, we would need local support to follow it up.

Chapter 42

As smart as Jià Zhú Táo thought she was, her security booth had left her trapped like a rat in a barrel. I would have thought it would have injected some civility into her, but instead she acted as though she had nothing left to lose.

Her two guards huddled in the corner, nursing their wounds and still coughing from the smoke left over from the Agency-issue breaching charge Paredo had used to fold the steel door like crumpled foil.

My own ears still hummed from the report of the Glock fired at close range, but it would have paled in comparison to being inside the booth when Paredo's charge went off.

Hector was rifling through desk drawers and files, as Paredo towered over a defiant Jià Zhú Táo, one great hand around her throat and another clasped over one of her balled fists. She must have been crazy to have launched it towards Paredo's scowling face.

"I told you, hag," Paredo barked, "the next time you do that, you would regret it."

He emphasised his point by squeezing on her clenched knuckles, which had nowhere to go. Tears of rage, pain and frustration forced themselves from her eyes unbidden, as she squirmed and then kicked ineffectually against Paredo's shins. But, to her credit, she refused to yield to his angry gaze and would not cry out. I could hear the ligaments and tendons within her knuckles beginning to give way, but he eased off the pressure before bones broke.

"Tell us what we need to know." Paredo said again with menace as he loomed over her, ready to deliver some other form of coercion.

"Look," I interjected, seeing that their clash of wills would only end badly. There was no give in either of them, but unfortunately for Jià Zhú Táo, I knew that Paredo would do whatever it took to save one of our relics.

"We don't give a shit about your usual business activities," I continued. "All we need to know is the whereabouts of Sierene and Brett Mason."

But even though she could see the way out I was offering her, Jià Zhú Táo was hard as nails and, most likely, criminally insane. The most I got out of her was a face full of spit and a tirade of curses, as she railed wildly against Paredo's grip.

Paredo clipped her with a sharp slap and instead hoisted her aloft by one of her feet. Her dress followed the path of gravity, so as she recovered from the dazing blow, she began to jerk and struggle all the more. She was like a scolded cat in a bag, intermittently trying, but failing, to restore her dignity.

"I warned you I would wring you until you told me where Sierene is." Paredo boomed. I could tell from the siphon-bridge that he was still angry, although he took no pleasure from this process.

But words were useless in the face of Jià Zhú Táo's fury. She had lost everything she had taken years to build and would not be reasoned with. As she frantically struggled, a lucky kick angered Paredo enough for him to catch her flailing foot and give it a mean squeeze. This time I did hear several bones pop, a fraction before Jià Zhú Táo's wailing made it impossible to determine what damage was being done. She continued to writhe and curse through her tears, but it certainly prevented her from kicking him again with her broken toes.

Through my Agency training, I was well aware of the numerous nasty options available to him, but the disgusting torture carried out at places like Guantánamo Bay were done over an extended time. And time was something we didn't have.

I turned away, a curious mix of disgust and shame gnawing at my belly, hoping to gain inspiration from something else in the booth. Paredo was mentally calculating his options and was about to go to work on Jià Zhú Táo, when one of her wounded guards broke his silence.

Like myself, he clearly had no stomach for what was about to happen, especially given that he might be next. We listened intently as he described everything he had seen and heard over the last week. It was patchy, because he hadn't always been around, but we gained enough. His fellow was less forthcoming, especially in front of Jià Zhú Táo, but when Hector flourished a gory blade, he broke like a dam.

He was still speaking when half a dozen field agents pulled up outside in unmarked cars. The camera feed may have been grainy and black-and-white, but I could still see them talking hurriedly into earpieces as they secured the perimeter and closed down the club. Paredo scowled at our prisoners, then snatched up the suppressed Uzi, as he went to check out our local support. After our incursion at the safe house, he wasn't going to take any chances.

Chapter 43

The midnight air was still balmy, although cooler than the day had been. A light breeze animated the nearby ornamental gardens and the profusion of street lights and infrared security cameras bathed the deserted street in intermittent pools of light and shadow.

This affluent location, near the Peak of Hong Kong, overlooked the iconic city skyline where high-rise buildings reflected their myriad lights in the inky water of the bay below.

The view was impressive, but we had our backs to it, as Hector, Paredo and I surveilled a mansion and it's grounds. The venue before me was overlaid with an implant-generated schematic, complete with camera feeds, satellite feed, triangulated cell-phone signals and more. We had even utilised the echo-mapping potential of stray Wi-Fi signals and the property's high-tech electrical appliances to flesh out the details.

As we crouched atop the perimeter wall, clad in urban camouflage and black tactical gear, I felt distinctly better to be fully equipped with the Agency's finest equipment. We had chopper support if it were required, along with 22 field agents dispersed across six different vehicles, each parked in different nearby streets. This was polar opposite to our low-tech and makeshift start to the day.

A litter of red-tagged personnel moved about the property, the walls made transparent to my eyes. Some of them winked in and out of certainty, as they moved beyond the net of surveillance created by CCTV, laptop webcams, cell phone cameras and smart TVs. A property loaded with such high-end electronics was a relic's playground when it came to spying.

We didn't have a precise fix on Sierene, but we knew exactly where Brett was. He sat on a soft leather sofa, distractedly channel surfing the 42 inch TV. One hand gripped the remote and the other alternated between his mouth, as he chewed his nails, and nursing a crystal tumbler which appeared to contain whisky. It was strange to have him seemingly staring right at me, but of course he was just watching the TV as I eavesdropped the camera it used for gesture recognition. He looked stressed. His suit was crumpled, his tie loose and his eyes swept to the doorway whenever any sound reached him over the distraction of the TV. He was only there to make sure Sierene made it to the meeting the following morning, but he clearly didn't relish the task.

The other cell phone signals from the property traced back to various known Chinese military personnel, some Triads and even a couple of CIA spooks. It was a mess, because we still weren't sure whether we would be compromising any other operations, or whether we had just uncovered dirty operatives.

A tray of meals had been delivered to the basement a few minutes earlier, but we had no intelligence on what lay below the main house.

It had been a temptation to try to reach Sierene with a siphon-bridge, but we couldn't risk alerting Brett until we had his head in a noose. As it was, Acertas and Canis had been forced to bring Major Winters into the loop in case Hiram was compromised.

The security camera directly in front of us whirred as it panned around in a continuous sweep, but Paredo's implant continued to cover us with the illusion of superimposed foliage via the hacked camera feed. Any human scrutiny could give us away, but whilst they relied on wireless electronics, we had a distinct advantage. In some respects, it was insulting that they had been so lax in their security, knowing who would come looking for Sierene.

'OK,' Paredo siphoned. *'We go on my mark. Lethal force authorised on all but four targets.'*

He didn't need to go over the plan again, but I suppose it was force of habit from working with non-relics. The security patrol in the garden was already out of sight around the other side of the building, but we were just waiting for a couple of red-tagged targets to step out of the line of sight created by a second floor window.

With a nod in the darkness, Paredo dropped to the ground inside the garden almost silently. Expensive rare ferns and flowers crushed beneath his combat boots, but he paid them no mind as he ghosted across the garden. Hector and I followed a moment later. Some of the camera systems were hard-wired, which meant we could not manipulate the feed, so our advancement around the outside of the building involved ducking under certain windows and timing our progress with the mechanical sweep of the cameras.

We reached a shadowed corner below the edge of a balcony some 8 feet above us. Hector and I put our backs to the wall and braced against each other for Paredo to climb us like a human trellis. It was a relief that he was able to use some of the brickwork to support himself, but his ungodly weight was amplified as he sprung upwards to grip the lower edge of the balcony. We had high-tech grapnels, but they were never truly silent.

Paredo hung from his fingertips, as Hector and I each scrambled up his dangling frame. In that moment, I better appreciated the physical modifications he had made to improve his grip strength. With barely more than a sigh of breath, Paredo hauled himself up and over the cast iron railing to crouch beside us on the first floor balcony. It was time to split up.

Paredo unholstered his suppressed agency-issue sidearm. Its matt black cylindrical silencer loomed darker than the night, ready to spit death in the face of anyone who got in our way. It was a Hollywood-created myth that guns could truly be silent, but this was as close as you could get. It used suppressed subsonic ammunition, similar to the Russian PSS silent pistol, where a clever mechanism kept the end of the case sealed after firing, so no gasses escaped - which is what creates much of the noise. The thick silencer screwed on to the barrel took care of the rest.

As Paredo set off in a crouch along the balcony, I boosted Hector up to the floor above us, then unholstered my own weapon and set off in the opposite direction.

As I ducked past windows, some lit and some dark, my implant flashed up camera feed images of the opulent rooms and corridors within, along with the map overlay and whereabouts of all tagged personnel.

The house was the private residence of a wealthy local banker, who had, for whatever reason, agreed to its use. As a result, the live-in staff were still present. I felt sorry for the chef, the two maids and the chauffeur, who had been dragged into this mess, as their names were not on the no-kill list. They had been forced to carry on about their duties as the home was taken over by hard men, who were no strangers to violence - and neither side would wish to keep them around as witnesses afterwards.

As I reached the darkened window I had been looking for, I unclipped one of my cargo pockets and pulled out the disk-shaped breaching tool I had been provided with. It was plain on one side, aside from a flexible handle, but the other had two concentric circles and a series of suction cups. I located the position of the window latch within and pushed the glass-breacher against the cool window pane nearby. There was a quiet hiss as the cups gripped the glass, then a piercing shriek as the device resonated the glass in a thin line to cut a circular section free. Paredo had warned me of the noise, which was in fact above the range of human hearing, but it still had me feeling as though it should have awoken half the neighbourhood.

The breacher came away cleanly, still gripping the severed portion of the window, which I discarded as I pocketed my gear.

'In position,' I siphoned to my brothers, as I reached through the hole and unlatched the window in anticipation of Hector's signal. Paredo's confirmation came soon after, but we were both waiting for Hector to clear the second floor.

My implant drew scattered impressions from Hector through the siphon-bridge as he breached a glass patio door and systematically worked his way through the top floor.

'Contact,' was all he siphoned to us as he dropped two armed men with as many silenced shots. The loudest noise his pistol made was the hammer hitting the firing pin and sound of the ejected brass shell casings hitting the wooden laminate floor. The clatter from the slumping bodies falling against

furniture and dropping their own guns was another matter, but Hector continued without a pause, as though he was on rails.

He had iced a total of 4 men, when I noticed Brett suddenly sit bolt upright in alarm. He looked up from the TV and turned to stare through the ceiling unerringly toward Hector's position, then scrabbled for his pistol, flicked off the safety and fired a round to sound a warning to everyone else in the building. I wasn't sure how Brett had detected Hector, but his actions would stir up a hornet's nest. A moment later, as shouts and walkie-talkie radio signals filled the mansion from every floor, Hector dropped out of our siphon-bridge.

My heart sank as everything unravelled before us.

I got the impression of a curse from Paredo an instant before he siphoned *'Weapons free. Clear this floor and secure Brett. I'll clear the ground floor and basement.'*

As I shoved the window open and vaulted inside, the outside flood lights were switched on from within the house, bathing the empty gardens. Well-trained men moved to create barricades or else search for intruders, most likely unaware that their every move was being broadcast through the property via the cameras and household appliances. I frantically tried to re-establish contact with Hector, but not only was he unresponsive, but he had now dimmed his implant signal as well.

I felt Paredo flare his own relic, as he broadcast to Sierene that we were here to extract her, but just like Hector, there was no response from her. It wasn't a good sign.

As I burst through the bedroom door and out into the corridor, I immediately had a fire-fight to contend with. At least 9 armed men occupied this floor and they were alert and ready to repel intruders. At the first instant of contact, they opened fire. Splinters of wood and showering plaster dust filled the air about me, as my implant had me sidestep the trajectory of incoming rounds. But these men may as well have been targets in a training simulator as my implant had me snap off return fire with lethal effect. I moved from room to room in pursuit of Brett and, one at a time, his fellow conspirators cut short their gunfire, snapping their heads back in macabre salute as my implant rewarded them with headshots.

I could detect the corresponding gunfire from below, steadily winking out in a wave, as Paredo strode over the bodies of the freshly fallen to reach his objective. He continued to call to Sierene, but I dismissed the impression as I entered a section of the house with very limited camera coverage. I had to concentrate and keep my wits about me.

Where a kitchen, dining room and home cinema joined a narrow atrium, I came upon Chinese military, fighting side-by-side with the CIA agents we had identified earlier. My pistol ran dry as some serious firepower from the Chinese obliged me to take cover. Brass shell casings clinked and skittered on the tiled floor of the kitchen as I hastily unslung my suppressed MP5 submachine gun. As I began to feel the edge of panic gnawing away at my training, my implant simply scanned my immediate surroundings, then laid the soldiers out by shooting a dozen rounds directly through the partition wall. The radio waves generated by the ionisation of their gunpowder had been enough to give away their position.

As I angled to look through the doorway, I saw that one Chinese soldier sprawled dead across the counter-top he had been standing behind, whilst the other lay to one side, moaning incoherently and bleeding out. I called to the spooks to lay down their weapons but the response I got was the telltale sound of the pin of a grenade being pulled, closely followed by another. Worse still, the bastards were cooking them before they threw them. My implant was already counting down the seconds as the two grenades came bouncing through the doorway and the kitchen door was kicked shut from within.

I was already moving before the two globes of death had come to rest, as my implant took over. It had me spray a line of bullets down the wall as I shoulder-barged the partition to burst through into a gallery of over-priced artwork. Thank goodness the stud wall gave way, because the double blast that followed was devastating.

What was left of the stud wall didn't do much to protect me. In the end, it was the Kevlar within my tactical suit that kept me alive. But even so, a piece of two by four had hit me with enough force that it drove the nails it bore deep into the back of my leg. I rolled over in the debris, coughing and trying to clear my eyes as the sound of sprinting footsteps fell away. I put thought toward my health and my implant helpfully displayed a diagnostic, showing that I was largely intact. It was only a minor injury, but it still made me wince as I gathered my gun and got to my feet. Up until now, I had been tackling this mission with relative calm, but this had made me angry. Brett was going to pay!

The dust began to clear, but as the receding footsteps had indicated, the spooks had retreated as soon as they had thrown the grenades and slammed the door in my face. Of course, they couldn't have known that they were on the do-not-kill list, but given their intimate knowledge of 'enhanced interrogation' techniques, they wouldn't have wanted to be captured either.

But it didn't matter. We had a positive ID and they could be picked up later on. My boots crunched broken glass and plaster as I pushed on through the first floor toward the staircase. I could only assume that Brett had made his way straight to Hector, as I hadn't spotted him on any of the other camera feeds.

The gunfire from below was now muffled, so I assumed that Paredo had cleared the ground floor and had breached the basement.

As I pushed on into uninhabited areas of the property, I paused only to swap out the extended magazine in my gun.

The stairway to the second floor came into view at the end of a short corridor. I say corridor, but it was more like a narrow conservatory, lined with comfortable cafe-style chairs and large potted plants. Tall windows overlooking another balcony and the gardens below, were interspersed with patio doors. Any other time, this area would have been a pleasant retreat in the warm Hong Kong evenings, but now it gaped ominously with just the illusion of cover.

As I began to advance, ahead of me I saw a set of boots begin to descend down the stairs from the floor above. My firearm came up reflexively, but after a second, the lower proportions of the figure were tagged as belonging to Hector by my implant. He strode down the stairs purposefully, with no indication of any caution. I anticipated his usual wolfish grin, but instead, he looked at me blankly and continued stair by stair. I automatically reached out with my siphon, but he was still dimmed against me. Something was badly wrong and no doubt Brett was entirely to blame.

My implant reacted before I did, bringing my gun up to unload a pre-emptive hail of lead in Hector's direction. But there was no way I could murder my brother-at-arms without even looking for another solution. So with all the will I could muster, I diverted the blazing barrel of my MP5 toward the windows, my finger tight on the trigger. As my eyes flicked back to Hector, I realised what my implant was reacting to. His hand was coming up, knuckles white on the grip of his pistol. Time slowed as my rounds hissed through the air, setting off a cascade of tumbling broken glass the length of the corridor as the windows shattered. I dove for the nearest window as Hector's subsonic pistol rounds tore through foliage in my wake. But there was no way I could avoid Hector's lethal accuracy.

My gun bucked in my hands as I clutched it in front of my chest as several of Hector's slugs flattened themselves against the powder-coated steel. The shock waves threatened to numb my fingers, but I was already rolling to my feet amidst the broken glass on the balcony and closing the ground between us as his clip emptied.

I vaulted the windowsill, back into the corridor through what was left of the window, but Hector flung his pistol at me and was already reaching for another weapon. His MP5 was gone, but as my boots crunched down and I thrust the foliage aside, he hunkered down into a combat ready position, brandishing a wicked 13 inch bowie knife.

I knew it was just a matter of seconds before my implant overrode my free will in order to eliminate this threat, but Hector was my brother. So although it may have been foolish and indeed beyond reckless, I hurled my gun away from me back down the corridor. My implant couldn't shoot him dead if I wasn't in possession of my gun.

As Hector advanced on me with a blank expression, I snapped out the stun baton I had selected for this mission. It wasn't cleverly weighted like the prototype I had practised with in Alaska, but Sericum's training had been very thorough in the use of this kind of weapon. But damn Hector's obsession with blades! He was like a magpie for shiny things and the near-shortsword he brandished was alarming to say the least.

My reluctance for combat almost cost me dearly in the first few seconds, as Hector's vicious opening flurry of slashes, stabs, punches and kicks encased me in a dynamic wall of threat and pain. My combat encounter earlier in the day had left me overconfident in my abilities, but Hector's forearms struck like crowbars and his kicks like battering rams. Even when I anticipated his blade, a failed slash or stab often resulted in him dropping it from one hand, only for it to be snatched up in midair by the other. Then it would be inbound again from an unanticipated direction. Even Chou would have been proud of him.

I took a slice across my ribs and a puncture to one shoulder before my elbow cracked across the bridge of his nose. I followed it up with a nasty head-butt, which slowed him enough for me to break off. But the respite was momentary, as like a machine, he dived back in with reckless abandon. Blood now poured from his nose, to trickle and drip from his chin, but he simply opened his mouth to breathe and advanced on me again with dead eyes.

As baton and knife whistled and parried, and our fists, feet, knees and elbows clashed like boulders in a landslide, our implants fought a war of their own. Hector's implant flared and suddenly we were wrapped in a raging sea of siphon energy as we wrenched at each other's implants and savaged each other's modules. The battle of our wills was like the flash and spark of static electricity between two Tesla coils, whilst our bodies raged like striking snakes.

Fortunately, I had the advantage of having more modules than Hector and my implant was faster. But every now and again, the perfect storm of combat and siphoning would either dim my vision or sap at my power, leaving me feeling sickened and disoriented.

But as my battle fury took hold and my implant managed to overwhelm Hector's, I struck the knife from his hand with a brutal wrap across the knuckles with my stun baton. Ignoring the pain, he went to catch it midair with the other hand, but I bull-rushed him and we both burst through a patio door to sprawl on the balcony amidst a shower of safety glass. I landed hard atop him and managed to jam the tip of my stun baton down the neck of his body armour and engage it. I knew his relic would eat up the worst of the electric current, but as he thrashed with the arcing discharge, the only thing I could think of was to scoop him up bodily and toss him over the balcony into the bushes below.

He landed ignominiously, a whoosh of air escaping from his lungs, but he was already struggling back to his feet and casting the stun baton aside as I turned from the balcony and rushed headlong toward the stairs. Brett couldn't be far away to be maintaining such control over Hector.

In my rage, I flared my implant until it felt like I was surrounded by a white-hot cloud of energy, then drew even harder from the siphon-bridge I still maintained with Paredo. To my eyes, my corona expanded even further, until I spotted a strangely dark patch above me. Handlers with control modules didn't give out a signature like standard relics, but something was absorbing the siphon energy I was blasting out in all directions. I caught a hint of Paredo's surprise mirroring my own, as I bounded up the stairs, three at a time, towards the dark spot in my vision.

As I rounded the corner, Hector's MP5, now in Brett's sweating hands, cracked the night with a vicious burst of gunfire designed to rend me from knee to skull. I was only missed by inches, but as I dared another look around the corner, Brett was already fleeing in the opposite direction. He gulped panicked breaths as he fired wildly behind him, not daring to slow his flight. He knew full-well what relics could do, and given that I had got past Hector, he wasn't going to let me get any closer.

Below us, I could feel Hector closing, as he made his way back into the building, so I threw caution to the wind and sprinted after Brett. As I ran, my body swayed aside and chose its footing carefully, as my implant assessed the constantly shifting angle of his weapon. Relics couldn't physically dodge bullets when fired up close, but through lightning-quick calculations of geometry and trajectory, our implants would evade the spots most likely to be struck when a gun was fired in our direction.

Unfortunately for Brett, he did not have implant-enhanced navigation and in his panicked headlong flight, he ran into a bedroom with no balcony and no way out. I pulled up short, anticipating further gunfire from Brett, when a triumphant Paredo siphoned to me that he had recovered Sierene.

'I have the package and it is secure. Agency support is inbound,' was all he said, but he was feeling well satisfied, so I knew Sierene was unharmed. We could both tell that Hector was converging on my location, but with Sierene vulnerable if left alone, there was nothing that Paredo could do to help.

My attention returned to Brett as I heard him readying his sidearm and checking how many rounds were left in his magazines. Not enough, I thought darkly. Every metallic chink and thunk he made with steel on steel only served to create an echo map for me.

As Brett hunkered down low in the corner of the room, guns in hand, the last thing he anticipated was my gloved fist bursting through the plasterboard to grab him below the chin and haul him backwards through the stud wall. His pistol fell from his grip and the MP5 emptied itself harmlessly in a wild spray as I rammed him by the throat into the floor. He tried to roll over dazedly, wheezing, his dark hair made grey by the plaster dust, but I gripped him by his lapels and hoisted him up against the wall.

The pungent stench of fear and urine filled my nostrils, as he lost control and pissed himself. It was only in looking down in disgust at the steady yellow stream falling from his leather loafers, that I realised I had lifted him a clear foot off the ground.

A proximity alert cut through some of my fury and drew my attention, as Hector entered the corridor behind me, walking with lethal intent.

"Call him off," I said, with genuine menace in my voice. But Hector continued to advance. A quick look over my shoulder showed he had retrieved his knife and that he clearly meant to use it.

"Call him off, God damn it!" I repeated, this time shaking Brett like a rag doll and planting his back against a different wall, hard.

The look of terror on Brett's face was real, as he looked down into the eyes of a lethal killing machine. But there was something more, another fear even greater.

"I can't! They'll kill my family!" He bleated pitifully, with the last of the wind in his chest.

I didn't properly register the importance of what he had just said, so intent was I on venting my fury and releasing my brother from Brett's sly control. He was on the no-kill list, but there was no directive against the use of excessive force.

Without conscious thought, I shifted my grip to clutch Brett by his throat with one hand and brought back my other with two fingers extended, ready to ram into his pudgy little cry-baby face. To this day, I don't know whether it was my own rage, or the compulsion of my implant, but God help me I would have done it if Brett hadn't issued further commands to Hector. As I readied myself for the cruel thrust of my fingers, Brett screwed his face up tight and flinched away, but a thin ribbon of orange force suddenly sprang into place between him and Hector, as he desperately siphoned for help. But instead of standing down, Hector suddenly bellowed and charged headlong towards us, his eyes wide with madness.

This fanned my fury to new heights and just like a bully snatching a jealously coveted toy from a smaller child, I mentally seized upon the orange thread between Brett and Hector and cracked it like a whip. With a savage flare of my implant, I ruthlessly yanked it from Brett's head like a pit-bull worrying a rat and visualised the connection turning to dust in the wind. There was no room for conscious thought, just bestial rage expressing itself through the super-technology of my implant.

Hector's bellow cut off as he sprawled to the floor mid-sprint, just feet away and lay there panting, whilst Brett fell limp in my grip. I turned back, to see his eyes rolled up in his head and blood coming from one nostril. His breath barely rattled in his throat.

My anger flowed out of me like an oil slick, leaving me empty, aside from the shame of my actions and my concern for Hector. What had I done? I didn't even know.

I hastily lowered Brett's senseless body to the floor and distractedly straightened his clothes, as though that would somehow make a difference. His heart still beat, albeit erratically, but horrifyingly, I could only detect trace levels of brain activity.

Our implants aren't able to determine precise thoughts in somebody's mind, but when in close proximity to a skull, we can still detect a swirl of electromagnetic activity and how it changes. It was just one of the many ways we could diagnose somebody's health status or state of mind. But as Hector began to stir with a groan and Paredo managed to coax him back into our siphon-bridge, I found that Brett's brain activity was gone.

Chapter 44

I felt terrible. What had I become? With a fit of temper, I had scrubbed a man's mind from his body. I had killed today, I had caused horrible injury in the heat of combat, but the cruelty of what I had done to Brett left me feeling sick.

With Brett's condition stable, I had forced myself to tend to Hector as he recovered and his weak smile was some consolation, despite him still clutching at his head.

'Thanks Homes,' he had siphoned through the bridge, conveying so much more than the words alone. It turned out that he had been consciously aware of everything as it happened, but Brett's orders had overridden his free will in every way. Hector had seen what I had done to avoid a fatal confrontation and was grateful to me. But more importantly to him, he was now free.

We sat around a stunning acid-etched brass table, made to look like an underwater scene involving a dolphin and her calf. The glass table top, representing the surface of the water, cleverly perched atop the sculpted sea mammals, resting on the points of fins, with the dorsal fin and back of the mother dolphin breaching it. We were in one of Sierene's private homes, which she had assured us was the most secure of her safe houses and off even the Agency's books.

Everything in this place was beautiful, not least the lovely Sierene herself. She was a figure to inspire lust in even a stone, but she almost glowed with a sense of peace and generosity. I knew much of her appeal came from body morphing taken to an art form, but even so, it was hard not to relax and enjoy her company. Like Sericum, she gave off waves of pheromones, far more than was natural, but she had a graceful and gentle way about her that disarmed even the most volatile.

She made you feel powerful and in control, yet inclined to follow her delicate suggestions as though they were your own. It felt good to somehow win her favour, as every smile she rewarded you with made your heart soar.

The bruise high on her temple was already fading as her relic-enhanced healing worked its magic. In all honesty, she was lucky that the blow hadn't killed her.

Although Hector was also conscious of the artificial and most likely non-exclusive nature of Sierene's charms, he was lapping up every moment of her company. I couldn't blame him, but I mentally stepped back. Let him have his day in the sun.

Despite my malaise of guilt, my subconscious mind was fickle like a butterfly and seeing Hector with Sierene was already dredging up unbidden thoughts of Jesse in Berlin, along with Sericum, I realised guiltily. Neither were right for me, and both would no doubt disapprove of my changing attitudes, but they both still had a forbidden allure that my mind had been toying with.

Paredo cleared his throat aloud as some of my stray thoughts hit the open forum of the siphon-bridge, much to my alarm and embarrassment. I coloured, adding to the amusement of Sierene and Hector, who laughed together conspiratorially.

"Back to business," Paredo began again. "Is everyone in agreement?"

The question hung pregnantly in the air between us. Sierene smoothed the expensive silk of her dress and took a delicate sip from a fine porcelain cup, apparently unaware of the hungry eyes upon her moist red lips and the shifting line of her pale and slender throat as she swallowed.

Hector's brown eyes broke away long enough to take in our small party of conspirators, sitting amidst the exquisitely tasteful finery of Sierene's home.

Paredo, Sierene and myself were already decided, but everything hinged upon Hector.

"Well Solus?" Paredo pressed again.

Hector let out a sigh. "OK. I owe you both. So I'll play along for now, but I can only take so much abuse. Don't keep me waiting."

The pretty smile on Sierene's lips in response, was enough to make Hector veritably glow through the siphon-bridge, and it was my turn to smile at his indiscretion.

Earlier, at the Mansion, as Hector lay groaning and as I fretted over both my actions and Hector's mental health, Paredo had hurried up to us, carrying a drugged and stunned Sierene with as much urgency as if the house had been on fire. She had been conscious, but in no fit state to walk, despite the assistance of her relic.

Paredo had felt what I had done to Brett with my siphon and had drawn upon the bridge to retrieve a full understanding in the form of my memories. He exuded such a sense of purpose and clarity, that when he had demanded that I held Brett upright next to me, I had woodenly obeyed.

I draped one of his limp arms over my shoulder, then stood, hauling his unconscious frame up alongside my own. I had been wondering if there were a better way to carry him when Paredo's pistol emerged from under Sierene's skirts and he put a slug through the centre of Brett's forehead.

I stood in shock, Brett's dead weight somehow even heavier. "Wha..." I managed to blurt, before Paredo cut me off.

"Drop him," Paredo said calmly. "You didn't kill him. I did."

I was about to rail at him for what he had done, but as the sound of vehicles converging on the mansion was overtaken by the sounds of Agents entering the property, he continued.

"You cannot be seen to have killed a handler, especially right after your last run-in with the Committee!"

But as he scanned for any cameras or listening devices in this part of the house, I sensed from the siphon-bridge that there was more that he wasn't saying.

"Trust me," he finished, "there is more at stake than you know. We will talk of this later." His eyes searched mine, before he reiterated through the bridge for emphasis, *'I killed Brett. Not you'.*

Paredo had handled the handover of the scene, including the prisoners he had taken in the basement, to the local Agency forces, whilst Hector, Sierene and I all did our best to overcome our recent traumas. But an hour and two vehicle changes later, we were in Sierene's private safe house.

Paredo wanted us to be entirely off the grid before discussing anything else, and even then he would only open up via a tightly monitored siphon-bridge.

'What I am about to divulge to you' he had begun, *'risks dozens of lives and could upset plans that have been decades in the making. But after the events of tonight, you need to know...'*

Paredo had told us of his bloody rise to prominence as the Lethal Hand of the Committee, earning the gratitude of many members by volunteering for missions that others would have baulked at. He explained that every relic, however miraculous, was just a glorified puppet, only tolerated because they completed even the most difficult tasks sent down from the Committee's table

He had shielded many of his peers from the darker tasks, but despite how high he had risen and how many favours he had done, he had hit a plateau. A relic, however talented, could never be on the same footing as a member of the Committee, because we were simply seen as tools to get a job done. We weren't there to think, let alone share in the rewards. We were there only to make the will of the Committee a reality, and with every relic at the mercy of their handler, we lived on a knife-edge.

I came to understand that however exalted (or detested) Paredo was seen to be by the other relics, he was still just another slave in the master's household. But more dismaying to him, was how schizophrenic and fragmented his orders had become as the Committee split down the middle over what to do in anticipation of the return of Nibiru.

But over the years, Paredo had been forming alliances - a secret network, if you will - in order to one day overthrow the yoke of oppression and to release mankind from under the boot heel of the elites. Yet he had never found a way to sever the command module from a relic without the death of the host of the relic. In fact, a relic could not deliberately kill a handler due to the inbuilt safeguards of relic programming. His ability to shoot Brett had been a complete surprise to him, as it should not have been possible.

'Tonight changed everything!' Paredo had exulted. *'We must take you back amongst your brothers and sisters, Lucidus. You must release them covertly, then when enough of us are free, we can overthrow our oppressors.'*

He didn't elaborate on what he would do with his new-found freedom, but his passion was contagious. Contagious to everyone except Hector. Hector was now free, (or as free as anyone could be whilst on the run from the Agency), but in order to give our plan a chance, he would have to return with us as a willing slave, maintaining the fiction of their control. He would have to tolerate the torments laid upon him by Hiram, until I was able to figure out how to covertly release our brotherhood. And that was assuming that I even could. Every newly released relic would risk exposing our plot.

The one saving grace was that Paredo's network had been divided into cells, so the discovery of any one conspirator could not immediately jeopardise all the rest.

Sierene was the head of one such cell and hearing her passion for Paredo's plan further emboldened me. This was a high-stakes endeavour, but I stood by my oath to Paredo and the brotherhood and would do my best.

Apart from anything else, I had already been pinioned by the merciless claws of the Committee and was lucky to escape with my life, so I knew I couldn't trust our fate to these power-hungry lunatics. They were madder than Paredo's plan!

So when Hector, the self-reliant loner he was, agreed to voluntarily continue his own captivity whilst we freed the rest of our brotherhood, our collective hearts sang.

Chapter 45

I found myself smiling at the memory in the darkness, as Decker and Darius came to inform me that the Titan series was under our control and was ready to be assisted back onto the metal gantry. Just as in those heady days of rebellion, there was an air of excitement building now. We had a new weapon in our fight against tyranny and it gave the men hope.

But as I crouched in dark ruins beneath a dead city, I couldn't help questioning the razor's edge that hope provided. The darker side of my soul, fed by decades of strife, sided with Nietzsche, who said that hope is the worst of all evils because it prolongs the torments of man. Yet as I watched my men working in concert to retrieve their prize, with smiles and laughter never far from the surface, I couldn't help but see the view from Samuel Smile's perspective. "Hope is like the sun, which, as we journey toward it, casts the shadow of our burden behind us."

"What was that?" Decker asked, turning towards me, a look of puzzlement on his lined face.

I didn't realise that I had even spoken aloud.

"Nothing," I responded. "Just something from another age. Let me help you with your new toy."

I joined the men and took hold of one of the ropes they had used to secure the stricken drone. We heaved in unison and, with the droid itself climbing, we soon had it safely away from the drop.

"I shall call it Deliverance", Decker drawled and the men about him excitedly buzzed their approval.

A few short minutes later, Deliverance was calibrated to recognise every man of our party by name, appearance, vocal recognition and smell. We didn't want any friendly fire accidents and this hulking android was the only member of our group that hadn't yet earned a position of trust.

Decker had Deliverance kneel and did his best to repair the illuminator and eye camera that I had blasted, but he was only able to replace the camera with a substandard alternative. The unit probably wouldn't have vision a great deal better than any of the men. The damaged hydraulics were more of an issue, but the unit was still mobile and had some 30 shells left in its midigun.

"It will have to do for the time being," Decker muttered under his breath as he worked, before stowing his tools.

We now had a choice. A set of heavy blast doors lay at either end of the roadway joining the end of the gantry. To the left, an 18 foot wide double door looked to lead back toward the under-city, so we concentrated our efforts on opening the 9 foot wide single door to our right.

The control panel beside the door, with its thick steel-reinforced keypad was functional, but the touch screen was cracked and the dialogue box it displayed was presented as crazed shards rather than a solid image. But when Decker hooked up a small console to interact with the security mechanism, none of it mattered. He hummed tunelessly under his breath as he worked, then nodded in satisfaction as he snapped shut and unhooked his console.

"Ready when you are, Chris," he offered up as he laid a callused hand on the keypad. "Deliverance had the access code," he added with a grin.

The other men fanned out cautiously and readied their weapons, as I gave Decker the go-ahead to raise the door. Nothing happened at first, but after a painful moment, a motor powerful enough to raise the thick, reinforced door squealed into life. It drowned out the noise of the cascading water to our backs, which only added to the tension.

Gaps began to appear in between the crenulations at the foot of the door and they widened as it lifted to reveal more darkness beyond. The air that it released smelled stale. As the door reached its apogee, the motor fell silent and we cast what light we had into the gloom.

The dust motes suspended in the air gave our torch beams texture, but despite this, as the tunnel within cut back into the dark bedrock, I could make out an open bay of vehicles on the right hand side and another large blast door ahead.

The door was stencilled with high visibility signage and authority logos were visible through the thick dust on the abandoned vehicles.

I had Deliverance take the lead as we entered, his long strides dwarfing our own. I followed a few paces behind, my senses alert for any sign of a threat, but we were alone. It seemed strange to be relying on a machine that only minutes before was trying to kill me.

"Facility 47," Darius read aloud, as we pulled up at the next set of doors. The others dispersed amongst the parked vehicles, where they also located the entrance to a small warehouse. Their roving flashlights caused the shadows to lurch and distort as they peered into the beds of pickup trucks and the backs of lorries. Their voices receded as they secured the area and hunted for supplies.

"I thought this was just supposed to be an A.I. substation," I queried with Darius, as I looked up at the vaulted rock ceiling and the painted doors ahead of us. "There was no mention of a fully fledged research facility down here."

"Judging by those cameras," I continued, pointing up towards a set of dented and scorched security cameras, which hung brokenly from their mounts, "we aren't the first to visit this place".

Darius didn't have an answer for me. The nav-band he bore contained the blueprint for the A.I. substation, but it didn't show whether the substation was within this facility, or whether it lay beyond it. The under-city stretched for many miles and had housed several million people at its peak. It contained hundreds of miles of tunnels. We couldn't afford to patrol them all.

"Alright," I said, coming to a decision. "We will check for supplies first, then we will make our way through this facility. If we are lucky, the substation will be here. If not, then maybe we will still find something of use. I am hoping those dead cameras mean that any other defences will be offline."

Even I could detect the hollow optimism in my words, but Darius and the other men nearby just nodded and took them at face value.

It wasn't long before a small stockpile of looted equipment and supplies was mounting up in front of the doors. Flares, ammunition, spare boots, and even some small remotely operated surveillance drones now lay atop boxes of long-life ration packs and out-of-date medical supplies.

Decker was pleased to have found some more ammunition and ordnance for his new Mech, along with some heavy duty body armour designed to enable a drone operator to travel more safely with their drone unit into hot zones. It was too heavy to wear on foot, but the harness and saddle for Deliverance to carry him with were unfortunately missing.

Clearly, the majority of the supplies would have to remain here until we left, but with Deliverance to help carry it, we stood some chance of taking it home with us after the mission.

My men pocketed and stowed any portable supplies, then assembled in front of the facility doors whilst Decker went to work on breaching the security. I was frustrated that I couldn't assist with my implant, but there was no point in wishing it were otherwise.

To a man, it made us all jump when a loud claxon sounded and the area in front of the doors was thrown into orange relief by a rotating hazard beacon mounted high on the rock face above us.

The doors were almost as noisy as the claxon, so between the two, our hopes of entering the facility quietly were blown away. This time, the steel doors parted in the centre and withdrew into the face of the building on great geared rails. Within, automatic lights flickered ominously, before firing into life one at a time. Some worked, some didn't and some continued to blink and buzz distractingly as the way before us was illuminated. Our night vision was all but destroyed by this unanticipated lighting, but we could now see at least 100 yards into the facility. Several of my men grunted in surprise. It was big.

Whatever this place was, it had been important. We cautiously entered the outer gates and Chavez and Petersen broke off to search the security office which lay immediately within the gates. A wide bulletproof observation window and a console of coloured buttons overlooked a metal barrier which was currently raised for pedestrian access, but 4 thick retractable posts protruded from sockets in the floor to prevent the passage of vehicles. It turned out that the security office was large enough to house 10 men on duty, including bunks and wash facilities to enable 24/7 operation.

Disturbingly, long-dried dark brown blood stains and drag marks were visible within, along with abandoned firearms, but there were no bodies to be seen. Whoever had been here, they were long gone.

It seemed that none of my men were too keen to press ahead along the main avenue without the rest of the group, so as I quietly conferred with Petersen about the blood stains, several men made a show of studying the large printed map of the facility, which was helpfully fixed to one of the walls of the tunnel. Its smaller cousin was mounted on the wall of the security office, but with the addition of coloured LED lights embedded in it to provide a status report at a glance. All the bulbs were dark.

I noticed that there was no reference to any A.I. substation, but four floors below us a robotics lab was listed. Many of the other areas were just identified as different 'sectors', each with their own colour, but the robotics lab was specifically mentioned by name. This was worth a look.

I was about to leave the security office when Chavez opened a gun cabinet under one of the counters and let out a low whistle.

"Hey boss," he called, "they left behind some nice hardware." He smiled as he reached in a gloved hand and pulled out a military issue AA-12 full auto shotgun and laid it on the counter top with a thump. This was soon followed by two drum magazines of 32 cartridges.

Both Petersen and I raised an eyebrow as more guns joined the first. Chavez was right. This was specialist equipment and not the kind of thing that would be used to guard a two-bit supply depot.

I knew first-hand what these rare guns could do. On full auto, they could fire five 12- gauge blasts a second, even soaking wet. They were constructed out of seven different types of steel and required no oiling or cleaning. Better yet, a clever spring mechanism in the stock meant the weapon had almost no recoil. Just point and kill - perfect to turn a guard or two into a small army in a confined space.

As I fitted one of the drum magazines and tossed the shotgun out to Decker, it conjured up memories of the first time

I had used one - as I fought my way clear of an ambushed convoy in Fallujah.

Decker caught it deftly in both hands and set about slinging it over his Titan's massive shoulder. I had no doubt that Deliverance would be loaded up like a pack animal before the day was done.

I was about to toss the next gun out of the door when a commotion amongst the men caught my attention, so instead, I shouldered the weapon and stepped outside.

To my left, I saw that Stephens, a short red-headed bull-dog of a man was already walking the main avenue, peering left and right through the wire-glass facility windows and checking the doors which lined the tunnel. But that wasn't the issue.

Several of the men were pointing back the way we had come and hushing each other. I was about to ask what the problem was when I heard for myself. A deep metallic thudding had begun on the double blast door linking to the under-city. Somebody, or more realistically, something, was beating on the other side of the blast doors.

My ears were better than theirs and it seemed to me that there was perhaps more than one source of the sound. I suppose it wasn't surprising. The fire-fight with the Titan series and the squealing motor opening the blast doors, followed by the claxons when we entered the facility, were all loud enough to wake the dead. The motorised doors could also have sent vibrations through the bedrock for miles. The question was, what kind of population was around to hear it. With the noise we had been making over the last half hour, there had been time to draw nearly half the remaining population of the under-city.

I was reluctant to risk sealing us in, but by the same token, I didn't want us to have any unwanted surprises to our back.

"Decker," I called, "see what you can do to shut the gate between here and the gantry. Take Murrin and Finch with you."

Decker nodded and set about his task, albeit with a light sheen of perspiration on his furrowed brow and an elevated heart beat. I stood to one side of the doorway, watching them go, followed by the hulking chromed figure of Deliverance.

The remaining men filed in and out of the security office, accepting additional firearms from Chavez and Petersen. There were only four more of the military shotguns, with a total of 7 drum magazines, but a few pistols and some 9mm ammo also found their way into pockets and packs.

Decker and his men were only half way to their objective when the strobing thunder of Deliverance's forearm canon lit up the darkness. The 50 calibre shells arced across my vision like tracer rounds on night vision goggles and in the momentary muzzle flash, I caught the impression of several ragged figures flying apart in a gory spray of body parts and entrails. Some of the 'lost' were in the caverns with us!

A curse erupted from me as I shouldered past the men too slow to get out of my way. "Defend the gate," I yelled. "...and look for the controls," I added as I unslung my shotgun at a full run. I didn't look back as their own curses faded behind me.

As I pressed forward, I could tell that this fresh gunfire had stirred up a fearsome clamour from behind the far blast door, but if some sub-culture had found its way in another way, then who knew how many could be following now.

"Abort! Abort!" I called to Decker and his men as I pursued. I couldn't have him tussling with the infected or psychotic denizens of the under-city, especially when our whole mission hinged upon his ability to hack the A.I. sub-station. He was irreplaceable.

As I neared, I could see several more ragged creatures barrelling towards us at full tilt, the bloodshot whites of their crazed eyes contrasting with their filthy faces. They wailed and howled incoherently, their gaping and snarling mouths rotten with whatever filth they had been scavenging. The only saving grace was that their emaciated condition limited their speed.

The 'lost' citizens of the under-city didn't usually congregate, as they were as likely to turn on each other in their rabies-induced madness, but we had drawn them with our activity.

Finch didn't need telling twice and turned tail, but at least Murrin had the presence of mind to attempt a rear-guard action as he covered Decker's retreat. My boots stirred up a cloud of rock dust as I skidded to a stop.

Past the armoured flanks of the Titan series, I could see more filthy figures emerging from the gantry. They must have found the same way in that we had. We should have closed the door behind us, but I hadn't trusted these neglected mechanisms. Besides, I was a big fan of leaving myself an exit.

Not all of the 'lost' citizens that followed were mad with sickness, but that only made matters worse as they hung back, awaiting their chance to kill, rob and feed. Some were still smart enough to open the doors we put in between us, but I fervently hoped they wouldn't be foolish enough to open the blast doors to whatever was trying to beat its way in.

I knew that as we retreated, we would lose the advantage that the bottleneck of the tunnel provided, but pressing forward would be a disaster for my men if the number of infected continued to swell. Our gunfire and their caterwauling would only steadily draw more and I couldn't risk my small band coming into contact with fresh contagion. A bite, or any stray drop of blood in an open wound or orifice, was a death sentence which would have to be served down here in the grim uninterrupted darkness.

"See what you can do with the facility gate controls," I called over my shoulder to Decker, whilst trying to maintain some semblance of calm in the face of the rising panic behind me. "Then have Deliverance broadcast his camera feed, " I added as an afterthought.

It helped to have a second set of eyes in the heat of combat, but it wasn't anywhere near as important as putting 4 inches of hardened steel in between us and the growing rabble ahead.

A milling mass of wretched figures was building in the darkness of the gantry. The echoes of their footfalls on the steel projected disturbing impressions of deformed limbs and grotesque leering faces, as they squabbled amongst themselves and pressed toward us. At this range, the micro-echoes didn't provide much detail, but it was enough for my implant to superimpose dark sockets where eyes and mouths should be.

Some of the wretches were already pounding on the inside of the gantry doors, irrationally enraged by the sound of their kin on the other side, but those with more awareness were meddling with the keypad.

I took aim and eviscerated two more screeching runners with my newly acquired shotgun, as the mechanised defence drone steadily retreated to stay close to Decker. Decker had taken it upon himself to programme in such priorities, but I was glad he had.

The spread of the 12-gauge shot made it harder to pick off the sickened misfits near the control panel, but I still took eyes, limbs and the tops of skulls from this distance. But every muzzle flash and corresponding boom served to enrage the milling denizens even more. They seemed to be building up to critical mass. There must have been upwards of 80 of them now, with clusters of four or five intermittently breaking off to charge us.

As Deliverance retreated, it was like a dam breaking. A trickle of infected freaks was becoming a stream, and I knew the stream would soon become a torrent, then a wave. I simply didn't have the ammunition to stop it. As it was, the stench of their filthy bodies was already rolling over me.

I took out several sprinting banshees as I backed up, their wild and matted hair streaming behind them as they ran. With my slow pace, I risked getting isolated from my men, but the further I retreated, the harder it was to clear the infected from the blast door keypad - and the more attention it was getting.

I risked a glance over my shoulder and saw, to my relief, that the men had largely finished dragging our supplies into the facility and that three brave men were closing the gap between us to help with the rearguard action. I was down to less than a third of my magazine and the milling masses were getting more and more agitated by the smell of blood and death in the air. Fights were breaking out and they were becoming even more enraged by the cacophony of gunshots.

Darius was one of the relief party and he pulled up with a fierce grin, before cracking off half a dozen blasts into a small group that was beginning a charge, emboldened by their sheer numbers. As the others opened fire, he was forced to yell that Decker was still working on the gate controls.

There was no doubt about it, the muzzle flashes were drawing the 'lost' like moths to a flame and they were losing any semblance of calm as the noise and crush of bodies pushed them into a frenzy.

We picked up the pace, but all chances of an orderly retreat vanished with the harsh screech of grinding metal as the electric motors fired up and pitted steel doors beyond the gantry began to open. One of the infected had either got lucky, or else they had retained enough faculties to deliberately open the floodgates to their diseased kin.

Before the blast doors were even a foot apart, a monstrous bellow split the night, its echoes reverberating around us, as a great brawny arm reached through the gap to savage the poor wretches unlucky enough to be within reach.

During the authority purges, different strains of infection had been released. Haemorrhagic fevers, which had proved to be far too indiscriminate to control, had been shelved in favour of genetically engineered rabies viruses, which pushed even the most mild mannered to extreme violence. Later iterations included an additional pathogen which ate away at the part of the brain associated with satiety, leaving the victims with unquenchable and unbearable hunger. I suppose this accounted for the variation in behaviour amongst the masses in front of us, but the pièce de résistance of the authority scientists was emerging from the doors ahead, with a shamble of infected following close behind.

In a botched attempt to create super soldiers, they had created a man-made virus that specifically targeted the endocrine system. In just days it forced the pituitary gland of otherwise healthy individuals to trigger a massive growth spurt, along with great volumes of testosterone and adrenaline to create super-compensated musculature and extreme aggression. This had been experimentally combined with mutagenic viruses which could force the expression of latent DNA with devastating consequences. What scientists used to call 'junk DNA,' was in fact the instructions left over from millions of years of evolution. It wasn't junk, it just wasn't being expressed because it wasn't necessary for our survival. We don't need horns, beaks, scales, feathers or whatever other remnants our own evolution has left behind. But tell that to the mad scientists who had created these horrors.

The one saving grace was that these beasts only had a limited lifespan before their biological changes killed them, and that those they infected with their bites were usually killed by the encounter.

The brute that forced itself between the doors redefined the name. I had experienced all manner of sub-culture, but nothing quite so monstrous. Jed, the infected engineer who had opened the way for us earlier, would have appeared slight in comparison to the towering mutant that bulled his way into the crowd, sending bodies flying.

"Run!" I barked, as it swept up a filthy, bare-chested female from the crowd and clamped its jaws down between her neck and shoulder.

I heard collarbone and ribs give way like snapping twigs, as her muffled shriek subsided to wet gurgles. But the brute cast her dying remains to one side in fury, as my men made the mistake of targeting it with their fire. Smaller wretches were swept aside or trampled underfoot as it recognised the origin of its pain and rampaged toward us, its bloody face a livid purple with infection and fury.

Its monstrous gait, augmented by two long, thick arms, enabled it to cover the ground like a gorilla at twice the rate that we could. So despite only having 40 yards between us and the facility gates, my implant alerted me that we wouldn't make it in time, let alone get the door closed.

In their panic, my men ran directly towards the gate, obstructing the covering fire that was coming from the facility.

"Run wide! Run wide!" I yelled as I saw the danger.

Darius angled across to myself as we sprinted all out, and Fenwick pushed to the other side. But in his blind panic, Norris carried on towards what he believed to be safety.

The force of men at the gate were frantically waving for him to clear their line of fire, but their gunshots were now only sporadic at best, for fear of clipping us.

Fortunately, as I made ready to turn and empty my magazine into the charging brute, Deliverance stepped out of the crowd and lit up the darkness with the rushing rip of midigun fire and a salvo of grenades from his secondary hard points.

Norris sprawled in panic, swiftly coming to his hands and knees. He scrambled under the flow of firepower which was clearly designed to miss him. Darius rushed to drag him out of the line of fire, as I skidded to a halt and emptied my last dozen cartridges of buckshot into the tattered wall of flesh behind us.

I turned in time to see the brute pin-wheeling as one of his arms was blown from his shoulder and as his chitinous flank was opened from hip to nape by shrapnel. More than forty of his frail brethren were laid low behind him, with many more taking horrific injury.

As Deliverance emptied his canon, it took the brute's varicosed and weeping legs out from under it and gave us the time we needed to get within the tenuous security of the facility.

The reassuring mass of the blast doors was already shifting with a squeal of gears and unlubricated metal as my men cleared a hole for us. Decker had timed it perfectly.

"Get in here!" He bellowed at the drone, who still stood with his back to us. "Double time!"

As Deliverance turned his grinning steel skull towards us and hustled his colossal bulk between the closing doors, the orange glow of fire behind him reflected the pressing mass of bodies. Those who were unhurt, or those who had shrugged off their injuries, were already feeding on the spray of flesh adorning the tunnel floor - their grasping hands gratefully pressing wet globs of unthinkable matter into their chomping mouths.

The brute still shifted weakly in its own viscera, but as the blast doors sealed with a dull boom of finality, the image of the wretches moving in to feed left me with an icy cold in my belly.

Chapter 46

My men were pale-faced at this turn of events, but several gave relieved pats on the back to Norris, who was standing bent forward with his hands on his knees, panting. Others praised Darius for his bravery in ducking under Deliverance's fire to help him. The truth was, they had all stuck their necks out for me, so I added my thanks.

Decker fussed about the Titan series, inspecting it for damage and attempting to re-arm it with the meagre supplies we had remaining. Unfortunately, we were now out of the 50 calibre rounds the droid needed and its thick metal fingers were too big to fit through the finger guard of most standard firearms.

The moans, hooting and squabbling outside was still just audible through the door, but with the smorgasbord of flesh available, none of the infected former citizens were directly troubling us. That wouldn't last.

Some of the more timid men were already fretting about our situation and spreading their anxiety to the others, so I gathered them all together.

"Hush. Settle down," I began. I waited patiently for quiet. There was still a buzz of conversation amongst the men, but the most disciplined waved them to silence.

"When Decker has locked down the facility door, we need to secure this floor. According to the map, lower levels can only be accessed by a main stairway, a smaller secondary stairway and the main service elevator. At the other end of the Avenue, there is another blast door and on the floor below us there are several passenger elevators."

As I paused to draw breath, Stephens cleared his throat and stepped forward. He was a head shorter than the men around him, but made up for it with his fearless attitude. In fact, his fiery temperament was only matched by his fiery hair. I nodded to give him permission to speak.

"I didn't see any sign of life." His voice was low and steady. "There's nothing but undisturbed dust along this avenue and the far door is closed and it's going nowhere. The control panel has been sabotaged. It's a mess of wires. Some joker has pulled its guts out."

I anticipated the exclamations from some of the other men and ploughed over the top of them.

"Thanks Stephens. Okay listen up everyone. Decker, make sure we can keep control of the facility door. We don't want any surprise visitors. When you're done with that, take a look and see if there's anything you can do with what's left of the other control panel. We may need another way out." Decker gave a sloppy salute and a grin in acknowledgement.

"Finch, Williams and Harris, secure and guard the doors to the two sets of stairs and the elevator," I continued. "No heroics! Keep it quiet and watch our backs whilst we consolidate our position. Murrin and Petersen, stay with Decker and watch his back. The rest of you, I want two teams of three to investigate and clear the rooms on this level. Nobody goes off alone." I made eye contact with the men in turn, to reinforce this point.

Satisfied, I looked back at the map and pointed. "Start with the mess hall and kitchens. I want to know if we can rely on any more supplies. Then move on to the stores and goods inwards. I think we can just seal the laundry, the sports hall and gym... and the conference rooms. I don't want any casualties. Don't take chances and do not leave this level."

The men nodded and broke off in groups to carry out the plan. As Darius was turning to go, he handed me another drum magazine for my shotgun.

"That's the last of them." He said, looking more serious than usual. "What are *you* going to do?"

Darius was a smart cookie. The only areas on this floor that I hadn't mentioned, were the toilets, the briefing suites and the offices. I assume he wanted to know my whereabouts in case anything happened to me, so I put his mind at ease.

"I am going to clear the bathrooms. We don't know how long we are going to be staying here. Then I'm going to see if I can dig up any history on this place via the offices. I don't want us stumbling into more than we bargained for downstairs."

I think the men felt better with some clear direction and over the next couple of hours, everyone did as they were asked. The dust had been a reliable indicator and there were no hazards on this floor. That's not to say that there weren't any nasty surprises. The men made such good progress that we did decide to investigate the other areas on this floor. It was much as you would have expected, except for the sports hall which had been used as some kind of emergency triage area. Besides the medical tents and scattered gurneys, row upon row of sealed black body bags covered the basketball court. In fact, there were so many bodies that at one end, they had started to pile them.

Peering through the wire-mesh and glass observation window onto the dark scene, Williams, the nearest we had to a medical officer amongst us, wouldn't even allow us to open the doors. There was simply too much risk of contagion. Instead, Chavez dead-bolted the doors, top and bottom, and zip tied the handles together using some of the polyalloy ties we had discovered in the store room. Goodness only knew why they needed such strong zip ties.

Whilst my men had been gathering more ration packs, ammunition, universal power supplies and tools, I had discovered very little of interest in the offices. Any consoles which could be fired up were either too heavily encrypted to hack, or else only contained mind numbing trivia such as rotas for staff, inventories, logs of deliveries or requests for further supplies. It was a frustrating waste of my time. The only thing of value, was the personal records detailing the extensive roster of scientists who had worked at this facility.

Having secured this floor, I gave my men a half-hour to rest and eat before we pressed on. Finch took Decker his food, as he preferred to work through and complete the rewiring of the control panel. There was no way of knowing if his efforts would be successful, without actually attempting to open the door, but when he was satisfied, he returned to the group with his escort. Deliverance's steel heels and toes clicked and scraped at the concrete as he walked. He now bore an energy rifle which had had its finger guard removed by one of the men. I smiled at that. It looked a toy in his oversized hands, but with the aid of a laser sight, Deliverance had been able to calibrate his accuracy without drawing any more unwanted attention. At least he wouldn't have to reload the weapon. But with his prodigious size, how he would fare in the confines of the lower levels, was yet to be seen.

Rather than chance the noisy service elevator, we worked our way down through the facility via the smaller emergency staircase. I reasoned that if there were to be a press of howling bodies to contend with, at least they could only come at us four or five abreast. Auto lights came on as we passed each section of stairway down to the floor below. The next floor, labelled as Level 1, was technically several stories below, but this deep underground, it was standard practice for engineers to allow plenty of bedrock to provide support and prevent cave-ins. As we emerged into the new floor, the auto lighting system continued to follow us from corridor to corridor. Having grown to appreciate the bright light after so long in the oppressive darkness, my men were initially disconcerted when the lights would wink out behind us to conserve power, leaving our trail in the pitch dark. It was a duel-edged sword. On one hand, we felt the fragile reassurance that anything warm-blooded would trigger the lights, alerting us to their presence. But on the other, this meant that the facility security system was keeping tabs on our location at all times.

Level 1 was clear, as far as the network of corridors were concerned, but each section housed a separate, self-contained block accessed solely through a large set of reinforced steel doors. Above each door, a trio of armoured security cameras mutely surveyed all possible approaches simultaneously. Large biohazard warning signs were stencilled on some of the walls and that certainly deterred us from meddling with the digital keypads beside the doors. It was anybody's guess what pestilences lay within and we certainly weren't here for a nasty case of the pox or a dose of rabies.

Having established that this level was secure enough to put at our backs, we pressed down through the eerie silence to the floor below. Level 2 was as silent as a crypt. If it wasn't for the whine of Deliverance's servos and the breath and heartbeats of my men, I would just have been left with the sonorous rumble produced by the earth itself.

The layout was very similar to the floor above, except one of the sectors was stencilled with warnings of high voltage and another warned of corrosive chemicals. Some sectors bore no warnings at all.

"What the heck were they doing in this place?" Darius wondered aloud, no doubt voicing what we all felt.

One of the sectors labelled with biohazard warnings had the addition of yellow biohazard tape zigzagged over the entire face of the steel door. A dark and crusty trail of dried blood petered out as it led away in a drunken swerve from the door, but a gore-caked claw hammer lay abandoned on the floor below a smashed touch screen used to access the lab.

"So, we aren't the only people down here," I mused out loud. Several of my men shifted uncomfortably, so I added, "this blood is old, but stay sharp."

Just like in any horror film from before the collapse, the worst part was the tension. Every stifled cough, or inadvertent scuff of a boot put us on edge. Occasionally the overhead ventilation ducts and air-vents would tick and click as the auto lighting also triggered the activation of the ventilation system. The sound of scuttling on one such occasion, had my men shining lights up toward the metal ducting as they readied their arms or sighted down their barrels.

Stephens blithely dismissed it as rats, which could be deadly enough if they were former inmates of a bio weapons lab, but I wasn't so sure. To my implant-enhanced ears, the gait didn't sound right as it receded from us.

As we ventured hesitantly down to Level 3, I caught traces of decay in the air, along with the pungent ammonia-laden scent of animal waste. This was most definitely fresh. We still had several flights of stairs to cover, so I warned the men. We did our best to advance quietly, but with Deliverance's motors and joints whining and creaking at every step, it was next to impossible.

When we finally reached Level 3, we were greeted by a widening of the corridor. At the far end, the stairs continued downwards to Level 4, but to our left was a wide set of wired-glass windowed double doors and to our right was an industrial storage area with a battered roller shutter. The shutter itself had been abandoned in a part-open position, it's chains hanging still and long-forgotten. Beneath the dusty shutter, a two-foot high rectangle of darkness gaped at us eerily, defying the auto lights which buzzed and ticked above us.

My men fanned out and more than one, including myself, cautiously took a knee to shine a light under the door, but it only revealed four bare concrete walls and some broken cabinets and racking. What little was left in the storage area looked to have been trashed.

But my attention was drawn by the hiss of an intake of breath as several of the men eyeballed the view through the windowed double doors opposite.

"Over here," came a harsh whisper from Chavez, who made some room for me amongst the growing crowd who were now staring through the thick wire-reinforced glazing.

Even with the strong scent of life and decay, I was just as surprised by what I saw. As far as the eye could see, which admittedly was only a few hundred yards, lay massively overgrown aquaponics systems in a vaulted cave. This level was much more open plan and great vats of flowing water, presumably containing edible fish, fed the roots of rack after rack of overgrown vegetation. Banks of red and blue LED lights illuminated the system to provide optimal growing conditions for both flowering and fruiting, and this created a strange purple glow to the scene, which distorted the perception of colour.

Gangly tomato vines laden with fruit, (both ripe and rotten), vied with dwarf fruit trees, beans, peas, pumpkin and squash, to outcompete each other and smother the lighting. As we watched, a great fan clicked on and began to jostle the foliage with its breeze. A moment or two later some form of timered mechanism kicked in and across each of the water tanks, dried feed was automatically dispensed for whatever fish still resided in the system. The sound of frenzied splashes over the bubbles of the pumps indicated aquatic life still survived down here, if it didn't flourish.

I had seen similar systems, albeit a little more polished, in the homes of the wealthy elite. Some of the more advanced systems were almost entirely automated for the production of food. Fish food was blown from a three-ton silo through a network of pipes using compressed air at regular intervals. Edible freshwater fish then fed on the food, creating waste as they grew. Plants were grown in soil-less pots, their roots exposed to the water as it bubbled through pumps to aerate it. It was in perpetual symbiosis. Through the action of bacteria in the system, the fish waste became perfect plant food and as the plants grew and produced food at unprecedented rates, it cleaned the water, ready to return it to the fish tank. Some of these systems were capable of producing thousands of pounds of fruit and vegetables, and hundreds of pounds of fish.

After decades of optimising such systems underground, I knew that many new perennial strains of plants, (that were capable of producing year after year), had been developed, but although the vegetation spilled out into the gangways knee-deep, this system could not have been left entirely unsupervised for more than two or three years.

Movement caught my eye as some form of winged insect zipped past the glass of the window at speed. It was close enough to make me flinch. Honey bees had virtually died out by 2025 due to the pervasive use of neonicotinamide pesticides, so I had wondered how they were able to pollinate all of these plants below ground without manual intervention. Obviously, some other form of engineered insect was doing the job. As I observed the scene and tuned into the natural rhythms and sounds of this new environment, I began to pick out the occasional sound of insect wings beating and wondered why I hadn't picked up on it before. Perhaps it was the fact that I naturally associated bees and insects with the 30 plus different staple foods that relied upon them for pollination.

The sight of fresh produce after subsisting for so long on dried ration packs made my mouth water, but with the area still unsecure and inhabited by an unknown species, (and who knew what else), I opted to stick to the task at hand.

The other men around me were also eyeing the fresh produce hungrily. Norris even went so far as to push one of the doors open a few inches, before I pulled it back shut again with a bang. He went from looking surprised, to disgruntled, in just a matter of heartbeats.

"What my Helena wouldn't do for a fresh apple," he began as justification, before I cut him off.

"Stay out of there for now," I warned. "There's something else in there. I can smell it." It only just hit me as I uttered the words. There was something alien and unknown to the scent of waste I was getting.

"Besides," Williams added with a grin, "if those are GMOs, Helena won't thank you for giving her infertile offspring and shrivelled organs."

Norris seemed affronted, so I did my best to pacify him. "Look Norris, we need to scope out the robotics lab down on

Level 4. You stay here with Stephens and investigate this floor with one of the remotely operated surveillance drones, ready for when we come back this way."

I stretched out a hand to Decker, who huffed and begrudgingly dropped a heavily laden rucksack from his shoulder and began to pull at items and tip them out onto the staircase.

"Watch your feet!" he fretted, as one or more of the men stood too close to the precious contents.

After a moment, he handed me a drone which was not a great deal larger than a hen's egg, with a corresponding wrist band. I put the wrist band on and stroked it with a finger. In a similar fashion to Darius' nav-band, a holographic interface appeared above my wrist. A few finger strokes later and the soft, folded polymer wings of the drone were extended, ready for flight. I checked the camera feed, before opening the door a crack and tossing the surveillance drone through. It automatically took flight and self-levelled, awaiting further instruction.

Norris still looked offended, but when I handed him the band and patted him on the back, his scowl lifted a touch.

"Don't go in there until we get back," I reiterated, as I jammed a heavy duty flashlight through the handles to hold the door closed. "We may be in a hurry when we come back. It depends on what we find."

Both Stephens and Norris nodded, then made way for the other men to pass by them on the staircase.

As the rest of us filed deeper into the bowels of the facility, a backward glance showed Norris frowning in concentration at the holographic display emanating from the wrist band, his thinning hair falling limply across his forehead. Stephens was pressing close to the door to peer through at the mysterious garden within, his breath misting the glass.

Decker had put Deliverance in the lead and his chromed feet clicked as they bit into the concrete steps with every stride. His enormous gait caused the men to walk wide of him and I could tell that several were concerned about the amount of noise his servos and motors were making. It was a tough choice between firepower and stealth, but with the auto lights flicking on as we entered each new section of the facility, it was a moot point.

I did my best to relax as my implant assimilated the images coming from Deliverance's camera feed and as it fleshed out a three-dimensional echo-map using the taps and crunches of his unforgiving footfalls.

The stairway was relatively sterile, with little but our own tension to break the monotony, until we happened upon some long-abandoned signs of combat. Brass shell casings and spent cartridges littered the stairs and bullet holes and buckshot peppered the walls. It was strange, because the fire appeared to only go one way. Downwards.

It wasn't clear at first whether this was the result of an attack pressing forward, or someone beating a retreat, but the deeper we journeyed, the more dramatic was the level of damage to the facility walls, floor and ceiling.

But as we came to the foot of the stairs, onto the landing of Level 4, the large stencilled signs for the robotics lab were upstaged by a great barricade. It was like a scrap yard of junk and broken furniture. Broken steel cabinets, metal racking, crates and assorted other items were jumbled into a ceiling-high pile, all held together by great billowing clouds of expanded foam. Judging by the wreckage, dozens of canisters of biohazard containment foam had been thrown amongst the framework and punctured with buckshot. The ground was littered with spent shotgun cartridges and empty cans, some intact and some just warped wreckage from their detonation.

I ignored the expletives and curses coming from my men as I approached the pile. It spanned from floor to ceiling and didn't present any obvious gaps. We had reached a dead end.

"What were they trying to keep in?" Darius wondered aloud as he came to stand alongside me. I had been wondering the same thing.

He rested a booted foot on the base of the barricade as he pushed and jabbed at the foam with the barrel of his rifle. The scrapes and taps he made showed it to be rock solid.

"Do that again," I said, as the resulting vibrations and sounds he created within the structure gave me a greater impression of what lay within. In my mind's eye, my implant constructed, then deconstructed the contents of the mound, to a distance of about 9 feet. It calculated the path of least resistance, if we were to use Deliverance to carve a route through, but my attention was drawn to the large ceiling-mounted air ducts which appeared to continue down the corridor through the mass of solid foam and steel.

I pointed out the weak spots to Decker, as I shrugged off my pack and began to scale the face, using the protruding and jutting pieces of steel for hand and foot holds. The foam was very smooth to the touch, as it had only microscopic pore sizes created by the expanding gas within, but there were enough jutting edges to help me reach the metal ducting above.

Decker tossed me a cutting torch, so rather than unscrew the nearest vent on the side of the ducting, I just sliced through the corners and it fell clear with a clatter. Some of the men flinched at the noise, but the hastily constructed foam monstrosity would stop the sound from travelling any further into the facility.

As I craned my neck to peer into the square void of the ductwork, I was greeted by two surprises. One was the persistent ammonia-laden sent of animal waste that I was growing accustomed to and the other was a messy trail of spliced wires, which ran like errant tree roots along the length of the duct. The multicoloured patchwork of cabling snaked off in both directions and from the electromagnetic cloud which followed the same path, I knew the cables and wires were live.

When I described what I was seeing, Decker tried to hand me his remaining surveillance drone, but I refused it and instead boosted myself up into the narrow confines of the crawlspace. The senses possessed by his drone would be too limiting. I needed to see for myself what lay ahead of us and so I said as much. The breeze running through the duct was noticeable now and even more so, when my body almost blocked it. As the air whistled by me, it carried sounds that had been too subtle to pick up before. I ignored the complaints and mutterings from some of my men as I eased forward on elbows and toes. The duct wasn't tall enough for much more than a prone slither.

Before I was out of reach of the open vent, I heard the whirring of Deliverance's servos and a hiss of his hydraulics as he passed up an unused canister of biohazard containment foam.

With him standing almost 9 feet tall, I was still within easy reach for the glinting giant. The can he passed me was several years out of date, but I made sure the lid and safety mechanism were still in place and dutifully stowed it in one of my cargo pockets. As I half crawled, half dragged myself through the duct, I could both smell and feel the greasy trail running along the centre of the crawlspace. Goodness knows how many hundreds of passes from rats and other vermin it would take to build up.

The broad cone of light from my head-torch fanned out in front of me, but despite the reassuring way it cut through the complete darkness in the duct, I didn't want to run into the usual traffic. I couldn't help but think back to the bizarre scuttling I had heard within the ducts on Level 2. As I moved, I noticed on more than one occasion that my leg failed to respond to my commands, as my implant over-rode the signal from my brain. But my initial concern subsided when it occurred to me that it was protecting the canister in my cargo pocket from any inadvertent puncture from the screws, rivets and bolts which perforated the passage at each intersection. They occasionally snagged on my clothing and harness, but that was a minor inconvenience compared with the devastation that would be unleashed if several dozen cubic feet of instantly-setting biohazard containment foam erupted from my trouser pocket.

As I paused to rearrange the canister, I noticed that the metallic knocks and bumps from my movement were changing pitch and the duct below me was now tending to distort slightly with my weight. It was subtle, but it was a definite change. I was past the barricade.

It wasn't long before I arrived at another vent in the side of the duct. I flicked off my head torch to assess what level of light was coming through from outside, but the auto lights in the corridor on this side of the barricade were dark.

To my brief annoyance, the quiet chatter leaking up through the vent behind me was polluting my ability to detect and listen to new noises from below, but at least I was able to mute the audio on the camera feed being broadcast by Deliverance.

As I strained my senses, I couldn't detect any further signs of biological life, but I could pick up the echo of an occasional metallic tap or click, along with traces of a very faint wireless signal. It was still too weak and patchy for my implant to eavesdrop upon it, but it was a clear sign that the robotics lab was still active to a certain extent.

I pondered the merits of removing the vent cover and dropping down to the floor below, but the very presence of the barricade gave me pause for thought. Whoever had made it had been highly motivated to seal the passageway. I had a choice to make. The alternative option was to continue along the claustrophobic air duct, knowing that any mechanised defence systems could perforate me at will with gunfire from below if I was detected. Perhaps Decker's surveillance drone idea wasn't so bad after all.

I was about to turn back when sudden noise and vibration, travelling through the duct from behind me, announced that I was no longer alone. I shifted my weight, and peered back past my prone body to see Darius shouldering his way into the duct. He squinted as the beam of my head torch caught him square in the face, but he simply pushed his rifle ahead of himself with determination and continued stubbornly forward before I could send him back.

"Bring Decker's drone with you," I hissed before he could get too far along the duct. "It looks like we will need it after all."

As I eavesdropped on Deliverance's camera feed, I couldn't help but notice the look of smug satisfaction on Decker's face, as he and Darius conferred about it. The Titan series was standing under the vent, like an adult supervising children playing on a climbing frame. But Decker and the rest of my men were completely oblivious to the fact that I shared the drone's mechanical eyes and ears.

Whilst I waited for Darius to return, I used the time to remove the vent as quietly as I could and set it aside. I didn't want stray light to give our position away, so I swapped to 'infrared-only' on my head torch. It was perhaps a hollow gesture, because any machinery or cameras operating in the gloom would probably still pick it up.

Beneath the duct on this side of the barricade it was a complete mess. Debris was strewn across the floor, which included what appeared to be the remains of a boot, a tattered lab coat and several discarded body bags. A broken pair of spectacles glinted at me from amongst the dust. Less obvious under the dust and detritus, were the series of dried blood trails which appeared to be the result of bodies being dragged away.

I inched forward to peak my head out and was greeted by the soft blush of wireless signal that had been too weak to penetrate the harsh metal walls of the duct. It was several stages more advanced than the Bluetooth we used to use, but its range was similarly short. As my implant decrypted the signal, I understood it to be instructions to run a specific programme and directions to move to a predefined location. The question was, was this coming from an automated source, or was there some active intelligence behind the signal? And what was receiving the instructions? Deliverance was ample evidence that we could be up against some serious hardware down here.

I was fairly confident by the nature of the signal that it couldn't be coming from more than 200 feet away and at that range, I hoped that my sensitive hearing would detect the footfall or caterpillar tracks of a mechanised defence drone. As Darius' shoulders buffeted the inside of the duct behind me, I extended a hand to silence him. He held his breath as I listened intently, my head protruding from the vent. But aside from our heartbeats, I could only hear a few muted metallic clicks and taps from ahead. I was about to pull back into the duct when my face was bathed in several other signals, coming from different directions. They provided progress reports and some requested additional instruction. Despite the desolation of the rest of the facility, this side of the barricade was most definitely active.

I gestured for Darius to hand me Decker's surveillance drone in the darkness. I wanted to see what was up ahead, but I was concerned that any wireless signal between the drone and its corresponding wristband could give away our location. So I disabled the wireless functionality and programmed it to fly parallel to the wall, at ceiling height, then return to me with the footage. The tiny drone would be there for anything with eyes to see it, but at least it would not be broadcasting indiscriminately and giving our presence away.

It was this thought process which triggered a sudden realisation that made my eyes widen. At my request, Deliverance had been indiscriminately broadcasting his camera feed for the last couple of hours for anyone to see. Not only that, but I worried that he could be hacked remotely in order to wreak havoc amongst my men. Until Decker was able to run a full diagnostic, Deliverance could be harbouring any number of back doors in his software. I had been very short sighted and this left me feeling unsettled.

I looked back over my shoulder, a look of consternation still playing across my features. "Have Decker either shut Deliverance down or disable any wireless access," I breathed to Darius urgently. "There are multiple signals ahead. The lab is still live."

Some tense minutes later, I was reviewing the grainy initial footage collected by our aerial surveillance drone. Mercifully, Deliverance's camera feed was now gone and the signals from the lab were unchanged. It seemed as though we had narrowly avoided detection.

Just as the map in the security office had indicated, the reconnaissance showed a central corridor which fed into numerous individual lab departments on either side, each specialising in different areas. But many of the doors along the main flight path of the drone were closed, thwarting my efforts.

The manufacturing stations for the heavier hardware were visible on the right hand side, via thick bullet-proof glass observation windows. Within, as I replayed the footage, I caught a shadowy glimpse of row after row of utilitarian work stations which sported large, dextrous articulated arms for assembling anything from air conditioning units to engines. But these appeared still and silent in the gloom.

A steel door labelled 'Artificial Intelligence and Software Dynamics' was firmly closed, retaining its secrets, but a brief look through an open doorway labelled 'Bio-integration' showed a hive of activity.

There were cables trailing everywhere and at least six or seven spider-like drones were going about their business as they dragged clumsy wire tethers behind them. Each chrome-legged contrivance was as different as the next, sprouting a primitive array of different navigational sensors from their heads and legs - ranging from head-mounted lasers to whip-like antennae. They were mechanical misfits in every sense, but they did not appear to be armed.

I couldn't tell from the angle of the footage, but I knew enough about such facilities to assume that there would also likely be a series of ceiling-mounted automated 'lab assistants'. But if they were present, they wouldn't represent a threat if you stayed out of their limited reach.

From this brief initial reconnaissance, I hadn't spotted the source of the wireless communication, but it gave me confidence that I wouldn't be shredded to ribbons by gunfire if I pressed on.

As I saw it, we had three choices. I discounted retracing our steps and using the main stairs or the large industrial service elevator, as we would entirely lose the element of surprise. This left us with the options of pressing on through the duct and maintaining our flimsy fiction of stealth, or else just using the duct to bypass the barricade and continuing on foot.

I must admit, having observed the eerie mechanical menagerie up ahead, I saw the multicoloured string of spliced cables running through the duct ahead of me in a whole new light. For all I knew, at any moment I could be face to face with a hostile mechanical freak and be severely disadvantaged by the confined space. Clearly whatever, or whoever, still occupied this graveyard was active and spreading their web throughout the facility. The only limitation to their progress appeared to be time and raw materials.

It was time for Darius and I to backtrack and speak with the men.

Chapter 47

"So it is agreed?" I asked the group.

As I scanned the faces of the steadfast men circling about me, several nodded emphatically, but Decker didn't appear so certain.

"You saw the body bags upstairs, Chris," he counselled. "They blocked this floor off for a reason. I don't doubt I could have a field day with the equipment and technology through there, but at what risk? This isn't what we came for."

We had been over this already, but he was always very cautious and meticulous in his thought processes. Finch and Chavez were much more cavalier.

"Come on Decker!" Chavez said, a sigh of frustration bubbling past his calm exterior. "What else are we going to do? Go back out there with the 'lost'?"

"Yeah!" Finch chimed in, his eyes bright with passion. "Just look at what we've gained so far." He was perhaps the most fanatical amongst us and hungered for any way to get even with the Authority regime. He clearly regarded Deliverance as a great step forward in our war. "If they leave hardware like that just sittin' on the porch," he continued, "then there's gotta be more down there." Some of the others nodded in agreement.

Decker wasn't placated. "That's what I'm worried about," he responded. "I'm a mechanic, not a god-damned miracle worker. I pick my battles... and work from the shadows. A sabotaged system here, a hack there. We wage guerrilla warfare, not full frontal assaults!" Some of the quieter men were also nodding at this.

We were going over old ground yet again and I couldn't have our fragile group bickering when so much was at stake, so I stepped in.

"OK Decker, we all hear what you are saying. But we are going to recon the lab, one way or another. We can't pass it over without taking a proper look. If there is some useful tech, that's all well and good, but I suspect there is a lot more to be gained here. If those manufacturing stations are viable, we can use them to fight the Authority forces from a distance. We could do a lot with our own force of drones. Worst case scenario, we can still manufacture things to make life easier for ourselves back at camp."

I knew that would strike a chord with him. As one of the few tradesmen amongst the Freemen, he spent his life constantly mending and repairing scavenged items and worn out appliances - a never ending cycle of mend and make-do. Having escaped the embrace of the Authority, we had chosen liberty over 'security', but as a result, we lived on the fringe of survival. The community children played in the wreckage of the fall of civilisation and our people were never far from starvation. Such was life in the dead-zone.

"If that food on Level 3 is safe, Decker," Williams put in, "it will make a big difference. Come on. Let's secure this facility."

He left much unsaid, but Decker wasn't stupid. He knew that the food and technology here would enable us to expand our community - and that meant liberating more people from the inner-city. Friends and family that had been left behind through necessity could finally be free.

To my relief, it was enough. Decker wasn't the only man with family and friends still working their fingers to the bone for the Authority, their every moment and biological function micromanaged by bureaucratic dictates enforced at the barrel of a gun. It was no way to live.

He looked over at the basketball-sized test holes in the containment foam barricade that Deliverance had carved out with a few brutal gouges from his titanium-reinforced steel fingers. We couldn't fit him through the duct, but Decker had ordered him to test his strength against the material, just in case we needed him to follow us in a hurry. His lethal fingers could claw great billowing chunks of material loose with relative ease. According to my implant, he could be through the barrier in under 4 minutes, but that was still a long time if we got ourselves in trouble.

"Alright," Decker replied with a frown of concentration which furrowed his already lined brow. "But I will instruct our mascot here to follow in 10 minutes if he doesn't hear back from us." I think working with drones again was putting Decker back in familiar territory and lending him some courage.

The mood lightened somewhat, now we were all in agreement, and I wondered at the fickle nature of the human heart. Just a few short hours before, the men had been lining up to vengefully drop Deliverance to the depths of the abyss. Yet now he was being viewed as our latest new recruit.

As planned, when we were ready to move, Deliverance clawed a series of hand and foot holds into the face of the barricade. He fashioned us a makeshift ladder then stood out of the way, awaiting further instruction.

Six of us, including Decker, made ready to navigate the claustrophobic confines of the cold metal duct. I left the others with instruction to await our signal, but in the meantime, to tell Norris and Stephens what was going on.

I was the first to drop from the duct on the other side. It was a relief to be clear of it, but as the corridor auto lights fired up, (perhaps for the first time in years), I felt somewhat exposed to whatever lay ahead. From this new vantage point, I could see that the interior face of the barricade was intact, as far as a random pile of plastic, wood, steel and foam could be. There certainly wasn't any evidence of attempts to breach the barricade from this side. That was good news.

As my men lowered themselves, or simply dropped from the duct, I was focussing upon the noises of robotic activity ahead. It all seemed to be consistent with the drone footage. But the peculiar scent from the duct and Level 3 gardens still hung thickly in the air.

Decker was the last of the men to drop from overhead. He rearranged his bag and checked his firearm, then nodded that he was ready to proceed.

"Let's go," I whispered, as I took the lead.

The knotted rope we left trailing from the open vent would suffice to retrace our route, but I didn't fancy trying to get six men past it during a fire-fight. I just hoped it wouldn't come to that.

We passed along the corridor, ignoring the steel doors that were already sealed. My ears strained for any signs of activity behind them, but there was nothing so obvious as the action happening in the 'Bio-integration' lab. Decker slowed to shine his lamp through the observation windows, in order to get a better look at the manufacturing stations. Row upon row of industrial assembly units sat idle in the darkness, but we could see part finished projects on some of them. Conveyor belts and racking were laden with raw materials and spare parts ready to go, but this section seamed as dead as the rest of the facility. The scale of the department was obscured by the limited range of our lights, but as our beams swept from side to side, it was reassuring that nothing moved.

As we neared the open door of the 'Bio-integration' lab, I paused and raised a gloved fist. My men obediently halted behind me and took up strategic positions. There was no adequate cover in this corridor, but at least they weren't all bunched together. We were as ready as we were going to be.

The metallic patter of robotic feet and the creak and whine of servos, hydraulics and electric motors was now blatant to all of us as it created a steady background noise. Occasional sparks from welding equipment added to the mish-mash of sounds, which helped my implant to paint a picture of the interior of the laboratory.

Decker and Darius both raised eyebrows in question, but the thin line of my pursed lips was the only answer I could give.

Our progress had been preceded by the awakening of the auto lights along the corridor and we were in plain sight of the wall-mounted security cameras above the open door, so there was no point in any attempt at stealth. I strode forward with an apparent confidence I didn't feel and stepped over the threshold into mechanical bedlam.

The brief glimpse of this animated freak show from the surveillance drone footage didn't do justice to the mechanised 'Alice in Wonderland' dystopia that greeted me.

There were perhaps twenty or so different robotic creatures amidst the chaos of spare parts, scrap, tangled wires and salvaged materials. They all competed to out-do each other in their level of strangeness, with no consideration for aesthetics whatsoever. I saw biomechanical shades of spider, caterpillar, hyena, centaur, snake and lama in the designs, where it wasn't purely based around the availability of parts. Robotic limbs vied with steel hooks, rubber wheels and even caterpillar tracks as a form of locomotion.

As I watched, each nightmarish contraption continued autonomously about their business, dragging spare parts into situ, removing waste, dismantling scrap or else assembling even weirder offspring. I took a step back, as one of the droids with whip-like antennae darted forward, propelled by a single rubber wheel mounted in the centre of its wire and mesh body. It dragged its power cables behind it, along with a scuffed and dirty prosthetic limb, which it deposited in a pile beside another work station.

No sooner had it done so, then one of the ceiling mounted arms, uncoiled itself from a deceptively small alcove and extended down to the pile to retrieve the macabre offering and drop it on a bench.

Another equally peculiar machine, scuttled across the bench to begin stripping and melting the plastic away, working to a design and specification known only to itself. Wisps of acrid smoke rose into the air to mingle with the stench of waste, oil, solvents and ozone.

All activity in the room, however unsettling, followed the same pattern. Useful parts were being extracted from useless scrap and moderate levels of assembly were contributing to the construction of additional robots. It would have been alarming, if it hadn't been for the fact that they were making so many mistakes. Not only were these oddities peculiar to look at, some were also incompetent. One unit was repeatedly trying to drive a screw into a metallic strut which had no hole for it, whilst several others had already collided with each other in their efforts to navigate about the room. It was no wonder, as the limited array of sensors for each unit were inadequate to the tasks they were being put to. Maybe there was a shortage of parts?

Beyond the benches and workstations of this perverse assembly line, there were two further doorways. One was sealed with a steel door, the other was an open portal to a second room of mechanical mayhem.

I moved forward experimentally, but the pace and activity in the room didn't change. Despite my instruction, my men had followed and were now gathering about the doorway to stare at the peculiar display. Chavez was wide-eyed and tense as he surveyed the industrious scene before him over the scope of his rifle, but he looked veritably blasé compared with Decker, who gaped open-mouthed.

My attention was drawn by movement in the next room. Passing across the doorway, was a stout iron-grey quadruped loaded up with produce from the garden on Level 3. It was clearly more sophisticated than the scavengers surrounding me, as it ran under its own power source and didn't require a clumsy tether. It was relatively swift on its feet, albeit a little jerky in its movements and apples, carrots, kale, broccoli, tomatoes and a number of other fruit and vegetables jostled and rocked in a deep wire tray mounted upon its back.

"Don't touch anything," I cautioned over my shoulder as I broke away to follow the walking hamper. I could see no reason why this assortment of drones would require food, except to feed whoever was in charge, so I resolved to follow where it led.

I ducked and sidestepped some erratic robotic activity as I made my way toward the next room, which was larger and contained more sophisticated equipment. The machinery here was obviously original to the laboratory and although it had been co-opted to help manufacture the next generation of drones, it lacked the shock value of their unique and outlandish design. What made up for that however, were the dozen or so gallon jars of 'micro humans' lined up on a worktop, next to a grisly desiccated human leg, laid open in vivisection.

Other machines fussed over and worked on more mundane tasks, but my eyes were drawn to the distasteful biological experiments. Fine gold and copper wires had been implanted throughout the withered thigh, which gaped open under the pressure of several surgical clamps. The remains of other similar, but perhaps failed, experiments lay discarded unceremoniously in a deepening pile on the floor. They smelled of formaldehyde.

The harvested and flayed limbs were relatively disgusting, but not a great deal different to pale beef jerky in appearance and texture, but the fleshy foetuses within the jars were still lifelike in their preservation, which saddened me. I remembered my disgust as the FDA approved the use of genetically engineered foetuses in 2017 for use in experimentation in place of lab animals. The giant corporations and their lobbyists claimed that a minor modification to DNA rendered these unborn human babies as nonhuman and therefore fair game for whatever sick experiments they liked, with no recourse. And as usual, the bought-and-paid-for lapdogs within the higher echelons of the FDA had pocketed the tainted corporate silver to rubber-stamp everything. Overnight, 160 million lab animals worldwide had found that they no longer had a place in the world.

I cast my eyes about the room for additional clues as I tucked in behind the droid, which appeared to be oblivious to my presence. Its feet were tipped with rubber stoppers, which squeaked slightly as it placed them on the grey linoleum floor. It was heading toward a closed door marked 'Section 4', but a sign on the wall helpfully listed 'Theatres 1 - 4', 'Wards 1 - 4', 'Bio Farms 1 - 2' and 'Data Centre'.

As I passed, I noted my reflection shifting and distorting across the surface of several of the jars, drawing my attention to the dismaying contents. Judging by their size and proportions, the foetuses entombed within appeared to have been harvested at around four months and they floated in synthetic amniotic fluid like little homunculi. Some of their dead eyes were open and their accusatory gazes were as cold as the glass of their jars. Or maybe it was just my imagination.

I cast my eye over bench after bench and was somewhat alarmed to also see components that my implant identified as being from mechanised defence drones. Although there were no complete units visible, a chromed hand here and a brushed steel rib cage there indicated to me that other lethal units must be present elsewhere in the facility.

My suspicions were soon to be confirmed when the steel doors hissed open at the approach of the tottering quadruped. This triggered the auto lighting system within, which flickered and ticked into life.

I stepped forward with the drone, as the pitch darkness was reluctantly pushed back. Through the doors, I was greeted by a wide atrium with several desks and computer terminals arrayed along the far wall. Further steel doorways punctuated the austere clinical decor, beneath industrial security cameras and stencilled department labels. Yet again, a thick, improvised tangle of coloured cables spread across the floor, this time sprouting from the computer terminals and stretching away to my right towards the data centre.

I could hear my small team of men advancing behind me, but as my eyes slid along the route the cables followed, they were instantly forgotten. With a jolt of alarm, my focus was drawn to settle wide-eyed upon a man-sized figure in the shadow of a doorway. What stood there, straddling the wires, in apparent defiance of all the laws of nature, was what could only be described as a meat and steel scarecrow. Part flesh and part machine.

It was horrifying. Despite the 20 feet between us, my shotgun virtually leapt into my hands unbidden and aimed itself at the scarred and weeping torso of the figure before me. Clumsy stitches created ridged welts where flaps of skin were held in place over whatever lay within. The gruesome patchwork of flesh sat atop the bipedal drone chassis of a Valkyrie unit, which were the smaller man-sized cousins of the Titan series. But this drone had been modified to house a cadaverous creature within it like an exoskeleton. If the thing's head hadn't been lolling to one side, with its jaundiced eyes rolled back in its sunken sockets, I would have flensed the leathery flesh from its steel bones with a blistering automatic burst of buckshot. But whilst my initial horror at this morbid apparition was still registering, my implant's threat assessment blessedly flashed into life across my vision.

Although initially shocking to me, the creature remained stock still, having displayed no reaction whatsoever to my arrival. It's flesh components were the same ambient temperature as the room and however the flesh was preserved, it wasn't breathing and had no heart beat. It wasn't even looking in my direction, if indeed it could look at all. My eyes were drawn to its bony chromed hands, which hung emptily by its sides. It didn't appear to be armed in any way, nor hostile, so my implant indifferently tagged it as an orange unknown.

That was some small consolation, but despite my implant's lack of concern, I knew that Valkyrie units were agile and easily capable of hand-to-hand combat.

Perhaps due to my continued alarm, my implant helpfully highlighted the bunch of cables coming out of the back of the scarecrow's skull, to drape down its back and join the others running toward the data centre. If it proved hostile, that would be where I would place my opening shots.

The smaller quadruped bearing the food, continued into the atrium, oblivious to my consternation behind it. As I covered the scarecrow with my shotgun, the mobile hamper angled right and continued to jostle and squeak its way toward the data centre, entirely unperturbed by the ghastly figure blocking its path.

The creature, if you could call it that, was clothed only in flesh and steel. In life, it had been male, or predominantly male at least, as it had patches of body hair and a brutal puckered scar where its genitalia had been excised and sutured.

I didn't take my eyes off the scene in front of me, but my echo-mapping placed two of my men through the doorway behind me and highlighted their startled reactions to seeing my shotgun aimed. They didn't yet have the line of sight to see what I stared at, so I called out to them.

"Contact. Hold your positions". I was pleased that my fear didn't bleed through into my voice, but I must admit that of all things I could have been presented with down here, this one chewed and worried hardest at my rational mind.

Being an amalgamation of man and machine myself, I must admit to having had more than my fair share of nightmares along this theme, but panic would not have been helpful down here, so I swallowed and mentally got a grip of myself. My own internal dialogue tried to reassure me with 'it's just a machine', but the fear in my belly made the words sound hollow.

At least now I could identify the smell I had been detecting. It came off the creature in waves.

A quick glance behind me placed Murrin and Chavez taking up defensive positions through the doorway, thankfully out of sight of the scarecrow. I didn't want any reflex shots to unravel our undisturbed progress. So far, nothing had behaved in a hostile manner towards us, which was more than I could say for the former inhabitants of the facility.

As the quadruped drew nearer to the aberration, I anticipated it changing course. But far more alarmingly, it was the creature of flesh and steel which suddenly animated. In one fluid motion, Its eyes rolled down and centred themselves in their sockets and its head straightened on its neck, as it smoothly stepped aside to make way for the delivery.

It was a miracle that I didn't open fire, such was my shock at the sudden motion. It was almost as though a video was unpaused, going from still to sudden visceral action in an instant. The creature followed the progress of the quadruped with its dead eyes, then with a couple of smooth steps, it resumed its position across the doorway, still ignoring my presence. Unlike the titan series, its steel feet were sheathed in rubber to provide grip and this muffled the tell-tale clicks and scrapes I had grown accustomed to from the footsteps of Deliverance.

Unlike before, however, the Valkyrie unit now remained stock still, but with its eyes straight ahead. It was no longer behaving like a puppet with its strings cut, and this lent it a much more fiendish air.

But Paredo's tutelage ran deep within me, so rather than dither, I broke through my fear with decisive action.

"Rally on me." I called out. "Potential Tango. Weapons hold."

The sound of leather boots creaking and packs shifting was enough to know my men were following, so I stalked forward. My men had their orders only to fire in self-defence, or if ordered, so I had faith that they wouldn't panic when they laid eyes on our company.

I had no idea what would be perceived as hostile by the creature in front of me, so I trained my firearm upon the thick trail of cables leading in the direction of the data centre. I hoped that it would appear less threatening, whilst it still gave me a vague sense of security. In reality, I had no idea if the wires were necessary for the zombie Valkyrie to function, but it was the best I could do.

When I came close enough for the scent of the creature to curdle in my nostrils, its dry eyes swivelled in its sockets toward me and a mocking grin began to spread across its face. It was the first response we had received from any of the machinery in this place.

The features of its clumsily assembled face were unfamiliar, but despite my hair involuntarily standing on end, I somehow recognised something very familiar in its expression, before it even spoke.

"Welcome to my parlour, said the spider to the fly." It croaked from a voice box which shouldn't have functioned at all. A slightly lagging metallic echo added an even more sinister quality to the sibilant whisper. "To what do I owe this fine pleasure, Lucidus?" It asked, the sarcasm not lost on me.

With the use of my relic name, my suspicions had been confirmed.

"I see you haven't changed a bit, Susurro," I barbed back, the shocking build up to this conversation lending my words a cruelty I might not otherwise have used. But goodness knows he deserved it. "Still whispering from the shadows I see? Come out where I can see you."

The realisation that this vulgar contraption standing before me was just another robot, stripped away its menace and just left me feeling angry.

Knowing that Susurro still lived, or Kester as I had known him at the Academy, didn't do anything to lighten my mood. Fortunately for him, I had believed him long dead. If I hadn't, there were many years where I would have gladly sought him out to make him so. But what was he doing here, and alive?

I flared my siphon for answers. An instant later, a red thread was leading off through the meat puppet in front of me, down a corridor toward the data centre, some 80 feet away. It was definitely him, although his siphon signature had changed since I last bridged with him.

"It is you who haven't changed," the marionette shot back with venom. "Where were you *BROTHER*? Where were you when the Committee turned on us?"

I had fully anticipated him to be dimmed, but his implant's signature was blatant. In fact, in his bitterness he flared even brighter. Something was wrong. Kester had earned his relic name, through and through. 'Susurro' meant mutterer, tale-bearer, or whisperer - and he had been all of those things. But he wasn't an overt fighter unless he had backup and an audience to play to. He had always preferred to goad others from the sidelines and watch the fallout, such as he had with Flint. This outright aggression wasn't his style, unless he had the upper hand - or was desperate.

"I'll tell you where," he hissed, in response to his own question. "You dropped us like a hot rock the moment your bit of skirt fluttered her eyelashes. She wasn't even one of us, yet you chose her and abandoned us without a backward glance."

My surprise must have shown, but it was soon replaced with a rush of white-hot fury. "You brought about your own downfall. Don't lay that at my door!" As my sudden anger roiled within me, my words boiled out uncontrolled. "I stayed as long as I could. But when they confirmed you were dead, what was there to stay for? Brotherhood or no, I thought it was your just deserts. But mark my words," I growled, "mention Ember again and I'll have your eyes." It was more than two decades since I had spoken her name aloud, but it still ripped my heart to say it.

As they gathered and fanned out behind me, my men must have thought me mad, haranguing an animated corpse I had only just met. But in my anger, they were outside of my notice. They stood with weapons trained on the frightening Valkyrie as Kester puppeteered it from behind the scenes.

"Enough of this mockery," I stormed. "You have no respect for anyone or anything. Get this *offal* out of my way so we can discuss this face to face."

I strode forward, my temper fanned and shoved the stinking automaton to one side. I was expecting resistance, maybe even physical confrontation, but the droid adroitly maintained its balance despite the shove and allowed me to pass unmolested.

It was silent for a moment as I walked on, perhaps whilst Kester absorbed what I had said. But then, with a quiet whir of motors and hydraulics, it turned to follow me. "I hadn't planned on receiving guests," it rattled from its dry throat as it hurried to keep pace with me. "At least, not yet."

The red thread of siphon-tracking, which was superimposed across my vision, showed that Kester's implant hadn't moved, as I marched down the corridor with purpose. The sound of booted and rubberised feet followed behind me, but above that, I could now hear the low hum of pumps, along with the strange random melody of bubbling fluid, coming from up ahead. It sounded different to the usual cooling systems that used to serve large data centres, but who knew what had been improvised to serve a function in this mad-house.

As we neared the data centre, there were several wall-mounted vents, whose covers had been removed and discarded. Trails of wires broke off from the main trunk of cabling on the floor, disappearing into the open ducts, presumably leading to drones which were scuttling about the facility on various errands at Kester's direction.

"Wait!" Kester called through the parched mouth of the droid behind me, the mockery in his voice now absent and replaced with concern. "You cannot see me yet. We should bridge first."

I didn't stop. What nonsense was this? We had never been close and despite our brotherhood, there had been many times when my brothers and sisters and I would rather have killed him. I am sure the feeling was mutual, so why all the concern all of a sudden? What was his game?

With my long, purposeful strides, I soon overtook the labouring quadruped and rounded the last corner before a tall set of open double doors, through which I could survey the data centre and presumably, the spider in the centre of his web.

"Wait. You need to understand..." he continued plaintively as I pulled up in front of the data centre.

My senses had been straining to detect any form of trap, but I didn't anticipate what I saw. As I took in the sight before me, my years of pent-up anger towards Kester drained out of me in a flood, like I had lanced a boil.

Surrounded by banks of organic gel memory packs, computer processors, cables and life-support systems, stood a large glass tank in which Kester floated - or, more accurately, what was left of him.

Chapter 48

Several hours later, with a heavy heart, I stood with one hand pressed against the cold glass, as I looked into the milky and sightless eyes of Kester's ruined face. In truth, I was the only one of our party who would.

He hung suspended in the liquid of the tank, a testament to the immeasurable cruelty of man. His lower jaw had been removed and an array of flexible segmented steel tubes fed down his throat to cater for nourishment and oxygen. A similar affair handled waste at the other end, robbing him of even the most basic dignity. But the scars of his mutilation were easily overlooked when your eyes were drawn to the complete absence of his limbs and the thick trail of wires which exited through his head and chest, to physically connect his implant to the hardware arrayed about him. They had removed anything which wasn't biologically necessary and, in doing so, had eliminated any hope of his escape.

Over the years, Kester's physicality had been maintained purely to preserve the function of his valuable implant, which served as an EMP-proof, secure, intelligent super-computer for the facility. It had been his processing power running all the simulations, experiments, drones and manufacturing robots - and without him, the facility couldn't have functioned, especially in the years just after the collapse.

When I had siphon-bridged with him, the horror of his experience and ensuing madness and despair had washed over me like a tidal wave, as I absorbed his memories. As Kester and I communed in silence, Darius had come forward to stand beside me, pretending not to notice the tears which welled in my eyes. Whether they were a product of my sense of guilt, or empathy, I didn't know, as I felt both.

But where I had let down others in the brotherhood, I now had the opportunity to make amends with Kester. I had shared my own memories with him, which had helped him see that I had spoken the truth, but over half a century of burning hate still left its indelible mark on him. The only consolation was that at least now I could help him salvage some quality of life and, if all went to plan, he could exact his revenge on the regime responsible. For once, we had a common enemy.

Decker and several of the other men were working on restoring Kester's access to the rest of the facility and, when some of the other departments were no longer locked down, I hoped we could finally liberate him from the tank. We needed access to some special equipment and in particular, the surgical station in the hospital wing, but I was confident that we could help. I just hoped I could break the encryption which still remained on certain functions of his implant.

It would be a delicate time, but knowing what Kester held in his head, we no longer needed to locate the A.I. substation. We had everything we needed and more, right here.

I cast my mind back over what I had learned from him. Our treatment by the Agency had a great many similarities, but he had fared much worse.

He had been betrayed by his Agency handler and, through the use of his control module, Kester's life had been turned into a living hell. After his capture and extensive 'procedures' to facilitate access to his implant, the Agency scientists had firewalled off his consciousness, so that they could utilise his hardware without his overt interference.

But when Kester had somehow awoken in the tank months later, dazed and confused, he had gone berserk, breaking free of his restraints and ripping loose any cables and tubes he could reach before they could sedate him again. They had made the mistake of keeping him whole.

After that debacle, anyone would assume that they would have learned their lesson and taken better care to keep him medicated, but unfortunately for Kester, during his awakening, they had detected an almost forty-fold increase in his processing power - which was a product of the implant interacting with his consciousness.

We still don't understand the inner workings of our implants, but they function at the quantum level, which is why they are able to wink in and out of our reality when they embed themselves in a new host. But when given unfettered access to the human mind, the result is processing power many magnitudes greater than anything mankind has been able to construct themselves.

Afterwards, although hazy, Kester recalled drifting in and out of medicated catatonia. The next time he truly regained full consciousness was almost a month later. This time, due to the modifications they had made to his restraints, combined with the physical functions of his implant having been disabled, he found his bindings were impossible to break. But in his desperation, he had been able to wrench and tear at them enough to damage his blood vessels. But his dropping vital signs and the billowing cloud of crimson coming from his wrists had triggered an alarm well before he had bled out.

When next he came around, his captors had taken no chances. They had stripped his body down to the bare essentials and he was both traumatised and helpless. Over the next couple of years, through a combination of torture, drugs and the more brutal functions of his command module, despite his horror and crushing despair, they forced his compliance. He lost count of how many times he had tried, and failed, to resist or even to modify his orders, but it was hopeless. They had complete control over him and worked him like a slave.

He operated hundreds of drones during the drone wars, indiscriminately killing his masters' political enemies from the safety of the facility. He ran the software simulations for their genetic engineering programmes as they created even more deadly bacteria and viruses. He even conducted cyber warfare through what was left of the internet, disabling reactors, crashing financial institutions, stealing proprietary data and more, all the while still running the day to day functions of the facility. They worked him around the clock, rotating in shifts and turning his life into one long arduous labour, enforced by unspeakable pain if he didn't comply.

But as the enzymes and harsh chemicals within the tank gradually ate away at the last of his remaining physical senses, Kester retreated more and more into his mind, living through his remote electronic connections to the real world. He found ways to take pleasure in expanding his sphere of physical influence through the machinery of the facility.

Over the years, he had tried so many times to sabotage all he was ordered to do, but it contravened whatever commands they had implanted and just resulted in failure and agony. So, in his depression, he had eventually resigned himself to his lot.

Until, quite accidentally, he discovered he could partition his mind. He was used to running hundreds, if not thousands of different programmes simultaneously, but he had never been able to hive off a section of his mind, free from the constraints of his captors. For the longest time, he had just used it as a refuge - a place he could go to be alone and free from the countless labours expected of him. He could daydream and spend time reliving his memories, or even create lifelike simulations of the life he left behind. Time moved differently there and he found he could salvage some joy whilst the rest of his mind continued to carry out the myriad tasks expected of him.

When the simulations of torture and bloody revenge over his oppressors eventually lost their lustre, he spent years simulating other lives and escaping the painful and cruel reality of his existence. Until one day, a freak accident changed everything.

He was immersed in a rather complex simulation when an explosion in one of the labs rocked the facility. One of the high-pressure vessels had failed during an experiment and according to the wall-mounted cameras, the surviving technicians were stumbling or crawling to escape the poisonous gases leaking into the section. Kester had absent-mindedly shut down the air ducts, turned on the extractors and initiated containment procedures without even considering what he was doing. It was only then that he realised that he had done this from within his private partition, completely bypassing the usual programming and safeguards.

He hadn't dared believe what he had done at first, but after sabotaging a few other minor lab experiments, trapping a technician in the doors of a lift and editing the outbound email communications of some key executives resident in the facility (to cause embarrassment), he knew that he had discovered a backdoor.

He jealously guarded his secret, being very cautious not to do anything which could give him away, whilst he spent his time simulating all manner of escape plans in his mind. But with his body so damaged and helpless and the facility so highly populated, it was next to impossible to pull off an escape. Besides, with the surface now largely an irradiated ruin, where would he go?

He had to think bigger! As the coming weeks became months, he realised that escape in his present state would be very difficult. So he set about his plan to empty the facility and build himself the means to escape the tank.

As he bided his time, he contented himself with creating an accident here, a poisoning there. Anything to undermine his masters. He compromised orders for supplies, disrupted staff rosters, created errors in the labelling of hazardous materials or biological samples and leaked sensitive memos. In short, he was helping to make Facility 47 one of the unluckiest places to live and work in for its inhabitants.

He was always very careful to leave no traces and even went so far as to raise alarms and report problems, when he himself had created them. When the pattern of mishaps was getting too blatant to ignore, he even framed new members of staff as terrorists or agent provocateurs before outing them to the facility security teams.

As the population of the surrounding under-city grew and available space and resources dwindled, he was able to extend his shadowy reach beyond the facility. There was already discontent amongst the survivors of the collapse as they bickered over privilege, resources and control - the usual things the wealthy elite squabble over. It was no surprise. Why would a bunch of moneyed psychopaths think life would be any different down here? They had still brought the hired help to fetch and carry for them, so the inequality they had fostered above ground in the past, now festered just as badly below. In fact, the tight confines of the under-city and the cheek-by-jowl living conditions of the three million inhabitants created even more of a powder keg.

Kester used this to agitate conflict. He used bogus communications to sow discontent amongst the populous. He targeted the political enemies of the facility whilst leaving behind a damning evidence trail to follow and even sabotaged trade amongst the various dividing factions.

Work had already begun on restoring and repopulating the city above ground, but it wasn't a popular move amongst the common people. Many feared that the high-tech materials, paints, filters and magnetic field generators would be insufficient to keep the radiation out. Even more feared that another debilitating series of solar flares could undo all the hard work. They reasoned that the survivors of the collapse had made the under-city their home for a reason. Here, they were free from the diseases which had run rampant, the effects of solar flares which had driven mankind underground in the first place, and safe from the radiation leaking from the dozens of failed nuclear reactors which had resulted.

But as usual, nothing halts 'progress' when it is being driven by those who stand to gain most from it. So work still went ahead, heedless of the risks. Let's face it, when people rely on the rations given to them by their government and the government hold all the guns, they generally get their way, regardless of cost or ethics.

More and more civilians were press-ganged into working top-side and the city was restored from the ruins. With every success, the activity snowballed. Kester found it fascinating how people's attitudes could turn full circle in just a few years. Before the collapse, almost nobody worried about the activity of the sun - despite NASA's warnings and even despite the Carrington event in the 1850's. The solar storm of 1859, was a powerful geomagnetic storm caused when a coronal mass ejection hit Earth's magnetosphere and induced one of the largest geomagnetic storms on record. It fried electronics across the whole of the northern hemisphere, but due to the lack of their widespread use, the biggest talking point was the glowing aurora it created in the sky at night.

By the 21st century, although people spent most of their time glued to their personal consumer electronics, they didn't pay the threat any mind at all.

The solar storm of 2012 was just a warning shot, but it passed Earth's orbit without striking us. It didn't even strike the headlines, because NASA didn't release the data on it until 2014 and the population was more interested in reality TV, celebrity gossip and sports, to pay it much attention.

So, having learned their lesson the hard way in 2025, attitudes were completely reversed. The sun was a killer, not to be trusted.

Yet as the city took shape and its large open spaces were populated and appreciated by more and more, caution was yet again thrown to the wind. Many of the new inhabitants had been born underground and had never even seen the sun, except in old pictures and magazines, or on electronic displays.

Kester himself was drawn into the building work as he remotely operated earth moving equipment, cranes, Titans and even some of the salvaged Goliath units, which towered over all but the cranes. He worked diligently, knowing that the more people went top-side, the less would inhabit the facility.

But to his dismay, as he watched the activity roll by, it became apparent that even the ruling elite were divided over whether the top-side was best.

Kester didn't cause the rift between the top-siders and the under-city dwellers. As usual, they could thank their own power-hungry leaders for that. The first few years were amicable enough, but as tensions mounted and top-siders and under-city dwellers began to grow discontent with each other, Kester knew that helping to build the city was no longer beneficial to him. So he helped to fan the flames of discontent instead.

He wasn't alone, in all fairness. Divide and rule has always been the preserve of the wealthy - and having top-siders set up a rivalry with the under-city dwellers was to their advantage. It started with the under-city folk being naive, then anti-science, then backwards, until it became a class war. When the populous of the under-city, viewing their self-sufficiency as their strength began to withhold supplies from the top-siders, it created the perfect environment for Kester to enact his escape plan.

When the bulk of the Authority leadership were living top-side, those remaining in authority below ground staged a coup and declared independence.

It was fascinating to see the bloody history I had lived through, from Kester's unique perspective, but his memories were no less harrowing as the lunatics running the show committed all manner of atrocities to purge and retake the under-city.

When top-side attacks were spreading all across the under-city, Kester had let hell break loose in the secret facility to drive out its inhabitants. When fire alarms and false containment breach alerts only went so far, he had released toxic gasses, allowed biological agents to escape and began to rend the more stubborn personnel with whatever machinery and drones he could. When some of the smarter facility technicians and engineers had discovered that he wasn't responding to their commands they had managed to stall him long enough to disable his access to most of the key systems. Over the course of 48 hours of bloody warfare, often having to counteract the actions of his own implant, he had managed to clear the facility. His final action had been to mobilise and send out the last three resident Titan units to prevent anyone from returning to retake the territory they had lost.

As the battle for the facility had raged, he had managed to lock down the blast doors surrounding the facility and delete records of its existence from Authority archives.

The facility location was already a closely guarded secret, but he didn't want any visitors whilst he made preparation to escape.

As it turned out, the damage done by the last of the facility personnel had been far more extensive and it had taken him years to get even this far, by engineering small drones to retrieve raw materials and manufacture successively larger units.

The pinnacle of his achievement so far was the flesh and steel drone which had greeted me. It didn't have a name, as Kester considered it to be an extension of himself, but it had been his prototype exoskeleton for when he could recover his physical body from the tank. He had been successful enough to create rudimentary sensations within the preserved flesh, but until the full functions of his implant had been unlocked, he wouldn't be able to replace his missing limbs.

"The men have made dinner," Decker announced from behind me, drawing me out of my thoughts. "We wondered if you would join us?"

He looked tired, but was calm. The haunted look he had been developing was gone, although judging by the way his gaze flicked towards the tank every few seconds, he didn't fully trust Kester. My assurances that we were locked down and that I was monitoring the facility through my siphon-bridge had helped, but he had always been a cautious man.

True enough, Kester, with his intimate link with the facility, could be dangerous to us if he chose to be, but right now he needed us just as much as we needed him. Besides, I knew from his memories that he had watched us on the facility security feeds ever since we arrived, without taking steps to harm us. There were no guarantees in this world, but although his loyalty was sorely tested, the brotherhood still meant something to him.

Kester had already been fed via a machine linked to his feeding tube, which mechanically blended and liquefied the produce that the quadruped had delivered. So despite his immobilisation, he had been eating better than we had.

He was resting now, so with a nod and a tired smile, I accompanied Decker.

After feasting on our fill of fresh fish and vegetables, conjured into a delicious meal by Williams and Murrin, my men had been full of questions. They were understandably concerned about our mission and our mysterious and horrifying host.

I had never given them much detail about my early history, but I told them what I could of Kester and filled them in on the memories we had shared. Some of the men weren't best pleased, as they had lost family in the conflict and subsequent purges, but I think they could see he was just another casualty of the regime, trying to survive. I hoped that eventually he would fit in and be accepted, just as Deliverance now had.

After all, when the facility was operational again, with Kester's help, we could safely house more Freemen, manufacture weapons, food and even drones. Most importantly, we could hack the Authority servers and drone network. I couldn't help but feel the stirrings of optimism. We finally had an edge we could use.

Although my men were now securely lodged in the abandoned accommodation on Level 3, we weren't in the habit of taking chances. So I took first watch. Deliverance had been sent to patrol the main avenue on Level 0, but that was just a precaution. I was weary myself, but my men were completely exhausted, so I contented myself with some time alone with my thoughts. I missed the verdant flush of nature that we had all taken for granted before the collapse, so I chose to sit amongst the aquaponics systems as I contemplated everything I had learned today.

My implant monitored the facility camera feeds, as I sat amongst the foliage, bathed in the magenta glow of the grow lamps and immersed in the kaleidoscope of scents.

The camaraderie amongst my Freemen over dinner reminded me of the heady days amongst my fellow relics. I had thought myself the last of them, but if Kester had survived, maybe so had others. Certainly the gang sign outside the facility was none of Kester's doing, if his memories were anything to go by, and remained a mystery.

I am not sure when my memories blurred into dreams, but as the bubbling water and buzz of insects lulled me, my mind fled back to the past. This time, to Berlin.

Chapter 49

Paredo and I had been greeted in Berlin by a small team comprised of local Agency staff, a US government attaché, two German secret service operatives from the BND, (Germany's Federal Intelligence Service), and a senior police officer who greased the wheels for the agency in Berlin. They were a serious bunch, but there was an undercurrent of excitement, as this wasn't their usual run-of-the-mill situation. The BND operatives courteously debriefed us in English, but explained that we would have to speak in German when we arrived on site, so as to not raise any suspicions.

It turned out that Sericum's overseas mission included checking in on the new relic recruits and making sure they were not being spied upon, but when news reached her of our experiences in Hong Kong, she had rejoined the team and taken control of the search. Her small team had successfully located the lost Nazi facility entrance, but it was yet to be breeched. There had been some internal resistance within the German government and the Federal Ministry of Health over the risk of pathogens or chemical weapons being released in a major metropolitan area, but the Committee of 300 had overridden them. They felt the risk of Chinese or Russian relics crashing the party was a greater risk and wouldn't tolerate any further delays.

Paredo had queried why so many bureaucrats had been told in the first place. In his experience, a fake gas leak was normally a good enough reason to evacuate a building and cordon off an area to work. Then you could just get the job done. He was old-school in his attitudes and couldn't abide the constant oversight and bureaucratic nitpicking that was encroaching on all walks of life, including ours.

We had left Sierene and Hector back in Hong Kong, with the fresh Agency relief team that had flown in with Canis at the first sign of trouble. They were still going to attend the meeting that Sierene had been abducted for, just to see who turned up and if they could get to the bottom of the whole mess.

She had claimed that her captors had been headed by the Chinese military, who had been very keen on her lending her diplomatic weight to serving their best interests at the forthcoming meeting, but to my mind, there had been too many factions involved for that to be the whole story.

Fingers were still being firmly pointed at the Chinese - for the missing relics around the globe - and this affair had only intensified the speculation. But with Hiram's man also being involved and so many operatives turning on us at the safe house, something didn't smell right to me. Paredo had cautioned me to keep my thoughts to myself until we were able to coordinate an investigation with the senior relics back in Denver. But it hadn't stopped him from dumping a complete log and footage of our encounters into Canis' mind, along with our suspicions, before we left for Europe.

En route to the dig site, we transferred to a small convoy of gas utility vehicles and were offered utility company overalls. It seemed that Paredo wasn't the only agent to use a gas leak as a cover story.

As usual, they had struggled to cater for Paredo's size, so he had to settle for a clipboard, a high visibility jacket, some safety glasses and a hard hat as a disguise.

Traffic through Berlin flowed relatively smoothly and with it being so flat, there were almost as many cyclists as there were cars. Pedestrians bustled along the wide pavements, engaging in window-shopping, when they weren't actively blowing their hard-earned Euros on ever-changing fashions and the latest gadgets. Others lounged in front of cafes, smoking or chatting the day away over expensive coffee.

With my chosen career centred around archaeology discovered off the beaten track, I had never been a connoisseur of city lifestyle, where you ran the rat-race just to finance your place in consumer culture. As we drove by them, I marvelled at how they lived their lives in total ignorance of the forces that shaped their world. But awake or asleep, I would still throw every fibre of my being into keeping them safe and preserving their freedoms.

When we arrived at the architecturally historic apartment blocks of Mommsenstraße, the road had already been cordoned off with orange mesh fencing and local police were diverting traffic. Inside, several men were taking measurements with various meters and an excavator sat idle, ready to start digging up the road if we needed to extend our cover story. A crowd of bystanders had already built up, including a photographer from the local press. It was out of the ordinary for such an occurrence to require a complete evacuation of the whole street.

An engineer in brightly coloured overalls was waiting for us and opened the barricade to let us through with the vehicles. Navy and white GASAG signs, advertising one of the main gas suppliers in Berlin, were plastered all over the temporary barriers and canvas tents which had been erected in front of several properties. We pulled up in between the tents, which limited the public's view of us as we exited the vehicles.

A couple of agents, dressed as engineers, emerged from one of the buildings and escorted us up three stone steps, through a thick oak and glass doorway, which was usually defended by an intercom system. Within, we found ourselves in a plush foyer. As we proceeded, marble and mirror-clad walls, with a black and white chequered tile floor, gave way to dark green carpets and wooden panelling. One of the engineers indicated that we should pass through a discrete side door, which opened onto another set of stone stairs, descending to a brick and stone basement.

"It's down there," he said in German, before standing aside to let us pass.

Through mutual agreement, we left the rest of our party to wait in the reception area, but the armed BND agents took up position either side of the stairway, to enable us to work without disturbance.

The basement ceiling was vaulted and divided into sections, but the space itself extended the entire length of the building. Motes of dust hung in the air as we passed boxes of stored household items and stacked furniture. We passed a large rusty boiler which presumably used to provide heating and hot water to the property, but this stood cold and redundant, having no doubt been replaced by smaller individual boilers in each apartment above us.

Great polythene curtains had been fixed across each section to minimise the spread of the dust and grit which was still coming from up ahead. Piles of brick and rubble were now pushed to each side of the basement and as we pulled aside the makeshift curtain and passed through into the last section, we could see where it had come from.

Amongst the broken brickwork of the floor, a ragged opening revealed a further stone stairway leading down to a large painted steel door. I say door, but it wouldn't have looked out of place on a bank vault. It hadn't quite been opened to its full extent, as rubble still created an obstruction. The view of the space beyond was obscured by a sweating Jarrod and Carmine, who were filing their way up the stairs with a large bucket of broken bricks and rubble in each hand. They wore dust masks and goggles, which didn't disguise Jarrod's scowl as he greeted us.

"You took your time," he said as he emptied out the excavated waste, heedless of the glare that Paredo was now giving him.

Carmine was more cordial, although I doubt any less impatient. "The way is already clear," he began. "Sericum just asked us to shift the last of the rubble whilst she gets final measurements from her air samples."

Sericum didn't want to take any chances with whatever lay down in Hitler's secret facility. With 70 years of corrosion, whatever was down there may no longer be properly contained, so caution was wise.

As Jarrod straightened and turned, Paredo was already on his way past, but he slapped his clipboard against the smaller man's chest, both as a way to be rid of it and to assert his dominance.

"Balatro," was all he offered in greeting as he swept past without looking back.

At least I assumed it was a greeting. Being omni-lingual, Paredo could have meant it as a flat statement. Jarrod's relic name, Balatro, meant bleater, babbler, buffoon, fool, jester, or joker in Latin. Any one of those descriptors suited him down to the ground, but judging by the sullen sneer he offered in return to Paredo's retreating back, he wasn't a fan of it.

I think Carmine must have been growing tired of Jarrod's attitudes, because his smile at Paredo's rebuke reached his eyes despite his dust mask.

I couldn't bring myself to blank Jarrod, as annoying as he was, so I nodded to them both as I eased past and followed Paredo down the uneven stairs. I refused to flinch at the sudden clatter behind me, as Jarrod petulantly tossed Paredo's clipboard down. It was silly really, as Paredo would only make him pick it up later.

Before I had reached the foot of the stairs, Paredo was siphon-bridging with Sericum, who was monitoring a second vault door, which must have helped form some kind of air lock for the facility. I felt the tug of Paredo's invitation to join his bridge. It put me in mind of a parent tugging on the hand of a distracted toddler, reminding him not to dawdle.

As I opened myself to the flow of communication, I caught the tale-end of Paredo and Sericum greeting each other with a flush of warmth that perhaps I shouldn't have been privy to, but this soon turned into a mutual sharing of information that had been gathered over the last few days.

Sericum's eyes flicked to me in surprise as she learned of my ability to break the commands imposed by handler control modules. I was certain the significance of that would not be lost on her. If anyone was in on Paredo's machinations, I thought to myself, it would be Sericum.

Dressed in a level 4 biohazard containment suit with portable air supply, Sericum looked distinctly fresher than my former classmates. It appeared that they had been doing the hard labour whilst she collected and analysed samples using several different hand-held analysers, which were slung about her person on shoulder straps. So much for being equals now we were all fully fledged relics!

Jesse was still loading a bucket with rubble when I arrived, her back to me. The way her slender waist met her hips wasn't disguised by her baggy overalls, as they had been pulled taught across her lithe frame. I pretended not to have noticed as she straightened and turned to shine me a broad smile through her mask.

I had to suppress the blush in my cheeks with the aid of my implant when Paredo's smirk revealed that my flush of sudden interest in Jesse's physique had dumped itself straight through the bridge, into the conversation that Sericum and Paredo were having. At least Sericum had the grace to overlook it.

"Chris! I'm so glad you're here," Jesse gushed. She was never one for holding back. "I was worried about you when I heard what happened in Hong Kong."

We exchanged pleasantries, or perhaps more accurately, Jesse fired off some excited chatter whilst I pretended to play it cool. But it was soon apparent that Sericum and Paredo were ready to open the second and final door to the facility.

I noted the Agency device mounted onto the inner face of the door she had been monitoring. It could breech the door via laser, then draw through a safely contained air sample. Very specialised gear, but if Sericum's work was complete, at least we could enter knowing that the air was breathable.

Jarrod and Carmine came down the stairs behind us, carrying lamps and respirators and handed them out. It was wise to shut the outer door before we opened the inner door, but I couldn't help feel nervous in case any of the doors jammed on us.

Before the door thudded home and the geared wheel drove heavy steel rods into the surrounding concrete and steel frame, with a nod of permission from Paredo, I drew upon the siphon-bridge and flared brightly, looking for any nearby signatures.

We were supposed to be the only relics here, but I didn't want anyone else sneaking up on us whilst we were vulnerable. To my relief, there was no sign of any relics but ourselves.

In the shifting shadows created by our lamps, everyone but Paredo donned their masks, but he just tucked the strap of the mask under his belt and let it dangle, to free up his hands. Ignoring the questioning looks, he simply nodded for Carmine and Jarrod to wrench on the geared wheel and open the door.

The grinding of the mechanism within the door jangled on my nerves as Jarrod and Carmine strained. Our agents had been abducted, or worse, to keep this place a secret, so who knew what we would find in there. Whatever it was, Hitler's finest minds had been working on it and he had considered it to be worth burying.

Chapter 50

With a deep metallic thud, the steel rods retracted into the vault door and it yawned inwards under the pressure of my Brothers' hands.

Past their shoulders, I saw a cylindrical tunnel angling down into the bowels of the earth. It was lined with riveted sections of corrugated iron, coated in a thick coat of grey enamel paint. They formed a patchwork as they receded into the darkness. The ceiling sported intermittent strip lamps every 30 feet or so, linked by piped cabling, but the floor was made easier to navigate by a six inch depth of white sand, keeping our work boots off the corrugated iron panels.

I could see now why Paredo had left his respirator off. I had only been wearing mine for a few seconds, but it was already hampering my senses. My breath echoed irritatingly and I couldn't get a sense of the movement of air, or lack of it, in the tunnel - things you take for granted when your bare face is open to the atmosphere.

My implant helpfully applied the data from Paredo's unfettered senses and began to construct a map overlay which we could all access through the siphon-bridge. It was strange to commune with so many at once, but as we spread out along the tunnel and pierced the stillness, it was reassuring to be connected.

We were yet to determine if this was a time capsule or a tomb, but with the extensive records of inhumane Nazi experimentation now in the public domain, I knew this place would have its own dark history.

As we walked, it seemed like sacrilege for our boots to overwrite the original footprints in the sand. A record of the comings and goings of the former occupants lay there for anyone to see, but as five sets of work boots disturbed the ground, they were erased from history forever.

After a couple of hundred feet, I succumbed to the frustration and followed Paredo's lead by removing my mask. Sericum was in the lead, her selection of analysers set to continuously sample our environment. She was on constant alert for volatile organic compounds, radiation, mercury, airborne pathogens and any other toxic elements, so until we opened any other doors, I reasoned I was safe enough. Paredo had clearly been satisfied with his own nose to tell him if there was anything to be concerned about.

It wasn't as reckless as you might think, as our implants could detect harmful substances in the parts per billion and through visual spectroscopy we could identify hazardous chemicals by sight. Beyond that, if my training was anything to go by, we could eliminate almost all harmful bacteria and viruses from our bodies by rupturing them with specific frequencies generated by our implants.

Just as Dr Royal Raymond Rife had discovered in the 1920's, microorganisms are vulnerable to certain RF frequencies and so pathogens can be harmlessly eliminated with the right wavelength. I felt very fortunate to house such amazing healing technology within my body, but at the same time, remorseful that this life-saving science was suppressed by the Agency and the Committee of 300, as it didn't suit their agenda on population control.

In the 1930's, Rife had cured over 1000 cases of cancer diagnosed as 'incurable', until the Agency funded crooks in the American Medical Association shut him down. When attempts to buy out his research and equipment by Committee-owned pharmaceutical companies failed, Rife's offices were ransacked, his research paperwork was stolen and the machine that healed all those 1000 'incurable' cancer patients was destroyed. After all, when each cancer patient is worth over a quarter of a million dollars to the medical system in ongoing treatment costs, the last thing our lords and masters would want is a cure. Cancer earned them more money than oil.

Just to be certain, all of the physicians who had used Rife's equipment were threatened by the AMA and Agency goons. Rife himself was dragged into court and the leading laboratory for electronic or energy medicine, which had been independently verifying Rife's discoveries, was mysteriously burnt to the ground.

But now wasn't the time for dark thoughts. There was nothing to be done about the injustices of the past. That was a problem for another day.

The air on my face, as I removed my mask, felt good - albeit stale. It carried away the light sheen of perspiration that had already built up and this cooled my skin as it evaporated. I don't know how Sericum was managing, sealed in her hazmat suit, but she continued on serenely at the head of our column. Paredo followed close behind, his impatience somehow telegraphing through his bearing.

After perhaps 300 feet, the corrugated tunnel levelled out. Ahead, we could see that the tunnel opened out into a larger, vaulted space. The sand-lined, corrugated tunnel gave way to gritty concrete floors and white-washed brickwork and plaster walls. The air was damp down here, and dirty runnels of rusty water had left tracks down the walls where condensation or groundwater had built up. Dark swathes of mould mottled the walls and in the light of our lamps, the facility was looking substantially more run-down. The vaulted ceiling arched away from us some 35 feet over our heads and ahead we could see at least three gaping, arched openings, as corridors or rooms branched off to our right at intervals.

Something dark hung from a verdigreed brass pole which jutted from the nearest archway. As we neared, it turned out to be a damp and well-rotted crimson flag, which was now more mould than cloth. The scent it gave off was just as dark and sickly as its appearance. But the disintegrating cloth wasn't the only source of rot I could smell.

As we gathered at this first intersection, Sericum attempted to draw a distinction with her instruments, but there was nothing conclusive to go by. As she studied her findings, Jesse cast about with her lamp, highlighting another tunnel similar to the one we had arrived by, exiting the vaulted space at the other end. Jarrod scooped up a handful of grit and without warning, flung it down the corridor. As it separated and came down, it clattered from walls and floor up the length of the tunnel, shattering the eerie and sombre stillness that pervaded the place. It struck me as somehow disrespectful, but nobody complained about the additional echo-mapping data that came back through our implants.

We had a choice to make. To our right, through the archway, the barren concrete continued, but I could just make out debris on the floor at the limit of the range of our lamps. Some additional archways and steel doors broke up the expanse of grimy painted brickwork, with wall-mounted plaques next to each. The sheen of reflection from our lamps made reading them at this distance impossible.

"Priebke's journal implied that this entrance was just an emergency escape tunnel, so it stands to reason that the main body of the facility will be this way," Sericum said, gesturing towards the archway with one of her instruments. Her voice sounded hollow within the confines of her helmet and as her hand returned to her side, the coated fabric of her yellow suit crackled noisily as it crumpled.

Paredo drew upon the collective power of our siphon-bridge and flared his implant. With our combined power, he must have reached a good 300 feet in all directions. It didn't help with choosing the best route, but we did get two very faint after-echoes, coming from slightly different directions.

"Bingo," he said aloud. "OK. Time to spread out."

I could tell that his usurpation of command from Sericum had annoyed her, but before she could object, he added, "siphon-bridge contact at all times. Nobody opens anything hermetically sealed, without Sericum checking it out first. We are just scouting the facility to locate the relic technology. Tag hazards, research materials and Nazi technology as you go, but our priority is securing any ancient tech first. Once we have that, we can let the other Agency crews come in here to wrap things up."

Through the bridge, Paredo's disdain for the mundane and tedious tasks that would involve, was obvious. He was happy to spearhead the treasure hunt, but someone else could clean up the mess afterwards and spend the countless hours cataloguing and reporting on the mundane minutia that a find of this kind would entail.

Salvaging some semblance of control, Sericum's voice rang out again. "Lucidus, Cordis, you two are with me. Balatro, Severus, scout these side tunnels and rejoin us when you can. Every 75 feet, flare your siphons to see if we can get a better fix on those signatures."

The blatant omission of any orders for Paredo made him smile. He flashed Sericum with a grin and an impudent wink and sauntered off down the corridor as though he didn't have a care in the world. Sericum was an odd mix of vexation and secret amusement. But she had something right, it was pointless expecting Paredo to stick to any plan, even if it were his own.

As our small unit split up and began to explore the facility, the visual overlay map in my mind expanded incrementally. New corridors and rooms added themselves as they were experienced and I found myself just as interested in the discoveries of my fellow relics as my own.

Collectively, we passed accommodation for staff, storage areas, engineering works and even abandoned design studios, where row after row of desks and drawing boards were overshadowed by tall chalk boards still covered in complex calculations. Anything perishable, such as soft furnishings or paper, was in a state of decay and as we moved further into the heart of the facility, the rushed nature of its abandonment became increasingly obvious. Many things had just been left where they lay, but a box of spilled papers lying in a doorway next to a lady's shoe, began to paint a darker picture.

Carmine and Jarrod were the first to find human remains. They had discovered the brig. Of a dozen or so large cells, 5 of them had occupants. Horribly, it looked as though they had been left to rot along with the facility. I don't know how they would have looked in life, but in death, their emaciated bodies were nothing but bones and corruption. Some had returned to their cots to die, but others still sat with arms and legs through the cold steel bars of their cells, waiting for rescue.

It was harrowing to think of the 3 or 4 desperate days it would have taken for the inmates to die of thirst, but a narrow drainage channel running along the wall of one of the cells had cursed the unfortunate occupant with enough water to draw out their suffering in the darkness for several weeks. From what I could see from Carmine's cursory inspection, they had tried to end their torment by dashing their head against the bars.

We might have received the best military training that money could buy, but nothing adequately prepares you for such scenes. We couldn't even offer justice. All I could hope for, would be for them to receive a decent burial.

As we each took different corridors, I toured a series of offices which lay behind frosted glass doors. These had been shielded from the damp and desks and filing cabinets still held their contents. Pictures on the walls showed various Nazi rallies, or portraits of Hitler himself looking on from balconies, from his motorcade or even in his private gardens. On one of the desks, a black Bakelite telephone with a braided leather chord lay with its receiver off the hook.

One of the offices was decorated with the framed schematics of various prototype weapons, such as a next generation version of the revolutionary Fritz X radio-guided dive bomb, along with assorted bat-like fixed-wing aircraft. I could see where later generations of stealth bombers had drawn their design inspiration from.

My implant tagged this location as potentially containing intelligence on weapons technology, but I moved on as instructed.

The visual map overlay we shared through the siphon-bridge was rapidly expanding in all directions as we each added to the data available. But more importantly, we now had a more precise location for the after-echoes we had picked up when

Paredo had flared. There was definitely some relic technology in this industrialised crypt.

Jarrod and Carmine seemed to have drawn the short straw when they found the barracks. The doors were unbarred and lay open, but a carpet of spent brass shell casings spilling into the corridor told a grim tale before my Brothers even cast the light of their lamps onto the dark scene within.

Behind dozens of rudely constructed wooden bunks, lay a mass of tattered bodies. The stripes of their clothing identified them as prisoners, most likely drawn from the surrounding concentration camps. Whether they were used for labour or experimentation, I didn't know, but the bullet riddled wall behind them and the way they had fallen in a huddle like ninepins told me they hadn't been given any respect, even in death. Some bodies still tangled amongst the bunks. I would have closed my eyes to it, but as Carmine's implant overlaid trajectory analysis and angles of fire, the way in which the cowardly guards had mowed down the occupants was indelibly printed across my mind.

We continued our search, our mood beyond sombre in the oppressive murk of the place. I could feel Jesse through the bridge as she moved from room to room, silent tears upon her cheeks, but her sudden interest in something important drew my attention.

Jesse had discovered a large and detailed map of the facility mounted on the wall of an intersection. It was exactly what we had needed. As our map overlay suddenly populated with new information, the vast scale of this facility became apparent.

The site sprawled across just over 75 acres and had been artfully worked around the Berlin U-Bahn - the underground railway that connected the city's 170 stations.

'I'm heading for Sonderprojekte,' Sericum siphoned, referring to the department labelled on the facility map. It meant special projects and was the source of one of the signals.

'Affirmative,' Paredo replied at the speed of thought. 'I'll take Fortschrittlichen Waffen. Severus, Balatro, you're closest. Meet me there.'

It made sense that the other signature was coming from the Advanced Weapons section, but the name designated to the location added some spice to the search. We were in awe of the wondrous Anunnaki technology which had been recovered so far, resulting in countless advances of modern technology, but who knew what marvels the Third Reich had recovered?

I already had the back of Sericum's yellow suit in sight when she siphoned for Jesse and myself to rally on her location. Jesse emerged from a side tunnel, with her respirator in one gloved hand and wiping her forehead with the back of the other. The hospital wing she had just been scouting held nothing but dark memories.

I caught up and we walked in companionable silence, but our collective apprehension began to build afresh as traces of radiation began to encroach upon us. It wasn't enough to cause us harm, but it was another indicator of the potential for danger down here.

I watched Paredo's feed with interest as Carmine and Jarrod helped him open an even larger vault door which would lead to the Advanced Weapons area. A long plate-glass observation window showed the immediate area to be free of hazards and even if it wasn't, I doubt that would have slowed him much, such was his eagerness to secure the ancient tech.

I was spared Sericum's laborious tests by the fact that the Special Projects suite doors already lay ajar. Jesse and I exchanged a look as I gestured for her to follow behind Sericum through the doorway.

As fortune would have it, we struck lucky almost immediately. Behind paper-strewn desks and laboratory benches kitted out with sinks and Bunsen burners, the walls were lined with row upon row of bell jars containing well-preserved biological specimens. Hands, eyes, hearts and other organs provided distraction to the eye, but Sericum's implant immediately highlighted some anachronistic robotic tech.

The most significant part was the mechanical hand of some kind of android. Its translucent gel-flesh coating didn't do much to disguise the polyalloy skeletal structure within. It had been sheared off at the wrist, exposing a thick bundle of fibre-optic like filaments, which reminded me of the filaments running throughout my own body.

Sericum wasted no time in scooping the jar off the shelf and dropping it into a net bag, similar to a diver's bag and passed it to Jesse. I could feel Paredo's interest piquing through the siphon-bridge as he eavesdropped on what she had found.

A fairly well-preserved notebook, containing documented drawings of similar tech, written in a neat hand, joined the jar soon after. Having seemingly exhausted the room, a door in the far wall opened onto another corridor, which presented four more doors to choose from.

Sericum took a moment to scan the mounted signs, then made a beeline for the door marked Leichenschauhaus, which meant Morgue.

Just to be on the safe side, I flared my implant again to be sure we hadn't missed anything. Only relics gave off their own signature, but I was pretty sure that any technology which could use siphon energy would show dark against the corona I was able to generate, because it would absorb some of the mysterious force. As a result of my encounter with Hector's late handler, Brett, I knew that at least control modules did.

Sericum and Jesse's signals were loud and clear, but they were joined by a third, which throbbed sullenly in resonance and formed a large dark patch in the field I was generating.

It was enough to make Sericum hesitate as she stared in surprise, but as my flare subsided, she set her jaw and pushed on with renewed vigour.

The Morgue had several large metal surgical tables in the middle, complete with guttering to catch any fluid and flexible metal hoses which hung down from the ceiling. A couple of small wheeled instrument tables were cast aside, still bearing their contents and a couple of rusty gurneys lay against one wall. To our left, cabinets and anatomical diagrams broke up the expanse of tiled wall, but what drew our eyes was the extensive arrangements for cold storage along the back wall. On one side, 8 banks of brushed steel mortuary drawers were arrayed three high, giving a capacity of 24 corpses on ice. One hung open, but the sliding slab within lay empty upon its rollers. On the other side however, was the door to a great walk-in freezer. The door must have been a good 6 feet across and was fastened closed with three sturdy chromed handles and a thick deadbolt and padlock.

As Sericum set about dealing with the antique lock, Jesse experimentally pulled open a series of drawers, which were blessedly empty. It seemed as though the power had been off for as long as the facility had been abandoned, so without any active refrigeration, any contents we found would be in a grim state.

Sure enough, when Jesse opened another of the draws on the second row, the stench that was released hit me before the steel door had even swung fully open. The body within had virtually liquefied on its bones to form a dark sludge that was impossible to identify except by its proportions. The scent was a combination of cloying rot and wet peat.

With such a grim discovery, Jesse had opted to replace her mask, and no wonder. But in my turning away from the greasy discovery, I had spotted a clipboard hanging from a hook on the side of one of the nearby cabinets. It contained a log of the Morgue.

It may have been a bit of a cop-out, but I opted to pursue the thinking man's approach to this investigation. My eyes scanned down the list until something drew my attention.

"Try number 18," I called over to Jesse as she slammed home another empty drawer. "It's logged as 'Wichtelmanchen'," which meant gnome.

Paredo's team was making steady progress towards the second signature, but they were struggling to get one of the metal doors open.

My mind turned back to the job at hand as Jesse grasped the handle to number 18 and pulled.

I have to say, standing in the transient darkness of that haunting place, enveloped in the stench of the grave, I wouldn't have expected my life to get any stranger. But it did.

When Jesse tugged on the handle and the metal door swung wide, the slender child-like body it revealed almost blew my mind. Jesse's gasp and her surprise through the siphon-bridge was no less intense. Sericum even ceased her attack on the thick padlock to come and look.

With unsteady hands, Jesse reached out and pulled. The slab rolled out quietly on its rollers to reveal what popular culture referred to as a 'Grey'.

The small humanoid's limbs were slender in proportion to its rounded belly and its dark eyes were as open as its gaping mouth, as it stared sightlessly at the ceiling. I couldn't believe what I was seeing, but Sericum's calm influence flooded through the bridge.

'You can pick your jaws up off the floor now, you two. It's a machine.' It took a moment to register what she was saying and I was already moving to Jesse's side to stare at the creature.

True enough, up close, it's skin resembled a very fine grey mesh, almost the texture of sharkskin. The eyes were a glossy jet black, like two ovoid pools of infinity. It was immediately obvious what had 'killed' it. Its bulbous skull, face and upper torso had been cleaved, in some sort of accident. There were scorch marks all along the damage and a dark ichor welled at the deepest reaches of the vicious cleft. Unlike the corpses we had discovered, this being had not decomposed at all and a quick look into the wound revealed why. Inside, several layers of its hide were visible in cross-section. The pale grey mesh at the surface, coated some sort of pearlescent insulation within, with a coarser mesh underneath to give it structural integrity and shape. But seen out of this context, I could understand exactly how these creatures had been mistaken as living beings. Suddenly the mass of sightings and abduction stories since the incident at Roswell in the 1940's had a very real basis in fact for me.

'They called them *the watchers* in Sumerian times,' Sericum added as she came to stand alongside us. 'I've only seen them twice before in person though.' She studied our reactions. 'This finding will be taken away from us as soon as we reveal it, so get a good look whilst you can. It'll end up at Dulce Air Force Base or White Sands. But,' she added with scorn, 'they can no more reverse engineer these than they can relics.'

With this revelation, I didn't know whether to be pleased or disappointed. Perhaps most of the value was in the mystery? But one thing was for sure, I had realised that there was another layer to the onion that even relics were not privy to.

Jesse seemed to be keeping her thoughts to herself, but she took off her glove and mask and ran a slender pink finger along the creature's grey brow and down the section of face where its nose should have been. It still had two small nostrils, but it had no external ears to speak of and its mouth was almost a slit. I followed Jesse's lead and lifted one of its thin arms. It was quite soft and spongy to the touch and as I raised it, it was surprising how extraordinarily light it was. The long-fingered hand lolled lifelessly at the end of it. When I gripped it, the fingers felt very dextrous, perhaps being articulated in more places than a human hand.

My fascination was disturbed by a sense of awe bubbling through the siphon-bridge as Jarrod and Carmine eavesdropped and were also marvelling at what we were looking at.

'Get back to the job at hand!' Paredo griped a moment later, out of sheer frustration. Clearly the blocked doorway was posing more of a problem than I had realised.

Having seen enough, Sericum turned back toward her work, electronic lock pick in hand. Her brows were drawn together, presumably wondering about the best way to defeat the lock she had been struggling with. But a moment later, she was chuckling to herself and moving towards one of the glass-fronted cabinets across the room. Her implant had spotted and highlighted the solution. A complicated brass key was hanging from a hook that had been screwed into the side of the cabinet and she retrieved it with a coquettish swagger only marred by her bulky and crackling suit.

"Simple solutions are always the best ones," she said with a smile as she placed the key in the lock and turned it. With a click, it sprung open in her gloved hand and she unhooked it and set it aside with satisfaction. I think she was pleased to have beaten Paredo to a prize.

The clipboard had listed the main freezer contents as 'Erste Menche (Base-211, Neuschwabenland).'

I was well familiar with the Nazi expeditions to Antarctica, having received my agency briefing in anticipation of going there. Neuschwabenland was the name given to an area claimed on behalf of Nazi Germany by Captain Ritscher in the late 1930's. By the 1940's the area had been stocked with substantial levels of supplies and materials in order to service the U-Boats operating in the south Atlantic. Serving as the southern-most point of influence, in a triangle including South Africa and Argentina, the Nazi base they constructed came to be known as 'New Berlin', or Base-211. It has often been regarded as a myth, such was the level of secrecy surrounding it, but what lay in this freezer must have been the product of their activity in the far south.

I found my heart racing in anticipation. The name 'Erste Menche,' or 'First Man,' held such promise, but at the same time, it sent shivers down my spine. What had they found there?

Sericum didn't keep us in suspense. She slid the deadbolt back and then pulled on the handles, in turn, until the heavy insulated freezer door reluctantly swung open. The air within was cooler, but my attention was immediately drawn to a large riveted steel sarcophagus, which rested atop a gurney. It had swastikas stencilled on the sides and at over 8 feet long, it overhung both ends of the wheeled trolley by at least a foot.

The hinged lid was glazed, to allow the contents to be visible and, arrayed around it on a couple of wheeled tables, lay a number of futuristic-looking artefacts which must have been removed during examination.

Sericum was the first to enter the freezer to get a closer look, her instruments all but forgotten. As Jesse and I crowded in behind her, offering up our lamps to improve visibility, we all stood in silence and stared down into a face lost to legend.

A muscular and blonde-bearded warrior lay within, looking impressive, despite how his flesh had sunken in death. He wore a glossy chromed suit, which seemed to be somewhere between skin-hugging armour and fish-scales. Perhaps even the scales of a serpent. His gauntleted hands had been laid across his chest, which would have been broad and deep in life. About his shoulders, his armour softened and appeared more like a mantle of gleaming feathers, terminating in a thick ridge of material about his neck which formed a collar.

If the Nazis had recovered him from the ice, who knew how long he had lain there, awaiting discovery.

In life, he must have stood well over seven and a half feet tall, but his noble features did not appear cruel. Was I looking into the face of a hero of antiquity? Or just an arrogant master of slaves?

I suppose the answer to that varied, depending upon which accounts from antiquity you favoured. Some had described the Anunnaki as wondrous benefactors, whilst others described them as ranging from capricious at best, to ruthless psychopaths at worst. The truth of this was yet another thing lost to the flow of time. But, I supposed, our own modern-day world leaders would seem no less polarised when viewed through the lens of history. They varied from mass-murdering dictators like Hitler, Stalin and Chairman Mao, (who between them murdered more than 100 million people), to magnanimous philanthropists like President José Mujica of Uruguay, (who gave 90% of his state salary to feed the homeless and declined to live in the opulent presidential palace or use its staff, in favour of living on a humble farm).

I doubted I gazed down upon the Incan god Viracocha, or Quetzalcoatl of the Aztecs, Ishkur of Akkad, Babylonia and Suma, or even the Mayan god Kukulkan, but this being fitted the descriptions offered for all of them. Every one of these ancient cultures had described a tall man (or men) with long beards and pale skin, at a time when scholars declare there should have been no contact with fair-haired Europeans. Some ancient accounts went so far as to describe the use of a rod that emitted thunder and lightning, and an extensive knowledge of agriculture, mathematics, astrology, or other such wondrous sciences.

I pondered all of this as I looked down upon the mysterious figure. Judging by his attire, the Aztec description of a feathered serpent, would have been remarkably apt. The metal scales and feathers were so smooth that they almost appeared liquid, with no trace of corrosion or wear. He would have appeared magical to any primitive people.

But whether you favoured the descriptions from Mesoamerica, or those of the Sumerians or Akkadians, they all pointed to this warrior being either an Anunnaki or one of their half-human offspring.

In death, he looked peaceful and it was hard to reconcile his gentle expression with the tales of ruthless overlords who would happily oppress us.

I had never learned anything more about the body my implant had come from, which would have been removed by the Agency at the time of my capture. But what I do remember clearly, was that it had lacked the extraordinary level of preservation shown here. I wondered if this was a product of the mesmerising suit.

"Is this an Anunnaki?" I asked aloud, to nobody in particular as my wonder spilled out.

Jesse didn't have any more of an answer than I did and simply moved closer to the metal sarcophagus to lay a hand upon the glass and peer at the features of the figure at rest within.

I had hoped Sericum would know, but instead she said, "I think only genetic analysis will tell us the difference. But I don't think such grand attire would be wasted on a half-human. After all, they were frowned upon enough by the pure-blooded Anunnaki to be left to their fate during the deluge."

She had a point. But then she seem to come to a decision. "Come around here and help me."

I was surprised to see that she intended to open the casket.

"We need to take some samples," she continued.

Opening the sealed coffin seemed to fly entirely in the face of the caution that she had been showing so far. Sericum must have either seen my furrowing brow, or else felt my confusion through the siphon-bridge, because she added, "Once we hand this specimen over, we will never know the answer. The same goes for the technology he bears. They will only restore to us anything which isn't considered a threat or which serves the Committee's ends."

I was surprised that she was being so frank, but being isolated in such an environment I suppose precluded the possibility of us being spied upon. Besides, the injustice of not being privy to the incredible scientific findings, from what we had just discovered, would rankle within even the most loyal relics. Intelligent people hate being kept in the dark.

She pushed one of the smaller wheeled tables out of the way and I, in turn, pushed the other toward Jesse, who took it in one hand and swung it out of our way. On it, lay a polished silver sphere, a dark metal rod and a small metallic container with a flared opening and a transparent, glassy lozenge within. They were all equally as mysterious, but I dismissed them in favour of moving around to help Sericum lift the heavy riveted lid. Jesse helpfully took my lamp and held it on high to give us maximum light.

We were about to heave, when Paredo's voice rang out through the siphon-bridge. 'We are through. Proceeding to the location of the second signature.'

He didn't say it, but he seemed pleased that we were taking matters into our own hands. My only concern was Jarrod and Carmine. Especially Jarrod. I wasn't at all convinced about his loyalties and suspected that our actions here today would be reported straight back to his handler and sponsor - and with the recent turn of events fresh in my mind, I trusted Hiram even less.

I am not sure what I was expecting, but there was no dramatic hiss, or anything untoward as we lifted the lid and set it back against its hinges. The body within remained at rest. Yet it still maintained an air of activity, as though it wasn't quite dead. It was bizarre. When viewed in full spectrum, it was slightly warmer than its surroundings, but that didn't account for it.

Sericum reached for a small satchel-like pack that was clipped to her belt and proceeded to open it up and retrieve three tubed sterile swabs for sampling DNA. Surprisingly, the Erste Menche's mouth fell open at the pressure of her thumb on his chin and, although her eyes widened at this, she proceeded to collect three samples of cheek cells. When the tubes were sealed, she respectfully pushed his jaw closed and poked one of the tubes into Jesse's jacket pocket and turned to hand me the other.

She didn't say anything, but she didn't have to. We would be complicit in concealing these samples from our masters. She repeated the exercise with three Vacutainer tubes where she drew what fluid she could from the jugular vein. She couldn't access femoral blood vessels or the heart, so this was the next best option for post-mortem analysis. Hair follicle samples came next.

The room was silent and still, as finally, she tore open a small sachet containing a disposable scalpel blade, in order to collect tissue samples. She aligned the narrow steel handle and clicked the blade into place, where its razor-sharp edge gleamed wickedly in the lamplight.

"This is going to be a little more obvious," she said, "but hopefully, they won't be able to date the incisions when they examine him. I'll try to be discrete."

I was mulling this over as she turned toward the body, scalpel in hand. But then it hit me.

"Why is he still intact?" I asked, concern in my voice, just as we received the startling answer.

As Sericum's arm stretched towards his neck, blade in hand, the quicksilver suit the warrior wore responded. In a ripple of liquid metal activity which confused the eye, the thick roll of material at the neck extended up to form a full-faced helm, which covered his dead face with the fierce, beaked visage of a great eagle. It happened so quickly that it could have easily protected the blonde giant from attack. But for good measure, the eagle was animated, its silver eyes flashing and its beak opening threateningly in warning, as Sericum snatched her hand back defensively.

If the sudden motion hadn't been so alarming, we would have been laughing and clapping our hands with glee like children at the fine display, but being on the receiving end of this threatening rebuttal gave it a different feel altogether.

We stood and gaped as the visor, or eagle, or whatever you wanted to call it, gave us each one last baleful look, gnashed its beak, then went still. A moment later, the threat seemingly resolved, it softened and the liquid metal withdrew back into the shape of the thick band of material about the Erste Menche's neck. His pallid, dead face still remained the same, with the same benevolent expression.

"Wow," I exclaimed. "Have you ever seen anything like that!" It was miraculous. "I guess that answers that!"

Jesse had been holding her breath and it came out in a whoosh of excitement and a grin spread across her face. Sericum had physically taken a step back and no wonder, after that display of super-technology.

"I think it is safe to say that this must be a full-blooded Anunnaki," she said, as she took the blade apart and stowed her samples. "Help me with the lid."

I wanted to see the response again, but Sericum was right to be cautious in this instance. Although the defence was automated, maybe the first reaction was a warning, but perhaps the second would be an attack. None of us were prepared for that. Who knew what capabilities the suit had, and we still hadn't even examined the artefacts that lay on the tables.

This find was beyond incredible to us, despite our knowledge of technology and our relics, but for the Nazi scientists of the 1940's, this must have absolutely blown their minds! No wonder the base was hidden before Berlin fell. This kind of miraculous technology couldn't ever be allowed to fall into enemy hands. Yet, with a sinking feeling, I realised that this was exactly what we were about to do with it.

I was about to say something to that effect, when Paredo siphoned.

'I have seen such only once before. A glimpse from the mind of a Russian relic. But this one had a snarling tiger for a helm.' For good measure, he flashed the image through the siphon-bridge.

'I assume it is the origin of legends of werewolves, minotaurs and even the animal-headed gods of Egypt. The Agency has working prototypes of this technology. Blades and such. But they are primitive in comparison and the power source cannot maintain the integrity of the shape for long.'

As Sericum secured the lid of the casket ready for transport, we carefully gathered the remaining artefacts and split them between us. I took the sphere and the stout metal rod and put them in opposite pockets to make sure they couldn't damage each other or interact in any way. A cursory check had revealed that none of them were giving off anything harmful, but you couldn't be too careful.

I must admit that having gorged on such incredible revelations, I was on a high, but I still wanted more. I felt disappointed that Sericum, Jesse and I, would now be leaving with our prizes for extraction. But the consolation was that we could no doubt share experiences with Paredo and his team when we met up later.

In truth, I had been hoping to siphon the warrior to see what I could learn from his relic, but I would have had to do that privately. I still hadn't revealed my progress with the decommissioned relic in Alaska, nor had I evaluated the packet of information it had left me with.

That was it! I would scratch my itch for discovery later on, by accessing that file. Given the trouble I had gotten myself into with the Committee over leaked data, I had been a little cautious, but in the face of today's encounter, whatever lay in that dump of data would surely be tame in comparison!

As we carefully wheeled the fragile gurney through the facility, it creaked and groaned under the weight. Its wheels were large enough to navigate the rough concrete when we had left the smooth tiled floor behind, but we were careful not to overdo it.

Our slow progress didn't require a great deal of my attention, so I allowed my focus to shift to Paredo's activity in the Special Weapons section. Jarrod and Kester had paused to look at prototypes for body armour, tanks and detailed plans for experimental aircraft, but Paredo was doggedly heading toward the location of the signature. He paused to flare his siphon, in order to get a more accurate fix on its location. His alarm hit us all through the siphon-bridge almost as fast as we realised the problem for ourselves. It had moved!

Chapter 51

My mind raced as it considered the possibilities. My instant, but perhaps fanciful conclusion was that the signature we had been detecting was from a relic that was somehow still alive down here, but as Paredo broke into a run and flared with even more intensity, he boomed through the siphon-bridge.

'Severus, Balatro, on me. We have company.' Paredo's small team sprung into action as Paredo himself unholstered his machine pistol and broke into a run.

'Secure your finds and get them back to base,' he threw in our direction as he burst through doorways and vaulted furniture and workbenches, with Carmine and Jarrod hot on his heels. With Paredo's blood being up, the excitement of his whole team flooded through the bridge. This was their first real action since leaving the Academy and Jarrod let out a wild whoop as he ran, pistol in hand.

As Paredo flared again, it became more obvious what he had detected. The original signature was now accompanied by another, which had been dimmed against us. Someone had beaten us to it!

As Paredo's siphon drew close enough to establish a red thread of siphon-tracking, it became obvious that the signal was receding towards the underground tunnels on the far side of the facility. I had been lulled into thinking we were secure down here, but if agents of the Russians or the Chinese had accessed the facility from the U-Bahn, who knew what we could be up against.

I was torn between extracting our find and joining the frantic chase, but as Sericum detached and discarded her helmet and air supply and left them where they lay, her voice cut through my indecision.

"Time to pick up the pace. Let's go," she said, her urgency writ large across her delicate features.

We didn't have any suitable way to transport the 'Grey' that we had discovered in the mortuary drawer, but we couldn't leave it behind either. So Jesse and Sericum lifted the limp figure between them and placed it onto the metal rack slung under the gurney that the 'Erste Menche' rested upon. One of its thin arms flopped over the side to slap onto the cold tiled floor, but I scooped it up and tucked it back into the basket.

I hastened to the front of the casket and gripped the sturdy metal handle with both hands behind me, as Jesse and Sericum each moved to a back corner and leaned into the task and pushed. The gurney, complete with its two passengers, surged forward, testing the rusted antique to its limits as the wheels bumped and skittered over the uneven concrete.

The payload must have collectively weighed over 700 lbs, so as we jogged down corridors and swerved around corners, the gurney had a tendency to keep on going, like an over-laden shopping trolley.

The feed from Paredo was becoming fragmented as we were separated by more and more concrete and distance, but before the signal gave out, we watched through Paredo's eyes as he ran toward a great breach in a corridor wall. As Paredo scrambled over bricks, stone, sand and rubble, bursting out of the facility into a subway tunnel, he was finally able to see his fleeing quarry in the distance, silhouetted as heat signatures in the carbon-black darkness.

But the blackness of the tunnel was suddenly dispelled in two great swathes by the xenon headlights of a couple of motocross bikes, as they roared into life and ripped away with matching plumes of exhaust smoke. A shower of pebbles and grit fanned out behind each of them as they sped away, their thick, knobbly tires making short work of the railway sleepers in between the tracks. Paredo's only recourse was to empty the clip of his machine pistol in the direction of the receding tail lights, the report of each round amplified by the confines of the tunnel.

Paredo ejected the spent magazine as he ran and was sliding another into place as his signal finally dropped out. As Jarrod and Carmine also went out of range, our siphon-bridge was finally severed. The last impression I got was of Paredo reaching out with his implant to the GSM frequency mobile telephone network that serviced the underground, in order to call for backup and update the Agency of the chase in progress.

His implant would no doubt find him the best footing as he sprinted through the darkness, but even with a relic's speed and endurance he wouldn't be able to keep up. All I could hope was that the lingering exhaust fumes and subway surveillance cameras would enable him to track their exit point and that we could use satellite support and local agencies to mount a pursuit. But what technology had they taken?

As Sericum, Jesse and I reached the tunnel we had entered by, the magnitude of the task at hand became more obvious. The wheels of the gurney soon got bogged down by the deep sand which lined the tunnel and our progress slowed to a standstill.

"We're going to have to carry the casket up first," I said aloud, as I inwardly groaned at the task. "Then come back for the little guy."

Without complaint, Sericum took one of the lamps from atop the casket and clipped it to her belt, passing the other to Jesse for her to do likewise. We had lost the third during our headlong dash through the facility. As the lamps swung, shadows lurched and shifted confusingly within the tunnel, but with our relic-enhanced vision, there was still plenty of light to see by.

I tested my grip and experimentally lifted my end of the casket. The pressure of the metal digging into the palms of my hands was unpleasant, but not unbearable. The weight itself was not the problem, but more so the fact that we had to haul this deadweight up a 300 foot incline with shifting sand for footing.

Sericum and Jesse were able to spread the weight between them, but as we lifted the sarcophagus clear of the gurney, my shoulders and trapezius muscles were feeling the strain. Given that I was at the front and had an end to myself, Jesse and Sericum allowed me to dictate the pace. My implant highlighted that it would be my grip strength which would likely fail first, so I put in a solid effort to reach the basement before that happened. After 50 feet I was sweating, after 100, my lungs were burning. Every step and stumble fatigued my back further still, as the lactic acid in my quadriceps turned this endeavour into a torture. But we doggedly continued on.

It was difficult to tell whether it was my implant's intervention, or merely the motivation that comes from being scrutinised by two attractive women, but mercifully, I made it through the first set of vault doors in one go. We lowered the casket to the ground as delicately as we could, but when I turned, exhausted, I saw that I wasn't the only one with pumped forearms and sweat running down my face.

I did my best to massage life back into my limbs, as Sericum and Jesse edged past me in the tight quarters to unlock the outer vault door. Jesse's jacket hung open and she tugged at the buttons of her shirt to allow herself some air. Her movement caught my eye and I couldn't help but stare as she swept fingers through her tousled blonde hair and wiped the sheen of perspiration from her forehead with the back of one sleeve. She was blatantly unaware of how her clothing clung to her as she brushed past me with a gentle smile. The distinctly feminine scent of her, along with her natural pheromones, filled my nostrils and settled on the back of my throat. I couldn't help wondering if she had been taking lessons from Sericum. Although, given my recent track record of inadvertently blasting my private thoughts through the siphon-bridge, I took some care to ensure my thoughts remained my own.

As Jesse and Sericum laid hands upon the geared mechanism of the vault door, I flared my implant to make sure that we wouldn't have any surprises awaiting us on the other side. I certainly couldn't hear any activity, but the way my blood pulsed in my ears, that didn't mean an awful lot. The space beyond was clear.

Over the next few minutes, we settled the sarcophagus down in the basement and covered it with canvas and polythene dust sheets, whilst Jesse went to gather additional agents to help carry. The invaluable and beyond-top-secret contents were no longer visible and I hoped that the enormous weight would throw off any speculation as to what lay within.

As Jesse headed for the stairs to gather some assistance from the other Agency staff, Sericum tipped the contents out of a large black plastic and aluminium trunk, which held scientific equipment, and shunted it across the brick floor towards me with a booted foot.

"This ought to be big enough for the second specimen," she said as she set about unzipping and climbing out of her hazmat suit. "We will load up and head for the airport. If you can catch up, we will go together in convoy. Otherwise, just meet us there."

She had set aside some of her usual polish and charm for a more utilitarian demeanour. But that was understandable, after such a gruelling extraction and whilst Paredo and his crew still faced danger without us.

So I snatched up Jesse's discarded lamp in one hand and the empty equipment case in the other and headed back down into the facility, alone. My arms and legs still burned, but as I took each breath, I could feel them steadily recovering. Certainly, the lightweight kit I now carried was no great hardship.

As I trudged back down the tunnel, along the uneven trail we had created in the sand with our heavy footsteps, I maintained siphon-bridge contact with Sericum and Jesse as long as I could.

A crew of Agents and operatives had already gathered above and were helping to carry the casket up and out of the basement. By the time I had folded the spongy body of the Grey into the trunk, the Erste Menche had been loaded into the back of a long wheelbase utility van under Sericum's supervision and a convoy of vehicles was forming up. Sericum was already in contact with Acertas, confirming our payload and status, whilst getting details of Paredo's pursuit. He had already commandeered a vehicle and was giving chase, with local BND operatives and German Police providing support.

By the time I had secured my package, Sericum and Jesse were already pulling away, but Sericum had arranged for a support team to escort me to the airport.

So I wasn't surprised when four men in overalls met me in the tunnel, the beams of their flashlights and head torches sabotaging my night vision as they swept about me. They smelled anxious and their elevated heart rates matched their nervous laughter as they studied the facility about them.

They greeted me and said that they were to escort me. A couple offered to take the case from me, but knowing what it contained, I politely declined.

As we cleared the tunnel and entered the basement, a scientific crew was already waiting to enter, to take over where we had left off. They sounded more excited than nervous, with this facility having been under their noses pretty much all of their professional lives.

My small party accompanied me back to the foyer we had originally entered by, where I waited for a utility company Land

Rover to be backed up to the entrance, ready to be loaded with my precious cargo. One of the armed BND operatives we had arrived with, who my implant helpfully identified as Agent Schultz, was waiting there and offered to accompany us. He justified it by saying that the rest of the team had already departed with 'Frau Sericum', but I suspected it was just an opportunity for him to fish for further intelligence. I had already eavesdropped on Sericum and Jesse's departure through the siphon-bridge and knew he was the last of the welcome committee, but of course he wouldn't have known that.

The rest of my escort appeared reluctant to have him along, which I put down to inter-agency politics and rivalries, but I felt that an extra gun between us was probably a good idea. After all, we had already been robbed once today, despite our precautions.

When the well-used 4 x 4 was in place, its diesel fumes steadily filling the air as the engine idled, the driver, a round-faced agent with receding hair and a scar running through one of his dark eyebrows, opened the rear door for me to load the cargo.

When it was secure, I slammed the door and he moved around the vehicle to re-enter the driver's seat. I slipped into the passenger seat to ride shotgun. Schultz slid in behind me and a scowling operative in utility company work gear climbed in behind the driver. The other two of our party headed to a second Land Rover, then waited for us to take the lead.

As we pulled away, I turned my face away from the Journalists and photographers, who gathered with the pressing crowds at the barriers. Goodness knew when the residents would be able to return to their properties, with such a find beneath their homes. But of course, they didn't know that, so no doubt some of them made up part of the crowd who rubber-necked at the flurry of activity.

As we drove, Schultz made small talk about local news and politics, but nobody else seemed willing to humour him with conversation.

He rattled on about the latest vaccine scandal in the news, where the risk of swine flu across the whole of Europe had been grossly overstated and hyped up by the World Health

Organisation, in order to greatly advance the profits of the major vaccine manufacturers. Millions of people had been exposed to poorly tested vaccines against a strain of flu that was vastly less harmful than the vaccines themselves, whilst a number of WHO pandemic specialists magically ended up with highly paid positions in the companies that directly benefited from the endorsement of the falsified pandemic.

I politely nodded and responded in the right places, but my eyes were scanning the traffic and buildings lining our route, looking for any potential threats.

The Professor and I had spoken of the corruption within the vaccine industry on several occasions when he had visited me after a hard day's training, so what Schultz was describing was tame. The Agency insiders and many government officials wouldn't touch the public vaccines and had their own special 'clean' batches specially made. No SV-40 monkey cancer viruses, or mercury-induced neurological or immune problems for them! As it was, millions of women in Africa and South America were being injected with tetanus shots spiked with sterilents as part of the Committee's population control agenda. If Schultz heard about that, his hair would stand on end!

We made steady progress, but as traffic began to build, our driver indicated and pulled off the beaten path. When he caught my look of surprise, he shrugged it off as a quicker route to the airport during rush hour, but although his voice didn't contain micro-tremors, I still sensed some sort of change in his demeanour. My implant rerouted its own inbuilt navigation, but as we drove, the driver's heart rate was beginning to climb and his blinking rate increased. Something was amiss. He was looking in the mirror more frequently, but I could see nothing untoward myself.

Schultz seemed oblivious to the change and was now lecturing us on the corruption scandal surrounding the recent resignation of the German president, when the dour Agent sitting next to him shifted in his chair slightly, to also observe the rear view mirror.

I considered reaching inside my jacket for my Agency-issue pistol, but that would have seemed most churlish if I were wrong. Maybe the driver was simply in a hurry to be somewhere after work and was nervous about being late?

I was about to broach the topic, but then it happened.

My galvanic skin responses changed and my pupils twitched. Before the flash of my implant's biofeedback alert had even cleared my vision, my implant was absorbing all of the data it could from around us and linking to the vehicle's onboard electronics.

I knew I had just a matter of seconds, but what was about to happen?

My answer came loud and clear when a second later, the Land Rover tailing us suddenly flashed its headlights. My reactions were faster than the driver's and I thrust my hand beneath my seatbelt and inside my jacket to pull my pistol from its shoulder holster, just as the driver reacted by slamming on his brakes.

The tyres shrieked and Schultz let out a startled yelp as the cab tilted forwards with the sudden deceleration and he careened forward in his chair, mid flow. But the sour-faced man next to him had been anticipating the move and was already bringing his firearm to bear. As my body flew forward and my seatbelt locked, it hampered my draw. All I could do was struggle against it as sour-puss unloaded several hollow-point rounds straight between Shultz's unprotected ribs.

As time slowed and fragments of lead burst mercilessly through Shultz's heart, liver and lungs, the round-faced driver was already reaching with one groping hand to hamper me further still. He just needed to slow me enough for misery-guts in the back to bring his gun to bear on me in the confined space.

As the marksman's barrel swung toward me with lethal intent and the light faded from Schultz's eyes, my implant wirelessly took control of the vehicle's anti-lock brakes and released the right hand set of wheels. With the wheels breaking unevenly, the vehicle slewed violently to the left, throwing off his aim. Another two rounds burst from his gun in quick succession, to spend themselves harmlessly. One exploded the foam from my headrest like a shower of popcorn, whilst the other burst through my window and continued on its path into a building, just as my palm made contact with the gun holstered under my armpit.

We veered into the flow of oncoming traffic, but I hunched forward into my seatbelt and took the powder burns to my ribs as I squeezed off half a dozen rounds of return fire, directly from within my holster. The gun bucked in my hand, but my implant took care of the targeting, suddenly giving my assailant a genuine reason to look grouchy. The rounds tore through my clothing and chair like they were butter and perforated him from crotch to chin.

I didn't expect the high pitched squeal that came out of him as he thrashed against his own seatbelt in a spray of gore and teeth.

Amidst a screech of smoking tyres and the swerving blare of car horns, we mounted the curb and slammed into the doorway of a grocers, sending a wooden display table and its contents flying. The screams of pedestrians and customers joined the kaleidoscopic peel of shattering glass and the damp thuds as melons, cucumbers and courgettes dashed against the pavement and came to rest.

I was already slewed around in my chair from the impact, so as the driver desperately fumbled for his own firearm, my implant took control. I have to admit, I was still trying to regain my equilibrium, but my implant wasted no time in bringing up one of my heavy work boots to stamp his pudgy head out through the driver's window with a vicious thrust of my heel. I was surprised it didn't break his neck, but as gravity brought his body back down into his chair again, he was still dazedly fumbling for a weapon.

The pierced wreck of an agent in the back seat was still wheezing out his last bubbling breaths as I drew my pistol. I had intended to threaten the half-conscious turncoat sitting next to me into surrender, but as my gun came up, my implant casually pulled upon the flexor tendon of my trigger finger and placed a round neatly in his temple. His eyes rolled back grotesquely and he slumped forward against the restraint of his belt. God Damn it! I railed in anger at my implant, feeling a deep stab of remorse at what it had just made me do, but in hindsight, the agent would have killed me if he had the chance and I still wasn't out of the woods.

As I sat there, surrounded by a fresh crop of corpses and hysterical passersby, my implant took note of the men getting out of the second convoy vehicle with snarling faces and pistols drawn.

Taking no chances, one of them ran wide, up the pavement, whilst the other began placing pot-shots into the back of the vehicle. I couldn't help flinching as the rear window exploded inwards in a spray of safety glass, as I fumbled to release the driver's seatbelt. In reality, my idea of fumbling would be near precision for any casual observer, as my implant slowed my perceptions of time to allow for a maximum chance of survival.

As the corpse in the driver's seat was freed from its restraint, it flopped forward to head butt the Land Rover's horn into a strident and continuous blare that drowned out the noise of the idling engine. I had never been keen on loud noises and wasted no time in reaching across him to release the door latch. Then, with my other hand, I toppled his stinking carcass out onto the pavement amongst the ruined vegetables and broken glass. The impact released the contents of his bladder.

The agent that had been hugging the shop fronts, cracked off a couple of shots as the body exited the vehicle. He missed his late colleague, but the muzzle flash that reflected in the wing mirror, as the door swung open, was enough for my implant to locate him and return fire, as I slid across into the driving seat.

The man was lucky that he only took a round in the collarbone. But as I slammed the battered Land Rover into reverse and bumped roughly over the legs of the freshly jettisoned corpse, I realised I was down to just three rounds in my magazine and had left the driver's gun on his body. It was a silly mistake.

As the vehicle dropped down off the curb and swung around with the tyres singing, the pistol being clutched by the agent in the back seat fell from lifeless fingers, to land on the floor behind me. There would be several rounds left in that, but now wasn't the time to reach for it. I could tell from the magnetic field disruption and the noise it made that it was behind my chair, but as more lead slugs lanced through the cabin from behind, I slammed the vehicle into gear and barged around the ruck of traffic the incident had created.

As I ignored the angry shouts, beeping horns and women screaming, I glanced in my rear-view mirror to see the agents retreating through the cloud of my diesel smoke to reach their vehicle. They were definitely going to give pursuit, even if one of them was losing blood.

Making use of the mobile telephone network, my implant patched a status alert through to the Agency, along with a request for backup. So it was no surprise, as I careened through the suburban streets on the outskirts of Berlin, that Acertas' voice came through loud and clear.

"I have your report, Lucidus," he rumbled, his voice resonating deep in his chest. "Assistance is inbound, but I have some Agency vehicles approaching your location without my order. Their intent is unknown. I am attempting to make contact now. Most of our assets and personnel are assisting Paredo, so you may be on your own for a few minutes."

"Copy that," I responded aloud, relying on my implant to broadcast my words.

I knew that it wasn't necessarily Agency vehicles I had to be worried about. Anyone could be a threat. But with their recent track record, I didn't feel inclined to trust anyone I didn't know.

"Patch me through to whatever satellite feeds are available," I added. At least then I could watch for inbound hostiles and plot my route to the extraction point. "I'll lose my tail and then change vehicles."

"Roger that," was all Acertas offered in return, as our channel of communication closed.

A few moments later, as I weaved between side streets, my vision populated with a satellite overlay. The second utility company Land Rover was still only a street behind, but with every bend I took, it followed.

I would have picked up on any form of tracking devices within my own vehicle, so they were either triangulating the phone signal coming from their expired colleague - who nodded and leaned around every bend in the back seat - or else they had some kind of aerial support themselves.

There was only one way to find out.

As I swung into the next street, my tyres humming and the Land Rover wallowing on its springs, I spotted what I had been looking for. Ahead, there was a row of parked cars with a clear run of at least 100 yards leading up to it. Well-kept gardens lined the street, with mature trees creating dappled shade.

I slowed to below 20 miles per hour and set my sights on the back of the row of cars in front. I didn't have my seat belt on, so all I had to do before bailing out, was to ease the vehicle out of gear and switch off the ignition. I intended the vehicle to coast onwards, providing a distraction whilst I set an ambush for my pursuers.

With my final moments within the vehicle, I groped one arm around behind my chair for the Agent's gun, but I was still empty-handed when my window of opportunity closed. The 3 rounds remaining in my own pistol would have to be enough.

I jumped clear of the Land Rover and hit the ground running. It coasted on silently as I veered off to double back on myself. Near the corner of the street, I skidded to a stop behind the green boughs of a sculpted conifer in somebody's front garden.

The crash of crumpling steel and glass breaking reached me a moment later, as the corpse-laden Land Rover shunted home, no doubt ruining the day of several careful motorists. The frenzied barking of neighbourhood dogs joined the chorus of car alarms and a quick glance back the way I had come, showed the vehicle was now stationary, with its door hanging open. It would have to do.

I readied my pistol as the pursuing vehicle slewed around the corner in a cloud of grit and tyre smoke. I waited a second for them to focus on the vehicle ahead, then I stepped out and took aim. The driver only had time to widen his eyes in surprise before the laminated glass windscreen in front of him sprouted a misted star-shaped hole and his consciousness fled from the expanding hollow-point round which turned his mind to grey jelly. The sound wave reached him a moment later.

His pallid colleague was busy trying to apply a field dressing to the spreading wet patch over his collarbone, so he was plainly startled by the incoming fire and the driver losing control of the vehicle. Rather than ducking, he instead grabbed for the wheel with his good arm. It was all my implant needed to carefully place a second lethal round, creating a matching set of dead agents. The rampaging vehicle continued on its route, mounting the curb, tearing through a white picket fence and half uprooting an apple tree, as it slammed to a messy stop in someone's garden. Apples raining down on the bonnet and roof of the vehicle added to the cacophony of the impact. But the most grizzly fruit on the lawn that day, was the dead agent who hadn't been wearing his seatbelt because of his injury. His limp ragdoll corpse had exited through the vehicle windscreen, clearing the bonnet, despite the resistance caused when his femurs had been snapped by the dashboard.

Any citizens concerned enough to investigate the initial impact of my abandoned Land Rover had soon beaten a hasty retreat when they heard my twin gunshots and the second wreck, so I now stood alone in the deserted street. As the car alarms subsided, I was left with the last of the sunshine and the barking of dogs.

I sprinted to retrieve the precious equipment case and Schultz's gun. Bless him for joining us. If he hadn't, I would have had two dirty agents behind me and would likely be dead.

I was tucking the spare firearm behind my belt and closing the passenger door, just as a BMW X5 pulled into the opposite end of the street. At first, I assumed the driver must have heard the crash and the ruckus, but rather than re-routing, their curiosity had got the better of them. But as they drew closer, the rich thumping bassline that preceded them told me that their stereo must have drowned it out. Unlike the residents who likely huddled in their homes, the motorist was blissfully unaware of what had transpired here.

I had time to unload the case and drag it out into the road before flagging the unsuspecting vehicle down.

Rather than looking concerned, the driver - an arrogant-looking sales rep in his 30's - saw only the uniform and just looked annoyed at being stopped. He wound his window down to tell me to get out of his way because he was running late. As the booming music spilled out of his open window, I pretended I couldn't hear what he was saying and approached the driver's window. He turned away to turn his radio down, but when he turned back, he was met by the harsh black barrel of my pistol thrust under his chin.

As he looked down his nose at it, disbelief soon turning to horror, I reached into the cab and pulled the interior door latch, triggering the central locking.

"Out of the vehicle and on your face," I barked in perfect German, with cold menace.

He barely had time to unfasten his seatbelt before I was pulling him bodily from the vehicle and slamming the air from his lungs with the unforgiving tarmac. He lay face down, his protestations quieting as my gun bore down on the back of his neck and my bodyweight pushed through one of my knees into his back.

As I pulled the leather wallet from his back pocket, I snarled, "I have your driver's license. I know where you live. You will not report this for 24 hours, and when you do, you were never here. Mention or describe me to anyone and I will kill you. Follow my instructions and you will never see me again."

He barely had room to nod his head, which translated into frantic vibrations running up through my pistol.

I felt terrible, but my Agency training dictated that brutally subduing civilians saved lives. If you were soft on them, then sooner or later someone would try to be a hero.

"Now get up and run back the way you came. Run like the devil is on your heels. If you slow down or look back, Mr. 9mm here and his friends will be chasing you."

I didn't have to do much more than lift my weight from him, before he was scrambling to his feet and sprinting off, his suit dusty and his tie askew. I had secured myself some transport and hopefully, when the police made door to door enquiries, people would be describing someone else fleeing frantically from the scene.

I loaded the vehicle and left the scene at a casual pace, but before anyone else arrived to trouble me. I had left a real mess behind for the Agency to clear up, but ultimately that was why we had a division of labour. I could better understand Paredo's outlook now. As relics, we took the largest risks, so if we occasionally made a mess getting the job done, someone else should mop up after us. It was only fair!

The satellite feed that Acertas had provided, proved invaluable in avoiding any suspicious vehicles - including the approach of a police helicopter, which I avoided by pulling up under a bridge.

In the end, I didn't trust Berlin's Schoenefeld airport enough to risk it. Nor the alternative, Tegel airport. So instead, I headed toward the airport at Leipzig, some 90 miles away. It took me around an hour and a half to get there - an unpleasantly tense and paranoia-inducing experience for a new Agent in the field, on their own for the first time. I spent much of the time scrutinising my rear-view mirror and intercepting police scanner radio signals in order to highlight any sign of trouble, but the journey was thankfully uneventful.

My implant frequently uploaded progress reports to Acertas, as he did what he could from the base in Denver to assign a safe and trustworthy Agency crew to bring me in.

Chapter 52

The quicksilver face which looked back at me, frowned in intense concentration. Its brows bunched together and its eyes narrowed, as they returned my stare like two perfect spheres of mercury. My peripheral view of the Professor's Agency laboratory faded into the background as I concentrated my flow of siphon energy into the experiment before me, shaping it to my will.

"That's it!" Thomas exclaimed excitedly, as the metallic mask took shape from the pool of liquid metal in the tray. "Now make it speak," he finished in an excited rush as I focussed my intent.

The mask's silvery features wavered as its eyes turned toward him, but as the lips of the glistening countenance parted, my tentative control slipped and the whole structure lost its integrity and collapsed inwards with a wet ripple. The liquid metal lay inert in the tray, only kept liquid by the flow of energy I fed it. I was tired and we had been at this for hours, testing both my patience and my mental endurance.

"It's no good, Professor," I sighed in frustration. I looked down at the tray of liquid metal in front of me, my expression reflected in its chromed surface. "The form is just too complex for me. I can't hold it together. Either the Anunnaki were far more skilled than I, or they didn't demand such fine detail from it."

I was referring to the spherical artefact we had recovered in Berlin, which was now the subject of the Professor's intense experimentation. The artefact had turned out to be a dense ball of liquid metal which could be reformed at will with siphon energy, to create all manner of shapes - and the metal face, which mirrored my own, was the pinnacle of my creative achievement with it so far.

In all honesty, given how promptly the other items had been shipped off to other Agency or military facilities, I was surprised we had been allowed to keep it. Thomas had suggested that it was because our masters considered it mundane technology, now that Agency experiments had managed to duplicate the amazing material, but I secretly suspected his own stretching of the truth had been something to do with it.

I had now seen the Agency prototypes for myself and Paredo was right. They were crude and incomplete in comparison. But however Thomas had manipulated his report to our superiors, it had worked and he had acquired a new plaything for his laboratory.

"It makes sense that you would have different tools for different jobs," I continued. "The helm and suit on the 'Erste Menche' was clearly more sophisticated because it had to do a lot more. And it no doubt played to Anunnaki vanity, so it had to be spectacular." I added as an afterthought.

The fact was, it was the display of such super-technology that had been the cement that had held our ancestors in bondage for so many millennia, believing their oppressors were actually gods.

"But this?" I said, severing the thread of siphon energy I was sending, "this is just a high-tech Swiss army knife."

The energy had been keeping the material malleable and dictating its form, so as I withdrew my efforts, the pool of metal promptly reformed into the shape of a perfect sphere, as its own innate surface tension reasserted itself. Thomas still looked in awe at the shiny globe, which now reflected a distorted mirror image of the room about it in its polished mirror surface.

He had named it an 'imitor', which meant *mimic* in Latin. I couldn't have named it better myself, as that was exactly what it did. True enough, Agency scientists had recreated the liquid metal alloy which could be hardened with one frequency of energy and softened with another, but what our prototypes lacked was the tiny module within, which received siphon energy as a power source and the thousands of microscopic filaments running through the material that delivered the energy in a much more directed fashion.

"Maybe you're right," he agreed reluctantly, his disappointment evident. It wasn't like I hadn't tried. We had been experimenting on and off for just over three weeks, since my return to Denver from Berlin.

"Just run through the forms we have been practicing," he said, "then we can call it a day. It's getting late."

It was an amusing comment, coming from this pale man who never saw the light of day and kept whatever hours his sleep cycle dictated. So I smiled and shrugged resignedly, before gathering my will to cycle the imitor through its paces again one last time.

I began with abstract shapes, a disc, a cube, a cylinder, a pyramid and built up to ever more sophisticated forms. My implant was able to assist more with every repetition, but the first time I formed a shape, it always seemed to have to come from me. So in truth, practice was beneficial.

The material couldn't shrink, so smaller tools such as spoons, blades, screw drivers and the like, had to have fairly hefty handles to compensate for the extra volume, but the imitor could incorporate hollow spaces to form larger objects. But an interesting property was that its hardness was directly related to how much energy you were able to sink into it. I didn't wield a great deal of finesse with it at the moment, but Thomas had theorised that I could maintain a form with just a trickle of energy, then spike the energy just before the point of impact when the imitor was used, in order to conserve my strength. Even relics had limits.

It took me the best part of an hour to fumble my way through all the forms we had practiced, as Thomas required a practical demonstration of each form. So I was grateful to bid him good evening and head for my bed at the end of it.

I had been assigned new quarters within the Academy facilities, which were a little more spacious, but they were located a tier above the student quarters - which simply involved more stairs to climb. So I wasn't sure if I appreciated the trade-off - especially after a hard session of training or experimentation with Thomas.

Many of my peers were cycled out on active duty assignments and the two new students were no doubt in bed, more exhausted than I was. So the only living souls I saw on my trudge back to my bed were the various security details.

It wasn't long before I was crashed out in my bunk, the memory foam mattress comfortably conforming to the shape of my body. But as exhausted as I was, sleep wouldn't come. I had found it harder to sleep as the burden of worry was steadily heaped upon my shoulders with every new revelation and my homesickness didn't help. Being allowed to pen postcards home, filled with lies of my fictitious jungle expeditions did my psyche more harm than good, but I did it for the sake of my family. At least it would ease their worries to a degree.

But what bothered me the most was what I had learned when I had finally unpacked the data file pushed into my implant by the disembodied relic in Alaska.

I did my best to relax my body as my mind wandered, inevitably drifting back to the source of my worry before sleep would take me.

I had been met in Leipzig, Germany, by a crew of decorated veterans who had been drawn into service by the agency at the end of their careers. Acertas had deliberately chosen older staff with a long service record who had only received light duties recently due to their ages. They had been valued for their experience and leadership skills and, as such, Acertas had gambled that they were less likely to have been compromised.

He had transmitted their service records as reassurance, without questioning my apparent lack of trust. I had expected to be brow-beaten into following my orders and handing myself in to whichever agents arrived first, but it seemed that Acertas himself had been rattled by how many agency staff had been compromised recently. We were unsure of the source of the infiltration, but for the Chinese to have been so successful seemed unlikely without inside help.

There were too many factions on the world stage to know anything for certain. Governments vied for power and even the assorted alphabet agencies struggled amongst themselves in a constant turf war to demonstrate supremacy and justify their ever increasing budgets. The Agency itself, which parasitically invaded all of the major centres of power, had its own internal power struggles - and who knew what private forces were in the employ of the individual members of the Committee of 300?

It seemed to me that every operational decision we made was based upon a bed of constantly shifting political sand.

"Don't worry," Acertas had assured me. "I have worked with Duncan and Franklin before. They are both good guys. Ex special forces. They are level-headed in a bind and won't let you down. I haven't worked with Schneider or Clarke, but their records speak for themselves and they get the job done."

They met me in an unmarked van just north of the airport, where we transferred my priceless cargo. I left the keys to my stolen vehicle in the glove box and pulsed a signal to lock the doors, but I was more concerned about keeping an eye on my new colleagues than looking back, as we drove away in a plume of diesel smoke.

Franklin was a broad shouldered silverback of a man, with a barrel chest and a greying beard, trimmed to the same grade as his hair with clippers. His brow ridges were thick and scarred from his days as the boxing champion of his regiment, but he was still a thinking man and his rich sense of humour shone in his friendly eyes. Acertas had read him right and I soon warmed to his friendly banter. Duncan was easy company too, although he let Franklin do most of the talking.

There was only room for three of us in the cab, so I didn't get to see much of the others, who remained in the back of the van to watch our six and guard the cargo.

I let Duncan and Franklin do all the talking as we passed through various security checkpoints at the airport, driving the van through to the private hangar where they said a military transport awaited me.

I had been expecting something like a Hercules cargo plane with a military escort, but instead, we were greeted at the hangar by a dozen anonymous men in dark suits, earpieces and even darker glasses. I flared my implant reflexively, but none of them proved to be relics.

Franklin and Duncan exchanged looks, which made me wonder if they too were surprised by the turnout.

"This is a door to door service, Lad," Duncan offered as reassurance in his native Scottish accent. "We're coming with you."

I don't think the agents in dark suits had the same idea, because at first, they moved to block my escort. But after a few terse words from Franklin and some swift dialogue via their earpieces, we were reluctantly all admitted to the hangar.

What awaited us within, was in fact another new Boeing - a 737 this time. It was painted white, with a broad red stripe that ran its length, across the numerous porthole windows. Other than its tail number, it was unmarked.

I had seen these before on the internet. It was a JANET plane. The 'JANET' flights usually carried workers from Las Vegas to the Base at Groom Lake (known popularly as Area 51), along with the Tonopah Test Range, Edwards Air Force Base and no doubt other secret military installations. They were called 'JANET' because they used this prefix, followed by a three-digit number, over air traffic radio transmissions both at McCarran International Airport and at Area 51. The public couldn't get near them, but dedicated UFO enthusiasts had documented them via long-range telephoto lens photographs and these now graced many UFO and conspiracy enthusiast web sites. In all honesty, without my implant, I perhaps wouldn't have recognised it for what it was, as it still blended in with the commercial aircraft unless you knew what you were looking for.

"You must have some interesting luggage," was all the comment that Franklin made as he helped me unload. Clearly he knew what this transport was too.

Duncan led the way up the mobile stairs onto the aircraft, but we left Clarke and Schneider with the van. I had barely said more than a dozen words to them, but they diligently watched us board and saluted us before they departed.

The plane had already refuelled over at Schoenefeld airport, so once everyone was aboard and buckled up, we were able to taxi out onto the runway.

As I watched the airport ground crews scurry about their duties down on the tarmac, I made a final progress report to Acertas, knowing that once we were above 10,000 feet, communication would be problematic. His response was brief. Sericum and Jesse were also airborne and en route to Denver, but Paredo's team were still attempting to recover whatever had been stolen from under our noses. I knew Paredo would be furious about that, so perhaps it was just as well I had a delivery to make before rejoining him.

As diverting as Franklin and his straight-man, Duncan were, I was glad that they treated this journey with professionalism. They didn't chatter much and spent more time watching over the spooks, which enabled me to get some rest. I had been itching to go over what I had seen in the facility and to unlock and examine the file that now was burning a hole in the back of my mind.

In all honesty, I was amazed at my self-control for this amount of time, but everything had been such a whirlwind since and I had barely had any time to myself. Beyond that, I had discovered from my close shave with the Committee that secrets carried a price. Maybe ignorance was bliss?

When I had gone over every last inch of my memories of the exploration of the facility in Berlin, and the mysterious specimens we had recovered, I turned my attention - with trepidation - toward the packet of information I had been given in Alaska during my encounter with the stricken relic.

The demise of its host wasn't going to be pleasant, whoever it was, or whichever side they were on, but I felt that now it was time for me to know. There were simply too many interests at work and I reasoned that any inside information may help keep me afloat in the turbulent waters that lay ahead.

Chapter 53

In hindsight, it may have been a mistake to access the data file aboard that plane, surrounded by potentially hostile agents, but the impetuousness of youth sometimes knows no bounds.

I can only be thankful that my relic enabled me to keep a poker face when I finally assimilated the information and the memories within, because the revelations slammed home with far more emotional impact than I could have anticipated.

The magnitude of what I learned was perhaps every bit as enormous as my initial Agency briefing, but in a much more visceral and gut-wrenching fashion. Learning of an extraterrestrial threat from mankind's ancestors, who have been lost to the dust of antiquity, doesn't quite have the same psychological impact as seeing recent human history through a completely different lens.

I don't even know where would be an adequate place to start.

The data itself wasn't one continuous memory. It was a collection of status reports spanning the life of an Agency relic known as Derexi. I didn't know her background or her age, but the reports spanned from the late 1940's through to 2001 and they seemed to hint a little toward her character, if you read between the lines. The persistent references to her handler's part in her missions made me think that she was kept under close scrutiny, but I think her name suited her character traits. She was well-organised and efficient. Derexi meant to direct, steer, guide, or set in order, and that's exactly what she did for the Agency until her reports ceased in 2001. She was a fixer, and seemingly a damn good one at that.

If the Agency or its masters wanted something done, she handled it - and in an era where women didn't usually occupy such high profile positions, she was able to work from the shadows without notice.

The early reports of her career, whilst often exciting and dramatic, didn't affect the world stage, as they mainly surrounded her hunting down former Nazi officers and scientists, in order to appropriate intelligence on technology or hidden assets for the Agency, before other world powers could. She did this efficiently and with a very high strike rate.

Over time, her skills were apparently noticed and she was given increasingly high profile operations to supervise. In the early 60's she was assigned to help co-ordinate and support Operation 40, a Central Intelligence Agency sponsored undercover group, which was active in the United States and the Caribbean (including Cuba), Mexico and Central America. The shadowy hit squad was approved by President Eisenhower in March 1960, after the 1959 Cuban Revolution and was presided over by Vice-president Nixon.

Operation 40 was formed to seize political control of Cuba after the Bay of Pigs Invasion, but when the invasion of Cuba failed miserably, the unit returned to Miami where their true value as ruthless assassins became evident. Wherever anyone became a problem for the Eisenhower and Nixon administrations, or by extension, the Agency, they were put to work - with Derexi in support.

The group included Frank Sturgis (who would later become one of the Watergate burglars), Felix Rodriguez (a CIA officer who was later involved in the capture and summary execution of Che Guevara in 1967), Luis Posada Carriles (who played a key role in the execution of the 1976 Cubana Flight 455 bombing), Orlando Bosch (founder of the counterrevolutionary organisation that facilitated the 1976 murder of Chilean former minister Orlando Letelier) and a host more, with equally grim resumes.

Wherever there was blood in the water, Derexi was there, making arrangements, observing and mopping up loose ends. She ensured that the Agency was kept in the loop, but out of the limelight.

She had always been careful, but she slipped up when she was captured on film at the Dealey Plaza, at President John F.

Kennedy's assassination. For decades after, she was known as the Babushka lady, a nickname for an unknown woman present during the 1963 assassination, who might have photographed the events at the time Kennedy was shot. Her nickname arose from the headscarf she had worn, similar to scarves worn by elderly Russian women - as babushka meant "grandmother" or "old woman" in Russian.

She was seen holding a camera by eyewitnesses and was recorded in the Zapruder film, as well as in the films of Orville Nix, Marie Muchmore and Mark Bell. What drew so much attention about her was that even though the shooting had already taken place and most of her surrounding witnesses had taken cover, she could still be seen standing with the camera at her face. After the shooting, she crossed Elm Street and joined the crowd that went up the grassy knoll in search of the gunman. She was last seen in photographs walking east on Elm Street. Officially, neither she, nor the film she took, was ever positively identified - and now I knew why. No known photograph with her in frame captured her face, because in all cases she was facing away from the camera, or in the case of the Zapruder film, she had her face obscured by her own camera.

But what her Agency reports filled in for me, (that the official narrative didn't), was that more than half a dozen of her Operation 40 assets were on the ground at the Dealey Plaza that day, to play their part in removing Kennedy from office. Two were trigger men, with the others helping to set up the hit and execute a clean extraction. The other two shooters on the day, were supplied by the mob and a group of high profile Texan Oilmen and Bankers. It was deemed that if each of the parties involved supplied trigger men, then nobody could point fingers later. They would all have blood on their hands, regardless of their motives.

The Cuban operatives felt JFK was a traitor after the Bay of Pigs and wanted to kill him. The CIA were under threat of being dismantled by Kennedy. The mob wanted to put an end to the 700% increase in prosecutions under Kennedy and his brother Robert, acting as Attorney General; and Kennedy's threat to revert the US dollar back to the gold standard and stay out of Vietnam was the final straw that effectively signed his death warrant with the Oilmen and the Bankers. He planned to sack the privately-owned Federal Reserve and begin the issuance of bills backed by precious metal - taking the profits and power from the bankers and putting it back in the hands of the people.

As history rolled on, the House Select Committee on Assassinations, established in 1976, concluded its investigation with a 95% probability that at least 4 shots were fired (by multiple shooters) and that Kennedy was killed as a result of a conspiracy, recommending that the Justice Department follow up with a further investigation. Unsurprisingly, this recommendation was never honoured and the spate of witnesses suffering mysterious deaths immediately prior to being able to give testimony, was ignored.

Lee Harvey Oswald was actually a dissenting CIA operative within an operation to eliminate Fidel Castro, who had become a security risk and the ideal scapegoat. His CIA handler, David Atlee Phillips was the operative who had recruited James Files, the self-confessed grassy knoll assassin, who, by his own admission, fired the fatal shot into JFK's head.

Now, knowing the truth, I felt terrible that Oswald was likely to have been a patriot who believed he was to penetrate the group of assassins, in order to sabotage the plot and prevent JFK's assassination. Yet he would unwittingly take the blame as the patsy, and his memory live on in infamy. He had been duped into meeting his contact at the Texas Theatre where they were to get him out of the country, then eliminate him. But things went wrong.

When Oswald was apprehended by Police, he had to be silenced. It took another asset under orders from the mob, Jack Ruby, to tie up the loose ends by publicly shooting Oswald. But when Ruby managed to overturn his subsequent conviction and force a retrial, he too was silenced by an injection of highly aggressive cancer cells.

But it didn't end there. Derexi went on to provide support for the assassinations of a number of other notable public figures, including Martin Luther King Jr and John Lennon - and anyone else who threatened to derail the profits of the war machine by advocating peace.

In the 90's, she was assigned to help the CIA in their dirty war in Nicaragua, where she helped facilitate the distribution network for the cocaine supply into the US. As her talents caught the attention of more exulted figures, she began to execute important tasks under the direct orders of the White House, including organising the air supply of weapons and explosives to the Contras in Nicaragua. Some of these operations later became known as the Iran Contra scandal, which were directed from the Vice Presidency, headed by George H.W. Bush.

As history later revealed, George H.W. Bush became the first President in American history to effectively grant himself a pardon in order to avoid prosecution for the Iran Contra affair, by pardoning his numerous accomplices in that operation - many of which ended up holding posts in his son's administration.

But unfortunately for Derexi, you can only handle so much dirty laundry before you become a target yourself. It gets to a point where you are worth more dead than alive. After all, dead men are supposed to tell no tales.

Her final job was organising the removal of the gold and silver bullion from the vaults beneath the World Trade Centre complex, prior to the collapse of the Twin Towers and Building 7 on 9/11.

Like anyone else following the devastating events of 9/11, I knew that on November 1, 2001, Mayor Rudolph Giuliani announced that "more than $230 million" worth of gold and silver bars, that had been stored in a bomb-proof vault under the complex, had been recovered. But the mainstream media had been conspicuously quiet about the further $750 million of precious metals which was unaccounted for in just one of the vaults. The Comex Metals Trading Division had been storing gold for Chase Manhattan Bank, Bank of America, HSBC, Bank of Nova Scotia and others, including almost 65 tonnes of gold and an incredible 102 million ounces of silver.

The news had reported that gold from World Trade Centre Building 4 was found under World Trade Centre Building 5, in the back of a 10-wheel truck with an empty escort of security vehicles, abandoned in a collapsing delivery tunnel. Certainly amongst the 9/11 truth community it was safe to say that the convoy carrying the bullion was running away from the south tower, even if the authorities preferred to avoid the topic. In actual fact, this evidenced that the attack on 9/11 was a cover for the greatest gold heist in history.

If only they knew what was in Derexi's reports. The score was many magnitudes greater and didn't just involve the gold.

There were also the insider trading profits made on the day of the attacks, as evidenced by hard drive data recovered from the wreckage by a German computer company, named Convar. Of some 400 recovered hard drives, 32 held evidence of insider trading which totalled hundreds of millions of dollars. Convar handed the evidence over to the FBI, who were legally bound to investigate, but by 2010, no investigation had occurred.

More widely publicised were the multi-billion dollar profits for the owner of the lease for the complex itself, Larry 'Pull it' Silverstein - who only acquired and insured it weeks before, despite his winning bid being $50 million lower than his nearest competitors. He and his cronies made almost $500 million from the insurance payout from building 7 alone, which wasn't even hit by a plane, but instead was brought down by a controlled demolition that he admitted to, live on TV. The destruction of the SCC Offices and several thousand files necessary for the ongoing investigations into Wall Street improprieties were just a bonus. The paltry $115 million or so that he and his backers had put down for the complex, just weeks before it was demolished, was dwarfed by the $4.55 billion insurance payout.

More subtle, yet even more important was Donald Rumsfeld's disclosure the day before the attacks, stating that there was a missing 2.3 trillion dollars from the books of the Pentagon. The following day, the accounting records and evidence for these missing trillions (housed in the offices at the Pentagon) were supposedly struck by flight 77 and destroyed. Unfortunately for any subsequent investigation, the rest of the evidence was in World Trade Centre Building 7, which collapsed at free-fall speed despite not being hit by a plane at all.

It was even leaked to the public that 35 out of 50 key military investigators working on the 'Able Danger' investigation into the theft of over 350 nuclear warheads, were killed at the Pentagon that day in the explosion, along with their computer records - with several more investigators being wiped out in mysterious circumstances over the coming days.

But nobody, not even the most passionate '9/11 truthers', knew the true extent of the gold heist that Derexi had been organising for the Agency and its masters. There was far more gold under the complex than what was publicly disclosed - and it was her job to steal it.

She had been working crews around the clock for three and a half solid days to remove the bullion before the attacks, but she still couldn't complete the extraction before the last load had to be abandoned.

I learned that in 1938, the Nationalist Government of China sent 7 US warships full of Gold to the US for safekeeping against the Japanese occupation. They were given 60-year US government bonds in exchange. The gold was recorded in the Global Collateral Combined Accounts. But these accounts were not legal and were part of a parallel financial system, known only to the elite few.

So after the 60 years ended, when the US and their bankers were supposed to give the gold back to the Chinese, they declined to do so. Unsurprisingly, the Chinese owners of the gold sued the Federal Reserve Board at the International Court of Justice at the Hague in closed session, but what very few knew, was that when the court ruled in favour of returning the gold, the deadline to release the bullion was September 12, 2001. The day after 9/11.

So whether you believed the official narrative about hijackers with box-cutters stealing planes at the behest of an ex CIA asset on dialysis in a cave in Afghanistan, or some other more rational version of events, the elites were able to make billions from the event itself, hundreds of millions from insider trading, and trillions in increased funding for the military and security agencies. Not only that, but they saved trillions in repayments to the Chinese, sparking an even greater and acrimonious rift between the power blocks.

Yet despite this blatant slap in the face to the Chinese elite, the black gold transferred from Fort Knox to the vaults of the World Trade Centre complex in the 1970's was secret - and it was in everyone's interests to keep it that way. The Chinese didn't wish to admit losing such an absurd sum, nor the extent of their ill-gotten wealth - and the Committee of 300 frequently illegally dipped into the secret stash to manipulate commodity prices for even greater profits, or to bankroll their black operations. So all-out war was not a viable option for either side. The conflict and retribution had to remain covert.

But it was all linked. Kennedy had known about the gold. In 1963, the original owners of the gold and President Kennedy had come to a secret arrangement known as the Green Hilton agreement. Under its terms, the gold entrusted to the Bank for International Settlements was to be transferred to the US financial system, (the Treasury, not the Federal Reserve), to underpin the US dollar in the capacity of an international currency. The secret black gold was to be gradually legalised and brought into economic circulation. These newly legitimised international gold reserves were to be used for funding large-scale programmes aimed at overcoming the third world's social and economic challenges, but this would have resulted in the private Federal Reserve System being deprived of the right to issue money. This was the final straw that saw Kennedy targeted.

So events had run full circle. Not only had the Agency and its masters eliminated the threat they saw in Kennedy and secured their ability to continue to print their own cash at will, they had now installed their own puppet governments and physically taken the gold into their own safekeeping.

Above and beyond that, they had given themselves license to do and say whatever they liked under the pretext of 9/11 and fighting terrorism. The Patriot Act, Homeland Security, Iraq, Afghanistan, NSA spying and any other affront to privacy and decency was now fair game.

From what I could gather from Derexi's reports, it seemed that in the run up to the inevitable clash with the emerging super-power of China, the grand plan was to grab the oil of the Middle East and Central Asia, consolidate control over the

Muslim world and then use Russia, Japan, NATO, Taiwan and India to crush China.

With the invasions of Iraq and Afghanistan, the plan was already well under way, but as we all know, the best laid plans of mice and men often go awry.

As I sat aboard that clandestine plane, hurtling through the night sky towards Denver, Derexi's reports had done nothing more than awaken a righteous fire within me. I was furious and resolved to dig out the corruption wherever I found it. The problem was that I didn't know where to direct my wrath. Her reports weren't clear on who had been issuing her orders and whether it was the Chinese or her own masters who had put an end to her. But I would find out.

In any event, regardless of what the Agency and their villainous masters feared about the return of the Anunnaki, their corrupt methods flew in the face of everything that was right. What I saw wasn't a coherent strategy to control mankind in order to save them, it was just the actions of remorseless psychopaths exercising power to their own ends. They just wanted control of the populous at any cost and I couldn't countenance that.

But as I sat and stewed, surrounded by Government yes-men, each and every one of them just pawns in a bigger game, the words of Winston Churchill came to my mind.

"Do not let spacious plans for a new world divert your energies from saving what is left of the old."

The question was, what parts were worth saving and what parts had to go? I was too new to the Agency to even know.

In my mind, the line between the Agency and the other power blocks had been an obvious one, until I started questioning the Agency's agenda and their methods - particularly where the general population were concerned. At least the line between the relics and our Agency masters had been clear, where I knew my side. But now, having observed Derexi's part in pivotal events of history, I wasn't so sure. How much of her activity was a result of her handler's coercion via her implant, and how much was her own naked ambition?

Suddenly, things weren't so black and white. It made me realise that I had received an easy ride so far, with minimal oversight and quite a lot of freedom. Other relics, like Hector, hadn't been so lucky.

So the question was, who was Derexi reporting to? That would be my trail to root out the corruption and rot. But could I do it without disclosing my own level of knowledge? Or, like Derexi, would I end up dead, with my implant being tormented by future generations of students, or worse?

One thing was clear, my conscience wouldn't allow me to sit idly by and do nothing.

Chapter 54

I shouldn't have been so distant with Franklin and Duncan for the rest of the flight, but my black mood wouldn't allow their easy smiles and wry quips to take hold. But I still hung on to my manners enough to be courteous, if not warm.

In truth, this aircraft and its entire complement of agents and crew flew in the face of everything I believed in - both in terms of the secrecy and their willingness to go along with or even perpetuate the corruption. Trillions were being hoarded and spent on trumped up wars, when just billions were needed to eliminate poverty and hunger. It was sickening.

When we touched down in Denver and my implant uploaded a status report, I was instructed by Acertas to turn over custody of the equipment case to the agents. But when he didn't mention the other artefacts, I stubbornly retained them in my pockets. I had resolved to change the system and this would be the first of a series of small victories.

As angry as I was, however, I had feared that the revelations from Derexi's status reports would have somehow formed part of my own implant-compiled report, sabotaging me at the outset of my quest. But it seemed my intent for this to remain secret was enough to make it so. Perhaps my relic was intelligent enough to know that such a revelation would put me at great risk?

I was met by a security detachment from the Agency facility, but my erstwhile guardians, Franklin and Duncan, weren't invited along. Instead, they were offered accommodation downtown, with return flights arranged for the following day. When it came to saying our goodbyes, I made a show of thanking them for their service, which made them grin - most likely at my naiveté. To them, this was just another job - and an easy one at that - but they deserved credit for a job well done.

The one good thing to come out of this whole debacle was how pleased Thomas and Jesse were to see me. Sericum and Acertas too, but perhaps to a lesser extent. They simply congratulated me on handling the extraction well, then returned to the briefing suite to continue monitoring our agents in the field.

Paredo, Carmine and Jarrod hadn't managed to recapture the technology from Berlin, but no doubt due to Paredo's stubborn streak, they were still running down all available leads. In some respects, I felt a pang of jealousy that my former classmates were spending time with my mentor, when I should have been there myself, but at the same time, I felt emotionally exhausted.

Thomas joined Jesse and I for dinner in the Academy canteen, to catch up on all of our activities over the last few days. He had seen the reports, but that wasn't the same as actually hearing it from us directly. He was fascinated by my descriptions of the 'Erste Menche' and the Gray, but his eyes veritably bulged when I presented him with the artefacts I still possessed.

I must admit, that surrounded by friends, and in the conspicuous absence of our Agency sponsors, (and the other lesser cogs of the Agency machine), it was hard to stay angry and distrustful. If anything, I just wanted to sleep and see how things felt in the morning.

Unfortunately, I couldn't say the same for Thomas, who would probably now pull an all-nighter, running tests on what I had found.

Chapter 55

The days that followed were a peculiar mix of training in the arena, hacking overseas computer networks to search for enemy power-block activity, and experimentation with Thomas in his laboratory. This was perhaps designed to deliberately keep us out of trouble whilst those higher up the chain of command were drawn into the inevitable bureaucracy and politics of the Agency. Given how our overseas staff and safe-houses had been so readily compromised, it was inevitable that there would be debate and even a Committee hearing on the subject.

Sericum told me that Major Winters had advised us to consolidate here in Denver, for a while at least, whilst the dust settles - but that I wouldn't be required to report in person. Although she didn't outright say it, Sericum hinted that Hiram's feet were being held to the fire over his potential involvement. I can't say I wasn't pleased at this news, as I didn't trust him at all, but he had friends in high places who might step in to protect him.

As much as I regretted what had happened to Brett Mason in Hong Kong, or more precisely, what I had done to him in my fury, I was more dismayed that we hadn't been able to identify the people behind his actions. He could perhaps have directly implicated Hiram, but as things stood, it was all circumstantial. Our only hope there, was if Sierene, Hector or Canis turned up any new information.

Reports steadily came in from numerous other relics, including Verity, Ben and Oliver, but aside from rescuing Sierene, we hadn't recovered any of our missing Brothers.

I was glad of those first few quiet days back in Denver for some much-needed contemplation, (and time in Jesse's company, if I am being honest), but it soon began to transform into frustration as it felt as though perhaps I had been mothballed.

But life in the Agency was never dull for long as I was called in to help work with the Russian Enforcer. The Agency scientists had been working on him for days, presumably in the same way that they had worked on me, and he was now able to recall his own name, Grigory.

The staffers and nurses had been doing what they could to rehabilitate him, but at best he was still only showing the mental age of a 9 year old and he was full of anger over what had been done to him.

When I took him for a tour of the academy with his cadre of armed guards, he took a shine to Jesse right away and asked if he could enrol to train with us. It was daunting, to say the least, because even if he had the emerging mind of a child, he was still brutally strong and uncontrollably large.

But when Acertas heard about his request, he insisted that we welcome our future brother into the academy. After all, it had never happened before.

Until now, hunting relics had been an activity to deprive our enemies of their assets and to steal modules to enhance our own abilities. Perhaps Acertas foresaw an era where falling into enemy hands wasn't a death sentence for relics?

We had to take things slowly with Grigory, as he was still emotionally unstable, but I did my best to avoid actually having to siphon him into compliance. Jesse made it easier, as her little 'Gory' would do, (or at least attempt), whatever she asked, with a foolish grin on his great moon face. But I wish she hadn't chosen that as a nickname for him. If she had been there when he was captured, she perhaps wouldn't find the nickname so appropriate. But I held my tongue, as it was a new start for him and not his fault.

Each day we made progress, in baby steps, until a few days later, at Acertas' request, Sagax, the relic from Alaska, had arrived to deliver two new Academy students and their Agency handlers. One was a young Turkish boy who had been implanted when he and his friends had broken into a previously undiscovered section of the ancient underground city in the Nevşehir province of Turkey. The other was a 19 year old African miner from Johannesburg. Their handlers were as different as chalk and cheese, but they both carried themselves like the Agency spooks they were.

Having been kept at separate locations, the new students were completely green to life in the Academy, so Jesse and myself did our best to make them feel at home and bring them up to speed. Their handlers would leave them in our care for the next month or so, before returning to check on them. I was glad to see the back of them, as the whole master and slave connection just made me angry. It was strange that I didn't see my relationship with Thomas that way, but I assumed that was because he hadn't ever wanted that power over me and certainly didn't exercise it.

'Gory' wasn't safe to leave with his new classmates unattended, so he continued to live in his own secure accommodation, but this was nothing new to him, so he didn't seem to mind. But with each new day spent with his new friends, he seemed to come out of his shell even more. They had been afraid of him at first, but now the three of them seemed thick as thieves. Jesse and I were barely out of the Academy ourselves, but we took to the role of tutors easily and our students were respectful and attentive, making them a joy to teach.

And so the days had passed. Oliver returned with his handler from Italy, but he was only back a couple of days before being sent off to support Verity in Indonesia. Flint had come and gone too, just spending long enough to take a class or two with the new recruits and to support his father, before being sent off to steal some new technology from Korea. It seemed to me that everyone else was spending more time on assignment in the field than they were back at base.

So as I lay sleepless in my bunk, thinking back over the last few weeks (and knowing all that I now knew), I could only come to one conclusion. Lulled into the string of day-to-day activities within the security of the Agency, there was a sort of institutional comfort - where every brick in the wall had its place and every hour of the day had its purpose. There was even a sense of momentum, with this colossal organisational machine ploughing on, regardless of the individual views and opinions of its internal working parts. But given the direction we were headed in, I knew it was only a matter of time before I would have to choose between doing what was safe, and doing what was right.

The question was, would it be a case of the squeakiest hinge getting the oil, or, as I feared, the tallest nail getting the first blow of the hammer?

The End of Book 1 - Author's Comments

I do hope you have enjoyed reading the first book in the Born Lucid series. If so, please take the time to tell your friends and family about it and review it online. Reviews on

Amazon.com, Goodreads.com and other book-related sites really help authors to attract new readers - which enables them to continue to weave more tales for you to enjoy. Shares on Facebook, Tweets, Pins and other social signals are also very helpful - and are always appreciated. Thank you!

You can read more about the world this book is based upon at:
http://www.LivingForLonger.com and
http://www.BornLucid.com

Aside from the fictitious characters I have portrayed, (and the mysterious Agency they work for), the facts presented in this work of fiction are either true or believed to be true. I am passionate about both entertaining people and providing useful, practical real-world information - information you wouldn't usually get from the mainstream media, due to politics and financial interests. In fact, even the incredible technologies I describe, (with the exception of siphoning), are all based upon existing science - albeit experimental or in its infancy. The world really could be a place of marvels, if we could separate the science from the money, power and corruption that unfortunately goes with it.

If all I do with this novel is to raise awareness of the darker forces at work in this world and inspire people to stand up for what's right, then I have succeeded. You CAN make a difference, because every voice counts.

Coming up in Book 2

In subsequent novels, the story continues to flit from the futuristic conflict between the Freemen and the totalitarian authorities, back to the main character's experience as an unwilling pawn of the Agency. The story involves politics, conspiracies, love, betrayal and intense action, as corruption within the agency turns the extraordinary abilities of the relics against the populous. The main character's escape from the agency, (combined with bitter-sweet revenge), coincides with a turbulent period of extreme societal upheaval, as economic collapse, natural disasters and a pandemic rock society.

The totalitarian police state that emerges is core to this tale of a people's struggle for freedom.

The novel is deliberately educational, with medical, nutritional and scientific facts littered throughout. The events leading to the collapse of society are all based upon existing legislation and US executive orders, combined with real-world financial and medical statistics. I hope to provide readers with a thrilling experience akin to the great Hollywood blockbusters, whilst couching a cautionary tale and health information within the entertainment.

* * *

"I know in my heart that man is good. That what is right will always eventually triumph. And there's purpose and worth to each and every life." - President Ronald Wilson Reagan

"I do verily believe that a single, consolidated government would become the most corrupt government on the earth." - Thomas Jefferson to Gideon Granger, 1800

"A diffusion of knowledge is the only guardian of true liberty." - James Madison 1825

"Government can't solve the problem. Government IS the problem." - President Ronald Wilson Reagan

* * *

Glossary

Acertas - A Relic Instructor. Ranged weapons and explosives expert for the Agency. Acertas means "Force". At almost 7 feet tall and at least 350 lbs of dense muscle, he is a tower of a man, but he is generally jovial and friendly.

Academy (The) - The Academy within the Agency facility under Denver, USA, is a marvel of engineering, which houses a great vaulted floodlit arena, along with several tiers of rooms overlooking it. It was constructed for the sole purpose of training new Relics. It also contains briefing suites, laboratories and communal areas for students.

Agency (The) - The shadowy and covert organisation which has been gathering ancient and occult technology from around the world for many decades. The Agency has parasitically infiltrated many institutions, governments, government agencies and secret societies around the globe. With such influence and power, the Agency is only answerable to the Committee of 300.

A.I. - Artificial intelligence, housed in a wide range of different machines. The bulk of the A.I. systems within the future storyline are lethal and were used for war, extermination during the purge, or to keep citizens in their place.

Alumnor - See Ben.

Anunnaki - The extraterrestrial ancestors of mankind. Large and Nordic in appearance, 450,000 years ago they combined their DNA with the primitive hominids of Earth to create modern man as a slave race. The resulting work-force was used to mine vast volumes of gold to be taken back to their home planet, Nibiru. The Anunnaki were using the gold, converted into its monatomic form, to augment their atmosphere. It is unclear whether the aerosolised gold was being used to reflect solar radiation, (to counteract global warming), or to reduce the escape of their leaking atmosphere. Anunnaki are tremendously long-lived by our standards, and intelligent. But unfortunately they still have a tendency to make war. Their society, whilst technologically advanced well beyond our own, is still based upon the primitive concept of Royal families with elite bloodlines, rather than advancement through merit.

Araneus - An agency relic who has been in deep cover in Russia for the last 8 years. His codename means the 'spider', which reflects his patience and ability to lay an effective trap.

Arena (The) - Part of the Academy training facilities. Divided into different training zones, the arena is a versatile space, adaptable to the needs of the academy.

Authority (The) - The ruling elite amongst the survivors of the collapse formed a group called The Authority. They use drones and militarised police known as Enforcers to run the society of the future storyline with an iron fist.

Balatro - See Jarrod.

Ben - An Agency student and Relic, codename: Alumnor, which means "nurture, nourish, rear, educate, or train". A nice guy, originally a country boy, from wholesome farming stock.

Biofeedback - A scientifically measurable change in physiology which occurs seconds before emotional trauma. This is also known as 'presentiment', or the subconscious 'feeling' of future events. Composed of pupil size and heart rate changes, along with and galvanic skin responses, Relics can use this information to alert them seconds before a traumatic event. They do not know what is about to occur, but they do get a few seconds of advanced notice.

Brett Mason - Hector's Agency handler, answering directly to the Agency Sponsor, Hiram.

Canis - A Relic Instructor. Canis means "Wolf, Dog or Hound". He is tall, thickly muscled and dangerous. He is serious and straight to the point. His dark, chiselled features frame hard eyes as blue as chips of sapphire. He is a man of few words and not given to explaining himself.

Carmine - An Agency student and Relic, codename: Severus, which means "grave, austere, stern, strict, severe". He is a dour, middle-aged Austrian relic with a military background and experience in seismology.

Central Banks - The privately owned banking institutions established in each country to create money and loan it to the government and smaller banks at a rate of interest. Every penny in circulation is constantly making the private owners of these banks more wealthy. The institutions masquerade as national or government institutions, known by names such as the Federal Reserve, The Bank of England, The Deutsche Bundesbank, etc, but they are just private organisations with undisclosed shareholders. Interestingly enough, the countries who haven't succumbed to the bankers seem to be the ones faced with invasion or perpetual conflict - Cuba, Venezuela, Iraq, Afghanistan, Libya, Syria, Iran, North Korea, China and Russia. Is that a coincidence?

Chavez - One of the Freemen from the future storyline.

Chris - The name of the main character, Chris Trent, who is narrating the story of his life. His Relic codename is Lucidus.

Collapse (The) - The popular name given to the series of economic, environmental and pandemic disasters which resulted in the collapse of modern society as we know it. Billions perished during the collapse.

Colligatio - See Oliver.

Committee of 300 (The) - The pinnacle of the world's ruling elite. It is made up of the most powerful, wealthy and influential individuals on the planet and answers to no one. It supersedes governments, the UN, the Trilateral Commission, the Bilderberg Group, The Freemasons, The Illuminati, the Central Banks and even the World's most prominent Royal families, although it is no doubt made up of many of the senior members of these groups.

Control module - A piece of Relic hardware which allows an Agency handler to control or interact with a Relic. Different power blocks have different views on how they should be used.

Cordis - See Jesse.

Darius - One of the Freemen from the future storyline. Darius is a seasoned veteran of the conflict between the top-siders and the Under-city - and the subsequent purge. He acts as a sergeant for Lucidus and the Freemen.

Dead Zone (The) - The deserted outer reaches of the main city of the future storyline, made up of ruined streets and derelict buildings.

Decker - One of the Freemen from the future storyline. He is a grizzled former drone mechanic. He is one of the few skilled tradesmen amongst the Freemen, spending his time constantly mending and repairing scavenged items and worn out appliances, or else engaging Authority forces via guerrilla warfare and high tech sabotage.

Deliverance - A mechanised defence drone liberated by the Freemen from the future storyline. Titan series units, such as Deliverance, stand nearly 9 feet tall and are designed to intimidate.

Derexi - A deceased Agency Relic, only known through her recovered status reports and memories. Derexi means "to direct, steer, guide, align, point, set in order, or form up." She was an Agency fixer from the late 1940's to 2001.

Dimming - A Relic ability to obscure the signal that their implant gives off, in order to remain concealed from other Relics.

Dr Levine - A Doctor operating out of the underground Agency facility in Denver. He is a specialist in treating Relics, in his late 50's with greying temples and has the bearing of a military man.

Drone - A remotely controlled or artificially intelligent machine. These come in many forms, from tiny flying surveillance drones, through to self-driving commercial and military vehicles, through to robotic machines resembling humans or animals. Drones will do what a human with conscience might not.

Drone wars (The) - An ongoing conflict which lasted several decades, resulting in the collapse of society as we know it. As technology improved, men were replaced by machines which would not refuse orders or baulk at killing the innocent. This war of attrition between the three primary power blocks could also be known as World War III, but the Drone wars was a much more commonly used name for this dark time.

Echo-mapping - A form of passive echo-location used by Relics, similar to that used by dolphins and bats. See also micro-echoes.

Erste Menche - A well preserved Anunnaki corpse labelled as the Erste Menche or 'First man' by the Nazi scientists. It was recovered from the Antarctic. See also Anunnaki.

Fenwick - One of the Freemen from the future storyline. He is both brave and competent.

Finch - One of the Freemen from the future storyline. He is perhaps the most fanatical amongst the Freemen and hungers for any way to get even with the Authority regime.

Flaring - A Relic ability to flood the immediate area with siphon energy in order to locate other Relics or Relic technology.

Flint - An Agency student and Relic, codename: Renovo, which means "to renew, to restore, to revive." He is inhumanly fast, but as fickle and unpredictable as a flick-knife in a baby's crib. He is the lean and muscular son of Hiram, an Agency sponsor.

Freemen - A ragtag group of liberated citizens who live apart from the main city. They are engaged in guerrilla warfare, trying to overthrow the oppressive Authority and restore the basic human rights that citizens lost before and during the collapse.

Gamma wastes - The area outside the city which are contaminated with radiation from failed nuclear reactors. The city itself is protected from the worst of the radiation through high-tech magnetic field generators and special paints, materials and filters.

Grigory - A Russian Relic who has been recovered and taken in by the Agency. The first of the successful Relic defections, he was formerly known as Enforcer-32.

Handler - The name given to an Agent or Operative who looks after or controls a Relic in the field. Handlers usually possess a control module which gives them complete control of their Relic, but the Western power blocks tend to advocate a little more leeway for the Relic to act autonomously. Handlers take their orders from Agency Sponsors.

Harris - One of the Freemen from the future storyline.

Hector - An Agency student and Relic, codename: Solus, which means "alone, or loner". He is a fierce and swarthy Hispanic Relic in his late twenties, who had been involved in digging tunnels under the US / Mexican border for one of the Mexican drug cartels. He was an urchin raised by the streets, earning him the respect and loyalty of the underbelly of society. As a result, he evaded the various Agencies for almost three months before capture and has always held himself somewhat aloof from his peers.

Hiram - An Agency sponsor with his own stable of Relics. He is the father of Flint and the sponsor of Jarrod, Kester and Hector, amongst others.

Implant - Another term for a Relic, or else a much less sophisticated man-made device with only a fraction of the integration and functionality.

Jacob - One of the Freemen from the future storyline.

Jarrod - An Agency student and Relic, codename: Balatro, which means "bleater, babbler, buffoon, fool, jester, joker". Strong willed and headstrong, but treats everything as a joke.

Jesse - An Agency student and Relic, codename: Cordis, which means "heart". She is a sweet young woman, who lives life as a free spirit, always led by the heart. She may seem shy and reserved at the outset, but her warmth soon shines through. There is no guile in her and her openness makes you want to reciprocate.

Kester - An Agency student and Relic, codename: Susurro, which means "mutterer, tale-bearer, or whisperer". He is one of Flint's close allies, along with Jarrod. But he is the shorter, more pug-faced of the two.

Lost (The) - The infected denizens of the Under-city from the future storyline.

Lucidus - The central character of the story, formerly known as Chris. Lucidus means "clear, transparent, easy to understand and unable to conceal the truth". But the name also has a dual meaning. If the world in which he lived was but a dream, then he was a lucid dreamer, able to recognise and distinguish illusion from reality. He had been born lucid - with eyes wide open whilst all around him clenched their eyes shut.

Major Winters - An Agency sponsor with his own stable of Relics. He is the sponsor for Lucidus.

Micro-echoes - Any noise creates micro-echoes which help Relic implants to form a 360 degree image of the surroundings. It is a form of passive echo location similar to that used by dolphins and bats. See echo-mapping.

Micro-tremors - Subconsciously generated tremors in a person's voice when they lie.

Modules - Interchangeable Relic components which grant the Relic greater abilities, such as faster reactions, improved targeting, greater strength or speed, faster communications and more. Modules can be stolen from other relics whilst siphoning.

Murrin - One of the Freemen from the future storyline. He is brave and competent under pressure.

Naming ceremony - The Academy ceremony used to signify that students have graduated and become fully-fledged Relics within the Agency. Their new name is selected by their peers and is inspired by their character traits.

Nibiru - Otherwise known as Planet X, Nibiru is the home world of the Anunnaki. It is technically a planet of our own solar system, but its deep elliptical orbit only brings it past Earth approximately every 3600 years.

Norris - One of the Freemen from the future storyline. He is brave enough to rush in and help, but not very experienced.

Oliver - A balding Agency student and Relic, codename: Colligatio, which means "the thing that binds or connects, or binding together." He is the warmest of the other Agency Relic students. He was a former structural engineer from London, who had been implanted when he had been inspecting a collapse in the London Underground subway system, which lead to the discovery of buried remains. He is talkative and operates as a grapevine for Agency gossip and intrigue.

Omar - An Agency student and Relic, codename: Sapidus, which means "prudent". Only having three modules and therefore the least technologically enhanced of his peers, Omar has always had to be careful around more powerful Relics.

Paredo - A master of the order of Relics. A keeper of the mysteries. The Lethal Hand of the Committee of 300. Paredo means "the devourer", or "to absorb, consume, corrode, demolish, eat away". He is a large and powerful relic who has a very powerful 'siphon'. He becomes the mentor of Lucidus and is covertly scheming to overthrow the masters of the Agency, who hold Relics to heel as slaves.

Petersen - One of the Freemen from the future storyline. He is a big, blonde man with an open and honest disposition.

Power Blocks - There are three major power blocks. The Anglo-American-Israeli power block being the largest, (sometimes known as the Western power block), followed by the Chinese and Russian power blocks. Other nations may exert their own power, but they are largely contained or influenced by the three primary global forces.

Purges (The) - The term applied to the genocide brought about when the survivors of the collapse split into two factions - the top-siders, who lived above ground and the rebels, who still resided in the relative safety of the under-city. The Authority, who had originally been in control of both factions when everyone lived underground, decided to exterminate the rebels, rather than allow them to separate.

Relic - Used to simultaneously describe the high-tech implants left behind by the Anunnaki, or the people who act as physical host for them. Relics are assets of the Agency, or of the opposing power blocks. The actual implant itself interfaces with every aspect of human physiology, granting the host superhuman reactions and abilities.

Renovo - See Flint.

Reperrio - An Agency Relic in the field. Reperrio means "to discover" or "to find out". He is a scholarly academic, with round steel-rimmed spectacles, a beard and corduroy jacket and trousers. But despite the scholarly window-dressing, he is still a 200 lb relic who knows how to handle himself.

Sagax - A Relic Instructor. Sagax means "acute, sharp, perceptive, or keen-scented". Currently stationed in Agency facilities in Alaska, he is a relic who spends his time training with exotic weapons technology and sparring with the special forces who are rotated in and out on guard duty.

Sapidus - See Omar.

Sericum - A Relic Instructor, whose codename means "Silk". She is a wiry, lean woman with iron-grey hair pulled back into a tight bun. She is an Agency hand-to-hand combat specialist who is elegant, charming, graceful, attractive, yet refined, with just a hint of a conspiratorial sparkle that never leaves her eyes. She has the unlined face and physique of a much younger woman, but the steel-grey hue of her hair confuses the eye and puts her at some indeterminate age around the mid 50's.

Severus - See Carmine.

Sharashka - A generic term for a Russian research facility using forced labour.

Sierene - An Agency Relic in the field named after the mythological Greek sirens. She is a rare beauty and the daughter of a wealthy Chinese family living in Hong Kong, who made their fortune exporting rare antiquities. She now works the elite social circles of Hong Kong for the Agency, loosening all but the most secure tongues and sowing disinformation when required.

Siphon / Siphoning - An ability unique to Relics, whereby large amounts of information or even memories can be shared. This ability gives the impression of telepathy between Relics, but it is a product of technology. The full extent of these abilities is unknown, but Relics can also hijack and physically steal modules from each other if close enough, in order to enhance their own abilities.

Siphon-bridge - An open connection between Relics where they can share information and visual input. Several Relics bridging during a combat situation can effectively multiply their senses and situational awareness.

Siphon energy - The mysterious force wielded by Relics, which makes siphoning possible. No other known technology exists which can replicate it.

Solus - See Hector.

Sponsor - The name applied to highly-placed Agency staff who effectively own and operate teams of Relics. The designation of 'sponsor' was selected as it didn't overtly have the same connotations as slave masters, but sponsors essentially 'own' their Relics. However, they do not usually take their Relics into the field. For that, they use handlers. See also handlers.

Stavka - Captain Lieutenant Stavka is the commander of one of the last Russian Sharashkas.

Stephens - One of the Freemen from the future storyline. He is a short red-headed bull-dog of a man.

Students - Civilians within the Agency Academy who have been implanted with Relic technology, but have yet to be fully trained and named at the naming ceremony.

Sub-culture - A broad term encompassing all forms of life within the Under-city, from the future storyline. Whilst some bandits and rebel forces still exist, most sub-culture are infected with man-made pathogens from the purge.

Susurro - See Kester.

Textor - An Agency Relic in the field and Academy instructor. Textor means "the weaver", and relates to his ability to wield siphon energy and his fondness and aptitude for political intrigue.

Thomas Sanders (Professor) - An Agency scientist who has spent most of his life working for the Agency in their underground facility in Denver. He has been assigned as a handler for Lucidus, but has instead befriended him.

Titan Series Drones - Humanoid bipedal mechanised defence drones which range between 8 and 9 feet tall. They sport grinning steel skulls, infrared illuminators mounted on the shoulder, grenade and missile hard points and a forearm mounted midigun. These units were the utilitarian workhorse of the drone wars. They were relatively simple to maintain, operated reliably in the worst conditions and were as lethal as anything that came later. Early models were designed with the same bipedal skeleton and proportions of a human to gain acceptance, but as the drone wars raged on, they were made increasingly large and menacing. Later models dwarfed their operators. They couldn't be trusted with any sophisticated missions, but if you wanted something dead or defended, the titan series were good units.

Under-city (The) - One of many deep underground military bases that were used to save the survivors of the collapse. As years went by, this enormous development was expanded many fold, to become a sprawling underground city.

Valkyrie units - The smaller, man-sized cousins of the Titan series mechanised defence drones.

Verity - An Agency student and Relic, codename: Verum, which means "truth, reality, or fact". She has the plain look of a librarian about her, perhaps in her late twenties. She is a former museum curator.

Williams - One of the Freemen from the future storyline. He is the nearest the Freemen have to a medical officer.

Zoe - An Agency student and Relic, codename: Pacalis, which means "associated with peace". Zoe was a former police officer and whilst she is relatively firm, she is fair and believes in law and order.

* * *

This novel is a work of fiction, woven in and out of real world events.

ABOUT THE AUTHOR

Christopher C. Evans is a lecturer, author and specialist in medical diagnostics. He was born in 1978 and currently lives in the Midlands of the United Kingdom with his wife and daughter. His previous works include "Cancer Uncensored - Your step-by-step guide to cancer prevention, early detection, and cancer survival," which is a "must-read" available from www.CancerUncensored.com and Amazon.com.

Look out for Books 2 and 3 in the Born Lucid Series, along with several other stand-alone novels that he is working on.

You can also see what makes him tick via the Facebook Fan Pages FB.com/LivingForLonger and FB.com/BornLucid and on Twitter under the handle @LivingForLonger and @Bornlucid

www.BornLucid.com
www.LivingForLonger.com
www.CancerUncensored.com

49159758R00200

Made in the USA
Charleston, SC
20 November 2015